Postcards From Another Life

Andy Paulcroft

This edition published in 2018.

Copyright © 2017 Andy Paulcroft.

All rights reserved.

1.

J eremy Paxman would not have approved.

One Saturday, early in my college career, I attempted to join the University Challenge team. I didn't do so because I was some sort of genius and wanted to test myself. Nor did I do so because I had delusions that I was some sort of genius. I didn't even have a quirky mascot that I was desperate to show on prime-time television.

I simply did so because I fancied one of my fellow contestants.

Well, I was very new to cruising.

I had had a good, if unremarkable childhood. At school, I got on pretty well with everybody, without ever having a friend who was likely to stay so until death. I was neither exceptionally brainy, or a cause of worry to any of my teachers. I was never the first to be picked for a team, but neither was I one of the daisy pickers whose eventual inclusion was met with groans of derision from their team mates.

As soon as my A-level exams had finished, I got a job in a local pub. I worked long hours over the summer, trying to earn a bit of money to ease the size of my student loan. With little spare time to meet up, I had already drifted away from the school crowd, almost by accident.

I went back to the school on our exam results day and found out that my results were, true to form, OK but not spectacular. At least they were good enough to get into my first choice of university. We congratulated, sympathised, and caught up with news of various summers. Feeling unusually reluctant to tear myself away, I followed as a group of my peers straggled their way across town. We found a pub with a large beer garden and reorganised it into our own private club for the lunchtime.

Sometime, on the mellow side of the third pint, I looked around at my classmates as if for the last time. All these people had grown up with me; had shared all the milestones of childhood. We had worked, skived, laughed and fought. Within weeks we would scatter in every direction, like the pack of reds in a game of snooker when the cue ball strikes it.

I must have been looking pensive as Dean Knighton pulled himself away from his harem of female admirers and touching me gently on the shoulder, sat down on the bench seating.

Dean couldn't even have been described as a daisy picker; he was famous throughout our year as being a lad who would do anything to avoid sport at all cost. He had also been outwardly gay since he was about fourteen. He was popular, and everyone accepted him for who he was and those who didn't, learnt quite quickly that you upset his smart mouth at your peril.

He was the closest thing I had to a best friend and the person who had eased me out of the closet door a few months before. He had become my self-appointed advisor and sometimes it had felt like he was tutoring me in a BTEC course on how to be gay.

Although I liked him a lot, he was also a complete control freak which possibly prevented me from falling in love with him. He himself, was far too sociable to limit himself to one lover, so we were free to experiment happily in the rugby club changing rooms with no expectations or awkward desires.

On the first occasion I had visited, he had guided me around in such a sure-footed way, like a tiger who really knew his territory. I smilingly suggested that this probably wasn't the first time he'd been there.

He had stretched himself to the full extent of his six-foot-three inches, hands on skinny hips, lips pursed and in comical outrage, spat out: "Are you accusing me of - playing rugby?"

I didn't argue with the fact that it was probably the only way that anyone could get him to go anywhere near a sporting facility.

True to form, he had come prepared. As we enjoyed drinking in the last dregs of our school days, he opened his ever-present Louis Vuitton man bag and produced a mass of literature. He had researched the area I was going to and had found out information on everything homosexual that you could wish to know about the place: from gay line dancing, to the rainbow canoeists, back to the pink pie eaters club. He had found the location of two gay pubs and a gay club in the town and even printed out a map with the best routes from the university's halls to all of them. I was really touched and told him so. I didn't tell him that I was unlikely ever to use the information.

I had come to a decision that I didn't want to start a new life defined by my sexuality, I didn't just want to experience the gay side of university life, I wanted to experience it all. I wasn't thinking about going back into the closet, once I'd made friends that I trusted, there would be no deception. Well, that was the plan, it just didn't turn out exactly like that to start with.

I might not have wanted to join an exclusively gay fraternity.

However, I certainly didn't want to be ensconced in the frat house from hell.

My neighbours, Faulkner: "Call me Foz," Jerrard: "Call me Jez" and Warren, you've guessed it… "Call me Woz" were determined to turn our corridor into party house and absolutely no-one was safe.

They also insisted on calling me the Pete-ster which, I thought, made me sound like a brand name for a composting toilet.

The final straw had arrived on the way home from the Freshers' Ball itself. I had managed to do a long-practised pattern at parties of floating round the room and joining each group for a small amount of time and then moving on to the next, but having quite a good time in the process. I hadn't yet developed a close bond with anyone, but it was certainly fun trying.

I was just leaving the venue, when I heard a huge chorus of "Pete-ster!" I realised with a slight sinking of the heart, that I would have their company on the walk home and started preparing my excuses for the inevitable invitation for shots and an all-night party.

We were taking a cut through down a back lane that ran parallel to a row of terraced houses, when Foz stopped suddenly, turned to face us and raising his hands above his head, pointed one finger on each hand towards Jez. He looked like a football hooligan taunting the opposition supporters on the terraces.

"I challenge the mighty Jez to throw a brick over the wall!" The fingers were still pointing in Jez's direction, just in case the rest of us were unaware of his identity. "If he manages to break a window, he will get the first jaeger bomb when we reach halls, if he doesn't, he will drink a glass of my piss!"

I don't think that Ant and Dec should adopt that idea as a challenge on Saturday Night Takeaway.

At first, I didn't think he'd agree to it, but I should have known even from our relatively brief acquaintance that you didn't welch on a challenge. Certainly, the forfeit made E. coli poisoning look like a preferable alternative, but I hope I would have stood firm against it, had the choice been mine.

Jez stooped, picked up a sizeable brick and launched the missile before I could even think of anything to say that might have stopped him. Seconds later, we heard the sound of smashing glass. This was greeted by a roar of triumph from Jez and whoops and hollers of admiration from the other two.

I was horrified. I've never thought of myself as a prissy do-gooder or a member of the fun police. However, to me this was not fun.

All I could think of was the poor people who were living in the house. Had they been woken from sleep to discover that a brick had crash landed in their lounge? Were they enjoying an evening at friends which would be ruined by the vandalism that greeted their return? Worst of all, what if they had still been downstairs at the time…?

Foz, Jez and Woz ran back to halls to avoid any consequences. I dawdled at a distance, I didn't even care if I'd been picked up by the police, I felt guilty just by association. They were waiting for me as I walked down the corridor with that offer of shots and an all-nighter. I pretended to be much drunker than I was, and raising a hand in a goodnight salute, fell through my door without a word before they had a chance to try to talk me out of it.

For them, Fresher's week hadn't ended. I don't think it would actually end before they graduated or got kicked out.

On Monday night they wanted me to join them paint-balling without protective googles and dressed only in Speedos. Luckily, I had arranged to go home to pick up some ear defenders.

Tuesday, I was invited to the Carrot Crunchers Club which apparently involved a full bar, a dice and a bucket. I probably don't have to explain the significance of the bucket. They were amazed when I cited the after effects of a long journey home as an excuse not to join them. They would have been even more amazed if they had found out that I lived just forty miles away: well the journey involved catching a train - and a bus.

Wednesday night was Jackass night. This idea was stolen from the television show and from their rambling explanation I gathered it involved being shot at with a BB gun at point blank range, being kicked in the scrotum and running barefoot over broken bottles in the quickest time possible. I said that unfortunately I'd had a dodgy burger at lunchtime, otherwise…

Thursday was student night in many of the local pubs, but rather than just go out and get pissed, Foz, Jez, Woz and the rest of the Carrot Crunchers had made it into a competition. Basically, you got a point every time you went up to a woman and touched her arse, two points if you squeezed her breast and five points if you managed anywhere even more personal.

This time I killed off my grandmother. She was long dead in reality, but I was getting desperate…

Friday night had already been described to me as "the big night." I had been hoping that after four days of excuses they might have got the message that "The Pete-ster" was happy doing his own thing. It hadn't worked so far, and I was beginning to worry that it never would. One thing was sure, I could not live my life at university constantly being over tired, sick, or disposing of already dead relatives. I was going to have to tell them, but how?

I decided to go out before they got home and not return until they were safely causing mayhem elsewhere. I took my Kindle over to the student bar, more to hide my Norman No-Mates status, than any particular desire to read. However, it was only open in front of me using up the battery, I didn't take in a word.

My mind was on how I was going to tell my neighbours that their idea of university life, wasn't necessarily mine, without giving them a reason to make my life hell on a daily basis.

And, it was this simple act of avoidance which led to that audition to join the University Challenge team.

My thoughts were disturbed by a lively group settling themselves into the table of four directly in front of mine. There was an attractive, petite oriental girl who was probably second or third generation Anglo/Chinese. She certainly had an incredibly sexy, deep Yorkshire accent and looked a real handful, but great fun. Her skin was clear and blemish free, requiring no make-up at all, saving a rich scar of scarlet lipstick that seemed to echo her personality.

There were two dark haired lads in the group, they were both about six-foot-tall, one with very thick set features that made his face look like it was made out of rubber. He had a deep lined forehead and thick, rather kissable lips. The other had a slightly softer face with smaller facial features and was in my mind the slightly more attractive of the two. Both had styled their jet black hair in exactly the same way, teasing it to within an inch of its life and using enough hair products to keep L'Oréal in business for the next decade.

Twins? It was possible, they had definitely attempted to look similar, even if basically, they probably didn't, so brothers or lovers? I wasn't sure.

However, it was the fourth member of the group that made me sit up and take notice.

I had spent two weeks in August enthralled by the success of the British team at the Rio Olympics and had developed an unrealistic but healthily hopeful man crush on one of the gold medal winning gymnasts. The lad in front of me bore a striking resemblance to him. OK, his hair was much blonder, and his physique didn't quite equate with someone who practised single leg swings and double saltos twenty-seven hours a day. However, the body that was hidden by a slim fit white button-down shirt was a long distance from shabby.

The moment that I zoned into their conversation, he was replying to some good-natured teasing by the girl.

"OK Chlo, I know I'm not Mastermind material like you, but I bet I could get at least ten of the questions right."

"Twenty-five per cent... wow!" This was said with a good deal of smiling sarcasm.

"Well, it's probably more than most people could do."

My gymnastic crush was on the defensive.

"Fair comment, so what will the forfeit be, should you not achieve your target?"

"Hey! I didn't say I would do it, just that I could get ten questions right if I was to enter. I might not want to spend my Saturday morning trying to get into a University Challenge team that I don't even want to join!"

"I don't think being selected for the team is the point behind this," the girl laughed. "But I do think the word bet was used, as in: 'I bet I could get at least ten of the questions right.' Therefore, where there is a bet, there must be a prize, or a forfeit involved."

The lad looked across to the twins who had said very little, but were grinning identically. "Never argue with a lawyer, even if she is only just starting her second year of university."

"Very good, Sam, you are learning! Now drink up your drink, we need to get to reception before seven, to make sure we get you entered."

The deep lined twin spoke for the first time. He had a slightly nasal estuary accent, which was not quite as masculine as I had expected from his gym honed physique. "The forfeit, Chloe. We haven't sorted out the forfeit!"

Chloe exhaled dramatically "Mmmm?" Although it seemed to me that she already knew exactly what the forfeit was going to be. "If you fail to get ten questions right, you will jump into the Millennium Fountain and submerge yourself totally at eight o'clock tomorrow night - and you will do it completely naked!"

Now, I was getting very interested…

"OK," Sam drew out the two letters, to give himself thinking time. "But if I do get ten questions right, then you three must perform the forfeit."

"Hey!" The twin with the smaller features objected, "this is between you two, don't bring us into it!"

"All for one and one for all amigos!" Chloe merrily cross referenced her classical literature.

"Ah go on Chris," said rubbery face, "Sam will barely get five questions right, never mind ten!"

"Bloody cheek, Dan!" Sam laughed.

"Come on, come on you lightweights!" Chloe chided, "If Sam loses he does the forfeit on his own. If he wins: not likely I know, but after all Leicester City did win the premiership. In that case all three of us will do the forfeit. Now drink your bloody drinks and let's get him entered!"

They bantered on until the drinks were finished and then they disappeared in a riot of good humour, leaving me to my thoughts. I liked them, it wasn't just a case of fancying the lad they called Sam, well OK, that was a definite factor, but they also seemed like fun.

I wanted friends like them, actually, I wanted them as friends.

Maybe it was the extreme void I had felt between myself and my corridor mates that exacerbated the feeling, but for the first time in my life I wanted to be in a close group of friends. I was no longer happy to be Pete, vaguely popular with everybody.

A little germ of an idea planted itself in my head. I could just happen to be at the Millennium Fountain at eight the following night and it would be win-win for me. Either Sam would be getting nude, or the twins would be doing so alongside Chloe. The twins were probably a bit buffed up for my personal taste, still very acceptable though; but that wouldn't give me an opportunity to chat to them. However, if I entered the silly quiz/audition, call it what you will, it should be fairly easy to make sure I bumped into Sam afterwards. There would be an easy opening gambit for a conversation to follow; if friendship followed that, it would be great and if it didn't, I wouldn't have lost anything.

I lingered over my drink for ten minutes to give them enough time to get Sam registered and disappear into the night, before I made my way towards reception. I only just gave it time enough, if the conversation of the two receptionists was anything to go by.

"Looked like that gymnast fellow, didn't you think?"

"Yes! He did! Fit as… Good evening!" Seeing me interrupted her flow, but she dealt with my request cheerily and efficiently and I did get a bit of a glow when I heard the other girl say to my disappearing back: "Wouldn't chuck that one out of bed either!"

By the time I had got back to my room it was mercifully quiet. I spent the evening texting Dean and a few of my closer school mates, who seemed to be getting on much better than I, if their replies were to be believed.

Dean seemed to have turned his halls of residence into a gay village in the space of a week. A girl called Mandy had met "A dreamy guy" and the other two were "Having a great laugh at Freshers' Week!" It reinforced my feeling that we were moving further and further apart. The full stop at the end of my childhood was soon to be printed in bold script.

I rang Mum and Dad and lied for fifteen minutes, but it was what they wanted to hear, so they were happy to believe it. I threw together a pasta dish and ate it in front of a David Attenborough nature documentary.

Friday night at university. Wild!

I didn't know it, on that evening, but I had just set into motion a chain of events that would change my life… completely.

2.

The audition was being held in a lecture theatre at ten o'clock the following morning. I saw Sam immediately I entered. He was three rows in front of me and slightly to the right, so I had to concentrate to stop myself fixating on his profile rather than the questions in front of me. At a guess, I was confident of about twelve of them, which was fine by me. Being on TV was not the reason behind this little adventure so I was more than happy to fail to make the team.

Happily for me, we were told before the quiz started that we all had to stay for the entire two hours, which meant we would all leave together. These instructions were given by a young man with goofy teeth, plentiful dandruff and the vague aura of someone who is too intelligent to wash. Once the allotted time was up, I faffed around getting all my stuff together, so that Sam could leave just before me and I could follow him out.

I was just building up to my opening gambit of "What on earth? Were half those questions even written in English?" when Chloe, Chris and Dan appeared and surrounded him, which would have made any interruption sound rude.

Chloe was vexed. "Bloody hell! I've just had the mother of all conversations with one of the organisers. Apparently, it's not in the ethos of the University Challenge committee to name and shame the stupid people, so they won't release any scores, just the people that have got into the team and the substitutes in a case of an emergency. I mean, what is enjoying Paxo all about if it's not watching him shame the stupid people!"

Sam was visibly relieved, "Oh, so the bets off, that's a shame… I reckon I did rather well."

"Not so fast Stephen Hawking!" Chloe laughed. "I did manage to nick one of the question sheets whilst he wasn't looking, and with a little help from Wikipedia, we have all the answers!"

Sam grinned wryly, "Chloe, you always do!"

"So, it's off to the bar, I will buy you a drink and then we will go through your answers which will confirm that you are going to have a nice cold bathe tonight!"

"Or, it could be you…" Sam countered, as if he were compering a reality TV show, but I could tell he wasn't overly confident. They had been walking down the corridor whilst having the conversation and I was following at a distance. I decided that I would head towards the bar, apart from all the obvious reasons, I was rather interested in finding out the answers.

The bar was fairly quiet at just after noon on a Saturday, so both Sam's group and myself had a bar person each waiting to serve us. This meant I'd been served, and had paid for my drink, long before the four of them were ready. I decided that people are generally habitual creatures, so I headed for the table I was sitting at last night, in the hope that they would do the same. I waited, trying to work out what I would do if I suddenly had to change seats to get a better vantage point. It wasn't necessary as they cackled their way towards the table next to me as soon as they had their drinks in hand.

I was a bit smugly chuffed with myself, as Chloe went through the answers, to work out that I had actually managed to get sixteen questions correct. Halfway through the quiz there had been one of those unfathomable maths questions that always pokes its head up during University Challenge. I was grimly amused when Sam said, "Oh for

Christ's sake Chloe, have you got the google translate version of that question?" If my timing had been a bit quicker, my opening gambit would have worked a treat.

They had reached question forty and Chloe was delightedly telling Sam that as he had managed nine correct answers so far, he had to get the final question right to avoid a soaking.

"Which artist painted the seventeenth century life sized portrait of Danae, the mother of Perseus, welcoming Zeus who impregnated her in the form of a shower of gold?"

"He's doomed!" Dan taunted.

"Samuel Morris, you are a wet man!" Laughed Chris.

"Actually," Sam said diffidently, "I think I know this," he paused for effect, "it's either Van Gogh or Van Dijk"

"Van Dijk?" said Chris, "hasn't he just signed for Southampton?"

"The painter, you twerp!" Sam dug him in the ribs. He had the air of a man who knew he had the right answer and was just taunting his audience before producing it.

The trouble was, I knew he was wrong. I had been to the Hermitage museum the year before on a school trip to St Petersburg and had seen the painting. I particularly remembered it because one of the group had said it looked like a Matt Lucas character from Little Britain and Dean had said in a very bad Scottish accent "Oooh ah Din nae!" This had stuck as a bit of a catch phrase for the whole trip.

Practically without thinking, I scribbled the name on a Tesco receipt that I found in my pocket and knocked my mobile phone so that it fell to the floor, just by Sam's chair. As I scooped down to pick it up, I surreptitiously pressed the piece of paper into Sam's hand.

He managed incredibly well not to look surprised, and also to glance at it without being seen by the others.

"Or it could be Rembrandt!" He grinned triumphantly.

"Yes, but what is your answer?" Chris was now getting concerned, he too thought that Sam had got the ten correct answers that he needed.

"Rembrandt of course!" Sam revealed the answer with a convincing panache, as if my words had always been his.

"Well done Sam," Chloe said without emotion.

Sam couldn't resist a taunt of his own, "It looks like you three are getting wet tonight after all - and I cannot wait!"

"Except Sam," Chloe interrupted his triumphant teasing, "I think you might have had a little help! Hold out your hands, please."

I held my breath as he did as he was asked, but somehow, he must have managed to drop the receipt onto the floor as his hands were empty.

"Leave it Chlo, let's face it, he's brighter than he looks!" Chris grinned resignedly.

"Not difficult!" Dan chimed in.

Chloe stood up and went over to where Sam was sitting, "It's just that I saw that young man," she nodded in my direction, "writing furiously, then knock his phone onto the carpet. He then stooped to pick it up right next to young Mr Morris."

She bent to pick up the receipt that Sam had managed to spill on the floor and raised it in the air dramatically.

We had reached the part of the courtroom drama where the young lawyer exposes the guilt of the criminal amongst them.

She turned to me.

"So young man, do you admit to the charge of aiding and abetting a thicko? Will I find the name Rembrandt written on this piece of paper and will it be in your writing?"

"It's probably quite likely that you'll find a packet of pasta and a pot of Dolmio sauce written on it actually…" I glanced up and was rewarded by seeing Sam laughing delightedly, but it was time to fess up. "OK, it's a fair cop; but in my defence, there were three of you picking on him, so I was just trying to even up the odds a bit!"

Chloe's face went from severe to genuine delight in the

passing of a second. "I love it!" She clapped her hands. "Funny, moral and brave - you are quite right, we always pick on him!" She bowed her upper body in an Oriental gesture of respect and I bowed back. We were suddenly involved in an orgy of body bowing at each other.

"However!" Chloe was suddenly dead pan serious again. "The fact of the matter is that Mr Morris failed his challenge and must accept the consequences. Therefore - at 8pm tonight - he will enter the Millennium Fountain, completely naked, walk to the middle and fully submerge himself." She paused for effect "…and I think that young Rembrandt here should join him, as a punishment for trying to help him, however noble his actions might seem to have been!"

Three thoughts flashed across my mind. Firstly, I certainly had got myself a way in to their group. Secondly, I would be in the best place to see Sam in his birthday suit if I was standing next to him. Thirdly, how was I going to stop myself getting an erection?

I was juddered out of my thoughts by hearing Sam pleading on my behalf. "No Chlo, that's not fair! Of course I'll do it, but leave him out of it!"

I had been in lust! I was now just a tiny bit in love.

I interjected, "It's OK, Chloe?" I nodded towards her to check I'd got her name right, she nodded back. "Chloe's right, it'll teach me for poking my nose into other people's affairs. I accept my shaming."

"Great that's settled!" Chloe dregged her drink and picked up her bag, preparing to leave. "Now, I've wasted too much time on you losers, I've got lawyery things to learn about, and I must look glorious for tonight!" She pecked the three lads on the cheek and beamed in my direction. "See you later Rembrandt!"

Chris and Dan said they really should do a session in the gym and asked Sam if he was going to join them. It seemed that just as I was getting to know them, the party was breaking up; still there was always tonight. However,

Sam surprised me by refusing.

"I think the least I can do is buy poor old Rembrandt here a drink." It seemed that the nickname could well stick before they even knew my real name. "After all, it was trying to help me out that got him into this mess." He smiled a full voltage smile in my direction and I practically melted.

"You'd both probably be better off pissed, to be honest," Dan laughed, "It might blank out the cold when you pay up tonight... see you later!"

Chris smiled at me, slapped Sam's hand in a high five sort of handshake and they were gone.

Sam tilted his empty glass in my direction, "That's if you'd like another drink, of course." he said.

No, I think I'd rather sit in an empty darkened room and talk to myself... I accepted and tried to sound nowhere near as enthusiastic as I was actually feeling. He had to queue a little this time as the bar was beginning to fill up with people who had at last fallen out of bed and were topping up from the night before, whilst I waited in a state of nervous excitement. It was ridiculous, I felt like I was waiting for a blind date to turn up. What would we talk about? Now that it was one on one, would I bore him to tears?

I knew within minutes of him returning with the drinks that I had worried unnecessarily. It started with the obvious ice-breakers, the course I was doing, how was I finding living in halls?

That was a very good question...

However, for the first time since I had met Foz and his crew, I was actually pleased to have known them. My tales of carrot crunching avoidance had Sam in fits of beer spluttering laughter. I missed out the glass breaking story as I didn't want him to say that I should have done more to stop it. I knew it was true, I just didn't want to hear it.

I also missed out the fact that to keep out of their way, I had been in the student bar the night before. Stalking isn't the most attractive hobby for a man to have.

When I had finally drained all the humour I could from my predicament, I asked him about his background. The Morrisses ran a hotel in Weston-super-Mare and the story was fairly romantic. His mum's family had owned the hotel; his dad had arrived to work as a deputy manager after travelling the world; they ended up falling in love, marrying and having two children, Sam and Emily. His sister was two years younger than Sam and was currently in her final year at school.

The way he talked about his family gave me a vision of an incredibly close knitted unit, something I couldn't actually say about my own. OK, our family story was if anything, even more romantic. My father, whilst twenty years of age and at university fell in love with my mother, a lecturer eleven years older than him and she became pregnant with me. The ensuing scandal had left her jobless and him with a degree to finish and no means of supporting us. My dad's parents who conversely had been over forty before my dad had come along, stepped in. Determined that their son and heir should finish his course and get a degree, they let us live with them, paying all the bills into the bargain. When my mum found a research job for an international chemical company, they took on childcare duties, looking after me, instead of throwing themselves into a retirement they had probably looked forward to. I adored my grandmother as had my grandfather - she died when I was eight years old and he barely lasted four months after her. I think she adored me too, I certainly never got the impression that she resented looking after me.

However, when my grandparents died, I never really forged the same bond with my parents. They kept me healthy and happy and I loved them to a fashion, but the woman that I really loved was gone. My maternal grandparents were both dead and our family of three felt a little limited sometimes.

By this time, we were three pints down and by the time we had discussed sport, music and films, we had finished our fourth. I was beginning to believe that if I didn't stop soon I wouldn't even find the fountain, let alone be able to climb in it, I said as much to Sam.

"Chloe won't make you do it you know," he said, and I noticed a slight slur in his voice as well. "She'll make me do it, but not you. Just ask her."

I was sure he was right, and I probably could have survived without a dunking in an autumnal fountain. However, wimping out in front of my new friends didn't strike me as a very inspiring alternative.

I know - "Baa!"

And of course, there was the small matter that Sam would be right there next to me.

Shallow?

It was three-thirty by the time I got to my room and the lunchtime drinking session made me pass out completely until I was rudely awoken by a banging on the door. I opened it to find Foz standing there dressed in a mankini and a smile.

"Pete-ster it's mankini madness night! How many council signs can you stuff down your mankini and can you get home without getting caught?"

"Sorry Foz, I'm meeting some mates tonight, sounds fun though!"

He was surprised but let it go, and as I closed the door, I realised that this time, only half the sentence was a lie… definitely an improvement!

Before I left, I got myself dressed in trackie bottoms and a hoodie, shoving a T-shirt, and a pair of jeans, along with a towel in a rucksack. I downed two paracetamol and a pint of water in an attempt to get rid of the headache that had come as a result of the over indulgent lunchtime. I made my way towards the fountain, never thinking that I would have trouble finding Sam and his entourage when I got there. As I rounded the corner, I was aware of at least a hundred people crowding around the small plaza that surrounded the fountain. They had no idea who I was, or that I would be providing the promised entertainment. I was pushing my way through the third row of the crowd when I heard Chloe's voice behind me.

"Hey, Rembrandt! Over here!"

I made my way towards them. Dan and Chris were looking mightily cheerful and smug, whilst Sam was looking rather apprehensive. The smile he gave me though, was as genuine as it was heart-warming.

"Hey ho Rem! Bet you never thought we'd gather such a crowd!"

I hadn't actually given it a single thought and said so.

"Isn't social media a wonderful thing?" Chloe looked very pleased with herself. She pushed her way to the front of the throng, and by so doing parted the crowds so that we could follow her. Once at the fountain she turned so that her thighs were touching the surrounding ledge, one small push and she could be in the water herself.

"Ladies and Gentlemen!" She roared, and the crowd hushed. "We are here today because one of these two men is educationally inadequate!" There were big cheers as Sam waved his hand, "and a cheat!" Now there were boos and catcalls and Sam waved again. "Whilst the other young man was caught aiding and abetting in an act of cheating!" This time there was a mixture of cheers, boos and catcalls and I raised my arm. "They have both been sentenced to a dunking in the fountain of shame!" The crowd erupted in a delighted cacophony of cheering. "Gentlemen... strip!"

I could see Sam out of the side of my eye, taking off his sweatshirt and then a Superdry T-shirt. I mirrored his actions and discarded my hoodie. I was now down to my bare skin. I risked a glance in Sam's direction: as last night's button-down shirt had hinted, he had the most exquisite torso, slim and hairless except for a treasure trail leading from his belly button downward to the top of his jeans. He had small nipples on tight pecs, firm without being overly toned. My own body reacted in a slightly worrying manner, so I forced myself to look away.

I concentrated on standing on one leg to remove a shoe and a sock, and then wobbled slightly as I transferred my weight to my left leg to do the same on my right foot. I was aware of Sam mirroring my actions, but didn't trust myself to look. On a whim, but slightly because of my predicament, after I had removed my trackie bottoms, I picked the towel from the top of my rucksack and wrapped it around my middle. This drew a great reaction from the crowd, so I teased them by shimmying my boxers down behind its maroon curtain in what I hoped was a seductive manner.

To my amazement, after a lifetime of hiding in the shadows, I was thoroughly enjoying being the centre of attention. A glance at Sam who was completely naked, but hiding his manhood behind his hands gave me an idea. I theatrically thrusted back and forth and after teasing the onlookers with a few false starts, suddenly ripped my towel off with one hand, whilst still covering my genitals with the other. The crowd loved it and out of the corner of my eye I could see Sam laughing. I also got a sideways view of a practically perfect bottom complete with dimples on the side of his arse cheek.

"Shall we?" I enquired of him. In answer he took one hand away from its sentry duty, grabbed my free hand with it, swivelled me around so that we were both showing our naked behinds to the great unwashed public. In one movement we climbed onto the edge of the fountain and dropped down into it.

September may have held the warmest day on record for over one hundred years, but on that night in early October, there was a definite feel of autumn in the air. I barely noticed it. I could feel the water around my ankles and Sam's hand in mine as we made our way towards the middle of the fountain. Just his touch was threatening to send the blood pumping to areas I would have preferred it not to go to. I focussed my thoughts on the results of a carrot crunchers club meeting to keep my body under control. All this and I still hadn't seen Sam's penis yet, he was defiantly keeping it hidden behind his remaining hand, which on balance was probably just as well.

I think we both felt the torrent descending from the top of the fountain at the same moment - because I felt his body shudder almost in time with my own. Suddenly, carrot crunching thoughts weren't so necessary as the bitingly cold water gripped my body. I turned to him, at last confident I could take in every detail of that beautiful form. The perfectly shaped legs, blonde hairs darkened and flattened by the water, then up past rounded knee joints, to the white and hairless quads, shimmering with damp in the fountain's spotlights. The hand at last removed from duty revealed a long, thin uncut penis surrounded by well-groomed pubic hair. Even relying on the incredible cold was suddenly quite risky, so I said to him: "Ready?"

He nodded, and we dropped to our knees, the shower of water from above drumming against the back of our heads as we readied ourselves for the final movement. I put my hand out in front of me, flat on the base of the fountain floor and dropped my back realising too late that I had probably given everyone a pretty decent view of my arse crack before I flattened my penis against the bottom of the pool. If I believed that I had got myself acclimatised to the intense cold, I was suddenly proved skin achingly, teeth janglingly, wrong.

An ice-wave crawled its way across my body that was like a pain I had never experienced before. The paracetamols that I had taken before leaving had seen the back of the post-lunch headache, but the pain that I now experienced spread across the whole of my forehead and down into the roots of my teeth. I sprang up at almost the same time as Sam, so we must have had the look of two synchronised swimmers dancing to Bolero. There was absolutely no feeling left in me, let alone blood, so when he turned and hugged me, I could enjoy it without the fear of my body giving me away.

We could hear the roar of the crowd even above the drumming of the fountain that cascaded down our backs. I could feel his genitals rubbing against mine. I hoped, against hope, that one day I would be in this position again. However, next time it might be nicer without the freezing water or half the university campus as onlookers.

We had shuffled our way from under the fountain towards the edge when I heard the distinctive tones of my next-door neighbour and looked up to see Foz standing there with Jez and Woz. Mankini madness had obviously been put on hold for a while at the discovery of a more interesting humiliation happening to someone else.

"Pete-ster!" We were sort of heading towards them anyway, so to ignore them completely would have been a ruder thing to do than I was capable of. I accepted the offered hand and he clung on to it. For the first time I was very aware of my total nudity. "Props, man! I was beginning to think that you were some boring fecker that we were going to have to bully into becoming a party animal, but hey toss face - that was rad!"

I think it was a kind of compliment.

Suddenly, someone in the crowd shouted, "Security!" Within seconds the plaza cleared. Foz and his crowd vanished like they had just nicked Harry Potter's invisibility cloak, and I couldn't see Chloe, Dan, Chris - or our rucksacks.

So, there we were, Sam and myself, stark naked and dripping contents of the Millennium Fountain onto the plaza as we were abandoned by the crowd that some thirty seconds earlier had been cheering us. We looked about as guilty as two cake covered kittens in a bakery.

If I'd chosen a time and a place to meet the college security team for the first time, that probably wouldn't have been in my top ten...

3.

"Quick! Follow me!" I saw Sam pull himself up to the ledge, and drop down onto the plaza. I did as he said and ran to keep up with him as he darted towards an area of shrubbery just underneath the windows of one of the lecture theatres.

There was only a small patch of ground that we could squeeze into before the bushes became thick and impenetrable; this meant I was forced to squeeze tight against Sam's body. My body had recovered slightly from the shock of the cold water and this final act was more than my flesh, or blood, could stand. I was beginning to get aroused and even carrot crunching thoughts were failing to have the desired effect. I knelt on my left knee and brought my right knee up to act as a barricade. Luckily, Sam was turned slightly away from me, so he probably hadn't seen anything untoward.

However, I was strangely disappointed that he wasn't trying to sneak a clandestine peek in my direction. Obviously, he wasn't interested in the way I would have liked him to have been.

My thoughts changed direction when I saw a torchlight flicker across the plaza and heard the security guards talking to each other.

"Aw Bill! They've gone, let's leave it - it's nearly break time anyway, I'm dying for a cuppa!"

"They'll be some of them round here, you mark my words - hiding, like as not!"

"Look, we've done our job, moved them on - it was only a bit of harmless fun, no need for stressing!"

"Harmless fun? That would have played havoc with the acidity levels in the water, that would!"

"Aw Mate! Not our problem, whadda'you say - tea?"

Bill mumbled and grumbled but allowed himself to be led away towards the warmth of a staff room tea break.

Once they were safely out of sight, Sam breathed a sigh of relief and although he was still turned slightly away from me, whispered in my ear. "Thank God for that! Now, where is that bloody woman with our clothes?" Trust me when I say that his breath, hot and warm against the side of my face, didn't help my predicament at all.

Almost as if she had been waiting for a cue, Chloe's voice rang out loud and clear in the cold night. "Hello! Are there any saddos and losers hiding in the bushes – and do they need any clothes?"

I scrambled out of our hiding place and could use the rucksack that Chloe handed me as a rather more substantial replacement for my hand. Slightly bragging here, but fully loaded my little man can over extend my hand by an inch or two.

Sam followed, unsteadily picking his way out of the undergrowth. He snatched his bag back from Chloe. "Where were you?" He said slightly grumpily.

"You practically ran past us," she said. "By the time we reached you, security was on the way and it would have been a bit of a giveaway if they'd seen us with rucksacks in our hands - calling across the dahlias - don't you think?"

We both went about drying ourselves and then covering ourselves up completely. I got one more view of his gorgeous behind before the red Hollister boxers with blue insignias, were pulled up to cover it. If Romeo wanted to be a glove to be able to touch Juliet's cheek, then I sure wanted to be those boxers… well I'm sure you can finish the analogy.

Once we were both dressed and vaguely respectable

again, we went over to where Chloe, Chris and Dan were waiting. Chloe was beaming at me.

"Well! What made you go all Magic Mike on us? And what about the manoeuvre with your arse in the air? Genius! There were a few girls near to us that would have willingly had your babies. I would never have had you down as an exhibitionist!"

"To be fair, neither would I!" I said, not mentioning that the bottom in the air bit had been a slight accident.

"I think you gained more fans than the Somerset Sex God over there!" She laughed hoiking her thumb in Sam's direction.

"Excuse me!" Sam was good naturedly outraged, "not possible!"

"Anyway," Chloe ignored the outburst, "we've got one of my fabulous curries bubbling away in the slow cooker, so if you're not doing anything more entertaining, you are more than welcome to come back to ours and tuck in - we might even find some booze. I reckon you've earned it!"

I'd had a bit of left over pasta before I had come out, but practically no more than a starter for a healthy eighteen-year-old appetite. I would have quite happily recreated the Christmas dinner scenario from the Vicar of Dibley, if it meant spending more time in their company. I didn't say that however, desperation is never attractive.

They lived in a house a mile away from the main campus and as we walked, we chatted about light-hearted nothingness in such a companionable way that I felt I had known them for a lot longer than twelve hours. It was so different from my last walk around the streets of town and I found myself mentioning the story. If they thought that I should share some of the blame for not preventing it, they didn't say so. However, by the end of the story Chloe was incensed.

"Rich, brainless twats!" she seethed.

"Oh, I don't think they're particularly rich," I argued, I certainly wasn't going to disagree with any other part of it.

"So, you think they came to university completely on their own merit, determined to work their arses off to get a good degree? Or, are they taking any old course, which they will probably never use, and have their lifestyle funded by their parents just so they can experience the university lifestyle?"

I thought the latter was probably more likely but, to be fair, I was affording it with the help of a loan that would probably take years of paid employment to get rid of. I never considered my parents to be particularly wealthy.

"It's people like them that made my dad's life hell. They used to come into the restaurant he worked in, pissed up and thinking they were so funny with their ridiculous impressions of his accent. They used to treat him like shit!" Chloe was getting visibly upset and Sam put his arms around her and whispered something comforting in her ear.

"Sorry Rem!" Whatever Sam said had the desired effect. Chloe mimed the action of climbing down from a high stool. "This is me getting off my soapbox and re-joining the party!"

"Nothing to apologise for, they deserve all of that and more, believe me."

"Does anyone fancy a pint in the Chequers before we go home for the curry?" We were passing a pub, so Chris' changing of the subject didn't seem overly obvious.

The pub was busy, but not heaving, and we were able to find a round table towards the rear of it that we could all fit around. We chucked a few quid each at Sam and he and Dan went off to the bar to get drinks. They had returned with five pints of beer almost before we had got settled.

Chloe raised her glass. "To friends old and new!" she said smiling in my direction, we all clinked glasses and laughed.

"So, Rem," Chloe continued, "it suddenly occurred to me, that I have seen you naked, started getting to know you and I don't even know your real name yet!"

"Just another Saturday night for you then Chlo!" Dan chimed in and everyone laughed. Chloe gave him the finger, but she too was laughing.

"Hi, my name is Pete Abrahams, I'm from Shaftesbury in Dorset and I'm studying Sociology." I mimicked a University Challenge contestant and they all laughed except Sam, who spluttered on his drink, remembering something.

"Of course! The Pete-ster!" The others look baffled, so Sam encouraged me to repeat the carrot crunching stories that I had told him earlier.

I was dubious. I didn't want to upset Chloe again and said so.

"Oh, ignore me! Sam will tell you, I've got a bit of a chip on my shoulder about people like that."

"One chip?" Sam laughed, "It's more like a consignment from a McCain's Factory!"

Reassured I launched into my saga. OK, so with each retelling, it was becoming a little crazier, but when you have that sort of material, it seems a bit of a shame to keep to the complete truth, doesn't it? By the time we had finished our drinks, we were all doing carrot crunching impressions that had us collectively gasping for breaths between the laughter.

"Enough!" Chloe finally said after Dan had mimicked Foz as Ozzy Clarke, except he was reviewing a vomit that tasted like a "Harlequin hooker's sweaty jockstrap," rather than a wine that had notes of elderflower and lime. "If we carry on like this, nobody will be able to eat my delicious curry, and that my friends, would be a crime!"

Their temporary home was in the street next to the pub. A spacious three bedroomed terraced house that had gained another two bedrooms courtesy of a well-designed loft conversion. They had split the rent between four of them rather than five, as they hadn't found anyone else they wanted to share with.

When the conversion had been completed, the owners had also knocked through the downstairs room so that it was an open plan kitchen/diner/lounge. This meant that we could still all chat as we lounged on settees and chairs whilst Chris and Chloe put the finishing touches to the meal.

They told me how they had all met at Freshers' week the year before, bonded straight away and spent the whole of the previous year cementing that friendship. It sounded like they had shied away from letting anyone else join their group, and I felt really chuffed that they had been deluded enough to revise that decision on my account.

We all piled around the large table in the middle of the room and started on the poppadoms and dips in the way of a starter. The little I had heard about Chloe's family had piqued my curiosity, so I asked her about them.

I had been wrong about her being third generation Chinese. It was actually her father and mother who had emigrated in the 1980s. Chloe was the fifth and final child, and the only girl. Her parents had arrived, speaking very little English, knowing very few people, just one rather odd second cousin and his extended family. Her father had built a life here, by working as a road sweeper by day and in a Chinese restaurant by night. First, as a pot washer and later, as the waiter who would be verbally abused by Foz-like students in another university town. In his spare time, he learnt his new language and helped his wife with their steadily growing family. He now managed the restaurant, with one of his sons helping front of house and another as his head chef. The other two sons were a plumber and a builder, but it was Chloe, who was the star performer of the family, according to Sam, who took up the story when the focus came around to her.

She had been a bit of a child prodigy, by all accounts, and passed a zillion A-levels a couple of years earlier than her contemporaries. This had labelled her, in her own words as, "A bit of a freak" and I got the impression that

Sam, Chris and Dan were her first real friends. She had been taken on by a national law firm who saw her potential and after initial training, sponsored her to go to university. She was now flourishing, with the help of her friends, but I knew that her sponsors would want their pound of flesh and she would be working harder than anyone else on her course. It was completely obvious that her father was her hero. Whatever she achieved in life, would be in her eyes, entirely down to him.

She jumped up to serve the main course, and it was, as promised, delicious. As we used dry-fried chapatis to scoop up mouthfuls of tender, spicy, meat, the focus of attention drifted on to Chris and Dan. They weren't brothers, but might as well have been. Their mothers had been lifelong friends and had given birth within a month of each other. The boys had grown up together, gone to the same schools, played in the same teams and been practically inseparable.

"But you're just good friends, not a couple as such?" I tentatively asked.

"Well we have sex, don't we Dan?" Chris asked, and Dan nodded.

"Yeah, we do, but I don't think we're actually gay," he said.

"Just highly sexed really, and when there are no women that take our fancy, well it is 2016, after all!

Dan suddenly grinned and I could see Chloe flinch, I think she knew what was coming. "What we really like is a threesome, don't we Chlo?"

Chloe said very slowly and carefully: "I was drunk and when you offered me a threesome, I thought it was…"

"A new brand of chocolate bar from Cadbury!" Sam, Dan and Chris completed the sentence in a rowdy chorus. Not sure why, but I got the impression that they'd done the routine before.

We then went on to discuss how people didn't bother so much nowadays about categorising sexuality, and how we were lucky to live in a generation where people didn't worry about whether you were gay, straight, bi or just plain curious. It was the obvious opportunity to tell them I was gay - but I didn't.

I guess I just wanted to keep the hope a little longer. If I had told them I was gay, they would have wanted to know the type of man I liked. I would have been truthful, because I was terminally conditioned to be that way, and would have admitted that I was attracted to Sam. I was convinced by his apparent lack of interest in the bushes that he didn't reciprocate that attraction.

I was sure he would have then let me down gently and we would have carried on being friends, but the hope of something more, would be gone. And I didn't want to lose it. What I didn't know then was that I would be opening myself up to months of torment.

My sexuality apart, there was little we didn't discuss that night - we even managed politics, religion and Brexit - without things escalating into an argument, and it became clear that we all shared a very similar sense of humour. At times we were all helpless with laughter. I slid off my chair twice in hysteria, which of course only served to rank up the hilarity another notch.

The curry had disappeared rapidly, but we carried on picking at the left overs, as the empty beer bottles made the table look like a recycling centre. Sometime shy of one o'clock, Chloe decided that an early morning cheeseboard was the way to go. We cleared the debris and replaced it with a mass of food that looked like the entire cheese export from a small Bavarian country. Sam uncorked the first bottle of port that his dad had given him from the stock at the hotel and we carried on as if no interval had taken place.

I was going to learn that becoming friendly with someone whose family owned a hotel, would be very useful as far as food parcels were concerned. Not to mention the alcohol...

Eventually, bodies aching, stomachs bloated and feeling three glasses on the port side of pissed - we fell into the lounge area. Everyone was really ready to go to bed, but no-one wanted to break up a wonderful evening, and I was definitely resisting the call of the one mile walk in the chilly October night.

At around four in the morning, Chloe, Sam and I were sprawled on the carpet discussing third party ownership and the demise of the England football manager. Dan was sitting on the sofa getting his daily social networking fix on his smartphone. Chris was lying across him, snoozing, using his midriff as a pillow.

"OMG!" Dan suddenly shouted, causing Chris to mutter an obscenity as he was rudely awoken.

As one, the three of us sprawling on the carpet, turned to see what all the commotion was about.

Dan was pointing at the telly. "We've got to see this wide-screen!" He was laughing, almost uncontrollably, whilst the rest of us were looking at him slightly perplexed.

Sam was the first to react, "Facebook?" he enquired. Dan nodded, still somewhat beyond being able to make himself fully understood.

Sam turned the TV and computer on. He found the Facebook page and pressed some buttons on the TV controller, so that the information was beamed through the TV screen. This enabled us all to see it without having to cram around a laptop.

Almost as soon as the page loaded, the cause behind Dan's hilarity was obvious to all. About halfway down the screen was a video from a Seth Berkely posted at 8:49. The man had wasted little time! The screen shot underneath his post was the Millennium Fountain, and my heart sank as I realised exactly what the content of the video would be.

Sam groaned as he too, realised that our little performance was now available for all to see.

Chloe clapped her hands in delight. "Sammy boy, roll the VT!"

Sam clicked on the video and in reply to Chris and Chloe shouting "Full screen! full screen!" did as he was asked.

I watched in slightly horrified amusement as the video commenced with both Sam and I fully clothed. Chloe had just finished her spiel and Sam and I started stripping. Just the sight of his torso had my nether regions interested, but at least this time I was fully clothed and lying, front side down, on the floor.

As we reached the part where I performed my impromptu stripper routine, Dan, Chris and Chloe started to hum "You can leave your hat on!" with increasing enthusiasm. I have to say that I thought my routine was more in the style of Chip'n'Dale, cartoon chipmunks - than Chippendales, erotic dance troupe. However, the audience in that five-bedroomed terrace were certainly enjoying it. Even Sam was starting to join in humming the Full Monty favourite.

Seth Berkely certainly had a steady hand and knew how to use a mobile as a camera. When I plunged into the water, leaving my bottom waving in the air, he zoomed in, leaving very little to the imagination.

Now the whole university would know that I manscaped.

"Oh, for the love of God!" I cried covering my face with my hands so that I watched the rest of the video through opened fingers. My friends laughed delightedly at my discomfort. This waned slightly as I watched the part where Sam and I embraced, and I had the memory of his crotch against mine. The video ended abruptly just after I was seen, full frontal naked, talking to Foz and his crew. There was a shout and then the video showed a fast-moving road as Seth Berkely started running along it, away from the security guards.

The video ended and went back to the still shot of the fountain. Chris started reading out some of the comments, which were overall quite complimentary, but my mind was on other things. Just when we were hiding from the guards I had started worrying about security cameras and being identified. Now that worry had been voided, but only because our faces (and indeed every other part of my body in particular) was now available to anyone who was on Seth Berkely's friends list.

Sam's hand grabbed my shoulder in a friendly gesture. "Hey Rem! 450 likes! We are pop-u-lar!" Then noticing that, for the first time that night, I had gone quiet he asked gently, "what's wrong? No one was particularly vile!"

I managed a grin, but it was nowhere near full voltage. "I was just thinking that I may well have the shortest university career on record!"

Sam snorted, "What! Because of that?" I nodded, and he gave my shoulder a full hug. "My dear Rem, you won't get sent down because of that! Christ! You should have seen what went on last year!"

Chloe joined in - "Bridget Yarrell got her tits out at a basketball match!"

"Rory Parnell broke into the swimming pool at night and his girlfriend filmed him skinny dipping, which ended up on YouTube." This was from Chris.

Dan whooped with laughter. "And... Dexter Whatshisface was dared to attend a whole lecture butt naked!"

"Honestly Rem," Said Chloe, "I would never have let you do it, if I'd thought there would be repercussions." She hitched a finger in Sam's direction, "him; yes... if I thought he'd get sent down - because it would mean I'd be able to claim the biggest room in the house - but not you!"

"Bloody charming! Apart from that..." Sam gave Chloe a comedic glare, "if anything did go horribly wrong you could always call on the female Anglo-Chinese version of Atticus Finch over there, to defend you."

"University wouldn't stand a chance!" Dan laughed.

"Case closed!" agreed Chris.

Who could despair in the face of such support? Well,

me being me, kept the niggle of worry that would continue until the following Thursday. It was during a lecture and I had raised my hand to answer a question, when the lecturer looked at me and said: "Ah! Peter Abrahams, our naked synchronised swimming wannabe thinks he can identify the key points in social differentiation, power and stratification."

After the boost of excitement that the video had given us, we chatted on for a while, but by five o'clock everyone was droopy with alcohol and dropping with tiredness. I decided I could outstay my welcome no longer and got up ready to attack the walk home even though, at that time, it held all the appeal of an Ebola outbreak.

"Where are you going Rem?" Chloe asked as I went to the hall to find my trainers.

"Well, back to halls I thought. I also thought it was about time I got out of your way and gave you chance to get to bed!"

"Don't be daft! You can have the spare room… can't he?" She glanced around at the others, daring them to disagree. No-one did.

"Course he can!" Sam said, "A naked swim and a night he doesn't get home…? You'll be like a god to your carrot crunching friends within a day!"

I laughed and accepted without a need for a second thought. At this point the party did break up and we made our way upstairs to bed. As it was, I ended up in the attic conversion on my own. Chris, who had the other room up there, disappeared into Dan's room with barely a hint of discussion. Obviously, one of those nights…

For my own part, I had worked out the geography of the house well enough to realise that Sam was lying in a bed, just beneath my own. Happily cursing the floorboard barrier, I drifted asleep…

4.

I woke just before midday to the sound of water drumming on a shower room floor, one storey down. I lay there for a few moments, smiling in memory of the events of the night before, the small nugget of worry, the only barrier to complete happiness. I was blurry, but not particularly hungover and after ten minutes or so I dressed myself in yesterday's clothes and opened the door to my room.

The muffled sound of the CD playing in the lounge area identified itself as Bastille's "Wild World," as I made my way downstairs. Chloe was scrunched into the sofa, dressed entirely in towelling, from slippers to robe right up to the turban style head dress she had loosely wound around her head.

She was clutching a mug of coffee, deep in thought, but she smiled when she looked up to see me padding down the staircase.

"Hi Rem! Sleep OK?"

"Like a dead man, thanks!"

"Coffee?"

She bounced up from the sofa to make me a cup and asked me if I wanted a shower.

"No, it's OK, I can get one back at halls."

She looked slightly disappointed, "Of course, I suppose you've got things to do, people to see, we've monopolised you enough."

"No not at all, I was thinking about getting out of your

35

hair, not becoming the bloke who came to dinner and just wouldn't leave!"

She laughed, "Absolutely not! I really enjoyed last night."

"Me too."

"I was thinking of suggesting to the lads that we went to the Stag for a Sunday carvery. They serve it 'til four, it's cheap, tasty and they've got a good garden we can sit in - fancy joining us?"

"I'd love to, but I must say my underwear is slightly on the smeggy side of disgusting and there's nothing worse than showering and putting dirty skiddies back on…"

"What sort of student are you?" She laughed. "That's no problem… Morris!" The last word she yelled up the staircase in the vague direction of Sam's room. There were the sounds of someone clattering out of bed and then, a door opened, and Sam poked his head out.

"For the love of God, what do you want woman?" I got the impression that Sam didn't do mornings very well.

"Chuck down some clean underwear and socks for Rem; and a clean towel if you've got one!"

Sam muttered something and disappeared back into his room. A minute or so later the door reopened, and he appeared at the top of the staircase.

He shambled his way down the stairs, dressed only in the Hollister boxers he was wearing the night before. His hair was tousled from sleep and the boxers had ridden up showing an expanse of pale soft skin at the top of his leg. As he handed me a pair of Calvin Klein boxers, Adidas socks and a mauve towel, it took a lot of self-control not to pull him on top of me and risk ruining a beautiful if embryonic friendship.

My little man was on the move again, so I thought it prudent to make my way up the stairs. Once safely inside the shower room, I stripped naked and treated him to a gentle massage as I soaped my body under the soothing hot water.

I dried quickly, shoved the pile of dirty clothes under one arm and carried Sam's clean underwear in my other hand before opening the door. I practically walked straight into Sam who was hovering on the landing with a T-shirt in his hand, but no more clothes on his body.

"Thought you might like to borrow this," he smiled, handing it to me.

"Thanks," I said, trying not to stare, but risking a sly glance before I left him and climbed the second flight of stairs to the room I had slept in.

By the time I had dressed, I felt pretty much human again. Chris and Dan had re-joined the living by the time I got downstairs, and everyone was sprawled around the lounge drinking coffee. All three lads were dressed only in underpants. Apart from the difference in the brand names, I felt like I had walked in on an Andrew Christian video shoot; believe me, I wasn't complaining.

We swapped morning pleasantries. I squatted on the floor trying not to stare too hard at Sam. He was sitting on the sofa, right leg crooked up against the side of his left leg, so that his toes were almost touching his knee. This seemed to stretch the fabric of his underwear so that his penis line was visible. Just above that, there was the treasure trail of hair that lead up to his belly button and a stomach that even whilst it was scrunched up looked muscular and flat.

I was drooling like a pug puppy in front of a rib-eye steak.

***

The pub garden was pretty full on a hazy October afternoon - it was as if the sun was struggling to make a last appearance before a final goodbye towards a dreary winter. People were making the most of it and although it wasn't exactly T-shirt weather, the dying sun was creating enough heat to enable us to sit outside and enjoy a huge roast beef dinner.

Without doubt, Dan had been the king of the carvery. Using mathematical skill, he had been able to fill every inch of the plate using balance and counter balance. He created a food tower that was impressive, yet stable enough to carry from bar to table without leaving a Hansel and Gretel food trail across the carpet and out into the garden.

We ate and drank, laughed and squabbled. I felt totally at ease in their company. Sam was generally the butt of their jokes and he handled it with such genial acceptance that I found I was defending him on most occasions.

"Hey Chlo," Dan laughed, "I think Sam has found himself a knight in shining armour who will defend his honour! Arise Sir Rembrandt!"

"About bloody time!" Sam said with dark humour, "I've suffered dog's abuse from you lot for the last year, it's nice to have someone on my side for a change!"

"Well, when you've been through hell and freezing water together, what can I say…?" I finished lamely, but thought I'd probably better be a bit careful in future. Soon one of them would catch on that I had a thing for Sam; because a thing for Sam I definitely had.

"Well my fucking God! If it isn't the Pete-ster!" Either there had been a government cloning outrage that I had been unaware of - and they had bizarrely chosen Foz and his mates to be the subjects - or they were stalking me.

However, there they were, larger and louder than life - again.

I got up hastily and walked towards them as I didn't want them to upset Chloe. I had caught her looking up sharply on their approach, so I moved quickly to head trouble off at the pass.

"Hi lads!" I said brightly, "what you up to?"

"Body shots!" I looked blankly at him, so thankfully, he explained. "We paint dartboards on our bodies, rough like, they don't have to be exactly like the real thing." He said this as if it would have been the obvious question on my lips... strangely enough, it wasn't.

"Oh!" I said, "then you get those sticky darts and throw them at each other?" I had a feeling I might have been heading up the wrong track as soon as I said it, the look on his face confirmed my thoughts.

"No mate, real ones, obviously!"

Obviously.

"This is a real stroke of luck, we've been looking for you all afternoon - you're not chickening out of this one bud!"

Beam me up Scotty!

Woz didn't often speak and when he did, he tried to sound like he was black and from the Bronx – in fact he was almost albino white and from Bromley.

"Hey Bro! Who's the Ho?" He pointed blatantly at Chloe, and to my horror, she stood up and headed towards us. She smiled as sweetly as Cinderella in a bubble gum factory and wrapped her arms around me.

"Peter, darling - do introduce me to your friends!" Bloody hell, she'd suddenly turned into Helena Bonham Carter!

However, the use of my real name gave me a sign that something was afoot, and whatever she was planning on doing, she was going to do it beautifully and without rancour.

"Oh Chloe, this is Foz, Jez and Woz," I played along with her and hoped that I would eventually work out where she was going with it.

"Right Love! Nice meeting you but I'm afraid we're going to take the Pete-ster away from you for the night - we have got darts to throw!" He then went into full Foz flirt mode. I'd seen it during Fresher's week, and believe me, it wasn't pretty. "But any time you want a man to warm up the cold winter evenings...?"

"Oh Foz, that would be too delightful, but I could never hurt my Peter." She surrounded me in a complete body hug. "And I'm so sorry, but you can't have him tonight either, as he has promised me supper… in bed."

If I could have filmed the look on their faces at that moment, I would have done so. It would cheer me up at any downbeat moment that I was likely to have in my life.

"Y-y-you're together? Fucking hell, I thought he was a complete fag!"

Well thank you Foz! For a start I am still here, so please don't talk about me as if I'm not - and for the second part - I don't really want you to out me to my friends. Especially when it's the first time you've ever said anything half way accurate in your sorry little life.

As much as I wanted to say that, I didn't have to, Helena Bonham Chloe was right back at him.

"Peter, Homosexual? If only you'd seen him last night, this morning and," she giggled, "just before we came out to luncheon - I can tell you, he was being anything but gay!"

For the first time since I'd met them they were lost for words and completely out of their depth, but I could see that I had risen somewhat in their estimation. To use their own words, the fact that in my first week at university I had managed to pull an older, fit, posh bird, was grounds for a little bit of jealous admiration. They managed to mutter a mumbled "…props bro, catch you later…" before they ran away to the prospect of piercing their skin with darts. An evening that suddenly didn't seem as exciting to them, as the one they thought that Chloe had planned for me.

We stood there with fixed grins on our faces, holding on to each other tightly, until they were safely back inside the pub and out of earshot. At this point we moved back towards Sam, Dan and Chris who were still sitting at the table turning puce with the effort of trying not to laugh.

"Don't you dare say a word!" I said threateningly, but on the verge of exploding myself.

That was all it took. For the next five minutes we were

helpless. Each time it looked like we might recover, someone said something, and we were back to square one - even the people at the next table started laughing at us laughing - it was contagious.

Eventually we recovered our composure enough to think about plans for the rest of the day. We were two thirds of the way back to the halls, I had my rucksack with me, so the obvious plan would be to head back and get myself ready for lectures on Monday. After such a wonderful interlude it seemed ten times worse to return to a life that last week had appeared natural.

"You can't really go, can you?" Chloe said, as I picked up my rucksack to leave. I looked blankly at her, so she explained in the patient, slightly exasperated way that a parent might spell out things to a child. "Your carrot crunching friends might return to halls to get their darts for their body shot game. As I remember it, you are meant to be serving me supper in bed!"

It didn't take a lot of persuasion to head back to the house with them for an evening of a "Breaking Bad" box set. The walk took slightly longer than it should have done when Dan grabbed Chris in a Chloe hug and said in his best cut-glass English accent - "If only you'd seen him, last night, this morning, and, just before you came out to lunch-e-on." The ensuing hilarity curtailed any chance of walking for at least five minutes.

It was midnight, before I finally dragged myself away to walk the mile home. I had been offered a bed again, but I really couldn't carry on borrowing clothes and I needed stuff for lectures the next day, so I sadly pulled myself away.

As luck would have it, I walked down the corridor just as the human dartboards arrived home. They had shots, the alcoholic type, and they wanted details of my sex life. "We can make a drinking game of it," Foz said brightly. I think he could have made a drinking game out of a weather report.

"Every time we mention a sexual practice you have done over the weekend, we'll drink a shot and every time we mention one that you haven't done, you have to down one!" I imagined that some of the practices they would think up could involve animals or dead bodies, so I thought it likely that I could be stitched up big time. I mimicked a sore saddle cowboy walk the best I could and said I'd love to, but I was literally shagged out.

After I closed my door on their impressed faces, I started stripping off my clothes - Sam's clothes in fact. I imagined him stripping off the same clothes and although they were covered in the odour from my own body, I fell asleep clutching his T-shirt, which randomly seemed to make him feel much closer to me.

5.

For the next two weeks I practically lived at the house in Moreland Road - they kept inviting me and I kept accepting. However, on the Saturday a fortnight after my impromptu swim, they all abandoned me. To be fair, they had had tickets to see Bastille at the Roundhouse in London since they had gone on sale. They were going to stay over at Dan's house in Brentwood afterwards.

They had tried to buy me a ticket, so that I could join them, but they were long since sold out. Because of this, I would have my first weekend since we met, without their company. I thought about going home, but my parents were away and none of my friends would be around either, so that would have been pointless.

My main plan was to avoid any carrot crunching activity. When some people on my course started talking about going to support one of the lads who was playing his first match for the university, I sort of invited myself along. The main beauty of the plan was that after the football, everyone was going to meet up for an evening of drinking. This would mean I would be nowhere near the halls of residence to get inveigled in any scheme that Foz and his mates were planning,

The day was a bit like a return to my old life. Everyone was quite happy to have my company, but not one of them would have missed me had I not been there. I liked them, but I didn't share an automatic ability to banter with them like I did with the Moreland Road crowd. We watched the match, we went drinking, we ended up in an Indian restaurant in the heart of town. It was all very pleasant but when it came to the time when we could go on, or go home, I said my goodbyes and made my way back to the halls.

I was relieved to find the corridor I lived on as quiet as the grave. I settled into bed and treated myself to thoughts of Sam at the concert, dancing until he was sweaty headed, stripping off his shirt as he overheated. With such pleasant waking dreams, I drifted into the real thing.

There are few things better at waking you immediately than the lock on your door being broken and the door itself, being kicked open.

"Pete-ster!!!"

You are kidding me.

"We heard that the bae was away so the Pete-ster can play!"

The Pete-ster had never felt less like playing with anyone, but even fuzzy headed from a rude awakening, I realised that: a) they weren't going to go away: b) I could no longer close my door on them and: c) they weren't going to go away…

With a reluctance that was Olympic standard, I muttered that I would join them soon, and they whooped and hollered their way along to Foz's room. I grabbed my recently discarded clothes and pulled them back on again.

OK, I know my room was a little prissy and pristine to be a student's bedroom, but that certainly couldn't be said of the room I entered a few seconds later. There were no surfaces that didn't have dirty crockery, glasses or mouldy fast food containers on them. The room smelt of rotten food, dirty clothing, stale alcohol and BO.

"Drinking game!!" Foz yelled at me as I arrived. No surprises there then. What followed was a series of games. Rock, paper, scissors and Chubby Bunny were two of the ones that I knew, but there were many others. The loser of each game had to perform a forfeit.

I guess I was lucky, I only lost two games. The first forfeit I had to perform was to lay there whilst Woz tea bagged me. Although you may presume that having someone's balls lowered into my mouth wouldn't be exactly an anathema to me, it is slightly different when the testicles haven't been washed since puberty. I'm sure that Foz was still testing the theory that I was "a fag" because the next time I lost a game, he and Jez put their members in my mouth at the same time. It was ironic really that I was lying there with two penises on my tongue, and yet I had never felt less homosexual in my life.

As I said, I guess I was lucky, Jez had one of his eyebrows shaved off and after another loss, lit cigarettes were stubbed out on his arm. By the end of the night he looked like a peasant, with the pox, from a BBC drama set in the twelfth century.

There was no fun in any of the games, no humour in their banter and the whole episode held all the charm of a walk in a sewerage plant. And yes, I now have heard the one about the African paraplegic lesbian - unfortunately.

It was a blessed relief when, after about two hours of adding to the drink they had already consumed, they all crashed out within ten minutes of each other. I took my leave, closed my broken door as well as I could, and slumped back into bed. I felt miserable and dirty and so far removed from the thoughts that had sent me to sleep a few hours before, that they might have belonged to a different man.

I slept a fitful, restless sleep and my irritated brain kept waking me. At ten o'clock I was so fed up with being angry at the Carrots and even more so, myself, for letting them bully me into playing their stupid games, that I got up. My dad had randomly given me a small tool kit with all the basics when I left home. I had laughed about it to myself after my parents had gone, but that Sunday morning I was pleased with something practical to do.

The door and lock had not been damaged too much and, within a couple of hours, I had managed to repair it to a state where it would at least lock again. Slightly satisfied from my success, I lay back down on the bed and managed to drift off into a more restful sleep. I was disturbed by my mobile phone beeping to let me know that someone had sent me a text.

If last night's disturbance had been unwanted, this was completely at the other end of the spectrum. It was from Sam - "We're back! Dan's hungry! Stag at 3. Fancy joining us?"

Well yes, actually.

It was strange really, although the events of the night before had seemed hideous, by the time I retold them and imbued them with a touch of morose humour, I felt much less angry about the whole affair.

They had all enjoyed the Bastille concert and from time to time Sam would burst into the chorus from "Good Grief" and wave his arms about. However, it was my middle of the night hazing experiences that monopolized the conversation.

By the time I had got to the pox and passing out stage of the story, Chloe said, "For goodness sake Rem, you have got to get out of there!"

"Agreed, Chlo, but how? I've signed the contract. The university make it quite clear that they like everyone to live in halls for the first year, so I don't see what I can do."

"You could move in with us" Chloe said. However, it was the enthusiastic reaction the suggestion received from Sam that had my stomach doing a loop the loop that threatened the stability of my recently digested roast beef. But...

"As great as that would be, there is no way the college are going to let me off paying, and I just can't afford to pay two rents every week."

"You could stay at ours for free," Chloe said, "We're paying for an empty room anyway, so it's no skin off our noses if we pay the same amount for a room that's occupied." I knew that even with the sponsorship deal, her family weren't wealthy, and life was a struggle for her.

I had already seen her with a needle and thread, creating something wacky and trendy from a jumble of charity shop purchases. "All the nice girls love a label," she'd sing Marilyn Munroe style, as she sewed some trendy logo into the top of a cobbled together costume. It might have looked like she had paid a fortune for it in some popular boutique, but I knew the effort involved. I loved her for the thought, but I couldn't accept.

"I'd just feel crap about it," I said, "you lot shouldn't have to finance me just because I haven't got the bollocks to stick up for myself with those arseholes. But thank you for the offer, it means a lot to me."

"Well at least try and go and see the accommodation people and ask them to release you from the contract," argued Chloe. "I'll come with you - call it a spot of work experience for me!"

"Welcome to Moreland Road!" said Sam, "they wouldn't dare say no!"

It was all very well for Sam to joke but at the meeting, two days later, we were faced with a rather stern professional lady. She had the look of someone who had seen and heard it all before and didn't possess the word "yes" in her vocabulary. I felt I was doomed, even with Chloe, Legally un-Blonde herself, fighting my corner.

Fair play to her, she had launched into a passionate spiel about how I was miserable, my work was suffering and how I dreaded going back to halls each night, but it didn't seem to be make any inroads with the lady of granite.

"I didn't want to say this, but I've found bottles of spirits, and a stash of aspirin, in his room!" She said dramatically.

Well, there was a miniature bottle of vodka and a packet of paracetamol on the bedside table, but it wasn't exactly life threatening.

The granite lady raised an eyebrow at that one.

Chloe turned to me, "Too much?" She asked.

I wrinkled up my mouth and put my thumb and forefinger together, "Maybe a touch," I agreed.

I looked up and granite lady was smiling a broad and natural smile at our exchange. This encouraged Chloe to plough on.

"OK, so he's not exactly suicidal - but he's not happy there - and he's our friend. We want him to be happy, and he would be if he moved in with us."

My mother has always said that she could cry at an advert for toilet rolls. It must be in the genes because I was close to welling up at that one.

Granite lady crumbled too.

"Look, I'm not saying the university particularly likes cancelling contracts - but it's certainly not impossible - it has been done before." She paused, and I think we both felt a nugget of hope growing. "To be honest, I agree that you would be better off living with your friends, and I'm sure we can sort that out for you."

She then fixed me with a full voltage stare, which suddenly softened, and she smiled as she continued. "It's possible to make some wonderful friends at university. I think you have made some, cherish them, won't you?"

Not really granite lady at all.

Once we had thanked her and left the room, I held out my arms with a beaming smile on my face. Chloe came in for a hug and suddenly before I knew what was happening, we were kissing; proper full on straight boy, straight girl, kissing.

Oh God! No! I felt awful, not because it was awful, it was far from it - but Chloe was the last person in the world I wanted to lead on and lie to. I pulled away.

"Ah!" she said, "I did have a feeling that we might not be boarding in the same skate park."

"Chlo, I'm so sorry!"

"Why? Because you're gay?"

"No, because I wasn't open about it and you might have felt I was leading you on."

She looked at me squarely in the eye. "Let's get a coffee and we'll have a chat about it."

Once ensconced in a café bar booth, with a black Americano for me and a caramel Macchiato or some such concoction for her, she told me the story of the last two weeks from her perspective.

She had noticed me on the Friday evening in the bar when I had first noticed them. When I was there again on the Saturday lunchtime, she was hopeful, then when I gave Sam the answer to the missing question she thought it may be because I wanted to see her naked and soaked. Apparently, she wanted to see me in that state which was why she had insisted on me fulfilling the forfeit when our cheating was exposed.

She had thought I was gorgeous, strangely enough, and as we got to know each other that night, she felt like I was someone that she would like to get to know a lot better, hence all the invitations.

But, over the course of the last fortnight, she had begun to wonder if we were riding on the same bus. She certainly had plenty of euphemisms to describe someone's sexuality, I had to give her that.

"It's Sam, I guess," she ventured.

I agreed that it was indeed Sam.

"And you didn't want to mention it in case you scared him off?"

Crikey, I hoped that we would never be at the stage when she was cross questioning me in court!

Holding my breath, I asked the question that I both desperately wanted to know, and was equally terrified of hearing the answer to.

"Do you think I've got any hope?"

She sighed and shrugged her shoulders. "It seems daft to say it as we've been practically living in each other's pockets for the last year… but I really don't know. When I first met him, I quite fancied him, but nothing ever happened and then over time I stopped seeing him as a potential partner and more like a brother. Why the hell I need another one, I have no idea, I mean I have four of the bloody things already, but that was the way of it."

She continued, "He has had girlfriends in the last year, but none of them have been serious or even particularly compatible - they've never lasted more than a week. It was almost like he was going through the motions as if it was something he was expected to do. And I do think that if he had been really interested, it would have got serious. Don't you dare ever tell him I said this, but Sam Morris is one of the nicest guys I have ever met in my life. But, in answer to your question, I don't know but I wouldn't lose heart."

I smiled cheekily, "Are you telling me, that you haven't asked him?"

She laughed, "Of course I bloody have. Always got some politician's answer though. He never really answered the question, and I'm normally quite good at getting a truthful answer out of people."

"Really?" I said ironically, "can't say I've noticed…"

I became serious, "I'm really sorry Chlo, I think you're bloody fantastic and if I were straight…"

She brushed it off, "I know, I know! You don't have to say it… Oh why are the good ones always gay?" Then she brightened, "Why don't I tell him that you really fancy him? Then we'd know for sure!"

"Don't you bloody dare!"

"Funny," Chloe laughed, "thought you'd say that!"

The moment I moved into Moreland Road, my life at university started properly. When we weren't involved in our separate university pursuits, we were together all the time.

For Halloween, we turned the downstairs of the house into Harry Potter's sweat shop, or Muggles in Muddles as

Chloe christened us.

On fireworks night we drank beer and ate hot dogs in College Park, whilst we watched a thousand pounds explode to an empty sky.

On the 11th November we stood together remembering people we had never known - but without whom, we might not have known each other.

Then suddenly, as town and university started to shimmer under a blanket of Christmas lights that threatened to destroy the ice caps…

Sam, with no reason or warning, started to avoid me.

6.

I'm not sure when it began. I had become slightly aware of the fact that he would sometimes disappear to his room when I appeared in the lounge, or he would turn away just slightly when I caught his gaze across the dinner table.

When I had first moved into the house, he would appear in my room and we'd chat, laugh and listen to music for hours – that all suddenly stopped.

Of course, I did the worst possible thing anyone could do. I over compensated. I became nervous in his presence and would babble on like a Teletubby on amphetamines. Even Chris and Dan looked bemused sometimes. I would try to grab moments with him alone. Then, I'd be devastated when he made an excuse to leave the room quicker than Lewis Hamilton had flown around the track at Monza.

The only person who understood how I was feeling was Chloe. We spent more time than was prudent, cuddling on the sofa while she tried to persuade me to let her talk to Sam on my behalf.

Poor Chloe, she had started off the term thinking she might have found herself a boyfriend. She ended it with the same man using her painstakingly crafted wardrobe, as a box of tissues.

One Saturday morning, early in December, matters came to a head. We'd all been slouching round the breakfast bar eating cereals and enjoying the fact that no-one had to run off for a lecture. Chloe, Chris and Dan were taunting Sam about a girl on his course. She had made rather over obvious suggestions, in his general direction, whilst we were at the pub the night before. For once, I joined in, rather than defend him in my normal manner.

"Rem, why don't you just fuck off!"

There was a stunned silence. I felt like he'd just stolen Foz's BB gun and shot me in the face. Point blank.

Sam jumped off his stool and ran out of the room before anyone had recovered enough to say anything. Chloe went to follow him, but Chris put his right arm out to stop her.

"Leave it Chlo, we were getting a little carried away."

"We were," Chloe was angry on my behalf and I loved her for it. "Rem only made one little comment – he didn't deserve that!"

"Agreed, but I've never known Sam to lose it before. Shall we just let him have that one?" He touched me lightly on the shoulder. "You all right with that Rem?"

I nodded, but I wasn't. I was as far from all right as it was possible to be. The man I loved most in the world had looked at me as if I was the man he hated most. I managed to mutter that Sam could turn his early morning grumpy persona into a speciality act for "Britain's Got Talent."

They laughed more than the joke deserved, mostly out of relief, I suspected.

I took my bowl of cereal and slumped in front of Saturday morning television. I wasn't really watching it though, I went through the brief exchange about a hundred times and made myself more miserable with each review.

The lads went out to the gym, Chloe set herself up at the dining room table with some work and I half watched a minor celebrity face food hell on Saturday Kitchen. I then watched some pundits talking bollocks about football on Football Focus, some dealers talking bollocks about antiques on Bargain Hunt. Finally, I watched some famous for fifteen minutes members of the public talking bollocks about the pluses and minuses of parquet flooring on Escape to the Country.

I think you could possibly say that I wasn't in a very good mood.

Just as potential buyers were coming to the end of their moments of fame and were deciding, surprise, surprise that they didn't like any of the houses they were offered, Sam reappeared. He looked dreadful, he had been crying I think, I just wanted to hug him, but I was scared to do so.

He glanced at me and muttered an apology, but before I could say anything Chloe looked up and said, "Oh Rem would you mind searching online for that reference we were talking about?" As we had said very little over the last few hours, other than her asking me numerous times if I was all right, I realised I was being dismissed so that she could have that word with Sam after all. I ran upstairs on the pretext of using my computer, then opened and closed my door to make them think I'd gone inside.

"Sam, what was that all about?" I heard Chloe say as I settled myself silently on the floor behind the bannisters where I could eavesdrop without being seen.

"He was taking the piss out of me, or did you miss that?"

"Oh, for God's sake Sam! It wasn't just Rem, it was all of us and we always take the piss – it's our way of letting you know we love you." I couldn't see the loppy-sided grin, but I knew her well enough by now to know that there would have been one.

Sam wasn't to be placated however. "Just sometimes you know, it gets right on my tits."

"But why did you lose it with him Sam? I mean, he is one of the nicest blokes I've ever met, and he's barely ever given you stick before. Chris, Dan and I have given you grief for a year and a bit, and you've never once lost it with us… why him?"

"Look Chlo, I did have my reasons." Chloe obviously had given him the look because he continued, whilst I waited crouched behind a bannister with my heart beating frantically, "but I can't even tell you, not now, maybe not ever."

"Come on Sam! We're soul mates! You can tell me anything you want to…" But it was wasted breath, and I heard Sam running up the stairs. I froze, in case he was planning on coming straight up to apologise and my eavesdropping would be exposed.

But he didn't climb up the second flight, he disappeared into his room and closed the door gently. I did the same on the floor above his. As I lay on my bed I was sure I could hear the sounds of sobbing drifting through the floorboards…

What did he mean? I could only think that I irritated him beyond belief and he was only putting up with me as he knew the others quite liked me. I lay on my bed and as silently as I could; cried my heart out.

Sam did apologise later, and I accepted, we hugged and made like everything was back to normal. But it wasn't, he was awkward around me and I was still trying too hard around him.

The house may soon have resembled a "best bits" montage from Kirsty's Handmade Christmas - but I was feeling as much enthusiasm for the festive season as a Santa Claus with a fear of flying.

Chloe tried her best with both of us, but even her more inspiring pep talks didn't work. Chris and Dan spent more time on their own in Dan's room, and I think it was a relief to all of us when the term ended, and we could disappear back to our homes and take a break from each other.

However, as soon as I got home, I missed Sam like hell. I missed them all, but with Sam it was like I was in some masochist's dream. It was painful when I was near him, and almost unbearable when I wasn't. After two days of moping in my room, under the pretext of doing coursework, I decided to answer one of Dean's many texts.

He dragged me out for a drink and I told him all about Sam. He threw his eyeballs skyward and said, "Peter, Peter! Do not fall in love with straight boys, you will be doomed to a life of heartache!" It was typical of Dean to be edging on the melodramatic, but nothing I'd seen so far made me think he was mistaken.

"But, you've had affairs with straight boys," I argued.

"But I never fell in love with them," came the sage advice, "we just enjoyed sex, that's completely different."

"We've never had sex," I said bitterly. "The closest I've come to that pleasure was when we were both naked and he hugged me under the Millennium Fountain."

"That was Sam?" Dean had seen the Facebook video, in fact he had told me that I was very big in NUTAS – Nottingham University Twinks Appreciation Society, because of him screening it at their inaugural meeting.

I agreed that it was Sam.

"Christ! In that case, ignore all my advice. Fall in love with him, you lucky bastard!"

That Christmas I realised that I had been wrong in thinking that I was quite happy to drift away from my school friends, they got me through that holiday. Dean forced me, through persuasion, blackmail, and to be frank: hideous bullying, to go out most nights with Mandy, her best friend Gemma and a nice lad from our year called Mark. I had known them since our days of MMR jabs and Bob the Builder. Somehow, I had completely misjudged how much they meant to me. Maybe it was something to do with my fragile mental state, but I realised that I didn't want to lose them.

However, mostly it was my friendship with Dean that surprised me. It was only when I was alone with him that I would mention Sam. I discovered that when we talked things through, they just became comical and we'd end up laughing about the absurdity of it all. It helped me more than I could say.

I told him this as we parted at the bottom of his street on the last night of the Christmas holidays.

"Peter, sweetheart as you know, I live to serve! But for fuck's sake, tell him how you feel! OK, so you may not get the answer you're wanting, but it has got to be better than this…" he waved his hands theatrically "…emotional void you've dragged yourself into. You will remain friends whatever, because you are very good at being a friend, but for once in your life - take a chance and go for it!"

I pulled him towards me and gave him a lingering kiss on the lips and said that I would do just that. I knew I wouldn't though, some habits are just too hard to break.

"Now!" He commanded. "Go! I have to dine with the whole Knighton family dynasty at noon tomorrow and if I don't get at least nine hours sleep, they will think I've been abducted by aliens and replaced by a doppelganger with blotchy skin!"

***

I'd had a few texts from Sam over the Christmas, although he had been silly busy at the hotel, so that gave him a good excuse not to be too in depth. They were chatty and friendly but nothing that gave me any real hope that we were permanently over the awkwardness of the end of last term. I had skyped Chloe quite a bit and the boys in Brentwood a few times. We decided between us to arrive back at the house on the Friday before term began, and learning started in earnest, so we could have a relaxing weekend catching up.

I had spent the morning slowly getting packed and ready to go. Then I took the a bus to Salisbury, and a train to town, arriving back at Moreland Road early in the afternoon. I had passed the journey in a state of nervous excitement. I was so desperate to see Sam again, and yet I was also worried about the reception I would receive from him.

I was surprised to see Chloe already there, she must have left Leeds at the crack of dawn. She was sitting on the sofa, coffee in hand, having a very intense conversation with Sam.

They both jumped up, came over and hugged me - but it was obvious that I had interrupted something fairly important, so I made excuses about unpacking and climbed the two flights to my room.

I was worried. The reunion that I had dreamt of with Sam held the natural intimacy of the early part of our friendship. The one I had just experienced was an extension of last year's tension.

I didn't have to fret for too long. Within five minutes there was a knock on the door, and in response to my invitation to come in, the door opened, and Sam did just that.

I wanted to cross the room and envelope him in a friendly embrace, but the look on his face made that option untenable. He looked scared to death.

"Chloe said that if I didn't come up and talk to you, she would rip my bollocks off and turn them into a table decoration," he said without any trace of the humour that the words should have held. He could barely look at me. I was getting nervous myself.

"Christ Sam, she normally only gets violent whilst watching The Apprentice! What did you say to her?" I was trying to instil a levity in the conversation that I really wasn't feeling.

He stood barely inside the door, almost so there was an option of an easy exit if the conversation took a turn for the worst. He rotated his signet ring around his finger and eventually managed to force himself to catch my gaze.

"Well first, I wanted to apologise for my behaviour at the end of last term." I nodded a nod that I hoped conveyed the message that it was water under the bridge, forgotten. "And I wanted to say that although you might need to bear with me at times, I will be all right with it."

Now I was confused. "All right with what Sam?"

He looked surprised that I needed it spelling out, "If you and Chloe make it official."

Suddenly it all made sense - his irritation with me and the awkwardness since. He thought I'd fallen for Chloe, the cuckoo they'd invited into the nest had stolen the affection of the girl he had secretly loved for over a year. A wave of relief swept over me. I knew that even though I had dreaded the thought that he might get a girlfriend, the fact that the object of his affections was Chloe, made it so much better than any of the alternatives.

"Oh Sam, what on earth makes you think we would want to do that?"

He counted off the points on his fingers. "Well let me see; it was Chloe who suggested you came to live here. She pretended to be your girlfriend in front of Woz, Boz and Noz or whatever they were called… Oh, and you're always mauling each other whenever you think that no-one is watching!"

I was suddenly reminded of Chloe's supportive embraces when I was unburdening myself from the horrors of unrequited love.

"Oh God Sam, we weren't "mauling" each other. We were just having friendly cuddles." I decided it was best not to tell him why… "Honestly mate, there is nothing going on between us." I paused to glance at him, but he was looking a little bit confused, so I continued. "I just can't believe that you've spent over a year pining after her and not gotten around to telling her how you feel - talk about slow - you make a tortoise look like Usain Bolt!"

He looked at me like I was the most stupid person in the world. I was beginning to feel like I was really missing something…

And I really was.

"It's not Chloe I want to go out with," he paused and looked at me meaningfully. I was still suffering from the same confusion I felt when I watched a BBC4 documentary.

I desperately needed subtitles.

Eventually, he had to blurt it out.

"It's you - you doughnut - it's you I'm in love with!"

7.

I suppose when I had dreamt about that moment, in the days when it had simply been a dream, I hadn't envisioned being compared with a sugar covered confectionery.

Quite frankly, I couldn't care less.

As soon as he had blurted it out, he looked stunned, shocked and nervous, all at the same time. For my part, I stood there opening and closing my mouth like a six-foot goldfish. I had gone from glass half empty to glass so full that even a professional bomb disposal expert wouldn't have risked lifting it.

I took a couple of steps so that I was standing right in front of him. Gently, I pulled his face towards mine so that our lips were within a shared revelation of actually touching. I could feel his breath on my face, it smelt mildly of coffee and started to affect me in the same way it had done on the night of our swim in the fountain. This time I wasn't worried about it embarrassing me, in fact I had a feeling it could be quite useful…

There was already a glimmer of hope on his face and this morphed into a full-blown smile as I whispered gently into his ear. "Well we'd better do something about that then, hadn't we?"

We kissed then; it was like birthdays, Christmas and any twenty-first century holiday the card shops wanted to invent, all rolled into one. I ripped at his clothes and he ripped at mine. We stumbled half-naked on to my bed where we continued stroking, pawing and stripping each other. It wasn't the best sex in the world, it was too frantic for that. We knew we had plenty of time to find out the things that each of us liked, and over the next few months we certainly had a lot of practice.

To be honest, on that first occasion, we could have both dropped our trousers and ejaculated on the duvet and I would have been satisfied.

Sam loved me!

Afterwards, I cuddled up against him, his arm around me and mine around him, tracing circles around his nipples and staring at the gorgeous body I had been dreaming of molesting for three months now. I had never once really believed it would actually happen. I asked him when he had first realised he was gay.

"Probably the day I shouted at you," he winced at the painful memory, "I've had little crushes before, but I always managed to convince myself that it was just a phase and I really liked girls. I do really like girls, I'm just not particularly attracted to them." He paused, then moved so that he was leaning on his hands which straddled either side of my body. This enabled him to fix me with the full force of his gaze.

"Then, I met you. I was attracted to you the moment I saw you, and when Chloe suggested you should do the forfeit, I was really torn. It wasn't fair to make a complete stranger strip naked in front of so many people, but I so wanted to get to know you, not to mention see that incredibly fanciable body in its natural state." I laughed, a delighted disbelieving laugh and he put all his weight on one arm so that he could stroke my face with his other hand. My sleeping appendage started stirring again. "Honestly Rem, the fact that you don't know how gorgeous you are, makes you even more desirable!"

He then continued his story: "I told myself that I would offer you a drink and if it was at all awkward between us, I would tell Chloe that it wasn't right to expect you to do it and that would be that. Except it wasn't, as soon as we started chatting, I felt like I wanted to talk to you forever."

"Why didn't you say something?"

"Well hang on, at that point I wasn't even sure myself what it was I was feeling, and I was convinced that you were interested in Chloe. I mean it was her you would have seen naked if our little bit of cheating hadn't been exposed. I knew she liked you, so for once there was something that I couldn't talk to my best friend about. Dan and Chris - well I love them to bits, but they are bloody hopeless with anything like that, so I just kept my own counsel."

You and me both, I thought.

We were suddenly interrupted by a furious rapping on the door. Chloe was outside.

"I've got instruments of castration ready here!"

Sam laughed, "You can put them away Chlo! I've told him!" He paused as a thought struck him. "You knew Rem liked me, didn't you?"

"Might have done."

"I can't believe you knew how he would react, and yet you gave me no inkling. I have never been so nervous in all my life!"

"So, everything is good...? Bloody hell! I can't have this conversation through a door, are you still having sex?"

"No!" Sam said with affected outrage.

"Are you decent?"

"No!" We both said it in unison this time, with slight desperation in our voices. It didn't work, because the door opened and Chloe marched in to see us desperately trying, and failing, to cover our semis with our hands.

"Good!" She stared at our bodies longer than was decent or necessary. "If I'm going to be your joint fag hag then I deserve a few perks - and this..." she waved her hands in the direction of our nakedness, "will do for a start!"

"What do you want Chloe? Apart from a cheap thrill?"

Sam asked with exaggerated patience.

"Oh!" Chloe dragged her vision away from our midriffs and focussed on our faces, "The boys are back and I'm dying to tell them everything, but I'm getting so good at keeping secrets that I found I couldn't mention it!"

"OK…" Sam waited, and when Chloe still didn't get the hint, continued. "Can you leave us Chlo? I take it we are allowed to put clothes on before we face them?"

"Oh, they've seen it all before," she said airily. "I mean, the whole university has seen it all before…"

With that, Chloe reluctantly left. Sam and I grinned, kissed and let each other go in order to dress ourselves and go downstairs to face our next inquisition.

***

"Praise the Lord! They've actually talked to each other at last!" Dan waggled his hands in the air.

"You knew?" Sam was surprised.

"Of course we knew!" Chris laughed, "Rem would stare at you when he thought you weren't looking, and you would stare at him when you thought he wasn't looking. It was like living through a very bad episode of EastEnders!"

"So much for Chris and Dan being useless to talk to about your feelings!" I teased Sam and he smiled grudgingly.

"Can we get back to normal now?" Dan asked, "the atmosphere around this place wrecked the end of the Christmas term for me."

"Quite," agreed Chris, "we didn't even have a house Christmas meal!"

I was feeling a bit guilty that Sam was getting all the stick when I was just as much to blame. "I should have said something too. Chloe was always encouraging me to, but I was so sure I was barking up the wrong…"

"Let's have Christmas now!"

"God! Now he's turned into Shirley Temple!" Chloe

had a box set of those black and white "let's have the show right here" films that the former congresswoman was so famous for when she was a child star.

"No!" Sam was getting excited, "It's now officially Christmas Eve!" We all looked at him like he was just slightly barking, but he ploughed on unperturbed. "Chris and Dan, get the tree and the decorations back down. Chloe you're in charge of decorating. Rem and I are going into town to do food shopping. And everyone has to buy a secret Santa Christmas present before the shops shut.!"

"Oh Samuel! I like it!" Chloe clapped her hands together in delight, then turned to me, "Does it slightly turn you on when he gets into his hotel manager bossy mode like that?"

"My dad gave me quite a nice little wage for working over Christmas as we had such a busy one," Sam ignored her. "Because I was a bit of a twat," he held up his hand to ward off dissenters and then pulled it back down when no-one disagreed... "Well you could have argued that one just a little," he said with fake annoyance. "Anyway, I would like to treat my best friends and," he turned to me, "my boyfriend, to a Holm View Christmas!"

God, it felt so good to hear him say it, I was grinning like Top Cat in a creamery.

We saw a bus drive past the end of the road as we left the house and were beholden to an old lady who had to search for her bus pass in the bottom of her bag, which gave us enough time to make it on board. Once we paid, we scrambled upstairs laughing and fell into the first available seat as the bus lurched town-wards.

I had drawn Chloe in the secret Santa. Sam, still in hotel manager mode, had insisted on half an hour only for us to sort out our presents. I went straight to the sales in the shopping centre, and within minutes had found a "Best Fag Hag in the World" mug in the bargain bin, which after her comments of earlier could not be ignored.

Once presents were sorted I reunited with Sam and we

crashed our trolley around the supermarket with great abandon. He had found a butcher who was still open and had bought the most enormous turkey. Progress was slow due to the bird banging against our legs, the trolley and any poor unsuspecting soul that had the misfortune to cross our path.

We arrived home laden with stores for the weekend, which should really in all honesty have lasted the month. The Christmas fairies had been weaving their magic and the place was fully decorated, like a Christmas card in stone and wood. Tinsel hung from every nook, cranny and bookcase. Lights were plugged in to every conceivable electric socket. Baubles were hooked to every plant and shrub in the building. The fibre optic Christmas tree that Chloe had discovered in a charity shop the year before glowed, gently changing colour every fifteen seconds or so. Of human life, there was no sign. Having followed the first part of their instructions, Chloe, Chris and Dan were now out completing their final task.

Sam turned on the coal effect gas fire that added to the various glows that flickered around the room. He held out his arms and I leant into his embrace. His cheeks, still cold from the outside chill, contrasted with warmth of the fire against our legs. He kissed me gently and traced a finger across my face, "Happy Christmas Rem," he said.

Our January Christmas Eve meal consisted of sirloin steaks cut in strips on a warm Thai salad with noodles, baby corn, mixed peppers and lemon grass. This was followed by a chocolate roulade, still slightly warm due to the constraints of time so that the cream melted and swirled around the chocolate sauce in a delicious gungy mess. We drank a lot and laughed even more. At midnight we had mulled wine and mince pies and sang carols around the tree - anyone passing would have suspected us to be slightly mad or drunk - and we were very happily a little of both.

I climbed one flight less to bed than normal, and I lay

wrapped around Sam after another exploratory session of love making. Slowly we were finding the things that the other liked and occasionally we both got it wrong. It was half trial and error, half puzzle, a sort of sexual Sudoku. It was certainly more fun than putting random numbers into squares.

I looked up at the ceiling and thought of the floorboard barrier I had gazed at on my first night in the house. How fantastic it was to be on the other side of that barrier.

January Christmas day dawned bright and clear. Sam had made a breakfast that would have kept a trucker happy for the entire length of the M1. We then went for a long walk around the quayside whilst the turkey cooked under a foil coat, so that it was ready on our return. Sam got it out to rest whilst finishing off the remainder of the feast and then popped the cork on a champagne bottle. He drank his glass whilst carving and we drank ours whilst making helpful comments which were treated with dubious disdain by our chef and host.

He even flamed the Christmas pudding and paraded it into a darkened room. It had taken Chloe ten minutes to locate all the switches to enable the effect - but it was worth the wait. As we flopped around the table afterwards, trying and failing to convince ourselves that cheese and port was a very bad idea, Dan looked at my boyfriend with a wicked grin on his face.

"So Sam, tell us. The night of the naked swim?"

It took Sam a few seconds to work out what he was talking about, but when he did, he groaned... "You noticed that?"

Dan and Chris nodded whilst I was still in the dark.

"OK OK! I know I won't get any peace until I fess up - as you are, quite frankly, bastards…!"

"Guilty!" They happily agreed with his assessment.

"Right," Sam smoothed his hands across his face in a gesture of embarrassment. "I know it's no good telling you lot not to laugh as you are quite frankly…"

"Bastards!" They shouted delightedly.

"Correct!"

Sam grimaced. "OK, I admit it, when I crawled out from hiding in the bushes, I did have the most enormous…" He mouthed the word, "stiffy…"

So that had been why he had turned away from me, and to think I'd been slightly disappointed at the time.

"Well, it's his fault!" Sam pointed at me with fake annoyance, "he shouldn't be so freakin' gorgeous!"

"It is a curse," I agreed, playing along. Although in truth, I was still amazed that someone like Sam should think that way about me.

"And this is why you've been so cranky, over the last few months?" Chris laughed although he very well knew the truth of it.

Sam nodded, serious for a moment. "If I was perfectly honest I've probably suspected for the last two or three years that I was attracted to men, but I was desperate not to be gay." He looked at Chloe, "what with my dad and everything." She nodded supportively. "And for the most part, I managed to hide it quite well."

Chloe, Chris and Dan nodded. The teasing was over. They were now supportive, loving and listening to every word.

"Then Rem appeared, and he turned my safe world to mush. I couldn't stop thinking about him, I wanted to be with him all the time and yet at the same time, it was torture." This sounded all too familiar to me, so I caressed his hand in solidarity. "I thought that he and Chloe were having an affair and that hurt me – my best friend and the man I had fallen in love with – yet neither of them had the decency to tell me about it." He shrugged. "That's how it felt to me in any case."

"So that Saturday morning…?" Dan asked gently this time, all taunting done.

Sam nodded but changed tack for a moment. "I have never minded you lot taking the piss," he grinned cheekily, "to be honest, I rather enjoy it, but I also liked the fact that since Rem has been around, he's stuck up for me." He took a deep breath. "Then suddenly that day, even Rem was mocking me, and I could see what it would be like when he eventually got together with Chloe. All of you laughing at the bloke who is hopeless with the opposite sex. The poor old gay boy who just won't admit it. For the first time in my life, I felt that I wasn't being laughed with... I was being laughed at."

That house in Moreland Road was seldom silent. It was silent at that moment.

Sam continued. "As soon as the words had come out of my mouth, I felt like shit. I also knew at that moment, just how much I loved Rem and that I was kidding myself, thinking that I may eventually find a woman who made me feel like that." I squeezed his hand again. "All through Christmas I've been trying to get my head around it, which wasn't easy when you've got a whole hotel of guests who are paying you a small fortune to give them the best Christmas ever. This morning, I finally decided that I had to tell my best friend about it at last."

Sam smiled across at Chloe, who returned it, beaming with happiness for us. "The rest, well you pretty much know..." he trailed off and once again there was silence as we all took it in.

After a few seconds I thought I owed it to Sam to take the spotlight away from him, so I said brightly. "Well I liked that story. Could you repeat that bit about how I was so lovely that I turned your world to mush?"

It certainly worked. I was suddenly submerged under a barrage of corks, party poppers, cracker presents, and it was topped off when Chris hit me squarely in the face with a large blob of extra thick double cream. As I mimicked the comedy wind screen wipers to clear my vision, I said wryly - "I'll take that as a no..."

"You do that young Rem!" Dan said sagely, patting my head as if I were three years old. "Otherwise we might just move on to the state you were in, when you came out of the dahlias…"

On a bright fake Boxing day, we got a couple of buses and ended up in the New Forest, where we had a long walk that ended at a pub with a log fire blazing. Back at Moreland Road we ended our house Christmas weekend with cold cuts and some actual Boxing Day TV that we watched on iPlayer. At the end of the evening, with college calling in the morning, Chloe summoned up her inner Shirley Temple once more. With a nod to Sam's words of the night before, she squeaked in a dubious American accent.

"Oh, my goodness! That was the best Christmas ever!"

8.

From the best Christmas ever to the best time of my life. The Easter term was a riot of hard work, laughter, friendship and a blossoming relationship which I really believed could last a lifetime. OK, I expect some of our contemporaries thought us a tad cliquey. We didn't go out of our way to invite other people into our circle, but in fairness, we didn't actively dissuade them either.

We sometimes went out with large groups to concerts or parties, but we always seemed to end up gravitating towards each other and were known as the Moreland Road lot, certainly to the people on my course anyway.

We did spend a lot of time at home, it was cheaper for a start and I was resisting getting a job in the evenings. Although, I suspected that it would have to happen soon if I wanted to pay off my student loan this side of fifty.

We would occasionally meet in the student bar or the Chequers after studies, have a quick drink before going home to supper, then coursework, TV or games depending on our mood or impending deadlines. Chloe was very good for us at this time. Her work load was quite a lot greater than ours, so she sometimes plonked herself at the dining room table after supper. She then demanded quiet and everyone would either join her and study, or disappear off to their rooms - surprisingly enough it was quite often the former.

Strangely, after the early days when everywhere I went I

would see Foz and his crew; after I'd moved out of the halls and in to Moreland Road, I barely saw them at all. It wasn't a great source of worry to me. One night when I was in the student bar waiting for the others, I heard the unmistakeable sound of: "Well if it isn't the Pete-ster! Where have you been hiding? Still having your fill of slitty-eyed sex I hope!!"

I don't punch people, I've never had the urge and if I tried I'm pretty sure I would hurt myself more than I would hurt them… and that's even before they punched me in return. But at that moment I never felt more of a desire to do so. However, a subtle revenge can quite often be sweeter, as well as causing a lot less trouble.

I had been talking to twin sisters who were on my course just before I'd been carotted and a little ruse came into my brain and out of my mouth before I'd had the chance to filter it.

"My lovely Chloe? Of course! She's possibly even more rampant than the day you met her - insatiable that one!" They were beginning to get a slightly envious emerald colour, so I thought I would ramp it up to gas mark nine.

"Christmas was mad! I went back to her house in the country. She has twin sisters slightly older than her and just as beautiful! And my God Fozzy! What can I say - they share everything…!"

With perfect timing, Chloe herself arrived at the bar, so with a quick - "Got to go! It's champagne and shower night tonight!" I swept away from them and towards Chloe, who clocked the situation as soon as I whispered quickly, "Chequers tonight I think, text the others!"

I would have loved to get a better glimpse of their faces but didn't dare to look back, so I whisked Chloe away and told her the story on our walk back to the pub. She was completely unperturbed by the fact that I had turned her into a bisexual nymphomaniac who enjoyed an incestuous relationship with her twin sisters. I never told her the exact words they had used to describe her, but she would have guessed the general gist, I'm sure.

Talking of twins – despite their bragging of women and threesomes the first night I had met them - neither Chris or Dan had had so much of a date since that time, either together or singularly. In fact, most nights they disappeared into Dan's room, just as I disappeared into Sam's. I asked Sam one night if he thought that they were on the same side of the church as us… Yeah, I know – that euphemism thingy, it's contagious.

"D'you know? I don't really think so, not like us anyway." We had a game we used to play when we were out in town - "Dishy young dad at three o'clock!" At which point the other would give him a mark out of ten, I know, ridiculously un-PC, but it's nice to share a hobby…

"I've never seen them look like that at another guy, I can sit in the lounge in my undies and they don't twitch an eyebrow and when you gave them the lap dance at Christmas…" After Sam's confession and the attack on my person, we had sung Christmas songs and played party games that had got a little rowdy… "They were laughing, but certainly not oggling you like I was!"

"Inexplicable!" I laughed, "So what are they?"

"I think," Sam said slowly, looking for the right words, "that they are basically straight, OK with strong bi leanings, but I think each of them have found their soul mate, who just happens to be the same gender."

"But what if one of them got a girlfriend?"

"I'm not sure they ever will, she would have to accept their relationship, and I think that's too much to ask of any woman."

Mind you, not that we could really talk about being out and open. Because we all went around in a group, no-one really questioned the dynamics of our tribe. I asked Chloe one night why she thought Sam was reluctant to be out and proud. "I just don't think he feels it necessary," she said, "it's not like he's looking for a playmate, he has the perfect one," she brushed my cheek with her fingers and I smiled. "He's quite private, is Sam, and when I met his dad I got the impression that he is a little last century on some of his views. Sam loves his dad so much, but I think he knows there may be difficulties there.

At that moment I didn't realise just how accurate his worries would turn out to be.

***

I was having such a good time and enjoying life so much that I hadn't really given a thought to the Easter break. As time went on, and clocks were due to go forward, I suddenly realised I was heading for another enforced break from my "Wonderful Life" - to borrow a title from an old song of the last century. Chloe had to work for her sponsors, Dan and Chris had got sports training jobs at an Easter camp in Brentwood and Sam had the delight of a Royal Holm View Easter to keep him amused.

I asked the Manager of the pub I had worked in last summer if he had any hours available. With the impending spring rush of tourists coming out of hibernation, he bit my hand off and gave me practically a full-time job for the whole of the holiday.

Although I missed Sam, this time we skyped each other whenever we both had a moment. It was more the absence of his physical presence. The blonde-haired arms wrapping themselves around me. The tousled headed grunts and groans as I forced him out of bed. The underwear clad limbs coming into view as I flopped on the sofa looking up at the staircase. These were the things I missed. I could see him, and I could talk to him, I just couldn't ravage him every day.

Apparently, he missed the intimacy too. He stunned me the Sunday before Good Friday by asking if he could come over to Shaftesbury to stay for a few days - was tomorrow all right? He had to be back in time for the Easter weekend rush, but his dad had said that he could do without him for a few days beforehand. As soon as I went in for my shift in the evening, I broached the subject of some time off and was given a similar ultimatum. As long as I could work all hours over the extended Easter weekend, the next few days wouldn't be a problem. It was a trade easily made and I quickly texted Sam with the good news.

Although I had been out and open at school, my sexuality was something I'd never discussed with my parents. Like I said, they were lovely, just a little remote maybe and we didn't really discuss stuff like that. However, earlier on in the holiday because of our frequent skyping sessions and the fact that I mentioned Sam in every other sentence, my mum and dad had calmly asked me if there was anything I wanted to tell them.

They accepted my news as if I had told them that Honey Nut Crunch was now my favourite breakfast cereal, which is an awful lot better than some gay kids experience after telling their parents. I guess I should have been grateful, but I was just a little miffed that my big reveal had been received so calmly... I guess we all have a little diva inside who wants their share of the limelight, and since mine had been awoken by the striptease at the fountain, it seems there was no stopping it...

When I skyped Sam, after our respective shifts on that Sunday night, I warned him that my parents knew about our relationship. Dean also knew - I had triumphantly texted him after our House Christmas weekend and had been rewarded with an incredulous reply of "FUCK OFF!!!"

We had met a few times since I had returned, and he had interviewed me with the tenacity of an investigative reporter sniffing out a government toppling scoop. Mandy, Gemma and Mark also knew, and I wanted Sam to meet my friends whilst he was visiting; call me old fashioned, but if you were dating someone as gorgeous as him, you'd want to brag too, wouldn't you?

He received all this information with an easy equanimity that made me wonder if he was getting to the point where he was comfortable in his own skin. Maybe it was just easier to deal with a bunch of strangers in the know, than a family you had left in the dark.

Our three-day holiday at home was magical. He charmed my parents instantly and by the time he left they had developed an easy rapport that almost made me jealous. He became instant friends with my friends - Mandy and Gemma gazed at him as if they were two Beliebers at a convention. Dean, of course, picked up on this and by the end of the evening, had started calling them the two Moreibers.

Not that Dean himself had any right to tease - I laughingly told him off at one point when he had yet again asked Sam if he was interested in a threesome. "Do you mind?" He exclaimed, "I've barely mentioned it!"

This drew laughing exclamations from around the table and I said sarcastically, "Oh pardon me! You've only said it about forty-five times!"

"Exactly," Dean said in a tone of someone totally exonerated from any charges, "barely mentioned it!"

We fell back into the summer term, with end of year exams the only blight on our perfect world. However, with Chloe's revision workshop in session most evenings, we all found that we did better than we expected.

Even though the Easter holidays had been bearable, I still didn't like the thought of Sam and I being apart for the whole of the summer, even with the joys of Skype and Facetime along with the prospect of the odd mid-week rendezvous in Shaftesbury. One evening, when I was talking to Sam about ringing the pub to sort out hours for the long summer break, he said "God Rem! I don't want us to be apart all summer." He paused, giving himself a chance to think.

"Don't ring tonight, let me talk to my dad and see if he needs a barman at the hotel for the holidays!" Just the fact that he felt that way made my stomach churn away like someone had switched on a stick blender inside it, but the next half hour was hell.

Sam's dad was in a particularly chatty mood and it seemed to take an eternity before Sam could ask the question. Suddenly the summer that I resigned myself to, looked like a very poor alternative to the one that was a simple "yes" away from being in my grasp. As Sam said the words, I held my breath. It was the massive smile on Sam's face that gave me the answer I'd been wanting. This was even before he said, "That's great Dad - I'll tell him. No problem about covering for you on the Monday either. We'll be down on the 18th."

Chloe had to leave fairly quickly after the end of term. Sam's dad wanted to go to a hotel conference on the 19th of June, which was his deputy manager's day off, so had asked if Sam could run the hotel for him in his absence. So, on Saturday before, we had our last house meal of the year. After dinner we played stupid games that seemed to involve a lot of movement, which after a huge paella on a stifling evening made us hot, sweaty and uncomfortable.

"We need a walk," was Chloe's pronouncement, but there was a glimmer in her eyes. I knew by now that this was a sure sign she had a plan.

She led us along the warm summer streets, only just dusk at 10:30, until we reached the deserted university quad from where we approached the Millennium Fountain once more.

"Right everybody! Strip!" She announced, standing in almost the same position as the night in October. This time, however, it wasn't just Sam and I that ended up totally nude. All five of us stripped off our clothing, Chloe's pert and beautiful body, dwarfed by Chris and Dan's gym toned nakedness. On a count of three we jumped in and ran to the middle, the cool shower as much a relief on the sticky night as it had been on that night in October, but for totally different reasons. Sam and Chloe started to trade insults jokingly, which was quite typical for them until Sam said something particularly rude about Chloe. I jumped to her defence and tripped him, so he fell face first into the water.

I submerged his head totally for a couple of seconds and then took the pressure off slightly allowing him to force his head back up. He was laughing, beads of water streaming from his soaked head. He stood up and ran towards me, catching me quite easily. If truth were to be told, I wasn't trying too hard to escape.

"Now I've got you my pretty!" he snarled, half pantomime villain, half sex god. He swivelled me around, his hands clasped me firmly on the arse and pulled me towards him, kissing me aggressively on the lips. This threatened to cause a reaction in my body that would have really had our friend the Security Guard worrying about the acidity levels in the fountain. As it was it provoked comments from our nearest and dearest friends.

"Please, this is a family show!"

"What is the matter with you!"

"Put them away you two for pity's sake!"

The last comment from Dan caused me to look at Sam and I could see he was suffering in the same way I was. Luckily our friends came to our aid. They bent down and scooped handfuls of water in our direction totally submerging us in a watery torrent until we were all laughingly exhausted, lying on the floor of the fountain, looking up at the stars.

"So, I've finished my year as I started it, naked and soaking wet in the bloody Millennium Fountain!" I laughed and then sobering slightly, looked at them all fondly. "Thank you all so much for the best year of my life!" This started a human equivalent of clinking glasses, each of us ensuring that we kissed and hugged each other in turn. It was only when we were all hugging someone for the third time that we laughingly called a halt. I had my arms around Chris at the time and I realised that Sam was probably right, because although I was stark naked in front of him, I could see that half of his gaze was on Dan. He in turn was hugging Chloe and Sam together - and his gaze was half on Chris.

"I'll miss you Rem," Chris said, "don't disgrace yourself at the Hotel de Morris, and I look forward to more nonsense come September!"

I didn't realise then, how much would happen, and how much would change in my life, before I was to see him again.

9.

As the train pulled out of Warminster station I shuffled around in my seat so that my back was leaning up against the carriage window. This way I could get a better view of Sam sitting in the seat to my left.

Well, a little bit of mild obsession never hurt anyone…

I loved to watch him when he was unaware that he was being observed. The little twitches, ticks and facial gymnastics reflected everything about him. His intelligence, his dopiness, his sense of humour and his kindness; they were all there to be seen, as clear as a mobile advertising hoarding. At that moment he was listening to music on his iPhone which seemed to be last year's White Lies album, if my reading of the lyrics that played across his lips was in any way accurate.

He must have sensed my gaze on him as he looked across and stopped his silent singing and giving me a huge grin, removed his ear phones and tucked them into his breast pocket.

"Stalker!" he teased.

"I'm just getting my fill of you - seeing as you have decided that we have to return to the closet for the summer…" I said with forced animosity, "…especially after all the time it took to prise you out in the first place!

He had broken the news me a couple of weeks before. We had been lying on the bed in his room after a particularly passionate interlude. We were both slightly sweaty on a warm and sticky night. I was just thinking about suggesting we shared a shower to freshen us up - and maybe prolong the intimacy - when he pulled himself up onto one elbow and caressed my face with his other hand.

"Rem...?" He started hesitantly, "please don't think that I'm ashamed of you - or us - but would you hate it if we pretended we were friends and not lovers to my parents?"

I guess it was a little bit of a blow, albeit not an unexpected one. Chloe had already warned me that she thought it unlikely that he would out himself to his parents.

"His dad's a bit of a troglodyte," she had explained, "a very nice one, but a troglodyte none the less!"

Sam mistook my silence for annoyance and hurried on to fill the void.

"It's not that I won't tell them, but can we wait until they get to know you? If we tell them straight away, my dad might just automatically take against you. But once he does get to know you - how could he not understand my feelings for you? How could he and Mum not love you?"

OK, I've always been a sucker for a bit of flattery and to be fair... that was pretty good flattery, so I let him off the hook; but that didn't mean I couldn't give him stick about it occasionally.

As a response to my latest bout of teasing, Sam sighed the melodramatic sigh of the perennially put upon - and then a sly grin crossed his face. "Of course, Mum and Dad have never allowed me to share a room with any girlfriends I've brought home, so if they thought we were a couple, it would be the spare top floor staff room for you, whereas..."

I interrupted him before he had a chance to finish his sentence. "Didn't I say straight away that it was far too early to tell your folks about us? Much better to let them get to know me first!"

Sam revelled in my instant capitulation. "You are as

shallow as a stream in the summertime!" He taunted whilst pulling his earphones back out of his pocket to return to the sounds of White Lies. I went back to watching the scenery, and it's not the rolling Wiltshire countryside I'm referring to.

***

I clattered my suitcase off the train at Bristol Temple Meads, whilst Sam was travelling rucksack light. I had ensured that I'd brought enough clothing with me to keep myself clean and smart for the whole of the summer, whereas Sam could rely on the comforts of an inbuilt wardrobe at home to manage the same result. I grumbled to that effect as I hauled all my worldly goods down the staircase to the subway.

"Oh, stop your whinging!" Sam laughed as he ambled along beside me, "look we've got fifty minutes 'til our train for Weston leaves - would a pint of ale shut you up?"

I thought it probably would.

He led me up the stairs to platform three of the cathedral like railway station, and onwards to a buffet bar that was probably part of the original structure. Inside it had stone walls and high ceilings and looked a little like a trendy café bar in the middle of a city. OK, some of the interior was a little battered and bashed by traveller and trunk, but it was still the poshest station buffet I'd ever seen. And it served real ale!

I manoeuvred my way across a floor strewn with enough obstacles to give an aspiring TV producer the idea for a television game show, and settled into a faux leather sofa at the far end of the bar. I watched Sam waiting at the bar to be served and remembered the first time we had been in similar positions. I had been waiting nervously to see if we had anything in common, or whether I had subjected myself to a two-hour quiz and a prospective soaking, just to discover he was an arrogant twerp with a lovely face. If you had told my October self the itinerary for this summer, he would have been delighted and disbelieving in equal measure.

The only niggle of concern in my practically perfect Mary Poppins world was Sam's dad. I must admit that I was a little nervous about meeting him. In my thinking, a troglodyte, albeit a nice one, needed a little bit of careful handling; especially if it was to lead up to a big announcement at the end of the summer. As you know, I could worry about whether I was going the wrong way up an escalator.

Sam returned with our drinks and we clinked glasses. "Here's to a summer of a bit of work, a bit of play and a lot of…" The last word he whispered in my ear to avoid the sight of three matronly ladies on the next table choking on their cappuccinos.

***

We had missed the day trippers by a couple of hours and the commuters by a couple of days, so the afternoon stopping train to Weston was practically an empty one. I could see Sam getting more and more excited as we passed through each of the stations on the line. By the time we stopped at the tiny halt of Weston Milton, Sam was already grabbing his rucksack and signalling for me to be ready with my suitcase.

"Oh my God! No!" Sam screamed as we pulled into the rather quaint station of Weston-super-Mare, full of hanging baskets and rustic charm. Slightly bemused, I picked up my suitcase and followed him on to the platform. By the time I had bashed my way from the train, Sam had his arms wrapped securely around a young girl, who I guessed to be Emily, his sister. She was as dark haired as he was blonde, but there was a definite family resemblance there. She was what my father would have called "a bit of a stunner."

"Please tell me that Mum is waiting outside in the car?" He pleaded in comedic disbelief.

Emily smiled and shook her head slowly.

"You came in a taxi then?" Michael McIntyre had nothing on him as far as comedy angst was concerned.

Again, the smiling shake of the head.

"I don't suppose you walked?" He asked hopefully, but there was another negative response.

"Please don't tell me that some bloody idiot has seen fit to allow you to drive a car legally?"

The smile was miles wide and hands resting on Sam's shoulder she jumped up and down in a jig of delight.

"They did Sam! I've passed my test!"

"It is an outrage! I demand a second opinion!"

"Just because I've beaten you to it there is no need to be such a grumpy guts!" Emily released her grip on his shoulders and turned to see me for the first time. "Or be so bloody rude…" She moved a couple of paces towards me and I held out my hand in greeting, she ignored it and went in for a full body hug, just like her brother would have done. "Hi, I'm Emily, the Grouch's sister and you must be Rem?"

"I guess I must be!" I agreed, realising suddenly that Sam had never called me Peter since I'd known him, so I guessed I was stuck with my nickname. I didn't mind, Chloe had been the first to call me Rembrandt and Sam had been the first to abbreviate it… I liked it.

We walked out of the station, Emily gabbling on about the end of her A-level exams. She had officially finished school. In three weeks' time she would go back for Speech Day and the Leavers' Ball, but other than that, she was done and dusted.

"Dad's got me waitressing of course," she said. "I keep telling him that I won't need to know about table service in veterinary college, but he just says…"

"Whilst you're under my roof young lady… you can bloody well help out!" Sam finished the sentence and they both laughed.

I liked her immediately and being an only child, I almost felt jealous of their intimacy. No matter what life had in store, they would always have each other. It must be a nice feeling, I reckoned; but not knowing anything different, I don't suppose they gave the alternative a second thought.

We walked towards a short stay car park with a large Tesco dominating the area behind it. We all got into the car and Emily drove down past what I was reliably informed was the Town Hall and beyond it, the soon to be opened multiplex cinema and on to the sea front itself. The tide was out, and my first view of the coast was a large expanse of mud flats that seemed to extend almost as far as an island between Weston and the Welsh coast called Steep Holm.

My tour guides reliably informed me that it was this tall outcrop in the Bristol Channel along with her lower slung sister, called imaginatively, Flat Holm, that gave the Morris Family Hotel its name.

As I bounced about in the back of the car, I had to admit reluctantly, that Sam was right. I had absolutely no idea how Emily had passed her test. She didn't seem to believe in stopping at roundabouts, junctions… pedestrians. The journey was like a Banksy version of a Royal Procession along the Promenade, but instead of a cavalcade of sleek Rolls-Royces and Bentleys being greeted by cheers and waves, it was a baby blue Fiat 500 being greeted by V signs and shaken fists. By the time we had reached the Royal Holm View Hotel, I was amazed that she had been driving for two weeks and the little car had barely a scratch on it.

Sam must have noticed my glazed expression because he whispered quietly to me whilst helping me take my suitcase out of the boot… "Don't say I didn't warn you!"

"Well, you didn't warn me!"

"I didn't know, did I?"

"Ignorance is no excuse!"

Once I'd sorted out my luggage, I stood and looked at the Hotel for the first time.

It had been built late in the nineteenth century and had been inspired by the design of the Grand Atlantic Hotel, a hotel that had been pointed out to me on our journey down the Beach Road. However, I had been more intent on keeping my head from drilling a hole in the car roof than looking at it properly.

From the safety of terra firma, I could at least look at the Holm View properly. It was a late Victorian building in the dark grey colour of an angry sky, with a turret at either end and a view from all the front rooms over Uphill Sands. Every storey had either sashed windows with a canopy above, or French windows and a small balcony.

To be fair, it was a little exaggeration to call it a balcony, you would be hard pressed to get one person standing outside, let alone a chair so that you could sit in the sunshine. Maybe the architect had wanted to add a little interest, or maybe the original plan had been to have proper balconies outside the French windows and money problems had forced a compromise. The wrought iron had then been added to stop a short-sighted person walking to their death in the middle of the night.

I glanced behind me, Emily had abandoned the car - even being charitable you could have barely called it parking - in one of the two taxi pick up spaces in front of the hotel. Across the driveway was an immaculate lawn packed with classy garden furniture. It was full of people enjoying a post dinner coffee, or summer Sunday afternoon pint. At the far end of the grass there was a gate that gave access directly to the beach. To my left, there was a golf course that Sam had told me gave special rates to guests and staff at the hotel. Not that I was likely to use it, Mark Twain had described the game as a good walk spoiled and I was right there with him on that one! I glanced back at the Hotel, as idyllic went, it was pretty much up there.

Sam and Emily were already half way up the entrance steps and I was just about to shout something rude about being left to bring all the luggage on my own, when I saw the reason for their haste. A woman had appeared at the doorway of the Hotel and Sam ran towards her and into her opened arms, enveloping her in a huge Sam hug that I had got to know and love so much.

Fiona Morris was a striking woman - think Downton's Lady Mary twenty years on and you've got the vague idea. After Sam had introduced me, she took my hand in such a way that I wasn't sure if I should shake it or kiss it, but rather luckily plumped for the first option.

"If you take Rem up to your room, get yourselves settled. Your dad said he'd see you in his office when you're ready."

Sam nodded, "Busy lunch?"

"Packed!" His mum agreed happily… "Oh Emily!" she called as she saw her younger child sneaking towards the staircase under the cover of our welcome. "Dad said to make sure you go back to the restaurant as soon as you arrived back and help everyone finish with the clearing up."

"Bummer!" said Emily, "So close to getting under the razor wire but the searchlight got me!" She changed direction abruptly and giving us a cheery wave, disappeared towards the call of duty.

Sam's room was at the rear of the building, overlooking the car park and the point where Beach Road turned into Uphill Road North. It was a good-sized room dominated by a king-sized bed. It was clean and tidy but going by the state of his room in Moreland Road, I guessed it was probably the touch of a chambermaid that had left it so, rather than the tsunami state it would have been in the day that Sam had left for the summer term.

"It's very tidy," I observed.

Sam grinned, "What are you insinuating?"

"Oh, I don't know, just that the young son and heir has a nanny to change his diaper and chambermaids to clean his room…"

"I'm not actually Prince George you know," he corrected with comedic patience. Then he continued more soberly, "Dad's very strict on making sure we don't use the Hotel staff for stuff like that, but Mum does always manage to sneak a girl into my room, just so it's tidy when I get home at least."

"Sneaking girls into your room?" I arched an eyebrow, "She really doesn't know you, does she?" I received a wallop for my cheek and Sam pushed me across the room.

"I think you'll find your area over there," he waved a dismissive hand in the direction of a camp bed erected in the far corner.

I turned back and stroked a placating hand across his chest, "But you have such a big bed and I would hate for you to be lonely…"

Sam sighed a big dramatic sigh, "Oh well! If you must…" He then added as an afterthought, "perhaps you better make sure you rumple the spare bed up sometimes in the morning though…"

I could almost feel the closet door closing.

***

As you can imagine, I was never in a lot of trouble at school, but I was once sent to see the Headmaster when I had poured Angel Whip down the back of Alex Garvey's trousers after a friendly tussle had got a little out of control in the dining hall. I had the same sense of nerves as we were walking down to see Sam's dad. The main difference this time was the absence of squelching sounds from my co-traveller's buttocks.

Mr Morris was a huge man in every way, tall, dominant and imposing, with a waist line that spoke of good living and a lack of a gym membership. He might have owned a

"Vitality Suite" but he certainly didn't use one. His hair had gone prematurely white and his face sported a matching moustache and beard. I was tempted to ask him how he managed to sort out the problem of finding a Santa Claus at Christmas - but decided that irony wasn't a good opening gambit.

Once we'd dispensed with the how do you dos and discussed our journey down, Mr Morris, or Ned as he asked me to call him, got straight down to business.

"So, Rem, I guess Sam will have told you how difficult it is to get staff to cover weekends here," I nodded. "Basically, if you could work long shifts Friday, through to Sunday, you can have the rest of the week off." He went into full details of the shifts he needed covering then turned to his son... "As for you Samuel..."

"I know!" Sam interrupted, "Wherever, whatever, whenever!"

Ned smiled the smile of a summer Santa with gifts to give. "Well actually... no. Your mum has persuaded me that as you have a friend here this summer," he nodded in my direction, "and unlike your sister you never seem to moan about the amount of work we expect you to do, you can do the same hours as Rem here." He paused to let it sink in, "the wherever, whatever bit is correct though!"

Sam had already told me that he was used to being deputy manager one minute, pot wash the next and a chef in between, He had also told me to expect that I wouldn't see a lot of him, so this was an unexpected bonus. OK I could have probably worked more days in Shaftesbury and earned more money, but thirty odd hours working followed by four days off seemed a good deal to me - and I would spend the whole summer with Sam.

Ned continued, "I still need you to cover for me tomorrow though," Sam nodded. "And I might have to call on you both to fill in if we have any sudden staff shortages, but they've all been pretty reliable lately." He flicked a finger to his head, "touch wood!"

At that moment Ned's extension rang and Sam signalled to him that we were going to leave. Before we could do so, Ned left the phone ringing for long enough to say… "And tell your bloody sister to move her friggin' rust bucket from the taxi only parking spaces!"

Five minutes later, message delivered, we were crossing the lawn area still littered with people enjoying a drink in the early evening sunshine and went through the gate I had seen earlier. The tide had come in since we had been inside and the whole look of the seafront had changed. With the blue sky above, it was much more Mediterranean chic than the mid channel mudflat look of earlier. Add on top of that, the news we had just received, and we were both suddenly in a holiday mood.

Sam made a funny noise, a cross between a yodel and a yell and tore his shirt off before tying it around his waist and setting off at a full paced sprint towards the water. He turned his back towards the tide, but continued running in reverse - shouting at me to join him and well, as I've said before, I'm a good boy and always do as I'm told…

Pulling off my shirt as he had done, I ran towards him and as I reached him, he turned, and we ran the final distance to the water's edge, side by side.

We then took our shoes and socks off and rolling our trousers just above our knees we paddled our way along the shoreline. Before too long Sam, as always, took the whole thing one step further than sensible and started kicking the water in my direction. Of course, I couldn't let this go without retaliation and before too long our trousers were soaked, and our chests were glossed with sea spray.

"Am I cursed to always end up soaking wet whenever I'm with you!" Sam wailed after a particularly violent kick of mine had sent a tidal wave in his direction, covering him from his flattened hair to his drenched jeans and all points in between.

I pointed out patiently that he had started it and then ran from the water before he had chance to finish it as well. He raced after me and caught me as the sand softened towards the dunes. He rugby tackled me to the ground and we rolled around covering ourselves, so that we looked like two sub-standard sand carvings; gaining ourselves a disapproving tut from an elderly couple walking a Jack Russell that was almost as sand blasted as we were.

We lay there for a while in companionable silence before we made our way back to the hotel. Sam led me up the dunes and across the gorse, then being careful to avoid any wayward golf swings, crossed the course at an angle until we reached a small lane that led to the main car park I had seen earlier from Sam's room. We reached a fenced area that seemed to hold a bin for every eventuality - and shook and rubbed the now dried sand from our bodies.

Putting our shirts back on we went through the back door. I could hear chefs clattering and bantering in the kitchen beyond, but even rubbed down and shirted we weren't in a fit state to meet anyone. We had just reached the floor below the Morris apartment when running down the stairs was a lean, tall young man with sandy hair and a hipster beard.

"Well hello Sam!" He drawled. "Have you had a fight with a Sand Fairy?" He managed to make it sound suggestive and contemptuous at one and the same time.

"Sort of!" Sam grinned being careful not to look at me as he said it.

"I believe I have the pleasure of serving you tonight when you dine en famille!"

I was beginning to believe that he might be a slimy toe rag.

Sam turned to me and explained - "The first night I arrive home, we always have a family meal" and then to the Hipster, "Oh Jack, this is Rem, a friend of mine who's staying the summer and working the bar at weekends for us."

"Yes... I believe I have the pleasure of training him

tomorrow." He made it sound as inviting as a cruise on the Costa Concordia and managed the whole exchange without looking at me once.

"OK," Sam said vaguely, "Dad hasn't mentioned that yet - but I'm sure you're right." He nodded in my direction. "Come on you! We'd better go and make ourselves look respectable, see you later Jack!"

Jack nodded, and we continued our journeys in opposite directions. Once safely inside the apartment I said laughingly to Sam:

"He so fancies the pants off of you!"

Sam looked at me with incredulity. "Jack?" He frowned as if I had tried to submit a word with five consonants in a game of Scrabble, "don't be daft! He lives with an uncle old enough to be his grandfather and he seems to be out with a different girlfriend every night!"

Sometimes he really does have no idea.

We stripped naked and shared a shower in his en-suite bathroom. My helpfulness in trying to ensure that he was completely sand free led to a love making session that was as easy to predict as a White Christmas on the Matterhorn...

But quite a lot hotter.

Once we were dressed and respectable we seemed to have enough time for a pint before dinner. However, I had reckoned without the Sam factor. As soon as we walked into the bar everyone wanted to talk to him.

A group of lads wanted to chat about getting a discount round of golf at the club next door. An elderly couple wanted to know if Sam could organise a special deal at the Hotel's Rugrats club for when their great grandchildren visited?

A family wanted details about a BOGOF scheme the hotel was running on weekday lunches - did that include

Sunday?

Staff wanted to know information about everything from wages to hours they were working. I was going to discover, over the next few weeks, that everyone went to Sam for information because he was much more approachable than his father. Ned Morris had a reputation for being slightly volatile - not always the sunny Santa Claus I had seen earlier.

Sam tried to include me in the conversation, but it was obvious that people only wanted to talk to him. I thought I would ease the situation by taking my pint outside and leaving him to it.

I had just settled myself on an empty table near to the Taxi parking spaces, now Fiat 500 free, when I heard my name being called. I looked up to see Emily emerging from the building sucking a carton of fruit juice through a straw. Completely oblivious to the sign that told her that only food and drink bought on the premises could be consumed at the Hotel tables, she joined me.

"So," she said after I had asked her about her afternoon and given her a censored version of my own, "which one of you is the top?"

I had a mouthful of beer at the time, so I moved my head quickly, to splutter my drink on to the grass rather than Emily or myself. I tried to look baffled and innocent, but Emily was having none of it.

"Oh please!" She laughed, "I guessed ages ago - I mean what fifteen-year-old boy do you know refuses to play Grand Theft Auto because he feels sorry for the prostitutes?"

"We-ll…" I drew the word out, I'd sort of worried about them myself.

"Exactly!" Emily said triumphantly, "you're both far too nice to be straight!"

"Why didn't you say anything to him? I asked

"Oh, I knew he would tell me when he was ready," she said easily. "And I wasn't completely certain. Then at

Christmas he was so down, which was really unlike Sam, but suddenly at Easter he was back to normal and I have never seen him as excited as he was when he was due to visit you in Shaftesbury. Then, when he asked if you could work here over the summer, well, I was pretty sure. As soon as I met you this afternoon I really knew for certain."

"Excuse me!" I pretended to be outraged, "Mr Straight-Acting, I am!"

"Oh please, you're like Norton and Carr's love child!" She teased, then conceded, "OK you're not that camp – it was just the way you were with each other, it was obvious to me."

The summer suddenly seemed a lot more awkward than I'd thought it would be.

"Do you think your dad...?" I was interrupted by a contemptuous snort.

"Dad? Never! It just wouldn't occur to him, Mum possibly - but she wouldn't say anything if she did."

"Would your dad be that worried?"

"That Golden Boy is gay?" she asked, and I nodded. "Possibly, he is a bit right wing in most of his views. You know - too many immigrants, homos, disabled people and scroungers - the country is full of Polish one-legged lesbians with sixteen children wasting our hard-earned taxes!" She paused for a breath. "I guess Sam is thinking that if he gets to know you and like you, he might take it a bit better"

"You know your brother well!"

"Well, to be fair, it worked with Chloe - when Sam told Dad that her parents were Chinese immigrants, he went a bit UKIP, but as soon as he met her and got to know her, he absolutely loved her."

"I can but hope!" I grinned.

"I guess my darling brother's plan would be to wait until the end of the holiday, tell him, then run away back to uni, leaving us to deal with the explosion; hoping that he will have calmed down by the next time he sees him?"

It was half question, half statement.

"Pretty much so," I winced. Putting it like that sounded a bit cowardly.

"Sounds like a bloody good plan to me!" She laughed at my discomfort, jumped up and came around to my side of the table. "Now brother-in-law, give me a big hug!"

We were in the middle of a half sitting, half standing, back to front hug come cuddle, when Sam appeared, pint in hand and a questioning look on his face.

"What are you two up to?" he asked

"Oh, just getting to know your boyfriend better!" Emily said easily.

Sam looked around quickly - as if to check that no-one had overheard - and then glared at us, before saying to me, "What have you been telling her?" I held my hands up in an innocent gesture and Emily came to my defence.

"Oh Sammy! I've known you were kicking the pink football for ages!"

This euphemism thing - it's an epidemic…

Sam squatted on the seat I had been sitting in previously, "You, er, you won't…"

"No, I won't tell Dad. Yes, I think you're doing the right thing to wait until later to tell him. Yes, Rem is absolutely lovely! And, I'm very happy for you."

This earned her another cuddle hug from me and a beaming smile from Sam.

"Tell me though," She smiled a wicked smile, "which one of you is the top?"

10.

There were three private rooms at the end of the dining room, just to the left of the doors that led to the kitchens. They were called Brean, Berrow and Burnham and were hired out for business meetings and private dining. The family dinner was to be held in Brean, the smallest of the three. By the time we had arrived, Fiona was already there, talking to a man seated in the chair nearest to the door.

He was tall, wiry and grey looking. He had a rather pathetic looking beard and moustache. It was as if he had started growing it when he was sixteen, and forty odd years on, it still hadn't quite taken hold. Opposite him was a lady who was so obviously Fiona's sister, that she might as well have been sporting a big game show badge saying just that.

"Oh, here they are," Fiona said. "Rem, this is Maureen my sister, and her husband John. Rem is a good friend of Sam's from university." Mumbled hellos were exchanged and Fiona organised Emily to sit in the middle next to John, I sat next to Emily with Sam sort of opposite me, next to Maureen. Fiona went to sit at the top of the table between "the two boys" leaving the other head of the table for Ned who arrived at that moment.

"Sorry everyone! Just checking on the beef, it looks fabulous! Rem you're just about to taste proper food after being a poor starving student for the last few months!"

I was tempted to say that with a hotelier and Chloe both living at Moreland Road we did pretty well food wise, but thought that it might sound ungrateful, so I kept my council. I could see Sam chewing on his cheek, to prevent himself laughing, so I knew he'd guessed exactly what I was thinking.

Jack arrived and started pouring the wine. I was amused to see that when he got around to Sam, he got so close to his body that his nostrils were practically touching Sam's earlobes.

As straight as a Spiralizer.

I was suddenly aware that Ned was talking and looking in my general direction, so I pulled my attention back into the room.

"… might have told you Rem, I don't really believe in having the staff running around after the family. I want them to concentrate on the paying guests but, just occasionally, it is nice to have a family meal like this."

I nodded and asked about the history of the hotel. Emily groaned a heard it all before groan but everyone ignored her.

"Did you see the Grand Atlantic Hotel on your way down the seafront?" Ned asked.

I nodded, but didn't add that I'd had the same view of the outside world that a mushroom in a Magimix experiences.

"Well, that was originally a nineteenth century boarding school for young gentlemen, a boring square building that looked more like a prison than a school. Then I think someone decided that the view it commanded was wasted on the youth of the day; so, the school was moved elsewhere, and the building was sold, extended, turrets added and was turned into the grand building you saw."

Ned was on a roll, Sam had told me proudly that his dad was a man who naturally commanded attention and respect. I was getting an idea of what he meant.

"A family called the Meakers already owned the land on Uphill Beach, so they decided to build a building in a similar style. I think they cut a few corners design wise…"

Sign me up as an expert on Homes Under the Hammer, if you would.

"… but we're left with the rather quirky, money pit of a building you can see now - and I must say that I love it!"

"The hotel has always been owned by families you know," John spoke for almost the first time. He had a light, slightly raspy voice and spoke as if he resented the breath he was wasting on the sentence.

"Yes," Fiona joined in, "although when our dad bought it in 1984, it had been owned by a succession of managers and it was a poor sad little building that needed a lot of TLC."

"He got it at a knock down price, didn't he Fee?" Maureen laughed a laugh of fond remembrance.

"He certainly loved to get a bargain," Fiona agreed with a similar grin.

"The girls' dad ran the hotel until…?"

"1990," Fiona came to her husband's aid with the date.

"When sadly, the old man had a heart attack and died very suddenly. The girls were left with a hotel to run and a lot of worried staff."

"We were approached by loads of hotel chains who wanted to buy us out, but Maureen and I knew that it was the last thing that Dad would have wanted. We were determined to keep the hotel in the family. Luckily we had the help of lots of local people including a young solicitor who had just returned to Weston." Fiona smiled a gentle smile in the direction of her brother-in-law. "Remarkably, we made a little bit of a success of it!"

"Auntie Maureen married the solicitor," Emily butted in with a mischievous grin. "In fact, both of the daughters married the hired help at one point or another…"

This gained her an "Emily!" from her father but there was a twinkle in his eye. However, I caught sight of John's profile as Emily rocked back in her chair whilst laughing - and he didn't look amused at all.

Jack chose a very good moment to enter the room and

clear the starter plates. I must admit, he was very professional, but rather showy. He went around the table, gripping the first plate between thumb and first finger then balanced all the other plates on his little and ring fingers, enabling him to scrape any debris onto the plate below. He did this with such pompous panache, that I was willing him to drop something.

He didn't.

Once he had left the room in the style of a contestant on a yet to be commissioned game show called Strictly Come Waitering, Maureen continued with the family history.

"Someone told me once that there were similarities between us and the Edwards family that owned the hotel before Daddy," she paused to take a sip of wine. "Mr Edwards had two boys, Dad had two girls. Mr Edwards died in 1980, Dad died in 1990. But whereas the boys couldn't work together to make the hotel work... us girls did!"

"Girl power!" laughed Fiona and the sisters raised their glasses in the direction of each other. Emily was appalled.

"Oh, please you two!" she moaned, "That Spice Girl stuff is so-o embarrassing!"

"Don't be rude Emily!" This time, there was definite annoyance in her father's eyes. I think only I heard the little "Whoops!" sound that came out of Emily's mouth as she realised she might have gone too far.

He was good at timing was Jack; I must give him that. At another slightly awkward moment he once again appeared, this time with a roast dinner that would have satisfied even Dan's monumental appetite.

The food seemed to restore Ned's equilibrium and the conversation moved to the safer waters of Hotel gossip and local news. The Royal Holm View Hotel should have had its own Sky Atlantic miniseries if some of the stories were to be believed.

Once the subject had run its course, Ned had obviously

decided that it was his son's turn to receive some gentle teasing.

"So Sam, have you actually got around to asking that lovely Chloe out yet?"

Sam groaned, and I held my breath slightly, wondering if it was the opportunity that Emily needed to make a little more mischief - but fair play to her - she didn't move a muscle. It was Sam who spoke and said, "For pity's sake Dad, how many times do I have to tell you that Chloe and I are just really good friends?"

"Yes, and how many times do I tell you that there is no such thing as friendship between a man and a woman? Get on with it boy, or some other bloke will be in there and you'll have blown your chance!"

Fiona shot a withering look in her husband's direction and I decided that all things being equal, the family history was a safer subject.

I glanced over at Maureen and asked her if she still helped to run the hotel.

"Oh no," she laughed, "this one," she nodded in Ned's direction, "arrived with impeccable timing. I had just become pregnant with my first son Rory and, to be honest, had become a little bit tired with helping to run the hotel. Ned was far and away the best deputy manager we had ever had, so I felt I could step back and give all my energy to being a mother. Then of course, Fee and Ned became an item, got married and I could well and truly become a sleeping partner."

"How are Rory and Tom?" Sam asked

"Tom's in his final year at Durham and Rory is settling well in Edinburgh. I was telling your mum earlier, Libby is pregnant and we," she nodded over at John, who seemed slightly less excited at the prospect than she was, "are to become grandparents!"

"Too quick if you ask me," John muttered tetchily.

"Oh, for goodness sake, John, Rory's nearly twenty-four with a good job that he loves. Libby's a little older and they couldn't be happier… and neither could I." Maureen stared at her husband defiantly.

I was now sure that Jack was waiting outside with a glass to the door ready to make an entrance any time the conversation became sticky. Once again, he appeared with impeccable timing and started to clear the empty plates. He moved round the room repeating the balletic stacking and scraping technique of the first course. He was so pleased with himself that I was still willing him to drop something.

Sometimes I'm not as nice as everybody tells me I am.

"So Rem," It seemed that the focus was now shifting toward me as Fiona smiled in my direction. "That's a quite unusual name, what is it short for?"

Sam sniggered in remembrance and I laughed too. "Oh no, it's not my real name, just a nickname really. I'm actually called Peter, Peter Abrahams."

My revelation was interrupted by my vicious wish being realised.

Jack had just cleared John's plate and added his cutlery to the already stacked plate, which seemed to be a piece of Jenga too many. A couple of knives fell to the floor.

I'm not quite sure why I had taken against Jack, a little bit of jealousy possibly. Oh, and the fact that he behaved like a pompous ass… Whatever it was, I was grimly amused when he decided to leave the room quickly and return afterwards to take Ned's plate and pick up the fallen cutlery.

Not so Strictly Come Waitering after all…

In between all these shenanigans that the family stoically ignored, Fiona asked me how I had come by my nickname.

After revelling in Jack's embarrassment, I completely deserved a little bit of comeuppance and I felt myself going red as the spotlight shifted on to me. I glanced at Sam who laughingly nodded that I could safely tell the whole story. I told the tale of the quiz, the bet and the cheating that culminated in Sam and me naked in the Millennium Fountain. I left out the bit about the hard-ons and the feelings of lust that got me in that predicament in the first place.

By the time I had reached the point where we were hiding from the security guards everyone was laughing and I felt that I'd got through a potential minefield with relative safety.

Even John was grinning... sort of.

"Like son, like father!" Fiona laughed and glanced across to Ned, who also laughed in remembrance. "Oh you mean...?" Fiona nodded, and the focus shifted to her husband.

"It was when I was cheffing at a beach hotel in Corsica during the eighties, long before I tipped up here. The kitchen had little in the way of extraction, or air conditioning, so by the end of a shift you were just a ball of sweat. Every evening, after we cleaned up, all the chefs got in the habit of running from the kitchen, down to the shoreline to go skinny dipping in the sea. It was fantastic! One week we had a group of Nancy boys from Brighton staying in the hotel, well you know what their types are like, they must have been eyeing us up all week. On their last night, they appeared when we were enjoying our swim. We'd gone a little further out than usual. By the time we had realised what had happened, they had nicked our clothes, run back to the hotel, and were waving our underwear at us from the balcony bar. We had to stagger up the beach completely naked to hoots and catcalls from all the guests who were enjoying a drink. Bloody poofters!"

Now I could see why Sam wasn't overly keen on sharing our news...

Emily looked desperate to say something and once again I was worried that the opportunity to spill the beans about Golden Boy might be too tempting for her. However, when she did get a chance to speak she simply said, "But Dad, were they impressed...?"

"Thank you," I said when we were alone together in the bar later. Sam and his dad were going through instructions for the next day in Ned's office. Fiona was saying goodnight to her sister and John on the front steps, and we were enjoying a brandy at a table in the corner of the room.

"What for?" She said with false innocence.

"You know exactly what for!" I laughed but explained anyway. "There were a couple of occasions in there that you could have dropped us in it, but you didn't."

She was as serious as I had seen her during the whole day. "I might tease Sam all the time, but I would never drop him in it like that. I love the bones of him. When he thinks it's the right time to tell them, it will be the right time. I will stick up for him if it becomes tricky - but I'm certainly saying nothing until then."

I told Sam this as I was lying against his chest when we were alone in his room after the brandy for two had become a night cap, or two, for the whole family.

"She's all right, my sister," he said proudly, then shifted our position so he could look at me properly, "she really likes you too."

"Impeccable taste obviously," I laughed and then told him a truth that he was desperate to hear. "Your whole family are great, but Emily is the complete business… and you're not too bad yourself!"

He laughed and viscously tweaked my nipple, an action that normally led on to other things and to be fair, the inevitable happened.

"I love you," I said afterwards and was rewarded by a smile that I felt as much as saw. He whispered "Back at ya," which was fast becoming our traditional statement and response. As lights from cars that travelled along the Uphill Road flickered shadows across our bodies, I waited for sleep to arrive. When it did so, it came with a dream that would change the course of the summer irrevocably.

11.

I've always dreamed a lot - and on wakening they would remain vivid for about two minutes and then disappear from my memory banks as real life intruded into my day. I learnt at an early age never to share my dreams with anyone. What seemed fascinating to your subconscious in the middle of the night, pails somewhat in the face of a bored look or a stifled yawn.

My dreams were always of the vague variety. I would dream of people I knew, yet their faces would be wrong. I would dream of people I didn't know, who were supposed to be my closest friends, and people that I could barely make out as having any features at all. There was always a surreal quality to them and the perception that I was viewing the whole scene through fog or dry ice.

The dream I had on my first night in Weston was different.

It was just like watching a movie.

It even began with an aerial shot, as if the titles had just finished and the director was manoeuvring the viewer into his world.

The scene started with a shot above the station where Sam and I had met Emily the afternoon before. There was a train arriving, it had a sloping orangey yellow frontage with InterCity 125 written in white on the side of the blue engine. The film panned in as the carriage doors opened and followed a young man as he swung an overnight bag over his shoulder and jumped from the train onto the platform.

He was roughly my age with a fresh face and straight shoulder length hair that looked like it had been especially chosen to be featured in a shampoo commercial. He was dressed in double denim with flared jeans and a cheesecloth shirt below the jacket. He looked like he had fallen from a different time zone.

He gave his ticket to the man on the gate, who took it from him, and they exchanged cheery words. The film followed him as he moved out of the station and stood on the pavement in front of a line of taxis. Ignoring the possibility of a taxi ride, he pulled a piece of paper from the pocket of his jacket. He crossed the road, whilst looking at the paper, and continued in the direction we had driven in about twelve hours before.

It was completely different though. Tesco and the car park had disappeared and in its place, a wall ran nearly the complete length of Station Road, which itself had shrunk to having one lane in either direction. Behind the wall, there was the vague impression of a disused goods yard. At the road end, the Town Hall extension had also disappeared and was replaced by a slightly sad looking area that looked like an abandoned car park. The only vehicles to be seen on it were a few children on bicycles weaving their way around some plastic discs as if they were taking some sort of test. An officious looking man with a clip board was watching them, which enforced the theory that they weren't entirely there for fun.

In the space where I had seen the multiplex cinema earlier, the young man passed a concrete building with the legend "Dolphin Square Indoor Market" above the entrance. I was suddenly aware just how few people there were on the street. Suddenly there was a roar from the pub opposite, and the reason for it was about to come clear. The lad crossed the road and opened the door to the bar. I could just make out a television at the far end of the room, but the pictures seemed to be in black and white.

Players in grey jerseys with white shorts were congratulating each other, whilst players in white shirts with grey rims and black shorts were looking disconsolate. All of the people in the bar were shouting, some in delight, some in despair and an almighty punch up looked to be one misjudged comment away.

The young man asked an old guy by the door what the score was, "2-1 to Manchester United!" came the reply. If the young man had thought about buying a pint and watching the rest of the match, he thought better of it. He left the pub and continued his journey, until he reached the sea front. To his right there was a pier, but it looked different to the one I had seen earlier.

He continued walking away from it along the sea lawns that looked wider, greener and more spacious, than those I had bounced past the afternoon before. He passed a building that my tour guides informed me had been used for Bansky's Dismaland. The fact that it was a sad abandoned Lido at the time, had made it the perfect venue. It was neither sad nor abandoned in my dream. A magnificent art Deco diving stage towered above it and you could see a few figures climbing up and diving from it. The man stood and looked at it for a while before continuing on his way - I now knew exactly where his destination would be.

The Royal Holm View Hotel looked similar from the front, except the grass lawn that housed the chairs and tables had been transformed into a car park. The gate to the beach was still there but was tall, painted green and metal with an arched top as opposed to the belly high varnished wooden gate of today. The young man took a deep breath and headed up the stairs to the entrance door. The open plan reception area had been replaced by a square box that looked officious and unwelcoming.

Behind it sat a young lady with hair that looked as if it had been shaped under a bowl. Shiny and straight, except for the fact that it curled under her chin and all the way around the back of her head.

"Hello there!" said the young man brightly, "has anyone ever told you that you look just like Purdey?"

The receptionist liked that, whatever it might have meant. She smiled a beaming smile and said, "Thank you very much, how can I help you?"

"I'm going to be working here, my name is Peter Abrahams..."

12.

1977

"Aah! The New Trainee Manager, welcome aboard! I'm Helen, I live in Strangeways, where you will also be living."

Peter wrinkled his forehead in a slightly bemused expression until Helen explained.

"It's a dreadful pre-fab building at the back of the hotel, most of the staff live there. Some comedian called it Strangeways, after the prison, and it sort of stuck! You will be sharing with Tony Dean, one of the chefs, room seventeen, your trunk has arrived, and they took it up there. Mr Edwards is out at the moment, but he wants to see you in his office at six."

Helen took a deep breath as if the effort of remembering everything had exhausted her. She handed him a bunch of keys, "Round the side of the building to the back. It'll be straight in front of you - you won't be able to miss it! I'll see you later no doubt!" Her manner was definitely flirty. Peter didn't mind but couldn't help thinking that she might be disappointed.

Helen was right though. The staff accommodation could not be missed. Unfortunately, neither of the keys he had been given fitted the lock, and on further examination it looked as if he had been given duplicates of the lock to room seventeen rather than one of each.

Deciding he'd rather get to his room and unpack, then

sort the key out later, Peter rang on the doorbell to the right of the entrance. A moment later the door opened and an extremely angry looking young man in an unbuttoned chef's jacket and blue chequered trousers opened the door. He looked at Peter with absolute hatred and practically spat in his face.

"Fuck...off!"

With that he slammed the door, leaving a rather confused would be trainee manager staring at a closed door. For the first time that day, probably for the first time in his life, Peter felt totally alone. He had a sudden yearning to see his mum, dad and the friends he had left behind. He was debating whether to go back to reception, or take the next train home, when a young West Indian man with a fantastic afro haircut came into view, heading his way.

"Hi there! You're looking a bit lost. Peter Abrahams by any chance?"

Relief flooded over him, not everybody in this place was a psycho! The other man held out his hand, "Tony Dean, we're going to be room-mates."

Peter grinned, "Call me Pete, I don't think I was given the right key to the outside door and I've just been told to fuck off by the most miserable man in the world!"

Tony laughed a delightful Caribbean cocktail of rarely tested good humour. "Well without a doubt that would be my second chef, Martin. You're absolutely right, he's normally pretty miserable, but he's also a Liverpool supporter!"

Understanding flooded through Pete's mind, "Aah, so they did end up losing then?"

"Yes sirree! No treble for them! I was just watching it in the staff TV room, Martin stormed out at the final whistle; you must have turned up just as he got back to his room, no wonder he was pissy!"

Pete grinned ruefully: "Me and my wonderful timing!"

Tony led Pete into Strangeways and up a flight of stairs.

The walls had been painted in a psychedelic design of pink, yellow, orange and purple by someone in an effort to brighten up the corridor, but that was a few years before and now it was looking flaky and neglected. The carpet had also seen better days, whatever colour it had originally been, it had been rubbed with grease from the bottom of many a chef's shoe. Of Martin, there was mercifully no sign. He had probably returned to his room where he was licking his wounds, getting prepared for the jibes he would receive when he went into work that evening.

"This is us!" Tony announced when they reached the door of number seventeen. He opened it to reveal a box sized room with a single bed against either wall and a window in between. There was a bed side table each and two chests of draws opposite the window.

There were three posters, one of Bob Marley, one of the Sex Pistols and one that contained the legend in a progressively frantic script: "As soon as the rush is over, I'm going to have a nervous breakdown, I've worked for it, I owe it to myself and no-one is going to deprive me of it!"

Abandoned in the middle of the room was a sizeable black metal trunk, bound around with belts and Pete's initials emblazoned in his mother's characteristic script.

Tony took a kettle from the top of the chest of draws, moved it onto the floor towards the nearest socket and plugged it in. Whilst he made tea, Pete set about the task of unbinding and opening his trunk. On the inside of the lid there was a very good reproduction of the Abba logo in gold acrylic paint with a picture of the Swedish Eurovision winners below.

"Save me!" Tony said in mock despair, "please tell me you don't like that sugary sweet pop crap!"

"Genius, I think is the word you are looking for! Don't tell me you are really into that Punk scene! Is there a tune anywhere?"

"Music of the future, my friend!"

Pete snorted in a derisory fashion then took a breath.

He had decided on the journey down to be honest about himself in his first proper job. He had done all the soul searching that he ever wished to do in the last two years or so, and he had got to a stage where he was just about accepted in his home town. However, if he was never again told to "Shut that door," it would probably be too soon. "To be fair to you, I'd better tell you before I settle in, just in case you want me to move to another room - I am gay…"

Tony barely blinked, "And to be fair to you, I'd better tell you before you settle in, just in case you want to move to another room, I am black…"

Pete looked confused for a minute and then laughed, loud and long… "Idiot!"

Tony laughed along with him, then sobered: "Brother, if you knew the shit I get on a daily basis because of the colour of my skin, you would know that I could never discriminate against anyone! All that stereotypical rubbish that some people think is so funny…? By the way if I catch you looking at my twelve-inch dick - you are a dead man!"

The tone was harsh, but the twinkle in his eyes gave the joke away so Pete said airily.

"Jeez! I've not been here an hour yet and I've already had a death threat and been told to fuck off; I feel as popular as Carrie at the senior prom…"

"I've even got some pig's bloody ready!" Tony laughed.

"You saw the movie too?" Pete enquired and when Tony nodded he continued, "That film scarred me!"

"Aww you are a poofter aren't you!" Tony mocked, "I mean it was scary, but…"

"No!" Pete interrupted him, "I mean really scarred me." He held up his arm to show a practically healed burn. "You know that bit at the end with the hand?" He mimed a hand rising through the earth and Tony nodded.

"It made my mate jump so much that he stubbed his cigarette out on my arm. I screamed, which made the woman in front of me jump up and scream. Well, within seconds practically everybody in the cinema was screaming... then of course when they had recovered, everyone started laughing! The people queueing to see the next showing of a horror film that had been billed as the most frightening of all time, must have been slightly bemused to see everyone leaving the cinema in fits of laughter!"

Tony laughed himself and said in a thick Caribbean drawl, "You and me, my skinny white gay friend - are gonna get on just fine!"

***

Mr Edwards, was not laughing. In fact, Pete wasn't sure he had ever laughed in his life. He had the look of Harold Wilson, but without the pipe or the occasional sardonic humour of the ex-Prime Minister.

"So, you have just finished your first year of an OND in Hotel Management?" He rolled the letters around his mouth with such distaste that they sounded more like a tropical disease than a recognised catering qualification. "The college agreed for you to leave a little earlier as they thought four months' work experience would be good for you?"

Pete nodded, he was not normally given to nerves, but the man at the other side of the desk was beginning to terrify him.

Mr Edwards shoved the papers aside irritably and continued without preamble, "We don't serve lunches in the hotel, we provide packed lunches for our guests on request. Your hours will therefore be: 6am 'til 11am then back in at 4pm to serve tea and get ready for dinner. You will finish at 9pm. Occasionally you will be required to help out in the bar until 11:30. Once a week you will be rostered on for a full day shift to cover the public bar or reception as necessary over the midday hours." He glared at Pete to ensure he had understood before continuing. "You will have one day off a week, which will be allocated as necessary. There will be no fraternizing with the opposite sex in your room. Your room will be inspected once a week and will be kept tidy. No smoking in your room, no visitors in your room. No fraternizing with the guests. However, you are to be professional and polite at all times. There will be no drinking on duty, if you are on the bar and are offered a drink, you are allowed to put ten pence in the pot and all tips will be shared out at the end of the day. Meals are provided, but you will eat what you are given, you will not help yourself to anything from any storeroom or hot plate. You will be issued with a uniform, you are responsible for all your own laundry. However, there is a washing machine and drying facilities in the laundry room that the staff can use. You will call me Mr Edwards at all times. My eldest son, Maurice is my assistant manager and you will call him Mr Edwards Junior, and you will be addressed by the staff as Mr Abrahams. Any breach of the rules will lead to instant dismissal. Is that all understood?"

Once Pete was dismissed he stood outside the office door and exhaled deeply. He felt like he'd just gone fifteen rounds with Mohammed Ali. The boxer might have been as famous for his rhetoric, as he was for his boxing. However, Pete would have defied even him to manage to get a word in edgeways with the boss of the Royal Holm View Hotel.

There was an area at the end of the dining room, just to the left of the doors that led to the kitchens. It seemed to be used as a dumping ground and a staff eating area. Out of sight of the main dining room, it was ideal for extra chairs, tables and table litter to be dumped if not needed. In the middle of this mayhem was a couple of tables, joined together, with a dozen chairs around it.

Pete had been given a few hours to sort himself out before joining the staff for their evening dinner. This was served at nine o'clock, once the guests had finished eating and the dining room had been reset for breakfast.

Tony was there and raised an arm in welcome. "Hi Pete, come and join this merry party!" His words were ironic, the people around the table either looked miserable, knackered or both. Unperturbed Tony carried on with the introductions. "Martin you've met, he's known to all of us as Smiler, for obvious reasons."

Martin managed a grunt in Pete's direction, but made no mention or apology in relation to their earlier meeting.

"Next to him is Helen, one of our lovely receptionists." Helen smiled, and Pete said they had met earlier.

"OK, next to Helen is Hutch, he and his mate Starsky are the full-time barmen. They came on a year out in between A-levels and law school and haven't torn themselves away yet. Starsky is covering the bar now, but you'll meet him later." The man Tony described nodded in Pete's direction and it was obvious how he had come by his nickname - he bore a strong resemblance to David Soul, all be it slightly younger with blonder hair. "Right, next to him we have Jackie, one of our waitresses," Tony indicated a pretty mousey haired girl who smiled shyly in Pete's direction. "At the head of the table is Dum and next to him is Dee, our two pot washers…" By now all the names and faces were beginning to blur into one and Pete didn't catch many of the rest of the names as Tony continued his tour around the table.

Giovanni the Head Chef called for Jackie and a couple of waitresses to come and get the food, then joined the table himself. The talk during a rather good beef casserole dinner revolved mostly around the FA Cup Final, and whether or not Liverpool would be able to redeem themselves the following Wednesday in the final of the European Cup against Borussia Monchengladbach.

"It'll probably be another disaster!" Martin proclaimed morosely.

"That's the spirit Smiler!" Laughed Hutch. "By the way, what was the score today?"

"Fuck off!" Snarled Martin. Not just me then, thought Pete. However, Hutch was completely unperturbed and started singing: "I don't want to talk about it…"

"Isn't it about time you went and relieved the other toss pot?" Interrupted Martin. Laughingly Hutch agreed it probably was and went off whistling the Rod Stewart number one.

People started talking more in groups once dinner was finished and Tony took the opportunity to grab Pete to one side and give him a less formal introduction of their workmates. "Tweedledee and Tweedledum are not only pot washers, but pot heads as well - if you want a little ganja them's the boys to see!" Tony was on Caribbean overdrive once more. "They've probably smoked away any brain cells they ever had, but they deal with a lot of shit from Giovanni and Smiler, you should see it! They don't bother taking any pans across to them, they just scream out "Dee" or "Dum" and launch the bloody things! If the lads don't get out of the way in time, they get a hot pan whacking them on the back of the head. It's funny, it doesn't matter how stoned they are, they've got quite good at ducking…"

Pete looked across at the two lads slumped at the end of the table. They were smoking, but their cigarettes had probably come from the packets of Embassy Number Ones in front of them rather than being anything dodgy. However, their faces looked blank and expressionless, like two adjacent hotels with "Vacancies" signs in the windows.

"Now Helen…" Tony surreptitiously looked over towards the receptionist who was deep in conversation with a waitress whose name Pete couldn't remember. "Isn't she gorgeous? I'd love to go out with her…"

"Well," Pete said reasonably, "why don't you ask her? You're pretty gorgeous yourself… and there is the twelve-inch dick!"

Tony laughed and nodded his head, "Yep, there certainly is!" He then sighed, "no, unfortunately she is going out with an older man with even more to offer than a large penis."

"Yes, but surely he doesn't have your fantastic charisma?"

"Actually, he's a bit of a toss pot. He thinks he's Weston's answer to the Godfather - he even calls himself Marlon," he sniggered, "I think his real name is Malcolm which didn't really fit in with his Mafiosa image!" Tony then nodded at Dee and Dum, "he's their supplier for a start - and half of the pot heads in the town for that matter."

"What on earth does she see in him?"

"Oh, she likes the bad boys does our Helen."

Pete looked at the animated face of the receptionist who was in the middle of a tale that involved lots of gesticulations. "She does look like Joanna Lumley, doesn't she?"

"Yeah especially now she's gone for the Purdey hairstyle," Tony sighed again, "lovely…"

At that moment, two young men appeared around the corner, one of them Pete assumed to be Hutch's co-barman, Starsky. He didn't really look like his namesake and Pete suspected that he only came by his nickname because of his association with Hutch. He was tall and lanky, his hair was darkish, but not particularly wavy, he had an anonymous sort of face with no strong features. He had even tried to grow a beard and moustache, possibly in an attempt to disassociate himself with his Paul Michael Glaser name tag, but it was definitely a work in progress. The other man was carrying a crate of beers and had dark hair and a moustache that made Starsky's look even more inadequate.

"Right! For God's sake don't tell my father, but we've had a good week, you've all worked hard, and we've got a newbie to welcome." He nodded at Pete, "Peter Abrahams, if anyone hasn't been introduced already, is going to be a temporary trainee manager for the summer." There were mumbles of welcome from the crowd around the table. "I'll leave you to introduce yourselves, if you haven't already - work hard, play nicely!" He dumped the crate of beers on a spare chair and retraced his steps back to the bar area to calls of "Thanks Mr Mo!"

"Mr Mo!" Pete whispered to Tony, "sounds like a character from Bod!"

Tony chuckled, "We're meant to call him Mr Edwards Junior, but no-one can be bothered! He's all right actually, got a bit of a temper on him, but he's fair... and not a complete knob like his father!"

***

The Weston lights were strung out before them, guiding their way along the promenade towards the town itself. A crowd of them had decided to visit a nightclub. This idea was mainly encouraged by Helen. She wanted to meet up with Marlon, the self-proclaimed man in charge of the Weston Mafia. Tony was decisively derisive about Pete's worries that he wouldn't be able to make his first six o'clock shift. He immediately quashed his new friend's concerns that it wouldn't be a brilliant start to his career at the hotel.

"Don't worry man! I'm up at 5:30 - I'll make sure you're there in time!"

Tony just wanted to be with Helen, Pete was sure about that. Helen's waitressing friend hadn't joined the party, so he had slipped in step with her, leaving Pete at the rear of the group with the shy and so far, silent Jackie. It gave him a chance to observe the crowd that may or may not turn into friends over the course of the summer.

Both Hutch and Tony had what Pete's father would have called, "a thing for the ladies." But whereas Tony really liked women and treated them with friendship and respect, Hutch acted like they were his possessions. Any good-looking girl they passed would be treated to wolf whistles and comments that Hutch obviously considered hilarious. Starsky would grin anonymously at his friend's dubious humour, but would neither join in or dissent, he just seemed to accept it as the norm.

The two other members of the small group were Dee and Dum, who trudged on stooped shouldered, cigarettes hanging from their mouths, barely saying a word to each other or the crowd around them. They might have been there to visit the same person as Helen, but what they wanted from him was completely different.

Gradually Pete managed to draw conversation from his mute companion. She lived in one of the roads behind their destination and had seemingly joined the party more for protection on her journey homewards than from any desire of visiting the nightclub. Pete was such a lively, friendly companion, that suddenly, in spite of herself, Jackie found herself talking to him.

They both loved Abba, that was the start of it. They dissected every track from the "Arrival" album that was currently at the top of the charts. Jackie favoured the anthemic "My Love My Life," whereas Pete was still bouncing around to "Knowing Me, Knowing You." He treated Jackie to a chorus of it in a wobbly baritone, but even if his pitch was defective, his enthusiasm caused her to join in and they both shouted "A-ha!" to the outgoing tide. This garnered them abusive comments from their fellow travellers.

She found herself sharing previously unspoken dreams about her future. She wanted to become a nursery nurse, but had no idea how to go about it. She had neither sought or been offered career advice at school and had reached the conclusion that a future as a wife and mother was her most realistic option.

"For pity's sake Jack!" He was the first person ever to shorten her name like that, and she rather liked it. "This is 1977, women can do whatever they want. There's a woman who will probably be Prime Minister at the next election - don't ever settle for being the little lady at home, unless you want to be!"

By the time they headed up Regent Street, Pete had persuaded Jackie to join the party on the understanding that he would take a detour with her to check that it was all right with her parents.

Regent Street was lined on either side with amusement arcades, now putting their shutters down for the night after a day of entertaining tourists with racing horses and penny drop machines. They turned into the High Street and halfway down turned right onto a small street that ran the length of Woolworths. The club they were going to was at the back of the department store. Pete quickly told Tony what he was doing and that he would meet them inside, before following Jackie towards her home.

Jackie opened the door and lead him into the hallway of the small terraced house. The hallway was wallpapered in a brick effect paper, which ended up looking like neither brick nor paper. It gave way to a snug at the end of the corridor. The TV was replaying the cup final and a small middle-aged man sat watching it, barely looking at his daughter as she entered the room with a strange lad in tow. The room itself looked like it had fallen out of Coronation Street. Pete stifled a snigger when that thought was followed by the observation that there were indeed three flying ducks on the wall.

"Mum, we're just off to Snoopys, Pete said he'd look after me and make sure I got home afterwards. There's a whole crowd of us from work!" She added, just in case her mother considered Pete a ne'er do well that couldn't be trusted.

Her mother was a woman in the Peggy Mount mould,

biggish and brash with the opinion that everyone in the world was a ne'er do well that couldn't be trusted.

"Waste of money and a waste of good sleeping time if you ask me. I'll be giving you one shout in the morning and if you don't get up I won't be chasing you, so on your own head be it!"

"Oh, I'll be up Mum, don't worry!" Jackie pulled Pete towards the exit before her mother had a chance to change her mind, Pete gave a cheery "Goodnight" as he was propelled towards the doorway. This was answered by the lady of the house with a noise that could only be described as "Harrumph!" The man was still enthralled by the football and seemed to be completely unaware there had been an interruption at all.

***

"Are you two twenty-one?" The girl in the paying booth looked as bored as a fifth former watching Shakespeare.

"Oh yes!" Pete lied, but was already regretting getting separated from the crowd. He reckoned that they would have had a better chance of sneaking in as part of a large group than on their own like this.

"Proof?" the girl was already trying to catch the eye of the bouncer lurking in the doorway, sensing a swift ejection would be the only outcome of this encounter.

"We're with Helen from the Holm View," Pete ventured, "they would have arrived about ten minutes ago." It was a bit of a desperate attempt, but he was rewarded when the girl exhaled something that could nearly have been called a smile.

"OK, she said there would be two more… It'll be £2 each"

Pete paid for both of them and they ran up the stairs behind her booth before she had a chance to let loose the bouncer on them after all. They entered a large room, packed with people. It had a dance floor at one end with a disco booth above it. Stretching the length of the room on either side was banquette seating in a cheap velour covering set out in rows of private booths. In the middle were wooden tables with stools around them covered in the same fabric. A large bar stretched across the wall on their left-hand side, directly opposite the dance floor. The Jacksons were singing "Show You The Way To Go" - far too loudly for the quality of the sound equipment.

Picking their way across the room, they were careful not to upset people carrying large glasses by knocking into them. They finally found the Holm View crowd on the second to last booth, close to the dance floor.

The Jacksons had morphed - although to say it was seamless would have been generous - into Joe Tex, who didn't want to bump no more with his big fat woman.

"Hi there - got in then?" Tony shouted at the top of his voice. He seemed to be slightly on edge and Pete realised the reason for it when he saw Helen. She was wrapped around a man with greased back dark hair wearing a black suit and white shirt and black tie. His Godfather fetish hadn't quite extended to full bow tie and dinner jacket, but he wasn't far off. Dee and Dum were sitting opposite them with Starsky. The pot washers were staring at the embracing couple with barely concealed desperation, and Starsky was staring ahead of him with barely concealed boredom.

A crash of piano keys and a Scandinavian chorus of "Aah aah aah" made Pete turn to Jackie and shout, "You are dancing to this!" As she took his hand he yelled in Tony's ear, "you too!"

"Oh Jeez, Pete - have a thought for my image - I can't dance to this Swedish shit!"

Pete shouted a whisper in his ear as Jackie threatened to pull his arm from its socket. "Would you rather watch the floor show?" he nodded at Helen and her beau as Agnetha and Frida started singing...

Tony took a wistful glance and joined his friends on the dance floor. Even dancing to a song he didn't like he had a natural rhythm, whereas Pete just exuded enthusiasm. He danced like a bowling ball on a skittle alley, and all the pins he knocked into simply laughed in the face of his innocent good humour.

They danced on through "The Shuffle" "Sir Duke" and "Red Light Spells Danger." They danced on for an hour. They danced on even though the heat was stifling, and sweat dripped from their foreheads and down the back of their clothes.

Eventually the DJ said: "So now we're coming to the end of the evening, just a few more songs for you lovers out there…" The opening chords to Deniece Williams's "Free" crackled across the sound system. Tony retreated to the toilets whilst Pete and Jackie stared at each other for a couple of seconds before coupling together for a slow dance.

Pete had mentioned his preferences on the way into town, so he didn't worry that Jackie would misinterpret his intentions. He did worry about Hutch though. For the last hour he had watched him use the music as a means to slide from one girl to the next, pinching their bottoms and sliding his hands down their backs. Pete had no idea how none of them had slapped him, although the fact that he was blonde and good looking probably saved him from that. However, how he had not been punched by a jealous boyfriend was another matter.

He had leached his way onto a girl for a slow dance and her short skirt was no defence for his probing hands that were practically performing their own medical examination. As the lights came on and the DJ played "Show Me The Way To Go Home" the girl whispered something in his ear. Hutch laughed derisively, sneered a short put down and left her standing on the dance floor, looking like she wanted to burst into tears.

Pete kissed Jackie on the cheek and walked over to the

girl, "Don't worry," he said into her ear, "I know him, he doesn't know a good thing when he sees it, he's a bit of an arse actually!" He then returned to Jackie and took her hand in order to prove to the girl that he wasn't trying to chat her up. Hutch's victim smiled and mouthed the word "Thanks," as Pete left the dance floor and re-joined the Holm View crowd.

"What did you say to that girl?" Pete asked Hutch. The music had finished, and it was now possible to have a conversation without straining the vocal chords.

Hutch snorted. "She wanted to take it somewhere quieter, but she had a sweaty arse, so I told her so... Filthy tart!"

"You have no idea how to talk to women, do you?" Pete was disgusted, and didn't hide the fact.

"Oh, and you do I suppose?" Hutch said disdainfully, "Fucking pansy!"

"You should watch how a fucking pansy manages to have a conversation with a woman, you might learn something."

"Who wants a conversation?" Hutch laughed like it was the most ridiculous idea he'd ever heard. Pete had a few observations he wanted to share, but was stopped from doing so when Starsky handed his friend a drink and pulled him away to have a chat.

Dee and Dum were still sitting in the same seats they had been sitting in an hour earlier. They looked like they had barely moved. In fact, they reminded Pete of two puppies waiting for their master to throw them some scraps from the table. Their master squeezed his way past Helen and, on a nod from him, the two pups launched themselves towards the fire escape where they had obviously done business before.

Helen grabbed hold of Marlon's hand. "Don't sell them that shit Marlon - please, they're getting more and more hooked on it!"

Marlon looked at her with displeasure but barely raised

his voice. "Do I come into the hotel and tell you how to run your little reception desk?" He enquired reasonably. He didn't wait for a reply before continuing, "so could I ask you nicely not to tell me how to run my business?" He bent down so that his face was two inches from hers and hissed into it. "Keep your nose out of it, you stupid little slut."

Tony had been talking to Jackie whilst this exchange was going on, but Pete was aware of him tensing up and moving to block the drug dealer's path. He pulled him back a little allowing Marlon to follow his customers outside. Before he did so, he turned with a smirk on his face and said: "A wog and a poof! What lovely friends you have!"

"Don't!" Pete whispered urgently into Tony's ear, making sure that he didn't release his grip in case his friend decided to attack the pusher after all.

Tony turned towards Pete and said, with slight anger in his voice, "You should have let me!"

"What good would it have done? You'd have ended down the cop shop, Edwards would have fired you and Malcolm Brando over there would have pissed himself laughing. Besides, I rather like my room-mate, he has no taste in music, but I'd rather like to share with him for longer than an afternoon!"

Tony visibly relaxed and laughed. "I rather like my room-mate too - even if he does force me to dance to music that is very bad for my image!"

It was then that they both heard the first sob that Helen had uttered. They looked, and she was sitting stock still, staring at the beer slopped table. Her shoulders were shaking in an effort to stop the tears from coming, but they were but a breath away. Tony shimmied into the booth and put a consoling arm around her. Pete chanced a worried glance towards the fire escape, but obviously business was still in progress as there was no sign of the drug dealer. The last thing he wanted was for the Mafia

King to reappear whilst Tony had his arms around his woman. He leant one knee on the banquette and whispered into Tony's ear.

"You get Helen out of here while the coast is still clear. I'll take Jackie home, then catch you up; but I think you'd better hurry!"

Tony whispered something to Helen, she nodded, and they joined the line of people leaving the club. Pete kept a wary eye on the fire escape whilst joining Jackie who was following on behind. Towards the exit, he caught sight of Hutch. He was practically welded to a tall good-looking brunette, whilst Starsky was talking to her less glamorous friend. He still managed to look like he was both there, and absent, at the same time.

Hutch saw Pete approaching and detached himself from his conquest for long enough to scoff, "Conversation!" in his general direction.

Pete laughed good naturedly and whispered "Tosser!" into Jackie's ear. She giggled delightedly but kept any observations she had about the matter to herself.

Once they had managed to squeeze their way out of the night club - there were too many people leaving and too narrow a stairway for a quick exit - he risked one glance towards the doorway before he turned the corner towards Jackie's house. There were no mad drug dealers following his friends as they went in the opposite direction. From what he knew of the type, Pete guessed that Malcolm Marlon would be so confident that Helen would come running back to him, that he wouldn't be the least bit worried where she had gone, or who she had gone there with.

"I've had such a lovely evening! Thank you so much." Jackie was turning the key in her front door and looked over her shoulder at Pete. "I think it's going to be fun with you around!" He kissed her on the cheek and sang half a line from "Dancing Queen," his shaky baritone in full effect.

Jackie joined in and they finished the chorus in unison, only to be interrupted by a roar of "Ja-que-line!" shaking the staircase as it descended from on high.

"Night Jack!" Pete gave a quick wink and blew a kiss to the closing door, before turning to make his way back to the seafront. There were still people leaving the nightclub as he passed it, but they were mercifully strangers to him. He walked quickly and by the time he had crossed over to the promenade that ran parallel to the beach and the bank of mud that was waiting for the morning tide, he could see Tony and Helen not more than thirty feet in front of him. He ran to catch them up, but just as he had decided to pounce on them, he could see they were locked in a walking embrace and kissing tenderly. They were completely oblivious to his presence, so he stopped to look at the seafront with the Welsh lights shining across the bay. After a minute or so, he followed on at a discreet distance.

He was happy for Tony, but he was also slightly worried, a state of mind that was unusual for him.

Marlon Malcolm Brando did not strike him as the type who would take getting dumped by his girlfriend in favour of a West Indian Chef, without a great deal of upset and recrimination.

As he walked, he gazed across the water. The lights from the Welsh coast were now being gradually hidden by a pre-dawn haze. The scene looked calm and innocent and held no clues or trailers about the story that was to unfold over the course of the summer; or the part that the sea itself would play in its telling.

13.

From the very early stages of our relationship, I had questioned Sam's decision to download a Broadway show tune and use it as the alarm on his phone. He argued that the sound of a stage school ingénue screeching in his ear, meant that he had to find the phone and put an end to it, rather than plant the pillows around his ears and turn over to go back to sleep. Personally, I thought that subjecting someone who was slightly cranky in the morning to that sort of abuse, was akin to giving a pasta sandwich to a coeliac.

"Fuck fuck fuck!" Sam had knocked his phone onto the carpet and was now trying to retrieve it. A bit of a bonus for me as it meant that I got to see his Calvin Klein covered buttocks crawling around the floor. However, it didn't do a great deal for his early morning grouchiness.

To be honest though, I was feeling slightly out of kilter myself. The dream had been so real that I could almost feel the breeze that accosted the other Peter's face, and still had the disco tunes that would have been stuck in his brain, rolling around in mine.

I didn't mention this to Donnie Darko as he stomped towards the shower room. He misjudged the step up to the en-suite and stubbed his toe, which brought another torrent of abuse in the direction of the step, the room and the world in general.

I smiled and snuggled down into the duvet. Even the stage school ingénue hadn't managed to drive a song from the dream out of my head. I was sure that I'd never heard it before, so maybe it didn't even exist. If I was composing songs in my dreams, then I was definitely emailing Simon Cowell as soon as I had the energy to grab my laptop…

Hot water drumming all over his body had performed the usual miraculous transition in Sam's character, and by the time he emerged from the shower room, his normal sunny demeanour had returned.

"Sorry 'bout that," he grinned sheepishly.

"After six months of hell… I'm finally getting used to it!" I put a hand to my forehead in exaggerated acceptance. Sam flung the towel that had been wrapped around his waist in my general direction. It hit me just above my chest and I was aware of the smell of him and the slight dampness of the material as well as his total nakedness in front of me.

Win, win, win.

He dressed quickly in a shirt, tie and suit - the first time I'd seen him so attired. I love a man in a suit and told him so in what I hoped was a provocative manner.

"Well we've no time for such shenanigans!" he chided mournfully, "now you know that you're due to join Jack in the bar at midday? He'll show you the ropes, so you'll be able to run the whole show on your own for the early part of Friday evening."

"Yes Boss!" I saluted, and he laughed. Moving across to the bed, he kissed me lightly on the lips.

"I'm really glad you're here" he smiled.

"Me too," I replied softly.

***

Emily was in the kitchen of the family apartment by the time I had showered, dressed and was ready for the world.

"Good afternoon!" she laughed sarcastically, "I have already served breakfast and cleaned several rooms in the time it took you to hoist yourself out of your pit!"

"You done for the day then?" I enquired.

"Nah!" Emily screwed her face up, "still a few more rooms to do." She nodded her head towards me conspiratorially, "I'm skiving off for half an hour actually, but for God's sake don't tell Michel Roux Jnr!"

"Your secret is safe with me!" I assured her. As I filled the kettle, I realised that the song I had dreamed about, was still in my brain.

"Em... have you ever heard of a song that is something to do with bumping and big fat women?" I enquired.

She looked at me quizzically and comically put her hand to my forehead. "No temperature, so my professional opinion is that the patient is completely barking" she concluded, straight-faced.

"Probably!" I agreed, but continued regardless. "It's just I had a dream last night, but it didn't feel like a dream. It was more like a movie." I paused, that wasn't quite right. "Well really it felt like a TV miniseries, and the episode I saw was the pilot, the one where they introduce you to all the characters and you establish the background."

"So, what was the background?"

"Well that's the thing - it was based in this hotel, but the hotel looked different and the whole feeling I got was that it was set in a different time zone... and..."

"Go on!" Emily did seem genuinely interested, so I continued.

"The main lad - he had the same name as me, but he wasn't me..."

"OK, but that's fairly staple stuff in dreams I'd say."

"I guess so, it's just that the whole thing was so..." I struggled for the right word... "cinematic."

"So, what about this bumping and fat women song then?"

"They went to a club and one of the songs playing was that one. It's just sort of stuck in my brain; even now, when normally I have forgotten my dreams five minutes after I've woken up."

"OK," Emily reached for her iPhone, "So I'm tapping in bumping big fat women?"

She did just that and her eyes widened when she looked at the results, "There was a song called 'Ain't Gonna Bump No More With No Big Fat Woman' by a bloke called Joe Tex released in 1977! Hold on, YouTube has got a version of it!"

She tapped again and the song from the disco in my dream, resounded around the kitchen forty years later.

"That's it!" I cried, "That's the bloody song!"

"You must have heard it somewhere," Emily said reasonably. "Your subconscious remembered it; and then you dreamt about it."

"Fair enough!" I agreed, "but humour me a bit. Tap in: FA Cup Final Manchester United 2 Liverpool 1"

"You dreamt about football?" She enquired, "Christ you are deluded!" She did as I asked and this time the result had her swearing softly.

"1977!" She looked up at me amazed, "So what you dreamt about happened forty years ago?"

"Well," I said reasonably, "We don't really know it actually happened, but it is weird that the two things that we know about the dream did occur in the same year - normally with dreams things are dotted about all over the place."

Before we could discuss the matter further, the internal phone rang. Emily answered her brother even before he could ask the question. "Yes Bro, I am skiving, well I'm being hospitable to your friend actually…"

At this point she was interrupted by her brother mentioning something about room thirteen and was Rem ready to be on duty in half an hour?

"God! He's such a bossy bore when he gets into his hotel manager mode!"

I remembered something that Chloe said at Christmas. "Yes!" I agreed, "but I do find it just a little bit sexy though!"

I had been dreading spending an eleven-hour shift being told what to do by Jack, as I had worried that even I might have wanted to punch him before an hour was out. As it happened, it was nowhere near as bad as I had feared. OK, so Jack had an opinion on everything from running the hotel, through Brexit, and back to whether the new flats on the street where he lived were a useful addition to the area, or an eyesore with all the appeal of a giant lavatory.

This led him to the subject of his family, his flat and his living arrangements. If the man he lived with was actually his uncle as he claimed, then I would quite happily walk around the town dressed in nothing more than a feather boa and a smile.

All that being said, he was a really good barman, quick, efficient with just enough chat to charm the customers, without ever going to the point of insolence. They all loved him and even if he was putting on an act, I have always had a lot of time for people who are good at what they do.

Of course, he gave me a running commentary on the histories behind several of the customers and just before six o'clock he looked at his watch and said: "Stand by your beds! Alf o'clock is nearly upon us!"

Alf was one of the regulars; and by the term regular, Jack explained that he was there every night from Monday to Friday on the dot of six o'clock. He had a favourite table next to the bar that he sat at religiously. One night, he had been beaten to that table by a couple of tourists. Although they were the only other people in the bar and he had the choice of any other seat in the room, that wasn't good enough for Alf. He stood by the side of the table, staring at them yet saying nothing, until they got so uncomfortable they moved to a booth as far away from him as possible.

Jack introduced me as a friend of Sam's from university

who was helping out for the summer. In the same way that Jack had a view of everything and everybody, so did Alf. However, he was a little less articulate in his views. In Alf's opinion, everything was shit...

"Waste of time university!" He told me. Jack had taken the first break and had gone off to find some food. I had a strange feeling that he had timed it to perfection. The bar was fairly quiet and there was little to do but listen to the words of wisdom from Lord Alf of Shitville.

By the time I had spent twenty minutes in his company I had learned that: the Government was shit, the England cricket, football and rugby teams were all shit. Weston in 2017 was shit, as were his offspring, his neighbours and the lollipop man who helped the children across to school at the bottom of his road. The children were also, no surprises here, shits.

In an attempt to get him away from all the manure in his life, I asked him if he had been coming to the hotel for a long time.

"Just over thirty years!" He agreed, "it's not too bad in here." I must tell Ned that, I thought. In comparison to all I had heard before, it was practically a glowing tribute...

"I expect you've seen a few changes in the look of the place," I was fishing a bit. To be honest, my dream was still very much in the back of my mind, and if Alf had been coming to the bar for thirty years, he might be able to confirm or correct some of the facts that were confusing me. Had it been a dream, or had I crazily gone back in time in some completely weird way?

"Too right," agreed Alf glumly, but without rancour. I was quickly coming to realise that with Alf, being morose wasn't necessarily a criticism, more like a way of life. On the other hand; it generally was also a criticism.

"The old man," I guess he meant Sam's grandfather, "knocked the bar through. It used to be three little areas, pool room, snug and lounge bar. He got rid of the pool table and opened the whole thing up." Again, the note of derision was there, but whether he was for or against the removal of the pool table was never quite clear.

I hadn't seen any of the bar area in my dream, so that confirmed nothing, but it did give me a natural lead in to talk about an area I had seen.

"Was the same thing done to the reception?" I asked, "I know that the open plan idea is fairly modern."

"That's right lad - I can remember it quite well, awful boxy thing it was, one of the last things The Old Man got rid of before he died." That sort of fitted what I had seen in my dream, but it wasn't exactly proof positive.

"Is that the main extent of the changes down here?" I asked, "the bar and the reception?"

"Pretty much, although one of the first things he did was to change an area at the bottom of the dining room into those conference and private dining rooms."

Now that really did fit in with what I had seen, and to confirm my facts, I asked him what it had been used for before.

"No idea lad, I never came in before the old man took over, it was shit…"

***

It wasn't a busy night, so by a quarter past eleven, we had closed down the main area of the bar, leaving just a small part of it for the night porter to run a late bar if the hotel guests wanted it. Sam was still busy telling his dad about the events of the day. Ned and Fiona had arrived back from the conference about an hour before.

I made my way upstairs and had a night cap with Sam's mum who was full of observations and funny stories about the people they had shared their day with.

"It's amazing the number of people who work in hospitality who hate people!" She laughed. "Talking to some of them, you would think that the people who put money into their tills were Beelzebub himself!"

"I did meet Alf today," I grinned wryly.

"On the other hand," she laughed, "sometimes they do have a point!"

She was bright and humorous and so similar to Sam that it was impossible not to like her.

By the time her son arrived upstairs, he was so knackered that I tempered down the fantasy I had been harbouring all day about stripping the suit from him piece by piece and royally molesting him. In the end, it was a case of a quick snog before we turned over and went to sleep. One day of working in the same establishment and we'd turned into an old married couple!

As I lay there waiting for the unemployment of sleep, I briefly wondered, whether I would return again to the previous century.

***

As it turned out, I didn't dream of 1977. I didn't dream at all, as far as I could remember. I woke to find Sam's arm flung wildly across my chest. I contented myself for a few minutes by staring at it and watching the morning sun glint across his blonde hairs, flecking them with shards of gold. I kissed the shards, but was rewarded by a very unromantic snort. It took three attempts over the next hour before the morning Grinch finally disappeared, and left me with a ridiculously randy boyfriend.

By the time we finally appeared in the kitchen it was after midday and Emily, having finished all her chores, was very quick to tease us about the fact.

"Oh, at last! Sleeping Beauty and Snoozerella have re-joined the land of the living!"

"Managed to get all your rooms cleaned without the need for a coffee break today?" her brother retorted.

"Are you kidding? The grand Suprendo is patrolling big time this morning. Twenty-four hours away and he's behaving like we've all forgotten how to cook, clean or breathe without him! The chefs are pissed - he's only gone and chucked out a whole batch of demi-glace because he said it wasn't up to standard. Mark's having a hissy fit downstairs!"

"Oh Christ! Perhaps I'd better go down and smooth things over," Sam said resignedly.

"Hold your horses Kofi Annan!" Emily said, "it's your time off with your boyfriend, they will sort themselves out - eventually!" As if she was regretting mentioning the subject of staff unrest, she turned to me and changed tack completely. "So Rem, did you end up in 1977 again last night?"

"What on earth are you talking about now?" Sam asked his sister. I saved her from replying by giving him brief details of my dream, including the song and cup final I remembered, and the changes in the hotel I had seen. The strange thing was that even after twenty-four hours, the dream was as clear to me as any film or TV programme I had seen, and much clearer than any dream I had ever had before.

Sam wasn't particularly impressed, I got the impression he had zoned out in that way that people do when dreams are mentioned.

"It's probably just sleeping in a strange room that got your imagination going. Also, don't forget, my dad was giving you a potted history of the place on Sunday night; your subconscious probably just added bits and pieces."

It all sounded reasonable. I could have heard the song without realising it. I could have seen something about the cup final that I'd stored in the back of my memory, and the changes in the hotel were vague enough to be a lucky guess.

"I suppose you're right. It's just the detail was so clear. I mean, the lad with my name had this black metal trunk with my initials on it..."

"Pa!" Sam interrupted.

"OK, I know, change the subject, I'm being boring!"

"No, you div... P . A!" Now Sam was getting excited and irritated by my inability to follow him. He continued in a slow and deliberate manner, the way some people might talk to a foreigner in the belief that if you say something clearly enough, people will understand you, even if they don't speak a word of the language.

"Are you telling me that the letters on the trunk were P and A?"

I gazed at Sam's excited face and wondered whether he was losing the plot, or I was.

"Well they are my initials," I said reasonably, "and inside the trunk..."

"...the Abba logo was painted in acrylic!" Sam finished for me. Now it was my turn to look confused. I looked at Emily who, by the look on her animated face, was definitely on the same wavelength as her brother. If we're talking old style radios, mine was still getting a lot of interference where I hadn't tuned it in properly...

"The Christmas decoration trunk!" Emily gasped. The static was receding, and I was finally receiving a signal.

"That trunk exists?"

"It certainly does my psycho boyfriend!"

"I think you mean psychic," I argued.

"No, it's OK I'll stick with my first answer," he said easily. "The trunk is up in the loft; do you want to see it?"

"No, I think I'll go downstairs and criticise the chefs and their demi-glace!" I said with very thinly veiled sarcasm, "Of course I want to see it!" Another memory entered my head. "Does it have a photograph of Abba underneath the logo?"

Sam shook his head, "Not that I remember, Em?"

His sister couldn't remember that either, but it sounded far too similar for that to matter. We made our way up the stairs to the staff corridor, and after grabbing a ladder, Sam climbed it, opened the trap door and Emily and I followed him into a cavernous, dusty, spider's heaven.

Not far inside was the trunk that I had seen in my

dream. My initials were on the front and when Sam opened it, the tinsel and paper chains pushed upwards for an early release, in the way that daffodils might poke their heads skywards during a mild January.

However, it was the inside of the lid that fascinated me. The acrylic paint had faded a little, but the logo was clear and unmistakable.

"Look!" Em said, pointing below the logo to where there were four pieces of sticky tape in a rectangular shape, each with a piece of yellowing paper trapped behind. "That must have been the picture you saw, it's probably been ripped off over the years, but something was definitely there!"

We squatted on our haunches and stared at the trunk. All their lives Sam and Emily had associated it with the commencement of Christmas. The excitement of childish expectation through to the present-day acceptance of hard work and enough mulled wine to keep a cathedral full of carol singers happy.

Suddenly, it was revealed as something else.

Someone else's story.

A postcard from another life.

14.

"What happened to him?" I asked, breaking the silence that had hung as thick as the cloud of dust motes that danced in the unexpected light. "Why did he leave and not take his trunk with him?"

"Perhaps he moved to a place in town," Mr Sensible suggested. "Perhaps he packed his stuff into a van and didn't need his trunk."

"But he was only staying until the end of the summer." I argued. They both looked up sharply, I hadn't even known I knew that until it fell from my mouth.

"Golly!" said Emily in a squeaky, lispy, public school voice. "What a mysterwy! I feel like one of the Famous Five!"

"Yes; exactly the same," Sam's voice rattled with sarcasm, "except there are only three of us, we haven't got a dog and none of us is a lesbian!"

"How do you know?" Emily asked archly, "I mean, I didn't know you were gay 'til the day before yesterday. I might be on the turn myself!"

"Not too likely, I think, having stalked your Facebook page." Sam laughed as his sister scowled at him, "come on Anne and Dick, we have the Internet to explore!"

"What exactly are we looking for?" I asked as Emily and I climbed back down the steps, leaving Sam to turn the light off and put the hatch back in place.

"Well…" Sam was doing his impression of Jessica

Fletcher, "We know his name," he nodded at me, "and we know the name of the hotel. We also know the year that he was definitely here. If we put all of that in the search engine, we might learn something."

"It's obviously his brains that attracted you," Emily grinned in my direction, then she scowled again at her brother. "It's obviously not his lack of charm or condescending manner that clinched it!"

We returned to the apartment and Sam retrieved his phone from the worktop he had dropped it on earlier. As his sister had done the day before, he tapped some information in to the phone. After a few seconds his question was answered, he stared at the screen and whistled softly.

"Crikey Rem my boy! I think you've seen a ghost!"

It was an article from the Weston Mercury, the local paper. It was dated 9th September 1977:

YOUNG MAN DIES IN TRAGIC DROWNING ACCIDENT

I heard my breath rasp, and saw the script blur in front of me. I felt a sudden sense of loss that I had only really felt once before in my life. To feel that about my grandmother was understandable, but to feel the same way about a boy who shared my name, a boy I had only known about in the form of a dream, was a completely different matter.

With a hollow feeling in my belly, I read on:

The body of a young man was recovered from Uphill beach in the early hours of Saturday 3rd September. Peter Abrahams (19) is believed to have been walking out to meet the tide for a swim late on Friday evening, when he became trapped in the mud and drowned when the tide came in. His death was witnessed by two of his friends who along with the dead man were employees at the Royal Holm View Hotel. Earlier in the evening he had been drinking with them in the dunes between the golf course and the beach, when he expressed a desire to go swimming. They thought he was joking, but when he hadn't returned after twenty minutes, they became concerned and started searching for him. "We had walked along the beach earlier and eventually decided to have a drink in one of the dunes nearer to Uphill village," said one of the witnesses named as Robert Morgan (21). "Pete had obviously walked back towards the hotel to try and find a safe place to swim. We only heard him calling for help when we emerged from the dunes and by the time we had reached him, it was too late." Mr Morgan tried to save his friend whilst Richard Townsend (20) raised the alarm. "The mud was too thick, the tide too rough and I just couldn't get to him," Mr Morgan told the Mercury. Inspector Edward Bickerstaff of the Avon and Somerset Police called for people to take care after this became the third incident of its type in the last year. Last October a Weston man nearly died when he tried to rescue his car that had been stuck in the mud as the tide came in, and in February a man trying to rescue his dog became stuck in the mud himself. He was only saved because his dog freed himself and ran to attract the attention of passers-by. "The mud is not as flat and firm as it looks, and the speed of the incoming tide is very deceptive" Inspector Bickerstaff warned. "It can be a killer, and sadly in this case, it was." He also warned against swimming whilst under the influence of alcohol.

"Bloody hell!" said Emily once all of us had read the piece, "what do you reckon? His friends were so pissed that they didn't realise he had gone, and he was so pissed he decided to go off for a swim on his own?"

"That was what the tone of the article was making me think," agreed Sam, "poor Peter."

"No!" I said it a bit louder and more insistently than I had meant to. "Sorry, but he wasn't like that, he was…" I struggled for the right word and stumbled rather unsatisfactorily onto "sensible."

The siblings looked at me strangely and I knew that I had to recount more of my dream to make them understand. "For a start, there were two pairs of lads that were friends and they all had nicknames. Dee and Dum, Starsky and Hutch."

"Not much help as to which one was Richard, and which was Robert then," Sam said, but at least he did seem like he was taking me seriously.

"No, and the thing was, Pete wasn't friends with any of them. Dee and Dum were potheads. Hutch was a misogynistic womaniser. Starsky was, as far as I could make out, a bit of a boring drip."

"Yes, but your dream took place on cup final day?" Sam asked, and I nodded, "so that's back in May - and the accident happened in September. There's plenty of time for them to become friends in between. First impressions don't always mean anything."

"Or maybe he hadn't even met Richard and Robert in May, they could have arrived at the hotel later?" Emily had been quiet since my mild outburst, but she certainly had a point.

"Right - let's rewind a little here." Sam had definitely moved on from humouring me. There was a glint of interest in his eyes. "Who have you met so far and what is their relationship to Peter, and what is Peter like himself?"

"OK," I shut my eyes as if the very action would make my dream clearer. I didn't need to; my dream was as real to me as anything else that had happened over the last few months.

"Peter is outwardly gay, which I would imagine wasn't the easiest thing to admit in the seventies - it had barely been legal for ten years and I got the impression there was still a stigma attached to it. This makes me think he was confident, sure of himself, unflinching."

Sam nodded, he was having problems admitting the fact to everyone forty years on. If he had been around in the nineteen seventies, I did believe that his story would have been a life of lilac marriages and bath house cottaging.

"He was also kind, he befriended a waitress called

Jackie, who was a shy girl with a dominant mother. Within minutes of talking to her, he was encouraging her to make more of her life. He had made another friend, Tony, a chef who was just starting an affair with Helen, the receptionist - who in turn was going out with a drug dealer called Malcolm. Peter was already worried about this."

I took a breath, but the information was falling from me like water from a broken jug.

"Malcolm liked to be known as Marlon and dealt drugs to Dee and Dum, two pot washers who might or might not be Richard and Robert. There were two barmen, they were the ones known as Starsky and Hutch because Hutch looked like the actor who played the part in the original TV series… They also could possibly be Richard and Robert, but less likely I think."

I took another breathe before plunging on to the conclusion. "There was a second chef called Martin, he was known as Smiler because he was so miserable. The hotel was run by a Mr Edwards, who was a bit of a bastard - and his son, who wasn't. There was a head chef who was called something Italian and various other staff that I haven't really met yet. Most of the staff lived in a prefab block they called Strangeways, which as far as I could gather was situated on what is now the car park. In those days the car park was out the front, it wasn't grassed over at that time"

I breathed out: "Now you nearly know as much as I do!" I looked at Sam and Emily, who were looking shell shocked.

There was silence for a few seconds. Somewhere a door closed, a radio played in a room on a lower floor and there were vague sounds of seagulls squawking outside the open window.

"You were actually there weren't you?" Sam whispered, "You really went back through time, in your dream…"

"Do you think this Peter is related to you?" Emily asked, "I mean you have the same name after all - is this why your dream is so…" she grappled around for the right word, "real?"

"Only child of an only child," I said simply, "could be a distant cousin I guess, but Dad's never talked about anyone - he doesn't really do family history stuff."

"Do you think, you will go back there again?" Sam asked, "Do you think you will find out what caused the accident?"

"I do believe there is more to it than this," I indicated towards Sam's iPhone with my hand, "but I don't want to wait for another dream - I want to find out more now!"

"But how?" Sam asked reasonably, "I mean the only person's full name you know is Peter's and he definitely isn't contactable!"

"Richard Morgan and Robert Townsend?"

"Common names I would say, and we have no idea where they are or what they are doing."

"His chef friend was called Tony Dean," I said, suddenly remembering. "I think I remembered that because of…"

"…your friend Dean in Shaftesbury?" Sam interrupted, and I nodded. "Well maybe if he still is a chef, he will be on Linkedin or he might even run his own restaurant with a website."

The trusty iPhone came back in to play and once again. Sam tapped information into it. Once again it came up trumps.

"Here we go! Tony Dean is a chef who owns his own restaurant called Deano's - original." I had noticed that Sam could get a bit hyper critical when it came to other catering establishments. Nobody could do it quite like the Royal Holm View Hotel.

I resisted the opportunity to say that for a hotel with views of two islands called Steep Holm and Flat Holm, the name of the family goldmine was hardly a tremendous example of ground breaking originality itself…

In reality, I was too excited to be bothered to taunt my

boyfriend - I know, I must have been really psyched up…

"So, where is it? Is there a number? Do you think it's the same Tony Dean?"

"Well, you'll probably know better than me, this is what he looks like now." Sam handed me his phone and I stared at a good looking, bald, man of colour - or whatever the PC term is at this moment. His age was difficult to gauge, but somewhere north of fifty-five would have been my guess, which would have definitely put him in the right age bracket.

"Christ Sam! It could be him!"

"OK. Deano's is in the Nicholas Market area of Bristol, so we could easily take a day trip to Bristol to meet him."

"I could drive you!" Emily volunteered cheerily.

"Or we could take the train?" Sam pondered comically.

"Train" I nodded conspiratorially.

"Bastards!" said Emily.

"But what on earth do we say? I mean we can hardly tip up at his restaurant saying: hello, I'm having dreams about your dead ex-friend who just happens to have the same name as me… like to tell me more?"

Sam nodded and grinned, "Aah, get your point, quick call to the police, hospital or home for the bewildered…"

"What if you said that you were working here for the summer," Emily said. "You were talking to one of the locals and the subject came up about people getting stuck in the mud. It piqued your interest and you started looking incidents up. You just happened to come across one where the victim had your own name, so you looked into it further."

"Not bad Sis!" Sam was genuinely impressed, but added reasonably, "but how are you going to explain to Tony how we knew about him?"

"Oh! We just tell him that Rem dreamt about him!" she reasoned, straight-faced.

Sam mimed whacking her across the face and she laughed.

"What if I say that we looked at the hotel records and saw he was on the books at the same time? You," I glanced at Sam, "as a fellow restaurateur knew of his restaurant and his Michelin star." OK, now I was taunting Sam, but that doesn't necessarily make me a bad person. "So, we just thought we'd get in touch to find out if he knew more than the newspaper article could tell us."

"We don't have hotel records that go back that far." Sam said reasonably, if slightly sulkily. I knew the fact that the hotel couldn't attract a chef with a Michelin star was still an irritation to the family. However, in my defence, he had been a bit pompous and sarky about the name of Tony's restaurant.

"Yes, but he doesn't know that, does he?"

In the end we decided I should ring him, rather than just turning up out of the blue. The call was answered by a deep, sexy voice with a Caribbean lilt to the accent. I launched into my story and when I had finished there was such a long pause that I wondered if Tony had hung up.

"Oh hi, are you still there?"

The voice was softer, like he was trying to get his breath back. "Pete Abrahams? I've barely heard that name for forty years." Then, in a tone that was half whisper - half expulsion of breath - he said, "but I think about him just about every single day."

15.

"Would you mind talking to me about his death?" His reaction had surprised me slightly and I was half expecting the line to go dead.

"Why?" he asked quietly.

"Because the story caught my imagination I suppose, same name and all that, but I know you're a busy man, so…"

"No! I'd like to talk to you about Pete. There was so much crap talked about him after the accident and I was completely useless at the time. I'd like to talk to someone about him."

We agreed that Sam and I would come to Bristol to meet him on Thursday at 10 am, before he got too busy in the restaurant.

I pressed the red telephone icon to hang up and Sam said in a whisper, "It was the same Tony Dean?"

"It was the same Tony Dean," I agreed.

I looked at Sam and Emily. "We're in!" I said with a shudder of excitement.

"But Rem," Mr Morning Grinch looked at me with barely contained horror, "we have to be in Bristol at ten in the morning - on my day off!"

For once, I didn't have an easy taunt on the tip of my tongue to launch in his general direction.

I believed that a man who had lived - and died - in and around this hotel forty years ago, was reaching out to me to find out the truth of his passing.

I was determined to discover that truth for him.

We had just arranged to meet the best friend of a dead man on Thursday morning.

Emily wanted to spend some time social networking as twenty-four hours had passed since her last fix and she was already feeling out of sync with all her school friends. "I feel like I'm going out without putting my underwear on," was her rather curious simile. Neither Sam or I asked for an explanation…

It was a beautiful day, set to reach thirty degrees in the middle of a mini heatwave, so we decided to make the most of our time off together. Sam suggested walking further along the beach to the village of Uphill itself and up onto the hill beyond the village. Neither of us was in the mood for frolicking in the surf as we had done on Sunday. We walked to the edge of the tide, close to the point where Pete had died. It was difficult to describe how I felt.

I suppose the feeling was close to hearing that one of your favourite characters in a long running drama is being killed off, but even that didn't cover it fully.

I had been struck by Tony's reaction to his name and the fact that there had been: "So much crap talked about him." I was convinced there was more to his death than just a misjudged late-night swim, but I had no idea what it might have been.

We walked along the beach and the colour of the sky was mirrored in the water. Today the blue won its battle with the swirling brown mud below the surface. On such a day, with Sam for company, it was impossible to stay broody for too long and soon we had relaxed into our natural banter.

Once we had left the beach, we walked along the road

before turning off into a boatyard on one side with a disused quarry towering above it on the other. The Wharfside café had been built into the side of the quarry and bits of it provided some of the interior walls. We bought ice creams and headed up the hill.

There were few people around, but we passed a middle-aged couple with a beautiful shaggy black dog as they strode down the hill. The dog seemed more intent on chasing seagulls than following instructions.

The lady laughed as she noticed us grinning. "I know! We seem to spend most of our time wading up to our knees in mud just because His Lordship has got a whiff of seagull!"

It brought Pete back to my mind, although I doubted that a dog had anything to do with his demise.

But what had?

We reached what looked like an old lookout tower and then walked back on ourselves, towards the most inaccessible church in the land. There were no roads leading to it, so the only access possible was on foot, either up a very steep hill from the village, or the long winding route that we had climbed. However, Sam told me there were still regular services in the summertime - even if only half of the building had roof cover over it.

On the way back to the hotel, we camped in one of the dunes and toasted our bodies, the day before the summer solstice and the hottest of the year so far. I wondered if this had been the dune that Richard and Robert had inhabited on that fateful night and just exactly what they hadn't told the authorities at the time.

"We could ask my mum if she remembers anything about the previous owners," said Sam at one point; "also, she could probably tell us a bit more about Strangeways."

"Uh huh," I agreed, "but could we stick to the story about it being gossip I've heard from the locals, rather than the truth? When we finally tell your parents about us, I don't want them to have already decided that I'm as nutty as the contents of a bird feeder!"

***

We found Fiona pouring through carpet sample books in the apartment lounge. "According to on-line reviews, the rooms on the second floor are badly in need of a refurb, so we've got to do that either in November or January," she explained. She was quite happy to exchange her homework for an early evening G & T. Once her daughter had sniffed the opportunity of a free alcoholic beverage; she, in turn, abandoned the social media sites she had been welded to for the previous few hours and joined us in the hotel garden.

I went through the preamble of the local gossip with a tale to tell.

"Alf?" she laughed.

I hadn't foreseen the possibility of her naming my fictitious source, so I just smiled in agreement.

"1977 was a long time before us," she said, "but fancy the lad having the same name as you, what a coincidence!"

"It was just that Maureen mentioned the family who owned the place before you, and I wondered how much you could tell me about them - as I guess they would have been running the Hotel at the time. It's just piqued my interest a bit, that's all."

"To be honest Rem, I don't know much about them at all. There were two brothers, can't even remember their names, but I think they both started with the same letter." Well I knew about Mo, the other I hadn't encountered yet - but of course I didn't tell Fiona this fact. "I know there was a big fall out when the father died, I think the older one blamed the younger one for his death. I don't mean he killed him or anything, I think it was just something the younger son... Mal, Matt, Max... it was something he did that caused his father so much stress, it lead to the old man having a heart attack."

"But no-one had said anything about a staff member drowning?"

"Well there were loads of horror stories about the mud - you can think it's firm enough, then suddenly…" She made a sucking sound and clamped her hands together… "but no, I don't remember that case at all."

"We were telling Rem about the Christmas decoration trunk with the letters PA on the front, we wondered whether that might have been his?" Ingenious Emily, ingenious.

"Gosh! It might well have been, it was certainly here when we arrived. The lads went their separate ways when their father died, and the place was put in the hands of various managers. The last one had been a bit put out when the Hotel was eventually sold and didn't bother sorting much out. Not that he had much to complain about; him and a succession of previous managers had made the most of the owner being absent, ripped the hotel off something rotten. This meant that as Maureen said, your grandfather got it for a great price, but there was an awful lot to do when we got here! I mean, for a start they had this whole area as a car park!" She waved her arm to signify the land that led from our bench to the beach. "Complete madness! That fantastic view and what gets the benefit of it… a load of flippin' cars!"

"So, what was on the area that we now use as a car park?" Sam asked, "or did they just have cars parked everywhere?" Smooth Sam smooth.

"Surely I've told you about Strangeways?" Fiona asked. Judi Dench would have been proud, they were both as straight faced as a nineteenth century spinster. Their mother chuckled, "to be honest, I haven't thought about it for years, it was the most awful prefab building that was used as accommodation for staff. By the time we bought the place it was rotten with damp, infested with cockroaches and there were holes in the floor. To be fair, it had been erected quickly after the war and it was only meant to be a temporary building, so it did pretty well to last thirty years!"

She smiled, remembering, "It had the most awful psychedelic style paintwork on the landing. I think the last time it had been decorated was the sixties and it probably looked all right then, but in the New Romantic eighties, when it was faded and pealing, it looked completely awful!"

I sucked in my breath gently, I had seen that paintwork. How could I have possibly seen it? The whole place had been destroyed over ten years before I was born. Somehow, during the hours of a sleep-filled Sunday night, whether my oh so sensible brain liked it or not... I had travelled back in time.

***

I think Sam sensed something in my demeanour, we were getting quite attuned to each other's moods by now. He steered the conversation towards more family orientated matters that I wouldn't be expected to contribute to. It gave me a chance to collect my thoughts and I was thankful for that. We finished our drinks whilst the family talked about very welcome normality.

Fiona said, "Right! That was lovely, but I'd better return to carpets. Sam, are you all right sorting out dinner tonight in the apartment? I told your dad that we'd eat about seven-thirty?"

As we walked into the bar, I saw that it was dead on six o'clock and right on cue, Alf was taking his place at his table. On the spur of the moment, I thought I'd better have the conversation with him that I'd told Fiona about, just in case they chatted about it at any time in the future. Telling Sam and Emily that I'd see them upstairs, I walked over to him. Unfortunately, I decided to be a little bit too clever about it for my own good.

"Hi Alf!"

"Lad."

"You know that conversation we were having yesterday about accidents when people have misjudged the mud and the fast-moving tide?"

"No. We were talking about changes I remembered in the Hotel, we didn't mention anything about mud." Sharp as a tack and just as pointed. I decided to backtrack somewhat.

"Oh sorry, thought it was you, must have been someone else, I chatted to so many people yesterday!"

He looked at me as if he didn't believe a word I was saying, but I carried on digging… in more ways than one.

"It's just the whole subject really interested me, and I thought I'd look particular cases up. It was really strange, one of the staff from this hotel drowned in that way in 1977 and he had the same name as me. Did you know him?"

I received a blank, yet calculating look.

"Peter Abrahams?"

"I told you lad, I never came in here back then… it was shit."

***

Sam was busy cooking when I got upstairs, and I knew how much he hated being interrupted when he was concentrating on food.

So, I went in to annoy him.

"That psychedelic paintwork your mum described?"

"You saw it in your dream, didn't you?"

"Yes Sam, is this crazy or what?" I nicked a piece of pepper he was chopping and after eating it, went back for another attempt and received a whack on the back of the knuckles with the flat side of the knife.

"We'll talk about it more later, now leave me alone to create!"

These prima donna chefs…

I blame Gordon Ramsay.

***

The dinner was good and on balance probably worth being threatened at knife point for, although the meal was a slightly strained event in other ways. Ned still seemed to be in a bad mood about demi-glace and was subtly criticising any decision that Sam had made the day before. Sam looked embarrassed and it almost seemed like his father was belittling him in front of me on purpose.

At least he was saved from the fate that had befallen Emily. She had been seconded, with very bad grace to help in the bar as they were short of staff.

"I am so getting Barney to stay next holiday, if it frees me from this slavery!" She flounced from the room and I helped Fiona clear the dirty dishes. She looked a little tense herself. Sam was receiving an extended pep talk from his father.

As soon as I had cleared up, I went in to save Sam by asking him if he wanted to watch "High-Rise" on a DVD.

Neither of us had any intention of watching a film. We had detecting to do.

"OK," Deputy Manager Sam was in action. "You concentrate on people called Mal, Matt, Mo and Max Edwards. I'll do Robert, Richard and the policeman. Let's see if we can find out anything."

We were both laying on the bed, I was sprawled on my front, across his body tapping on my laptop, whilst Sam was using my back as a table for his. OK, it wasn't the most comfortable of positions, but I just loved any contact I could possibly get with him, so I was more than happy.

We ended up surfing the net separately for about an hour or so. I had found some music related links. I plugged in my headphones, so I could listen to them without disturbing Sam.

Eventually, Sam did back to front press ups against my

stomach. Thinking that I had restricted the blood flow around his body for long enough, I shuffled my own body so that we were side by side, sharing his pillow. I ripped the ear phones from my ears and looked at him.

"Hello you!"

He smiled, "Hello you yourself! So, have you found anything?"

I grimaced, "Well, I entered just about every derivative of the names I could think of for Mal, Matt, Mo or Max Edwards – there are loads of them, but I'm not sure that anything I've found fits in with either of the brothers. I'm just listening to a singer songwriter called Max Edwards who does the rounds of the Brighton pubs, he's not bad, his lyrics are very Gay Pride though." I closed my eyes to remember the first line of the song that I had just started listening to. "Umm… 'The ruthless church that hid our love from the world.' Good tune though, great guitar introduction!"

Sam gave me that look… "Well I haven't just been scouring YouTube for new talent, I have been researching your mystery." He sniffed and maintained a superior countenance, "I have been detecting!"

"OK Jessica, what have you found?" I teased.

He lost the attitude and decided instead to pass on the information that he had discovered. "OK, I didn't manage to find anything from the police side of the investigation. The policeman is no longer with us, he had a fatal heart attack in 2008."

"So, a bit of a dead end then," I smirked and had to dodge a flailing hand.

"If you're thinking of a life as a stand-up comic, then I think you should prepare yourself for hard times," he said bitterly, then brightened. "Do you want me to tell you what I discovered about Richard and Robert or not?"

OK I admit it, I did want to know.

Of course, it wasn't that easy, you know what it's like. All the suspects are in the room and Jessica Fletcher mentions each one of them in turn, padding the story from one advertisement break to the next, until after three more minutes and yet more chances to buy sofas, beds and holidays - you finally get to the denouement...

Well, Sam was exactly like that...

"So, to start with, I tried their names alongside Weston-super-Mare. The only proper result I got was the article we have already seen. So, I took Weston out of the equation, and discovered that Robert Morgan is the name of a director animator; as well as the name of an actor who has been in everything from Grange Hill to Mr Selfridge and that Rich..."

"Excuse me! Is this the same Samuel Morris that was having a go at me for researching songs on YouTube?" I was deep in revenge mode. "Is there any hope of reaching a point some time before the next millennium?"

"Ok Ok, I was only pointing out that I had a lot of searching to do before I found this...!" He pushed his laptop towards me triumphantly.

And there it was:

TWO MEN DIE IN PUB FIRE

The joint publicans of the Grey Horse Public House in Swanton Morley were both found dead after a fire swept through the Inn just after daybreak on Thursday morning. The investigation into the cause of the blaze is still ongoing.

Two men called Robert Morgan and Richard Townsend were the only witnesses to Peter's death.

Two men called Robert Morgan and Richard Townsend were killed in a pub blaze in Norfolk early in 1987.

Coincidence?

16.

We looked in vain for any follow up information, but whatever had been discovered in 1987 was not revealed to us thirty years later. After all our investigations I was sure I would have another dream that night. However, when I woke up the next morning it was with the vague memory of Foz and Alf cooking huge vats of demi-glace, which Ned served to the customers in bowls made from carpet samples.

The next day, Sam decided to show me the other end of Weston. His father was still a little cranky. I was getting a slightly different view of Ned from Emily than the one I had got from Sam. She was obviously fond of him, but had admitted to me that he could suffer from moods that went on for weeks at a time. I was hoping for Sam's sake that this one would burn itself out before September. I was beginning to believe that he had a good reason to be worried about his confession.

I had a feeling that it might not go well.

I think that Sam was keen to get away from the Hotel for a day, so we walked up to the Marine Lake and beyond to Anchor Head where we played a dodgy game of tag on the rocks. Managing not to cause ourselves or anyone else any lasting damage we re-trod our steps. However, the journey back which started with a quick pint at the Captain's Cabin, turned into a massive pub crawl which ended with a drunken Indian takeaway on the beach.

We lay together in a sand dune afterwards, yards away

from discovery, but the cloak of alcohol rendered us oblivious, and we barely gave it a thought. Sometime after midnight, we staggered back to the hotel. Despite making an awful lot of noise by sniggering, shushing each other and sniggering again, we managed to reach the apartment without anyone seeing us. We collapsed immediately onto Sam's bed.

Oblivion came quickly.

And with it came my second visit to 1977.

17.

1977

During the summer of '76 the earth blistered, yearning for a drink like an alcoholic during prohibition. Pete had already heard all the stories of the ladybird summer where millions of them carpeted the seafront like a scarlet snowfall. The owners of the Arnold Palmer crazy golf course employed three people to continually hoover the fairways and suck out the little insects that were threatening to suffocate the mini windmill.

Children, who would pause from eating an ice cream to pet their dog or try in vain to find wind to power their own plastic windmills, would turn back to find the ice cream covered with the bugs, like a coating of hundreds and thousands. Crunchy, but slightly less appetising.

By mid-June the summer of 1977 was threatening to be much more like a traditional English summer, nice days and nasty days - but mercifully without drought or ladybird.

Pete had settled into his new life like the ladybirds had settled on the sand the year before, with an ease as if he had been there forever. His fledgling friendship with Tony was already mutating into something stronger. It really shouldn't have worked.

As well as the obvious differences of skin tone and sexual orientation, they agreed about absolutely nothing.

One of them described himself as a vague liberal whilst the other had copies of the Socialist Worker on order from the local newsagent. One of them was a monarchist, the other a staunch republican. One loved going to concerts and theatre whilst the other thought that Albert Hall was a lesser known brother of a BBC presenter. Their arguments about music could go on for hours, and were already legendary throughout the hotel with staff and customers alike. But the glue that held their friendship together was the laughter they shared. If humour was represented by a number, it was much larger than the sum of all their differences.

On a sunny but windy Tuesday, early in June, the car park had been turned into a massive street party to celebrate the silver jubilee of the Queen. Pete had served cakes on paper plates disguised as the Union Flag with the enthusiasm of a toddler at Christmas. Tony had sneered and taunted, every time the Trainee Manager had appeared for another plate of sandwiches or red white and blue painted fancies, "Come the revolution, all this will be mine!"

An interchanging group of them had taken to debunking after work and carrying beers that had been begged, bought and in Hutch's case, stolen, over to the dunes on Uphill beach. Depending on work schedules it usually comprised of the crowd that had visited the night club on Cup Final day along with Smiler, the second chef.

Pete had developed a grudging liking for the youthful curmudgeon in spite of the fact that he was twenty-eight going on eighty-two. On the night that Liverpool had beaten Borussia Monchengladbach to claim the European cup, he had grabbed Pete in a brief hug and said, in relation to their first meeting, "You were in the wrong place at the wrong time."

Pete took it as an apology.

Jackie and Pete had also formed a close friendship. Under his tutelage she had blossomed, and she was beginning to show more confidence. The caterpillar was slowly turning into a butterfly. He had accompanied her to the local technical college to find out what qualifications she needed to become a nursery nurse. She was a few GCE grades shy of acceptance, but Pete had persevered, and with the help of a friendly college receptionist, had discovered an access course she could sign up to in September. On completion, it could lead to the course she really wanted to take.

The only slight worry was the fact that because her confidence was growing, she was taking more pride in her appearance and people were noticing how pretty she was. For people, insert the name Hutch.

Hutch was the one person who worked at the hotel that Pete still had a problem with. Starsky, he had discovered, held a quiet charm and a dry sense of humour that had grown on him over the course of the month. When Hutch wasn't around, they seemed to have developed a relationship that even if it wasn't quite a friendship, was getting very close to one.

Hutch on the other hand was everything that Pete didn't like. A loud-mouthed braggart with far too high an opinion about himself. If someone shot a hole in one on the golf course, he had done it one handed, blindfolded, whilst travelling on a moving golf buggy.

He was racist, homophobic and Pete's opinion on his first night that he was also a misogynist had proven to be bang on the money. The only person that seemed to like him besides Starsky, was Helen. Although he would never say so to Tony, Peter had formed the impression that this was because he was blonde, good looking, had two legs and a pulse.

Helen worried Pete. He liked her a lot, but she reminded him of the femme fatales so brilliantly played by Barbara Stanwyck in the black and white movies that were shown on BBC2 before the channel closed for the night. She and Tony were getting closer by the day. Whenever she allowed him to, he would disappear along to her room and reappear in room seventeen in the middle of the night. His white teeth stretched into a delighted rictus that shone through the darkness.

However, she still went off to see Malcolm Marlon whenever she felt the need. The drug dealer was so far, mercifully oblivious to her double life.

Playing with fire, Pete thought.

He challenged her about it one day and she simply said that she thought it was better that Marlon didn't know about Tony, he tired of everything eventually, she reasoned. She was hoping that Marlon would tire of her sooner rather than later and after a decent period of heartbreak, she could make her relationship with Tony official. Pete could see her argument. However, there was something about her manner that disturbed him.

She was enjoying the attention.

On this night in mid-June they had once again had a few beers on the beach and were nicely relaxed when Hutch suggested a game of cards in the room he shared with Starsky. Their room was the biggest of all the staff rooms, so it was the obvious place to meet whenever the weather was wet and cold and a party on the beach was unappealing, or as on this occasion, there was something else to do. There was a murmur of agreement and a few abstentions. Smiler was far too busy the following day to stay up half the night playing cards, whereas Dee and Dum were nowhere near stoned enough to leave the dunes and be anything close to sociable.

They had played a few rounds of poker for pennies when Hutch suggested they played another game. "How about a few games of high card?" he asked. "Everyone gets dealt one card and the person with the highest card is the winner and the one with the lowest card is the loser. Aces high."

"Christ Hutch!" laughed Tony, "how long did it take you to come up with a complicated game like that?"

"Shut it Nig-nog!" Hutch said offensively, but without malice. "Before you turn over your card, everyone writes a forfeit on a piece of paper, and the loser has to perform the winner's forfeit."

Pete was sensing a plan. However, everyone else was up for it, so he decided to join in, but he intended to watch Hutch like a hawk.

The deal rotated around the room and Tony had to perform Minnie Riperton's "Loving You," in a voice that threatened to attract all the dogs within a five-mile radius.

Pete had to pretend to be John Wayne and he did such a camp impression of the ageing cowboy that even Hutch dropped his normal sneering superiority and laughed along with everyone else.

It was then Hutch's turn to deal. Because he was watching him so closely, Pete noticed that there was something slow and deliberate about the shuffle. When he had dealt his round of poker, he had done it in his normal showy manner… this was different. Just after everyone had written their forfeits but before the first card had been turned over, Peter exclaimed as if an idea had just come to him.

"Why don't we do it a bit differently this round? Why don't you give me your card, Hutch? I'll give mine to Tony and so on round the room until Jackie gives her card to you?"

"Well what is the point of that?" said Hutch arrogantly, but there was a slight edge of tension in his voice. Pete had surreptitiously nudged Tony who took his cue well, even if he wasn't completely sure what his friend was up to.

"I'm with Pete!"

Starsky couldn't see the point, so was against, but Helen and Jackie allied alongside Pete and Tony, so Hutch had no choice but to comply.

The look on his face when he handed Pete his card told the Trainee Manager all he needed to know. When he turned it over, it was the ace of spades.

What a surprise.

When all the cards were revealed, it was even less of a surprise to Pete to find that Hutch was holding the two of diamonds, the card that had been intended for Jackie.

"OK poofter!" Hutch conceded, "what's on your piece of paper? Bound to be something gay no doubt. Were you hoping your nigger boyfriend would lose and he would have to kiss you?"

"It's a bit more pathetic than that I'm afraid," Pete said with false apology. "I couldn't really think of anything fun, so I just put this…"

He unwrapped his piece of paper so that the other players could see. Tony whooped with realisation whilst the others looked confused. Hutch, for once had lost his arrogant air and looked horrified.

"The loser will perform the forfeit he or she wrote on their own piece of paper."

"So!" said Tony a little smugly. "Let's see it Hutch! What did you have in store for the loser, if you had won?"

Hutch stared at him, for once at a complete loss. Tony stretched over and took the piece of paper lying in front of the barman and with exaggerated care, unwrapped and snorted with laughter.

"Oh my God Hutch! You were a naughty boy! Talk about being hoisted on your own petard!" He then read out loud whilst trying vainly not to laugh. "The loser will strip completely naked, each player in turn will have a minute to tickle, grope or do whatever they like."

"Well I'm not bloody doing it!" said Hutch aggressively. "If the bum boy over there can't think of a forfeit of his own, then he's certainly not stealing mine!"

"Well" said Starsky quietly and reasonably, "It's just as valid as anything anyone else wrote. In all fairness, you would have expected the loser to go through with it if you had won."

"Oh, don't be such a fucking solicitor!" Hutch snapped at his friend scornfully.

"What is it Hutch?" Helen teased, "are you ashamed of your naked body? Is something not right?"

Hutch scowled at her as the others started chanting "Strip! Strip! Strip!" To stop them, Hutch held up his hand.

"OK OK!" With barely disguised bad grace he started by pulling his tee shirt over his head and threw it into the corner of the room. Far from confirming Helen's taunt, Pete was impressed by the summer tan, the firm muscles and flat stomach. Hutch scowled in his direction as he took off his shoes and socks, undid his belt and dropped his trousers. He then started to lay down on the floor, still in his underpants, ready for the next part of his forfeit. Tony and Helen shouted in derision.

"I think you'll find that it said completely naked!" they laughed. Starsky nodded whilst Jackie just looked on, amazed.

"Oh, for Fuck's sake!" He stood back up and slowly dropped his blue Y fronts with white edging. He tried to hide his manhood, but his tormentors were having none of it, so eventually, when he lay on the carpet, he was fully exposed. Pete was grimly amused to see that although by no means tiny, he wasn't quite as well-endowed as he had wanted everyone to believe him to be.

Jackie was the first to have her minute and she giggled her way around his body like she was sightseeing in a strange town. Helen, on the other hand, knew that sort of town very well and explored every area of it with great enthusiasm - even the suburbs that were very rarely seen.

It was clear that Hutch was not into receiving humiliation, even the soft caress of Helen's hands failed to cause any excitement.

Starsky viewed his friend's body as if it were a burger engorged with maggots and resisted any contact at all. He filled his minute solely by scraping a feather across the bottom of Hutch's feet, causing him to squirm with humourless laughter as his cock and balls slapped from side to side like a pin ball collecting thousands of bonus points.

Tony on the other hand, enjoyed himself unapologetically. He had been eyeing a can of shaving foam that was poking out of a wash bag on the chest of drawers. He took off the top and waved the can in front of Hutch's horrified eyes. He then squeezed the button, emptying the contents all over the barman's face, torso and legs. He then took great delight in using up the rest of his minute by rubbing foam into Hutch's hair and face before moving down his body. He didn't follow Helen's example when he reached the genitalia, and decided instead to use the barman's thighs as a ring road to find a detour around them, before moving on to the safer areas of legs and feet. By the time Peter shouted, "Time's Up!" Hutch was pretty much covered from the top of his hair to the tip of his toes. The only untouched area exaggerated his nakedness even more.

"Well Hutch!" Laughed Tony, his exaggerated Caribbean accent on full show, "you'm even more of a white boy than normal!"

Hutch growled, jumped up and grabbed a towel to remove as much of the foam as possible. He turned to Peter with a look of barely disguised dislike. "All of that and I've still got to suffer the gay boy molesting me. I bet you can't wait to get your limp wrists working on my body! But..." he turned to the others, "I don't care what it says on that stupid piece of paper, he can't do anything he likes, he's not allowed to get his fucking hard-on anywhere near me!"

Pete wouldn't have done that in any case, but other than that he was torn. He had to admit that he would have liked the opportunity to get his hands on what was irrefutably a very nice body. But this was all about revenge for what Hutch had wanted to put Jackie through - and he thought he had an even better plan.

"To be honest Hutch, I hate to break it to you, but

you're not really my type. I prefer a bit more to my men." Pete nodded at the area he was referring to. "Would anyone mind if I defaulted on my turn?"

***

"My skinny white gay friend! You are my hero!" The party had broken up soon after Hutch's humiliation. After making sure that Jackie was safely in a taxi home, the boys of room seventeen were getting undressed and ready for bed.

"So, you agree that I am a god and right about everything?" Pete laughed.

"Hell no! You're not right about anything!" Tony retorted laughingly, then sobering up said, "how did you know what he was planning? If he was planning it, of course."

"Oh, he was planning it. I've been a bit worried about the way he's been looking at Jackie lately, he's practically been licking his lips like Kojak when he's unwrapping a lollipop!" Pete shrugged, "I just watched him when he dealt those cards, it was so dodgy that the idea popped into my head. It was just perfect the way everyone was sitting, it worked like a dream!"

"I don't know why Helen likes him so much, I think he's creepy as fuck!"

Pete decided to keep his own council on his views behind that one and got into bed. Tony did the same, but as he turned out his light he said: "Be careful Pete, I don't trust that arsehole. You made him look a complete nob tonight and sure as I'm black and beautiful, he's going to be out for revenge!"

***

Over breakfast the next morning, Helen was trying to organise a picnic on the hill at Uphill. She was on a day off from reception, and although Starsky was on bar duty until two-thirty, the rest of her closest friends were free until four. Pete was rather hoping that Hutch would refuse to come if he knew that Pete would be there. Surprisingly though, the barman had jumped at the offer. Of course, this was after Jackie had agreed to join them.

Helen was dishing out instructions. Pete had been entrusted with the task of shopping for the picnic whilst Tony was to make the ingredients into something edible afterwards. Just as she was asking Hutch to bring his radio along in order to have a bit of music, Mr Mo appeared.

Pete liked the son of the owner and got on well with him. Once, in his first week, he had dropped back off to sleep after Tony had got up and was still sleeping when Mo had rapped on the door. He told him, in no uncertain terms, to get his backside down the stairs and get to work if he valued his job. As soon as the breakfast rush had died down, Pete had sought out the Deputy Manager and officially apologised. Mo liked his directness, had shook his hand, told him that they would say no more about it and there was no need for his father to know.

Since that day, Pete had worked hard, not been late and shown a real aptitude for the work. Mo had taken him under his wing and trained him in areas that he had never trusted any other trainees to learn.

On this day, he had a favour to ask. "I heard a rumour that some of you were planning a picnic?" There were murmurs of agreement, some slightly reticent, as if they were worried that the management were going to quash their plans.

"Don't worry!" He laughed, "as long as you're not on duty that's fine. I only wanted to ask if you would mind taking Max along with you. He broke from university yesterday, but all his Weston friends are away on holiday, he's at a bit of a loose end, that's all."

No-one dared to complain in front of the Deputy Manager, but as soon as he had gone Hutch voiced his opinion.

"Fucking Hell! Now we've got to babysit Little Lord Fauntleroy in our spare time - be careful what you say everyone, it'll go straight back to Daddy or big brother!"

Smiler moaned along with him, but it was almost a case of being on automatic pilot rather than the fact that he was particularly bothered.

"What is the problem?" Pete said in a slightly irritated manner. "We've just been asked if he can join us on our picnic, we've not been asked to change his nappy or burp him!"

"Well fancy! Perfect Peter is sucking up to the management! What a surprise!"

They had all assumed that Mo would have to go back up to the flat to collect his brother. However, he must have been much nearer to hand because the staff were suddenly aware of them coming back around the corner from the restaurant.

Mo stood stock still and gazed at his staff without expression. Pete could see his moustache was twitching, a sure sign that he was holding on to his temper.

"Is there a problem?" He asked neutrally, there were murmurs of denial, but no-one held his gaze fully. His brother, Pete thought, looked terrified.

Pete hated anyone to feel like an outsider. To take against someone just because of who their family were, was the kind of inverted snobbery that he couldn't stand. He held out his hand to the lad. "Hi, I'm Pete, I've been told by she who must be obeyed," he smiled at Helen, "that I'm on shopping duty, d'you want to come with me?"

Pete laughed at himself quietly. Yes, there was the inverted snobbery. Yes, there was the fact that it would piss Hutch off. Yes, there was the fact that Pete himself was naturally friendly. However, there was also the fact that Max was absolutely bloody gorgeous...

Max smiled shyly and said, "Thanks." He was just slightly shorter than Pete's five foot eleven with wavy mousy hair that stopped short of his collar. He had an open, even face with friendly features that lit up when he laughed or smiled.

In all honesty though, the conversation as they walked along the streets in search of provisions, was a bit of an effort. Max was obviously aware of the dissension in the ranks that had arisen when his brother had added an unwelcome guest to the party. As they neared the bakery, when his opening gambits had been met with one-word answers, Pete decided to tackle the problem head-on.

"Look, I don't know how much of that you heard, but all I can say is that some of them are wankers! Most of us are quite happy for you to join us - to be honest, they're probably having a go at me more than you."

"OK…" Max looked doubtful and again they walked along in silence. He might be gorgeous, thought Pete, but he seems like he might be slightly hard work…

"Hello Pete!" The lady behind the counter called cheerily as he entered the shop, "you're a bit of an early bird today! Your usual?"

"No thanks Vi! We're all going on a picnic, so about eighteen white bread rolls would be great thanks." He explained to Max, "they have the best Cornish Pasties in here." He then paused and laughed, "but you probably know that better than I do!"

Max smiled, but said nothing. Vi obviously didn't know who he was, and Pete thought it a little strange that whilst they were on first name terms after a month; Max had lived there practically all of his life, but was still a stranger to her.

In the butchers it was the same story, Pete ordered some sliced ham and bantered away with the lads whilst Max was treated like a visitor from another planet. Into the dairy, by which time Pete was beginning to think the whole trip was beginning to resemble a Janet and John book - they bought cheese and once again he joked with Nan behind the counter. However, she obviously didn't know

Max at all.

Into Liptons for odds, sods and chocolate. Within fifteen minutes of returning, Tony had turned it all into a picnic and they were marching en masse through the car park to the tall gate that led to the beach.

Pete stayed at the back with Max as Hutch had made it obvious that he would be ignoring the Manager's son. Smiler walked with him, but seemed vaguely embarrassed by the barman's thinly veiled antagonism. Tony and Helen were joined at the hip, Dee and Dum mooched, heads bowed like the branches of a birch tree in autumn. Jackie hovered, unsure of which pair she should join. In the end she gravitated towards Pete as she normally did.

They gossiped and bickered in a way that had become normal to them, but had been unheard of for Jackie until she met Pete. They were halfway along the sands towards the road that led up to the hill, when they realised that Max was being left out of the conversation somewhat.

"Do you like Abba?" Jackie asked Max.

"They're OK," he said.

Well, thought Pete, that practically doubles the number of words he's said in one sentence up to now - carry on like that and I won't be able to shut him up.

"They're our favourites aren't they Pete?" Jackie said brightly and then followed the adage: if in doubt – sing. They launched into the whole of the "Arrival" album, from the opening number, "When I Kissed The Teacher" right through to the instrumental title track. The bagpipe sounding keyboards that Benny Anderson had created sounded more like a distress call to the lifeboats when recreated by Pete and Jackie, but everyone got the gist.

"Is it ever going to end?" wailed Tony as they walked into the track that would take them past fishing boats on the right and a fishing equipment shop, built into the rocks of the quarry, on the left. They made their way along the track, and after passing through a gate, headed up a grassy hill dotted with buttercups towards a tower that topped it.

Under its lea they settled, and various blankets and foodstuffs appeared from bags and sacks until they annexed a much bigger area than nine people needed. Hutch turned on the radio and the sounds of Olivia Newton-John rattled from its speaker.

Tony groaned, "Lord save us! Another of your favourites Pete?"

Pete laughed, "I do like a bit of Olivia, yes."

"She's meant to be filming a Hollywood movie called Grease." Helen said whilst digging into one of the bags and pulling out several of the filled rolls.

"And to think they said her career would be over when she appeared in her mother's net curtains at Eurovision!" Pete paused, thinking about the information he'd just been given. "What's the film about anyway?" he sucked in his breath as a thought occurred to him. "Please don't tell me she's playing a mechanic?"

"No," Helen giggled, "It's a musical set in a high school in the fifties, apparently."

"Sounds shit!" Smiler was on good form.

"I like a group called the Jam," It was not certain if he'd been building up to it, but Max's longest sentence of the day was a bit of a shock to them all.

"Now!" said Tony, impressed, "their stuff is quite good."

"Punk crap is it?" Pete enquired and received a withering look from his friend.

"Sort of," said Max, "but they're more based on sixties mod groups like the Kinks."

"Oh, there is a tune then?" Pete said.

"There most certainly is my fluffy friend," laughed Tony rubbing Pete's hair in a friendly, mocking fashion. "Not sure about their politics though, some of their lyrics are a bit flag waving pro-empire for my liking."

"It's just that whereas punk is about tearing things down and destroying, the Jam are about changing things, saying that this country is great, but there are many

problems and we need to work together to change them."
Bloody hell thought Pete, I was right! Once you get him
going there really is no stopping him.

As though he could read their minds, Max grinned
sheepishly, "Sorry!" he said.

"So," Hutch had been quiet for a while. He stopped
chewing on a cheese roll to ask, "they'll be against a world
where all the rich get richer and the poor get poorer?" He
had the sly look he usually wore when he was plotting
something.

"Absolutely!" Max replied enthusiastically, falling into
the trap like a snared rabbit.

"Easy for you to say though isn't it?" Hutch countered
with thinly veiled animosity, "you've got your rich daddy to
run home to any time you're short of funds."

Done up like a kipper, Pete thought. He felt sorry for
Max. Just when he had found his voice, he had run into
Hutch in a power to the people mode. But Max was just
about to prove that shy and quiet he might be, a walkover
he wasn't.

"So, you're saying that just because my dad is rich, I
shouldn't care? I'm not allowed to want to change things
because I'm one of the privileged few? Decency is only for
the poor? Tell me Hutch, what have you done to make a
difference?"

There was no anger there, that's what impressed Pete,
the lad was calmly making a point. It did rather shut
everyone else up though. People returned to munching
their rolls and listening to the chart show.

Gladys Knight was up seven places to number seven.

***

They finished their picnic in relative peace, half
listening to the Newsbeat programme that broke the chart
show in two. When the top five was revealed and Hot
Chocolate had a big climber at number three, Pete

shouted, "I love this!" and grabbed Jackie for a dance. Tony and Helen joined them whilst Hutch sneered, Smiler frowned, and Dee and Dum were too busy rolling a joint to care. Max just grinned.

Next up was "Lucille" and if dancing to that was difficult then it was a comparative breeze compared to trying to boogie through the chart run down. However, when all was revealed, and the Jacksons had claimed the top spot, normal service could be resumed. The song would always remind Pete of his first night in Weston and once again he was amazed how close Tony and Helen were happy to be in front of Dee and Dum. Her boyfriend supplied their drugs, and one loose word could bring down the wrath of the mighty Malcolm Marlon and all his nasty little associates.

After the chart run down came Paul Burnett's "Fun at one" spot. Dancing to Bob Newhart's comic monologue was a step too far for all of them and they slumped back down on to the grass.

Max had been silent since his brief, but memorable interjection and Pete didn't want him to feel that everyone was siding with Hutch and excluding him.

"Do you know what the tower used to be?" he asked him, pointing to the building they were currently using as a windbreak.

"Oh, it was an old windmill - seventeenth or eighteenth century I think," Max said, "It's got fantastic views across the estuary from the top."

"Fancy a climb?" Pete asked, only for Hutch to latch on immediately.

"Make sure you keep your back to the wall Maxi! I mean, I know you're all for helping the poor and needy, but there are some things, that even you wouldn't want to give him!"

Pete was just about to poke a V sign in his face when help came from an unlikely source. Smiler had had enough.

"For fuck's sake toss pot! Would you give it a rest! OK, I heard what happened last night and I'm sure you're very upset that Pete doesn't fancy you, but I'm afraid you'll have to get over it!"

There were various sounds of spluttering and giggles from the group whilst Hutch contented himself with a dark stare in the direction of the second chef. Pete shot Martin a grateful smile and received a morose grin in return - the curmudgeon had just about left the party momentarily.

"Hutch is a moron, isn't he?" Max said as they climbed the rickety iron steps that coursed through the middle of the old windmill. However, he said it without any malice at all, he could easily have been asking for a dozen iced fancies from the bakery.

"He certainly is!" Pete agreed.

Max's hand momentarily brushed against Pete's arm as they neared the top of their climb. "I mean, how does he know that I would be against the idea in any case?"

Pete felt an unusual lurching feeling in his chest. Did the lad know what that sounded like? Did he mean it?

Max grinned, in a slightly embarrassed manner, and decided that scenery was the best policy. He described the undulating Somerset hills from one side of the tower, and the Bristol Channel with Wales and Devon in the distance from the other. Two areas of Britain that looked miles apart on a map practically wrapped themselves around each other, like lovers' fingers, from their viewpoint on the hill.

"See the church over there?" Max pointed unnecessarily, but Pete nodded nonetheless.

"Race you to it!" Max was already careering down the stairs and had a good head start. Pete, always up for a challenge, followed laughing and stumbling down steps and across the grassy hillside. He caught up with him just as Max played tag with the kissing gate. Unable to stop in time, Pete crashed into both Max and the gate and the lad caught him before he stumbled backwards. For a moment they held on to each other, laughing, coughing and breathing heavily. Each of them wondering if there was to be a next move and whether they should be the one to make it.

In the end Max relied once again on scenery...

"So, this is St Nicholas' church, built around 1100. It is now half in ruins, the nave doesn't have a roof, but there are still services in the part that does. It's a bit of a climb from the village though, I think you'd have to be pretty God fearing to be bothered!"

They walked through the gate and across the old graveyard to the church itself. They entered through a door in the side and stood in a roofless area that was carpeted with tufted grass, weeds and stone. Pete was once again aware of the closeness of Max. He was giving him signals he was sure of it, but like a smuggler on a Cornish beach, Pete was unsure whether he should answer them or run across the cliff top to the safety of home. In the end he did neither, he walked towards the inner door that led to the rest of the building and looked inside the tiny church with its few rows of pews and cloth covered altar. Bare and barren and as simple as silence. He felt Max's presence behind him.

"Beautiful, isn't it?" He whispered. Pete nodded and turned towards him. However, in his mind, it was Max who was without doubt, beautiful.

Should he?

Afterwards, neither of them could really agree who made the first move. But the move was made, and the kiss was gentle and passionate... and beautiful.

"Well!" Max laughed gently and nodded to their surroundings, "If Anita Bryant is right and we're going to go to hell, at least we've done the job properly!"

They moved back into the sunlight and Pete propped himself up against the ancient wall with Max leaning next to him. They chatted softly about nonsense and laughed disparagingly about their hopes and dreams as the afternoon drifted across the summer sky. Occasionally they would stop and re-enact that moment in the church, but this was more about verbal discovery than physical. The monosyllabic lad of earlier was gone and in his place, was a man of soft words and gentle humour.

"I'd love to play the guitar better," Max said.

"I'd love to play the guitar at all." Pete grinned, "you might have noticed that I have no musical talent whatsoever!"

"Mmm," Max mumbled his assent and Pete tickled him mercilessly.

"Disagree, damn you!" he laughed and eventually let him go.

"So, what can you play?" he asked

"Well at the moment it sort of starts and stops at: 'If Forever Ends With You.'" Max laughed.

"Bennie Gold?" Pete pretended to be astounded.

"Yeah," Max grinned.

"You act all cool and hip about music and the only song you can play is Bennie flippin' Gold?"

"Believe me I've tried 'In the City' but it sounds a bit pathetic without drums and amplification!"

"And," Pete nodded sagely, changing tack completely, "Bennie Gold is pretty cool."

"Bennie Gold is very cool, especially the way I play it!"

"I can't even imag… Crikey look at the time!"

Suddenly the wayward clock meant that they had to fly away from the church towards where the picnic party had been. Where there had been a shanty town of picnic debris, there was now only Tony and Helen looking worried.

"Where the hell have you been? The others have gone on. We need to shift or we're going to be late. What on earth have you been doing?" Having his friends acting like parents amused Pete and added to elation he was feeling. He giggled with the innocence of a mischievous child.

"Looking at the church and discussing Bennie Gold," he laughed, grabbing a bag from Helen who looked at him with humorous bemusement. He slung it over his shoulder and with Max by his side, they ran down the hill singing…

"Time and tide it waits for no one, you'll do what you want to do, but I will wait forever, if forever ends with you."

18.

I woke to a dry mouth, a pounding head and another strange song buzzing around my brain. My feet found the floor and the room lurched as if I was on a cross channel ferry. The sickness I felt had more to do with the number of hostelries we visited the night before, than the sea, however. I decided not to move until the nausea had subsided and the room had returned to port.

Once I felt that I was safe to move without my stomach exploding, I looked across at Sam, his peaceful sleep twitches camouflaging the pain he would feel when he awoke. If Sam didn't do mornings, he most certainly didn't do hangovers.

I found my phone and tapped the Internet icon. It took me three attempts, my blotchy fingers managed to find Music, Messaging and Maps before I finally got there. I typed: "If foreber emds with yoi" which the smartphone miracle worker correctly translated as a song by a man called Bennie Gold. So far, so right.

It was weird and a little creepy, I had to admit to myself, especially when the song started and mirrored the tune that had caught itself on my brain.

"Whar the fuck! Oh my God! Oh my God!" Sam had stirred, and the anaesthetic of sleep had worn off spectacularly. "Did you have to wake me with that racket?" he implored.

Well, to be fair, Bennie Gold sings a very gentle folk rock song, so it gave a very good indication of the way he was feeling, but oblivious to his tender state, I retaliated anyway.

"Well it has got to be easier on the ear than Stage School Stacey; who, thanks to you, has woken me up every day for the last six months!"

He looked at me as if he couldn't believe that I wanted an argument considering his poor state of health. Quietly, firmly and with as little head movement as possible, he said very carefully…

"I'd – like – you – to – leave – right – now…"

I decided that, on balance – it wasn't the best time to sing the Will Young song from my childhood into his unenthusiastic earlobes.

It was lucky that I had woken at seven o'clock, because it took the Grinch a good hour to pull himself from his pit, get washed, dressed and stagger, groaning at the self-induced pain towards the apartment kitchen. Since I had known him I had irritated him with the fact that no matter how much alcohol I had consumed, after two Anadin Extras and a glass of water, I was back to normal again. It took poor Sam most of the morning to feel halfway human.

"Hello lads!" Fiona said brightly, then grinned at her son, "Oh my God Sam! Feeling well?"

I think Sam grunted, if that is what you could have called the strange noise that came from his mouth.

"I had a feeling you would be a little fragile this morning, after the state you were in last night!" She laughed.

"Christ Fiona, I'm so sorry," I said, horrified. "We were trying to be so quiet when we got home!"

"I know!" she laughed, "you made so much noise shushing each other, you might as well have gone the whole hog and invited everyone from the lounge bar to come up to the flat for a party!"

I must have been looking very embarrassed because Fiona stroked my arm sympathetically and said: "Don't worry, it wasn't a problem. I had the Jolly Green Giant snoring beside me anyway, so a bit more noise made little difference."

She gave us coffee and toast and we chatted whilst Sam conversed, mainly in grunts, groans and mumbles.

If Fiona thought it unlike her son to decide to take the 9:11 train to Bristol for some retail therapy whilst under the influence of a first-class hangover, she didn't say so.

I wasn't sure I could explain how I knew about Tony Dean. She would have known that my tale of researching through hotel records was a load of rubbish, so I was glad about her lack of interest. However, as we left the apartment, she called to Sam, almost as an afterthought.

"Oh, I was thinking last night about your little mystery. Why don't you go and see your Uncle John? He's a Weston boy, he was definitely around in the seventies and if I remember rightly, worked at the hotel for a while when he was a lad."

***

As we left Bristol Temple Meads station, I looked back up Station Approach to view the cathedral like building. Although Isambard Kingdom Brunel built the original station in the 1840s, the main building wasn't added until 1875. Opinions vary as to whether it was the design of Francis Fox, whose signature was on the drawings; or Matthew Digby-Wyatt, who was a former associate of Brunel.

There was originally a wooden spire rising from the clock tower, but that was destroyed by German bombing in the Second World War.

Sam had told me all this when we were having a drink in the Station bar on Sunday afternoon. Any words he had managed to mutter on that morning, four days later, were mostly indecipherable.

We arrived at Deano's just after ten o'clock. We had,

more or less, followed the river across the City. Although the sign on the door told us the restaurant was closed, the door opened to our touch. A middle-aged woman in cleaner's scrubs was sweeping the polished oak flooring and seemed just about to reiterate what the sign on the door had told us, when the man from the website picture appeared.

He smiled a greeting, confirmed who we were and led us to a table out of the sight of any people passing by whilst he went to make us coffee. The place was a small palace of dark oak, combined with the bright modernity of the chrome fixtures, fittings and stair rail that went up to the mezzanine floor covering the back half of the restaurant. Noises off told us that people were already preparing for the lunch time special menu on the other side of the door, behind the table we were seated at.

"So," Tony appeared with the coffee and set it in front of us. I was relieved to see that Sam was beginning to lose the colour of death that he had been sporting all morning. All things being equal, I didn't think that a spot of projectile vomit was likely to endear us to our host. "What can I tell you?"

"Well as I told you on the phone, Sam's family now own the Royal Holm View and I'm working there this summer. You know what the locals are like, they love telling newbies about all the disasters that have happened locally over the years. The idea of the tide coming in so quickly it can drown someone who is stuck in the mud struck me as unusual. I'm from Dorset and the tide barely goes out at all. I was looking stories up on the Internet and came across this one that involved a lad with the same name as me. I thought it was a bit of a coincidence and when I looked into other cases, this one came across as a little different."

"How?" Tony asked.

"Well in all the other cases there was a reason behind it. A man's car got stuck in the mud and with another bloke it was his dog. With this case, apart from the vague suspicion of him being drunk, there seemed next to no explanation for it. We found you because luckily, they keep staff records a ridiculously long time at the hotel…" I trailed off with a lie.

"There was so much shit talked about Pete after he died." Tony hadn't changed tack from the views he'd expressed over the phone. "He would not have gone swimming drunk; he would have not been high on drugs, which was another tale that was bandied about, and he probably wouldn't have hung out with Dee and Dum on his own; in a group, yes, but not on his own."

So, Dee and Dum were Richard and Robert.

"What was he like?" I asked. I wanted to find out whether my impressions of Pete were matched by someone who knew him.

"If he was alive, we would still be friends." Tony said with certainty. "I only knew him for just over three months, but I will always consider him the best friend I have ever had." Strong praise indeed. "For a start he was the first person that I ever met who didn't even notice that I was black. I don't mean that he was quite happy to be friends with a black man, it was more that the difference in skin colour meant as little to him as the fact that I liked ladies and he liked men." He paused to explain himself, "he was gay, you see…"

"Oh yes, that was funny on the first day…" I stopped suddenly after receiving a kick from Sam's size nines. Of course, there is no way I could have known about their first meeting and it would have been almost impossible to explain how I did know of it. Tony was waiting for me to continue.

"Sorry…" I said vaguely, "I was going off at a tangent! Ignore me."

"Most people do." Sam was definitely feeling better.

Tony laughed and looked sad at the same time. "That was just the sort of banter we used to share," he looked at me, "you even look a little bit like him you know."

I was surprised, but for obvious reasons I wasn't going to tell him, I didn't think my leg would have survived another attack. However, I didn't think I looked like Pete at all.

Tony took up his story again. "Your generation probably wouldn't understand, hopefully not anyway, but in those days, it was different. If you went to try clothes on in a shop you felt you were being watched like a hawk. Some people would edge slightly away from you, if you passed them in the street, and quite often a stranger would shout an abusive remark for absolutely no reason at all."

I thought of Foz and the louts who abused Chloe's dad in the restaurant. It still goes on, I thought, but it was nice that Tony thought it was better now, at least.

"We laughed for most of those three months," he remembered, "the day he died was part of the worst twenty-four hours of my life."

"You can remember it?" I held my breath, I still found it weird to think that people in my dreams had actually existed, events that I had dreamed about had actually happened.

"Well - most of it," he laughed bitterly. "I had been going out with a receptionist at the hotel called Helen. My mum would have said she was the kind of girl who couldn't wait for one loaf of bread to prove before she started kneading another!" We laughed, I guess it was a nicer description than calling her a right old slapper.

"She had another boyfriend who was a nasty bit of work. He knocked her about, but never anywhere that could be noticed. I think I was the only person she told, and that was only because I saw them when we - you know."

We did.

"I kept urging her to break up with him, I didn't care what he thought of me, or did to me. I just wanted to be with Helen." Another slightly bitter laugh. "I was definitely young and foolish… but she said that it was best to wait, he would tire of her soon and then we could be together properly."

"But he didn't?"

"No, but gradually, over the summer, the bruises got worse and worse."

"So, you went to see him?"

"Yes, on the day that Pete died, but sadly not to protect her - to punish her."

"Punish her?"

"I'm afraid so. It was just a matter of bad timing. Dum had dropped a load of oven cloths in the sink by accident; probably still stoned from the night before, if you know what I mean."

I did, but didn't tell Tony that. I was getting better at this!

"I had to go to the laundry to get a handful of dry cloths and there she was."

"In the laundry?"

"In the laundry, but sadly not alone. The first thing I saw was the window cleaner's bare buttocks and Helen was with him, legs akimbo on top of a pile of tablecloths." He chuckled, not without humour this time. "It shows that I'm getting old, if it happened now I would probably be more worried about the food hygiene laws and the cost of re-laundering the tablecloths than anything else!" He paused whilst we laughed along with him. "But of course, at twenty-one, I didn't feel like that at all. I slammed the door on them, just about finished the last half hour of my shift, ignored Helen when she tried to come and find me and headed into town. I went straight to a back-street pub that I knew paid no mind to the licensing laws and stayed there drinking all day."

"And that's all you remember?" I was feeling a little cheated, I had hoped for more than a loose girlfriend and a day on the booze in a sordid bar.

"Not quite, OK it gets a bit hazy, but I do remember

deciding to go and see her boyfriend to tell him everything about our affair. It would have been madness, as I said, he was a piece of work and it would have been slightly suicidal to upset him."

"So, what happened?"

"He was a regular at this rough pub in town and I knew, even in my pissed state, that he used to hold his drug dealing "surgeries" there early in the evening. I went to the bar and found him, but just as I was about to confess everything, the cavalry in the shape of my friend Pete arrived. I don't know what he said or did, but I vaguely remember him bowling me out of there just as some sort of riot seemed to be happening. He got me back to our room, I should imagine that was fairly difficult, it was a twenty-minute walk and I can't imagine I was being much help."

Tony paused, dredging up a memory from three quarters of the way through the last century. "I'm not sure if I remember this correctly, but one moment he seemed really excited and the next, he was really reflective. That wasn't really like Pete at all, so it may be a false memory. I was certainly not in any fit state, it's just an impression that's always stayed with me about that walk home."

Tony pinched the bridge of his nose with his thumb and forefinger, "When he had got me safely back on my bed, he gave me a hug, kissed me on the cheek and left."

Tony then rubbed the bottom of his eye lid.

"I never saw him again."

"So, what do you think was making him a bit bi-polar?"

"I wish I could tell you, I have no idea. I've always thought the excitement was something to do with a lad called Max who he was having an affair with."

I heard Sam quietly take a sharp breath. He obviously recognised the name from the ones I had been researching on Tuesday night. I hadn't told him about the latest update yet. When your companion on a train journey is as happy as a vegan in an abattoir, you tend not to tell them anything.

"Who was Max?" Practically seamless!

"He was the younger son of the owner, Old Man Edwards, a complete and utter tyrant of the old school. If I treated my staff like he treated us, I would spend my whole life answering constructive dismissal suits!"

"So, Daddy would not have been happy?"

"Daddy most certainly did not know!"

"When did you discover that Pete was dead?"

"The next morning, I woke up with the hangover from hell and saw that Pete's bed hadn't been slept in. I went downstairs expecting a truck load of shit as I hadn't turned up for my shift the evening before, but firstly I was asked if I was feeling better. Pete, of course, had invented a dodgy tummy to explain my absence for the evening in order to save my hide. Secondly, I was told about the robbery, someone had broken into the office and stolen the takings from the safe. Finally, Giovanni, my head chef broke it to me that Pete had been found drowned on the beach."

"Shit, that must have been rough!"

"Deadly! I sort of collapsed, weeping and shaking. I was in a terrible state. They calmed me down and put me back to bed, I stayed there for three days. I only got up because I was told the hotel had organised an unofficial memorial service for Pete. I desperately wanted to show my respects to the man who probably saved my life on the evening he died. Well, at the very least, he saved me from a beating that I would have struggled to recover from. I went to the service and it was strange. Everybody who loved him when he was alive, were now saying that he had got drunk and drugged up with Dee and Dum on the beach. Oh, they were the lads that found him by the way."

"They were called Robert Morgan and Richard Townsend in the article I read"

"That's right, they were nicknamed Tweedledee and Tweedledum after the pair from Alice in Wonderland."

"They weren't best mates with Pete then?"

"No not at all, I mean they hung around with us, but I would never have said we were mates. They were so drugged up most of the time, they barely said a word to anyone except each other."

"There was quite a speech by Robert in the paper about Pete saying he was going swimming, then how they searched for him and tried to save his life."

"Nope, doesn't sound like them at all. Anything more than a one-word answer was unlikely from either of them."

"Did you ever hear what happened to them?"

"Not at all, never saw them after I left."

"We did find an article about a Robert Morgan and Richard Townsend who died in a pub fire in Norfolk, early 1987."

"Now that does sound more like the sort of thing that could have happened to them, they weren't very bright or very lucky." He paused, "you have really researched this haven't you?"

"I get a little obsessive!" I laughed.

Sam had said little but had listened intently, he changed tack just in case Tony was getting suspicious. "There is a trunk in our loft that we keep our Christmas decorations in. It has the letters PA on it and the Abba logo on the inside of the lid?"

Tony gave a small gasp. "Oh my God! That bloody trunk… Oh yes, that was Pete's - he was obsessed by Abba. It's a funny thing really, I used to take the piss out of him over his fixation, and now I can appreciate how good the music was!" He laughed at himself, "I must be getting old!"

I loved the music of Abba myself and I wasn't yet twenty, but I was more interested in an old abandoned trunk than discussing trends in popular music. "So, his family never collected the trunk?" I asked.

"No, I don't think so. Well they couldn't have done, could they? I vaguely remember hearing something about the mother being too distressed to come anywhere near the hotel, I don't think any of his belongings were collected."

"What happened after the memorial - I suppose the hotel went back to normal?"

"I don't actually know. I was so angry about the way that people he called his friends, people that he treated so well when he was alive, were treating his memory once he had died. I walked from the memorial service and never went back to the place again."

"And Helen?"

"She tried to placate me after the service, she said that it was all over with her boyfriend, he'd had to leave town and she would never have to see him again." He broke off as he remembered something else. "I've always wondered if that was something to do with what Pete did to get me out of the pub that night."

He paused and gave a self-deprecating smile as he continued.

"She even came clean about other affairs, admitted that she enjoyed the excitement of her duplicity. However, when she thought she had lost me, she had realised how much she loved me etc etc. Do you know, I might have been stupid enough to go back to her?"

Sam and I raised our eyebrows at that.

"You would?" I said incredulously.

Tony nodded. "I was besotted by her enough to forget all the lying and cheating, but there was just one thing I couldn't forgive."

"What was that?" I asked

"She was one of the people I had heard slagging Pete off after the service - I probably could have forgiven her any of the other shit she did, but not that."

His voice went into a whisper, as if he was talking more to himself than us. "Not my poor, lovely, skinny white gay boy…"

Hearing him actually say those words made my

stomach lurch. Luckily Sam was there to step in when I couldn't find anything to say.

"Have you seen anyone from the hotel since you left?"

"There was a girl that Pete was very friendly with, another Abba nut called Jackie Trevellyan. About six years ago, just after I opened this restaurant, she popped in. She had recognised my name and wondered if I was the same person. It was the only time until today that I had talked about Pete, it was lovely." He smiled a genuine smile of memory.

"She was with her second husband, living in Clifton and doing really well. I was rather hoping that she might pop back in again, especially since I broke up with my partner two years ago," he laughed, again slightly mocking himself. "I did even think about contacting her, but it didn't seem fair, when she was happily married at last."

"She wasn't one of the ones slagging Pete off at the memorial service then?"

"No, definitely not, she loved that boy as much as I did. Funny," Tony screwed up his face with the effort of trying to remember, "she would have been there, I'm sure… but I just can't recall seeing her." He paused, a thought just crossing his mind, "tell you what though - Max was definitely not there."

Now that was strange.

"I don't suppose you have any contact details for Jackie?" I asked on the off chance.

"Oh yes, she gave me her card, I've never quite convinced myself to chuck it out!" he laughed again. "I've got it in my contacts folder, hold on a sec!" I looked at Sam, a real gleam in my eye, he smiled at me and mouthed "So Max Edwards was his boyfriend?"

Tony was back quite quickly; his filing system was certainly better than mine…

"It's a long shot, I know, but if you ever find out what actually happened to Pete, would you let me know? I've kicked myself because I never did anything at the time and there was something definitely dodgy about his death." He paused, then gave Sam the offer I could tell he was itching for: "Can I give you a guided tour of the kitchens?"

***

After we left Deano's we walked around the shops, in a side street, a block away from St Nicholas Market. On a whim, in a record store that sold old vinyl, I asked the store holder if he had a copy of "If Forever Ends With You," by Bennie Gold.

He was a man who seemed to be growing his beard to provide extra bedding for the winter. He dismissively flicked his head at a sign that read: "We stock everything except Middle of the Road or Elevator Music." I got the message. I was nowhere near cool enough to be in his shop.

Luckily, an American tourist asked if he had a rare Plastic Rainbow LP and he left me with a look that said: "Thank God for serious music lovers!"

To be honest, I had listened to the Bennie Gold song and liked it - the Plastic Rainbow stuff I'd heard had sounded like a bit of a discordant mess to me.

I didn't say that though.

"What was all that about?" Sam asked as we left the shop.

"It was the song that woke you up this morning… I dreamt about it last night."

"You had another dream?" It was nice that Sam was as excited about this weird experience as I was.

"Yep…" We were walking back to the market. Street food sellers were packed on both sides selling North African flat breads. Spiced meats were punching the air with an appetising aroma and bowls piled high with spiralised carrot or courgette were alongside those topped with red or white cabbage; it looked like a Gay Pride flag in the form of food. "Look, I'm starving, shall we grab something to eat and I'll tell you all?"

Now, even though Sam's face had held the colour of seven shades of sickness throughout the morning, it only takes a brief moment of recovery before he's ready for food again, so he didn't need asking twice.

We chose our flat bread which was filled with meat, salad, hummus, baba ghanoush and mayo. One bite into it and there was a risk of spray painting an unfortunate passer-by, so we decided to retreat to a bench table in an attempt to eat it with a small amount of finesse.

On a balmy June day, it felt more like we were in a souk in Marrakesh than near the banks of a muddy river in Bristol.

Between mouthfuls I filled Sam in with details of my latest dream, from the card game to Bennie Gold. I was just coming to the end of the latest episode, when Sam interrupted me.

"Hold on, say that bit again..."

"Well, they went out to the roofless bit of the church, you know, the one we saw on Tuesday..." I wasn't quite sure what was confusing him.

"Yes, yes, I knew where they were," he said irritably. "But tell me, when I was doing all the research on Tuesday night and you were watching music videos on YouTube," I made a face in his direction, "you were prattling on about a song you had just started listening to..."

"Oh yes, that anti-religious one." I had no idea where he was going with this.

"What was the lyric again?"

"Oh my God!" I strained my brain, "something about the ruthless church that hid our love from the world, why?"

Sam paused as if he was David Blaine on the verge of performing his Dive of Death to a breathless nation.

"What if it was - the roofless church that hid our love from the world?"

He emphasised the letter F.

I suddenly realised that we had probably found Max.

19.

"**O**M G!" I stretched out the letters to give myself a chance to let the information sink in, "you mean it was a love song to Pete?"

"Exactly!" Sam was triumphant. "Max Edwards who plays pubs in Brighton is the same Max Edwards who had an affair with Pete back in the seventies!"

I grabbed my phone, but the mobile data wasn't strong enough to enable us to watch the video again.

"So," I asked, "is it back to Weston so that we can watch the video, or do we try and look Jackie up now we're here?"

"Let's go and see if Jackie is at home," Sam was decisive. "Now where does she live?" He grabbed the card when I held it out towards him and he snorted… "Jacqueline Ellis-Lyke, do you think her husband is called Willie?"

I played the name across my brain and grinned. "Bloody idiot!"

We walked across the city to the centre, stopping off at a book store to look at an A to Z of Bristol in order to find the road that Jackie lived on, then caught a bus over to Clifton.

A helicopter mother with two small children opened the door of a Georgian town house in a street a few minutes' walk away from the centre of Clifton Village, where everything was either artisan or bespoke.

She seemed to be a mistress of multi-tasking. Aside

from opening the door, she was in the process of feeding her children if the bowls of granola that were clamped in their hands were an indication. She was also organising viola lessons for a child called Hermes via a phone that was lodged underneath her chin.

"Four-fifteen next Monday?" She stopped to look at us vaguely, then looked away to hover over one of the children.

"No Dante, don't throw granola over the carpet… Sorry Mrs Humphries, yes that will be lovely… Goodbye! Hermes darling, viola lessons, won't that be super? Dante sweetheart, what did I say?

"I'm trying to grow an wanola tree," the child stated firmly - I was beginning to get an inkling that we'd called at a bad time.

"Oh darling! How lovely! But it's not like the seedlings we planted this morning, do you remember? We said they needed time, water and nutrients from the earth…" She turned to us, "can I help you?"

"Mrs Jackie Ellis-Lyke?"

She looked bemused for a second then remembered who we were talking about. "Oh no! We bought the place from them about two years ago now. I think they were splitting up, it was all a bit messy I believe, sorry I can't help!"

"I don't suppose you have a forwarding address?" I asked hopefully, but she shook her head, "Sorry, no, we kept in touch via Facebook for a while; but once housey things were sorted out, we didn't really have a lot in common."

I thanked her anyway and she closed the door. The last thing we saw was Dante still seeding granola into the carpet…

✳✳✳

Sam was on cooking duty in the apartment again that

evening and I was his self-appointed helper. I was practically indispensable, twiddling the knobs on the cooker and putting the things away that Sam had left out on the side. Eventually when I had put the milk back in the fridge for the third time whilst he was making the cheese sauce, he said, non-too politely: "Will you just fuck off and leave me to it?"

I think he meant it lovingly.

We had ended up in Cabot Circus and did a little bit of shopping that I couldn't really afford, but was obviously essential. We caught the train back to Weston and had time to investigate the Max Edwards song on YouTube. Emily had heard us arriving back and had crashed into Sam's room to catch up on all she had missed over the last few days. The song left very little room for interpretation, and if Sam hadn't interrupted me after the first line a few nights before, we would have realised so a lot sooner.

I thought it important to mention this to him…

"The roof less church that hid our love from the world
the rocks that both shaded and covered us
the estuary walks, the coffee bar talks
the world that shared in its love for us.

How I curse the tide that took you from me
I curse the cruel and taunting sea
the only thing left to ease the pain
would be to hold you in my room again.

"So," said Emily, "Pete Abrahams falls in love with the son of the owner of the Royal Holm View Hotel… Can anyone see any similarities?"

"Hell Em! Don't let me anywhere near the beach at night on my own!"

"As usual, you two are completely missing the point!" Sam chided us in that patronising way that we both loved so much.

"I actually thought it was a very good point," I argued.

"You might not have any choice in the matter if you carry on like that," Sam said with black good humour. "No, what I meant was, we have a way to contact Max Edwards." OK it had been a long day that had started with a hangover, I looked at him blankly. He paused the video and pointed at the screen. Behind Max was a sign that read "Kruz @ Brighton."

Within minutes he had phoned the venue, expressed an interest in Max's material, got an email address and even found out that Max himself would be performing at the bar a week on Tuesday. The barometer of his smugness was practically at the point where the mercury would explode from the glass tube.

We sent an email to Max with our generic explanation behind the story. I guess we could have just turned up at the gig on Tuesday week, but we thought it fairer to give him the chance to refuse to see us, just in case it was a painful memory he would rather not revisit.

Once that was done, we turned our attention to Jackie. We knew from the helicopter mother that she had a Facebook account, but nothing for Jackie or Jacqueline Ellis-Lyke bore any fruit.

"What about her maiden name?" Em suggested. "Lots of women can't bear to be shacked with the name of an ex-husband, who they can't stand, and go back to their original surname instead."

"Good point Em, but what the hell was it?" I turned to Sam, "Tony mentioned it didn't he?"

Sam nodded and chewed his lip in the way he always did when he was thinking things through. "Something Cornish? Tremellon, Tremellyon?"

"Trevellyan!" I jumped up and nearly bounced the other two off the bed in my excitement. Unfair slights on the legitimacy of my birth were thrown in my direction.

There were a few Jackie Trevellyans on Facebook. The fourth one down had a picture that bore little resemblance to the girl I had seen in my dream, but it was forty years on, so that was not particularly surprising. The information to the right of the picture was much more enlightening. "Works at the Bright Start Nursery school. Lives in Yatton, Somerset."

"That has got to be her!" I bounced on the bed again and received more insults, but I carried on unperturbed. "Pete was trying to persuade her to follow her dream of working with children, it looks like she did it."

I sent her a private message similar to the norm, but added the fact that we had met up with Tony, hoping that it would add a little weight to our request. We had sent two little pigeons into the night, now all we could do was wait and see if either of them returned with messages around their necks.

***

I must say the cauliflower cheese was very good. I took full credit for it. Well, I'm sure my input was vital. Sam laughed good naturedly, "Yes, thank you Jamie Oliver, we look forward to your next triumph!"

We were eating in the apartment again. Ned again had arrived in something approaching a bad mood, which I was beginning to think was par for the course with him.

Fiona delicately sliced a piece of gammon and manoeuvred some cauliflower cheese alongside it, onto her fork. "Oh boys!" she said brightly, "I had a chat to Uncle John today and asked him about your namesake." She nodded her head in my direction, then frowned slightly, "he said that he wasn't around Weston at that time, but I was sure he was..." she trailed off as Ned, totally ignoring her, started giving Sam instructions for the next day.

"I want you in the kitchen tomorrow."

"OK Dad."

"I want you to watch Mark like a hawk, and report back on everything: his organisation, delegation skills, cleanliness, how much food does he waste… everything!"

"I'm not comfortable being your spy, Dad." Sam said it firmly yet calmly, but his father was not to be dissuaded, and when he spoke next the irritation was definitely up a notch.

"Christ Sam! This is not the school yard where I'm asking you to dob on your mates. This is business and you're going to have to learn to be more professional and follow my lead better, if you are ever going to make a success of this hotel when I retire!"

"Did I complain when you told me that every single decision I made on Monday was wrong?" Sam was still outwardly calm, but I could tell he had a point to make. "I am more than happy to learn from you, it just irritates me that your biggest gripe against Mark is simply that he hasn't got a Michelin star." His father started to interrupt, but Sam calmly talked him into silence. "We went to see an award-winning Chef today, Tony Dean from Deano's in Bristol." His dad looked surprised at Sam's vehemence whilst I was worried about explaining why we were at Tony's restaurant in the first place. Sam however, was not to be stopped.

"Do you know what Dad? His kitchen was no better run than Mark's, the food we saw being prepared was wonderful, but no better than the stuff we produce and the same could be said for the menu." He paused for breath but wasn't letting go.

"Mark has worked for you for bloody years, he has sweated blood for this family and he puts up with you poking your nose in to his kitchen with remarkable tolerance. OK he hasn't won any awards that you can brag about on the Hotel website. But his loyalty and the way that every day he keeps standards high in that kitchen, are worth much more than any Michelin bloody star… and I don't need to watch his every move tomorrow, the day after, or any other freakin' day for that matter - to be able to tell you that."

I wanted to give him a standing ovation.

However, his father didn't necessarily agree with me. He looked like he was going to ignite like a firework in November. Emily looked nervously impressed, whilst Fiona stared at her husband and gently nodded in my direction. Her intimation was clear, "Not in front of the hired help."

I personally thought she could have been a bit more supportive of her son, but it did the trick. Ned decided not to say anything, but took his aggression out on the piece of gammon steak in front of him instead.

For my part, I have to say that if Sam in his hotel manager mode turned me on - then Sam in his passionate, articulate, protector of the workers persona, was simply off the scale.

I had to cross my legs unobtrusively under the table.

***

"Sorry about that." We had gone back into Sam's room after a rather uncomfortable end to the dinner. Emily had been asked to help in wash up as one of the staff had been sent home ill. Tonight, she had gone without comment or complaint.

"Nothing to apologise for." I said gently.

"I love my dad to bits!" he said, and I could tell that the incident had upset him more than he had let on before. "But there are times when he is a complete tosser!" I felt strangely honoured. Sam was not the type to criticise his family to anyone. The fact that he trusted me enough to confide in me made me puff up my plumage like a proud cockatoo.

"I thought you were absolutely brilliant!" I complimented him, which since we'd actually been together was rarer than a steak tartare, "it made me a little bit horny actually."

"Christ Rem! Opening an envelope makes you horny!"

He laughed.

"So, you don't want to do anything about it then?" I said with mock disappointment.

"Did I say that?" he countered, then as he grabbed me in for an embrace, he whispered in my ear, "thank you."

***

The next few days were the ones where I earned my keep. From four o'clock on the Friday I was pretty much on duty until the same time on Sunday. I didn't mind, the other barmaids were a good laugh, although I had to be a bit careful when they asked me for details of Sam's love life at university. They obviously both had designs on becoming Mrs Morris the younger, so I made a girl on his course at uni into a fairly steady girlfriend for him.

I made a mental note to tell him about it later.

Jack and I, after my initial dislike, were getting on very well. Yes, he was a bit of a prissy Queen and nowhere near as humorous as Dean, but underneath it he was kindly and well meaning. At one point over the weekend I nearly told him about my relationship with Sam, but decided at the last minute that it would be a mistake. For his part, he mentioned nothing of his own relationship with the "Uncle," so we both stayed firmly on the Narnia side of the closet door as far as each other was concerned.

I was hoping to see Alf as there were questions I wanted to ask him. I had decided to be much more direct with him on this occasion, after my mistake earlier in the week, but six o'clock on Friday arrived and Alf failed to arrive with it. Jack said it was unusual but not unheard of. Alf could be a bit of a hypochondriac and had a strict rule that had obviously been battered into him as a child. If you didn't go to school, you couldn't go out to play.

I barely saw Sam or Emily either, apart from the fact I was sleeping with one of them… After my shift on Friday night, I checked my Facebook page to find a message from

Jackie saying that she would be happy to meet us and suggested The Railway Inn at Yatton on Tuesday night after she had finished working at the nursery.

Once we had finished work on Sunday, Sam and Emily arranged for the three of us to get a picnic together and go to the top of the hill in a sort of recreation of my dream. However, with less people and focaccia bread instead of baps. I think they were hoping to incite another incident as my inability to go back to 1977 at will was frustrating them. Whatever, there was food and booze involved, so I was quite happy.

Before we left, I checked my emails as I had been doing religiously since Thursday evening. This time there was something a little more exciting than a phone bill or a chance to win a year's supply of peanut butter. There was an email from Max.

With a surge of nervous expectation, I opened it to read:

"Dear Peter,

How strange that you discovered about Pete's death and that you share his name. However, it doesn't surprise me that it came about due to locals talking about tragedies in the mud, they could be a morbid lot and that was always a favourite tale of doom - obviously not much has changed in forty years! This you may not know, but Pete Abrahams was the love of my life, I would be so happy to talk to you about him. Funny also that you should be so complimentary about the song 'Tides', as it was written about him. Please introduce yourself if you can make it to the gig on Tuesday week. I really look forward to meeting you.
Max."

Sam was reading the email over my shoulder. "Love of my life? That's a big statement for someone he only knew for half a summer."

"First love, Sam - it's very very special," I grinned at him meaningfully and he twisted my head fully around in order to kiss me on the lips.

"So true," he said.

***

When Emily said picnic, I was thinking of a bit of food and a bottle of wine between us maybe. What transpired was a bottle of Prosecco to go with the focaccia and meats, red wine to go with the cheese and a bottle of home brewed sloe gin to go with anything we had left at the time.

It was early evening by the time we made it to the tower that I now knew from my dream as the old windmill. The air was warm and still, although there was enough breeze and sunshine to keep the midges away. We discussed the prospective meetings with Jackie and Max, what had happened to each of us at work over the last few days - and their father.

"I don't know what's the matter with him at the moment," Emily complained, "he has got such a grump on!"

"Do you think it might be to do with the fact that he can suddenly see you running the hotel, sooner rather than later?" I suggested to Sam, "everyone asks you about everything when you're around, do you think he's feeling rather redundant. Maybe that's why he had to make a point of criticising everything you did on Monday?"

"It's possible" Sam conceded, "but ridiculous… I mean, he knows all there is to know about that place, I'm barely scratching the surface. I've got another year left at uni and I'm probably going to need a lot of hand holding after that. What's he like, daft bugger?"

There was another idea that I didn't voice, but it was battering against my brain. Had Ned found out about us? Was he making everyone's life difficult because he'd worked out he had a homosexual son?

Sam had a chat with his dad on the Friday morning

where I believe he had received a rap around the knuckles for disagreeing with his father in front of me. I was angered on Sam's behalf, after all, Ned had been quite happy to criticise Sam in front of me on Tuesday - and who the hell had started the whole argument in the first place? Sam had told me that he had accepted the telling off, but had stood firm on everything else he believed in.

"Anyway Bro," Emily said, "I was proud of you on Thursday night - I must admit I've always thought you were a bit of a push-over as far as Dad was concerned, but not anymore!"

"Jeez! A compliment from my sister!" Sam picked up the bottle of Prosecco from the cool bag and popped the cork, "that deserves a toast…" He poured the bubbly liquid into three glasses, expertly stopping before the froth cascaded over the sides. We tipped our glasses towards each other "…to us!"

We dived into the picnic after this and managed only tiny bits of nonsense between mouthfuls. By time the red wine bottle had followed the empty bottle of sparkling wine into the recycling bag, I was only about two scrumpies away from squiffy.

"Do you want to have a look inside the church?" Sam asked as he sliced off a healthy chunk of Stilton and washed it down his gullet with the last swig of wine.

I said that I did, but Em said she'd stay with the bags, she had social networking to do… I think she was giving us a bit of time on our own.

It hadn't really changed much from the church I had seen in my dream except the inner door was locked, I guessed vandals had been the reason behind that. Certainly there hadn't been much in there to steal unless the crown jewels had illogically been transferred there since 1977. We sat against the wall looking up at the blue summer sky, still the colour of a Coventry City shirt even as the warm evening wore on. I thought of Pete and Max and how they'd shared their first kisses in this very spot. What had happened on the evening Pete had died? Had they been together that night at all? What was it that had made Pete both excited and distracted, if Tony's drunken memory could be trusted?

I shared my thoughts with Sam and we chatted it over for a while - however, I knew one way or another now, that I would eventually get the answers I needed. The only thing I couldn't tell Sam was that Pete was becoming more important to me than just a character in a reoccurring dream.

Every time I dreamt about him, everything I heard about him, made me like him that little bit more. I was beginning to wish I could have known him properly.

When we returned to the old windmill, Emily was discussing the finer points of Sia's latest outfit with a friend via email, but she put her phone away after we had slumped back down on the grass.

"Sloe gin?" She enquired whilst wobbling the bottle back and forth.

"Couldn't possibly…" I said, then almost immediately, "Go on then!"

When our glasses were primed Emily asked about the song that Max and Pete had sung whilst running down this very hill forty years before. I had downloaded it onto my phone, so we had it on repeat as the sloe gin bottle evaporated and the sky darkened through never ending shades of blue: cyan, periwinkle, Oxford; until the bottle was empty, and the sky was dusk. Running down the hill was risky, but we did so to the strains of the old song we had just learned, and we reached a crescendo chorus loud enough to frighten the cattle.

"Time and tide it waits for no-one, you'll do what you want to do, but I will wait forever, if forever ends with you…"

20.

1977

Max appeared in the staff area of the dining room just as Pete was spreading marmalade on his third piece of toast. He hovered uncertainly, his feet tapping an unaccompanied tango as if he was unsure whether to make an appearance or not.

Pete could see that Hutch was just about to unleash some unpleasant sarcasm in the direction of the Manager's Son, so he said brightly, "Hi Max, can we help at all?"

"Oh, umm, well," slightly reassured, Max manoeuvred himself fully into the staff area. "I was just thinking about going into town to do a tour of the record shops. I wondered if anyone would like to come with me?"

It was one of those days when most of the members of staff that lived locally were on the split shifts, and all the live-in staff except Pete had to go back to work until two-thirty. The staff members that lived locally were older and tended to go home until tea time and didn't socialise with the others quite so much.

The chefs had started at their normal time, but for them the shift was nowhere near over. Old Man Edwards had inspected the kitchens the night before and found some crumbs under a chopping board. That was enough for him to insist that all the kitchen staff, from pot washers to head chef, would be on deep cleaning duties all day.

"I'll come with you," Pete leapt up and staring at

Hutch, silently dared him to make a flippant remark. For once, the barman managed to keep his counsel.

"I checked the rota actually," Max confessed as they were walking across the yard to Strangeways for Pete to change into something less formal than his trainee manager's uniform. "If you'd been on duty, I wouldn't have bothered to ask anyone else."

Pete was happily gratified by this. Even though there had been no doubt of the attraction between the two of them yesterday, a night to sleep it over can bring unwanted doubts and his perception of the whole incident had changed somewhat. Max's confession was very timely and reassured him that they both probably wanted the same thing.

However, when they reached room seventeen and he started stripping off his shirt and tie, Pete was amused to see that Max was a little unsure of where to look. He pretended to look out of the window whilst risking sly glances in the direction of the body that was gradually being revealed. It reminded Pete of his 15-year-old self in a newsagents at home. He would try to get a glimpse inside a Health and Efficiency magazine in order to see a naked penis, whilst pretending to thumb through a Beano three shelves down.

Pete, his cheeky confidence in overdrive, decided to prolong the tease a little. Instead of replacing work shirt for T-shirt, he decided to strip down to his underpants before re-dressing. Once naked save for the skimpy pair of white Jockeys that were the only clothing protecting his modesty, he even treated his guest to the view of a quick stretch, before he reached for his T-shirt and jeans and got dressed again.

Any doubts as to whether Max was actually interested were dispelled by the fact that Pete could see his friend's face reflected in the window. His eyeballs were almost being ripped out of their sockets in an attempt to look behind him, whilst outwardly pretending not to notice.

They walked into town along the seafront. After the heatwave of the day before, the day was revealing itself to be a typical smorgasbord of an English summer. Sun and showers combined with a viscous breeze that worried the fine top sand and blew it in their faces. The journey became more of a recreation of a scene from Beau Geste than a summer walk along the front and they talked little, preferring to keep their mouths closed to the invasive sand.

Once they had turned inland towards the High Street, the wind died down somewhat and with it the risk of inhaling a lunch of dusty sand, which meant they were able to talk more easily. They decided to start in WH Smiths where they both bought music papers.

Pete had had a weekly subscription to Disc in the latter years of his childhood and when it had been incorporated into Record Mirror in 1975, had moved with it. Max who was a bit more of a serious muso, bought a copy of Melody Maker. They disappeared into the back of the shop where all the chart singles were on display in wall mounted racks numbered from 1 to 30. Pete glanced along the rows and his hand hovered over number three. He picked up "So you win again" turned it over and read the title of the B side. He'd never heard of it, but he loved the thought of getting a bonus track for nothing. He also liked to feel the paper covered vinyl in his hand. Once he'd read all the details on the disc twice, he put it back in the rack.

"Aren't you going to buy it?" Max asked

"What on the wages your dad pays me!" Pete laughed, then nodded, "probably, but I never like to buy something from the first shop I see it in... I like to savour the moment."

To Max's amusement, he repeated the dance in Boots, but still refused to buy the record. After this they went through a gap in the wall that took them straight into Owen Owen next door. "Two shops that you can go into without going outside," Max laughed, "it's the closest thing

Weston has got to an Arndale centre!"

The handbags, scarves and belts on sale near them didn't hold too much interest, so they traversed the store and disappeared out of the side door, crossed Cambridge Place and went straight into Woolworths. In here Pete once again repeated his routine. Max was getting slightly exasperated at not being able to find the LP he was looking for, especially when Pete had already given up two chances of purchasing the record he so obviously wanted. Max pushed his new friend in the direction of the counter before he had the chance to return it to its slot yet again.

"Oy!" Pete complained good naturedly.

"Three refusals and you get disqualified!" Max laughed and refused to let him go until the record had been safely bagged and money exchanged.

"Fancy a bit of lunch?" Max asked, "I think the only place I'm going to find the Jam is in Exons, but that's on the other side of town, on our way home."

They went back out of Woolworths and Pete glanced down Cambridge Place in the direction of Snoopys, the club he had visited on his first night, and wondered briefly about Malcolm Marlon and his cohorts. He hadn't met the pusher since that first night, but his exploits were widely talked about. The general consensus was that you crossed him at your peril... Pete thought about Tony and decided that, on balance, sleeping with his girlfriend could have been described as crossing him.

Back once again in Owen Owen, Max turned towards the café area at the back and they ordered two bowls of oxtail soup.

The woman behind the counter opened two tins and pushed a long metal tap that expelled steam into each one in turn. She stirred the contents, repeated the process, then poured the now hot liquid into two bowls. She carved off a couple of slices from a bloomer loaf and putting each of the bowls and the pieces of bread on a plate, handed them over to the two lads.

They found a table by the window overlooking Cambridge Place and started to eat the soup, but not before Pete had once again removed his purchase from the bag and turned the vinyl over in his fingers. "Just checking for scratches," he chided as Max rolled his eyes roof wards. "Anyway, I have no idea why you forced me to buy this, I have nothing to play it on! Tony and I keep talking about picking up a second-hand record player for our room, but we haven't got around to it yet." He grinned ruefully, "we'd never be able to agree on what to play anyway!"

"Mo bought me a music centre for my birthday," Max offered, "you can come up to my room and play it on that when we get back if you like."

It was said lightly, but the part of the invitation that remained unsaid lay heavily between them. As usual Pete dealt with this by using light humour.

"Blimey! All we're looking for is an old Dansette!" He laughed and ignored his thoughts. "I'm not sure my ears will be able to cope with stereo!"

They relaxed into companionable silence whilst they ate their soup, but Pete knew there was something he needed to say, his obsession with the direct approach required it. Tony had brought it up the night before as a friendly warning, but he knew that he wouldn't be able to follow his friend's advice.

"Look Max, I really like you," he rested his spoon on the side of the plate, "I don't want to upset you, but I know what I'm like. If I've got something on my mind, then sooner or later I'm just going to blurt it out. I think I'm just wired a little strangely, to be honest."

Max looked slightly worried, but simply said, "Go on."

"O.K" Pete drew the words out, "Tony said not to mention your mother," he tried to gauge a reaction from Max's face and when he couldn't, he ploughed on regardless. "Now, if you don't want to talk about her, fine, just tell me - but I'm sorry, I couldn't just leave it as a subject unsaid."

Max smiled a smile of relief, "Oh crikey, I thought you were going to tell me that you weren't actually gay!"

Pete laughed inwardly, to think he had thought that he was the direct one! In the same way as the day before, the more time he spent with Pete, the more Max's confidence seemed to grow, the shy boy of the bedroom had disappeared.

"Well if I'm not, what on earth was I doing kissing you in the churchyard yesterday, and why does Hutch keep referring to me as one?" he laughed.

"Because he's an arsehole?" Max suggested. Pete nodded slowly, screwing up his mouth muscles, as if he was pretending to give the statement a lot of thought.

"Yeah, there is that I suppose!" he paused, "is the change of subject an indication that you don't want to talk about her?"

Max shook his head vehemently, "God no, not at all!" he waved his spoon around, threatening to redecorate the café walls with oxtail soup. "It's actually a breath of fresh air that someone will talk to me about my mother. Ordinarily no-one will say a word to me about her. All I ever hear are vague whispers and I guess that people are saying, don't mention it, he must really miss her."

"Well I suppose that is a fair comment," Pete observed.

"But that's it really." Oxtail soup splattered walls were very shortly going to be en vogue, "I don't really miss her. I never knew her. I've been very lucky. Hutch will tell you. I was brought up by a man who was rich, could give me everything I needed financially and loved me after a fashion. I also have a brother who loves me unconditionally," Max's eyes shone when he mentioned Mo. "He's the best," he said simply, "I know he'll always be there for me."

He stopped for a moment, trying to find the words to describe the tricky bit. "My mother? I admire her because she was single minded and stubborn enough to do exactly what she wanted against all the good advice. I love her because without her sacrifice I would not exist. She is my heroine because she seems to have been determined, stupid, selfless, courageous and bloody wonderful. I want to tell everyone all of these things; but you can't miss what you've never known, so I don't - miss her."

He took a huge breath, "But everyone thinks that it is better if they don't talk to me about her and it isn't. I want to know all about her, I want people to tell me tales of her until I know every detail of her life."

The eloquence and passion in someone so young were a heady cocktail and Pete knew that he was on dangerous ground here. This was a young man he could easily fall in love with.

"Tell me about her," he said quietly.

"She nearly died when Mo was born, she had a congenital heart condition that had not been diagnosed before and childbirth triggered an attack. They were absolutely adamant afterwards that she should never risk giving birth again." He paused to scrape around the bowl, picking up the last remnants of soup and licking it off the spoon. "Mo was healthy, and my mother had recovered and was being monitored, she could have lived for a long time had she been careful. I don't know what went wrong, whether they took precautions and were unlucky, or whether they just ignored the advice. I could certainly believe that of my dad," he smiled wryly. "However, when the deed was done, and every professional advised them to abort me, it was my dad that agreed with the doctors, and my mother who flatly refused to go through with it."

"Did your dad tell you all of this?" Pete said gently.

"Well sort of," Max's blue eyes flashed a reprisal to his absent parent. "Most of the story I've just told you I heard from Mo and his memories of her are sketchy in the least. He was six when I was born and remembers the arguments in the months leading up to my birth, the other facts he's cobbled together since."

"Mo told you that your father wanted to have you aborted?" It didn't sound like unconditional brotherly love to Pete, it sounded like cruelty.

"No, he just explained the facts after my father had told me himself." Max said quietly, "I went through a stage in my early teens, Mo was either working at the hotel or going out with his friends and Dad was never around. The nannies who had been there during my younger years had gone and I felt neglected I guess." He paused, picking his way through the tale. "I started stealing, anything and everything. I didn't steal because I needed the stuff, I stole because I wanted attention."

"And you got it?"

"I got it." Max confirmed grimly, "I got six lashes of his belt, but much more painful were the home truths he told me." He took a huge breath; the tears of a memory were forming faintly around his eyelids. "He said that I was a disgrace to my mother's memory and if he'd had his time again he would have forced her to abort me. He told me that she died so an ungrateful shit like me could live. It's the only thing he's ever said to me about her." He grinned a sad, ironic grin. "It sorted me out on the stealing front though, I never did that again."

He looked at Pete and said, almost as an afterthought, "I've not told anyone this before... but it is an awful thought to know that you have murdered your mother."

Pete wanted to push the table barricade aside and hold Max until the hurt had gone. However, mindful that the restaurant was filling up rapidly and most of the people would only accept two men hugging if it was on a football field, he contented himself with saying a quiet yet urgent - "Don't!"

Max looked up and Pete continued, "Don't you ever think that you were responsible! Do you really believe that your mum would want you to think like that?"

Max shook his head slightly and Pete continued. "She took a gamble, I expect she really believed she would prove the doctors wrong, after all she had survived the scare when Mo was born and we all like to think we are immortal." He risked grabbing Max's hand under the table and he held it behind the screen of table cloth that was hiding their contact from the café customers. "She believed you were worth that gamble then and, I think that if she knew you now, she would know that she had been right!"

Max smiled a sad smile of thanks and they sat clutching each other's hand for a while, relishing the contact. Eventually Max had recovered enough to say, "Tell me about your mum and dad, what sort of childhood did you have?"

It was hard to tell someone who had just opened his soul to you about a childhood that was blighted, about your own that had been almost perfect. Max however, was determined not to be palmed off with Pete's first answer, "It was fine."

"For God's sake Pete! It's not going to upset me, I think it's wonderful that you have a really close family. After all, I have Mo... it's not like I'm an orphan from a Charles Dickens novel!"

Pete told him then. He told him about the mother who had treated him like an adult from the moment he could talk and how they could both act like children, now he was grown. He told him about the family picnics, the times at home when his dad would bang out show tunes on a piano and his mum and he would screech the lyrics in discordant harmonies. The nights they went en masse to the theatre. The days they would find a bridge over a river and play pooh sticks 'til lunchtime. The afternoons when his friends were otherwise engaged, and his mum or dad would crouch on the floor and play Subbuteo, and how his mother could flick in a wicked free kick with her finger.

He told him how on Valentine's day that year they had been at a packed Royal Albert Hall when Abba had played there. His mother had presented the tickets to him just before they had sat down to eat their Christmas dinner. According to his father she had been in a state of excitement all day waiting for Pete to finish his shift at the restaurant he was working at. When he opened the envelope and yelped with excitement, the look of joy on her face mirrored his own.

"Over three million people applied for them Pete - and your dad, me and you… we were a few of the lucky ones!"

It was the best Christmas evening ever, the food tasted better, the Liebfraumilch was flowing and the Abba soundtrack on their old Baird record player and radiogram wasn't too bad either.

Finally, he told him how one rainy day in springtime, his mum and he had sat on plastic sheeting in front of a roaring fire and painted the Abba logo onto an old black trunk.

By now the café was nearly full, people were glaring at their empty bowls and they were beginning to feel like they'd taken up squatters' rights. In the interests of harmony and to prevent an OAP uprising, they took their bowls and plates back up to the counter and disappeared through the shop towards the main entrance.

They re-emerged into daylight opposite a ladies' fashion store called Trevors. The whole of the shop itself was hidden by glass boxes that stretched from pavement to ceiling and housed mannequins clothed in the latest fashions. The gaps between the boxes created corridors that ran up to the front door. Max said that as a youngster, he had a favourite nanny, and this was a shop they loved to visit. The nanny, so that she could look at fashion she couldn't afford; and Max, because it gave him the chance to run up and down the box corridors, catching his reflection in each glass as he passed. A free version of the crazy mirror house on the New Pier.

The whole street had recently been semi-pedestrianised, but because someone had forgotten to reroute the buses at the same time, they were nearly swept aside in the wake of a green 105 double decker on its way from Worle to Oldmixon.

After they had let it pass, Max said that he wanted to look in Rossiters the jewellers, as he was hoping to buy a watch for Mo's birthday at the end of July. As they glanced at the window display they could see a young couple inside. A girl who had an unhealthy look of innocence, was being fitted for an engagement ring; whilst a young lad, decked out in Sunday clothes midweek, watched on with nervous excitement.

Max sighed, "It must be lovely to be given a gift from someone who is telling you that they want to be with you for a lifetime."

Pete teased: "Now Max, I never had you down as a soppy romantic!"

Max laughed at himself: "I'm not really, I suppose I'm just a little jealous because it's something I'll never have."

"How do you know?"

"Well gay men can't actually get married, can they? You wouldn't see two men in there exchanging rings."

"It's all moving on Max, ten years ago it was illegal for two men to have a sexual relationship, now it's accepted."

Max scoffed, "Accepted! Allowed maybe, but do you really think, if you and I had held hands above the table in Owen Owen, we wouldn't have been given abuse from at least one person?"

Pete knew that Max was right, but his sunny optimism refused to accept defeat. "I'm only saying that in years to come, ten, twenty possibly - maybe not even in our lifetime, but I believe that eventually a man will be able to marry a man, and a woman will be able to marry a woman."

Max snorted a laugh, "Can you imagine my dad walking me down the aisle and Mo giving a best man's speech that embarrasses me with tales of my exploits with a male stripper at my stag night!"

Pete laughed at the thought: "Well maybe not this

weekend! To be honest, it will probably never be accepted by people like your father, but it will happen young Max, it will!"

They crossed the town and went into Exons. The independent record shop smelt of warm plastic due to the transparent sleeves that covered all their records to protect them. The prices were slightly more expensive, but the choice was much better and the chances of finding an LP on the edge of the charts was also more likely. As Max thumbed through the J's in the rock/pop section, Pete idled his way through the ex-chart singles that sat in an old shoe box on the counter. Eventually he found a record that made him grin, he sorted out twenty pence and went to stand behind Max in the queue.

"What have you found?" Max twisted his head to ask. At last his own quest had been successful and he stood with a copy of The Jam's "In the City" LP in his hands.

Pete just smiled an enigmatic smile and said, "Wait and see!"

They walked back along the seafront and although the sun had burnt the rain showers away, the wind was still howling and occasionally would try to inflate their carrier bags and float their purchases off to Wales. They clamped their records to their sides and fought the breeze, as sea salt stung their eyes. Their noses were turning as red as Dee and Dum's on the experimental evenings they seemed to be having more of lately.

They reached the point where Max would turn to go through the staff entrance and up to the Edwards' flat, whereas Pete would go straight on to Strangeways. Max looked at his watch and said, slightly morosely, "Hell! It's later than I thought, I suppose you have to go back to work?"

Pete chided him, "I thought you said you'd read the rotas?"

"Only for this morning," Max admitted.

"Ah well, if you'd read the whole thing you would have

known that I was off 'til 6:30… I'm working the bar late tonight, so I get a longer afternoon."

Max's face changed countenance as quickly as Red Rum had flown round the Aintree track. "Fancy listening to the records in my room?"

Pete grinned, "Thought you'd never ask!"

As they entered through the back door of the hotel, they could hear the dull sound of Martin moaning whilst Giovanni and Tony were chatting and clattering in the kitchen.

Pete gave Tony a small thought of sympathy, but it didn't last long. He was certain that Max's invitation was a subtle subterfuge - he was excited, nervous and full of strange feelings that were difficult to describe. He felt as if a whole batch of bubble gum were being blown up and popped inside his body.

They danced to Hot Chocolate first, although dancing was a slightly optimistic description, then turned it over and played the "B" side. After this Max slipped the Jam vinyl out of its casing and gave Pete his first taste of the three-piece band from Woking. Despite all his misgivings, Pete had to admit he rather liked it. Raw and loud it might have been, but it was also tuneful, and a few riffs bore their way into his brain immediately. As "Bricks and Mortar" came to an end, Pete grinned, took it from the music centre and replaced it with his surprise purchase. As soon as he heard the intro, Max laughed and sidled across to where Pete had plonked himself after playing disc jockey. He slid a hand across his friend's cheek and pulled Pete's face towards his own. They kissed as Bennie Gold played on.

They had just started to play it for the third time when Max pulled his lips away. "You know this morning in Strangeways?" he asked, and Pete nodded. "You were a right old tart trying to wind me up with that striptease!"

"I couldn't help myself, you were like a moral campaigner at a Mary Millington film – desperate to look, yet pretending you were horrified at the same time. You were asking to be teased!"

"I was very shy," Max said, "I really wanted to watch you, but I wasn't sure whether I should be so obvious."

"OK," said Pete, "I admit I was being a bit of a tease, but it was very funny seeing you trying to turn your eyeballs around corners!"

They both laughed, then Max stopped suddenly, "Strip for me now," he said quietly but firmly.

Pete was slightly taken aback: "What if your dad or Mo come in?"

"They won't, they'll be downstairs 'til about eleven I expect. Dad wouldn't stray too far from the kitchen area in the case the chefs escape from their penance!" He then repeated himself. "Strip for me."

Pete grinned, the popping bubble gum had reached a crescendo in his stomach. He pulled his T-shirt over his head before kicking off his shoes and peeling off his socks. He undid his belt and slid his jeans around his ankles then removed them by performing a wobbly arabesque. He stood in front of Max and looked him squarely in the face.

"Stretch like you did earlier." Pete followed the command and once his hands were safely above his head, Max got a full revenge for that morning's teasing, by deftly pulling his friend's Jockey Y-fronts to the ground. Pete laughed, a little surprised to be totally exposed whilst his body was in a state of growing excitement. He pulled Max to his feet and towards him. Max's clothing felt strange against his erect nakedness and gradually he reduced Max to a state similar to his own. They traced their fingers round the other's body, like they were trying to read a story in Braille. They stumbled, staggered and fell towards the bed as Bennie played his final chord and the needle ran through to the centre and mechanically clicked back to its silent resting place.

They lay against each other afterwards, elated, excited and unable to stop grinning. Max was the first to move and leaping up, ran over to the corner of the room where his guitar was propped against the wall. He bent to pick it up and Pete noticed a small beauty spot on the right-hand cheek of his perfect buttocks and felt his own body promise the possibility of a repeat performance. However, when Max returned to the bed, he leant against Pete and played his version of their song. His voice was earthy yet gentle and his fingers meandered around the strings with a grace that belied his inexperience. As he finished, Pete gave him a round of applause and a quick kiss, feeling the guitar digging into his belly as he did so.

"I must say I like the naked guitarist look," he said, "did you realise that your willy gives a little twitch when you're stretching for the high notes?"

"It wasn't the high notes that was making it twitch!" Max shot back at him, and Pete laughingly accepted the compliment.

"Well I haven't got an engagement ring for you," he said as he jumped off the bed and knelt beside it. Instead he produced a rubber band that he had found on the bed side table and laughingly triple twisted it and placed it on Max's finger. "Max Edwards, would you do me the honour of going out with me?" he asked.

Max laughed, a toxic mix of surprise, excitement and a happiness that had sometimes been a stranger to him. "I will" he said.

21.

I was beginning to become acquainted with the Weston to Bristol railway line. On that Tuesday night, we left the train at the halfway point, Yatton, and made our way from the platform to a pub that was practically in the station car park. It was called "The Railway Inn" - sometimes these breweries amaze me with the way they think outside the box…

Monday had been a very lazy day. Sam had needed his normal amount of alcohol recovery time, and I had been slightly wrong footed by my latest dream.

"Although, in some ways it was the same as before," I was trying to explain it to Sam, a late brunch finally having had a settling effect on his stomach. "The times when I was seeing the whole thing from Pete's perspective, well it felt like I could feel exactly what he was feeling."

I had wanted to say that it had felt like I was inside of him, but decided that it sounded a little bit too sexual.

I had told him about the sex scene, but not of how I felt like I had experienced it through Pete's body. I didn't tell him how I had woken in a state of excitement either… Although to be honest, morning wood was not an unusual experience for me since I had been sleeping with Sam.

The other thing that I didn't tell him was that I was beginning to become slightly obsessed with Pete and his story.

After I had woken, I just wanted to return to Pete's world again. It was becoming more and more like a favourite book that you wanted to spend every moment of the day reading. However, I had read the last page first and knew the ending. Part of me wanted to reach that ending, but another part of me wanted to savour every moment and hope that the conclusion of the story wouldn't happen.

A strange plan had caught itself onto my brain and I was finding it difficult to convince myself of the fact that it was completely barking.

I loved Pete. I loved his innocence and his worldliness, his humour and his sympathy, his integrity and his naughtiness.

I didn't love Sam any less, that was the absurdity of it. I could still look into his eyes and that stick blender would switch itself on in my stomach. However, I felt a connection with Pete that was something more than a shared name.

"Max's room was the same one as yours," I had told Sam. That had been strange as well, apart from the fact that there had been no en-suite shower room in those days, the room had looked so similar, and yet so different. I couldn't resist a dig, of course. "It was a lot tidier then!"

He hit me.

***

We saw Jackie as she entered the garden. She was scanning each table to see if she could find two men that she had only seen from photos on a Facebook profile page. I caught her eye by waving in her direction and she came over.

I offered her a drink and she said that she'd love a large white wine. "After a day helping to look after a room full of terrible twos, I could certainly do it justice!" she laughed.

By the time I'd bought the drink and taken it back into the garden, Jackie and Sam were already laughing in easy conversation. I watched this lovely man with a talent for putting people at their ease, and it re-enforced the fact that this rather strange development would never change my love for him.

I still thought it best not to mention it to him, nonetheless.

I repeated the story that was becoming so familiar to me that I could now believe it was the whole truth and not the slight variation on a theme that it was. It ended with our trip to Bristol to see Tony.

"How is he?" she asked. "I did pop in to see him when I first moved up to Clifton with William."

You are kidding me, I thought, what are some parents thinking of?

I could almost feel Sam biting the inside of his cheek.

The ex-Mrs Ellis-Lyke seemed to be oblivious to our musings and continued. "I always had a bit of a soft spot for Tony, but he was head over heels in love with a receptionist when I first knew him. I certainly couldn't compete with her. I was a shy and mousey thing back then," she nodded over towards me. "It was my friendship with Pete that brought me out of my shell. He was the first person to really believe in me and the main reason why I'm doing the job I'm doing today."

She smiled a wry smile and raised her glass to her lips, "I can't say that I thank him for it every single day!"

We laughed, personally I couldn't think of many things worse than looking after a classroom of other people's children, but each to their own.

"Do you remember the day he died?" I asked.

"I could never forget it," she said softly, "Pete probably saved my life that day."

Oh, for goodness sake! Not another one, surely?

Jackie looked up at our surprised faces, so I told her that Tony had said a similar thing.

"Do you know? I knew nothing about that," she said, genuinely shocked after we had told her the story. "When I saw him, and we talked about Pete, we both said how much we owed him, but neither of us really went into details. To be honest William was getting a bit jealous and a little bored by this point, so he hurried us out of the restaurant quite quickly. That was my first clue to how self-obsessed William was, if he wasn't involved then he wasn't interested!"

"Yeah," I said conspiratorially, "I've got one like that!"

"Bloody cheek!" said Sam, but he didn't seem overly worried that I was mentioning our affair in public. He was either getting more relaxed about it, or he thought that Yatton was far enough from home for it not to matter.

"So how did Pete save your life that day?" I asked Jackie.

"Have you heard of Desmond Marsons?" she asked, I screwed my face up in concentration, it did ring bells, but…

"Popularly known by the press as The Planner?" The light bulb came on and I knew exactly who Jackie was talking about.

"Serial rapist and killer from the eighties?" Jackie nodded but Sam looked a bit blank. "Surely you've heard of him? We studied him in history along with Sutcliffe, Neilson, Bundy and Fred West."

Jackie squirmed, "Thanks lads, you know how to make a lady feel old," she laughed, "my youth is being taught in history lessons!"

I apologised but she was taking it in very good spirits.

"Well I've never heard of him," Sam admitted which led to my favourite taunt.

"How much did your parents pay to have you educated?"

"We did the cultural and sociological changes that the fallout from the second world war caused, we did America and the cold war, South Africa and apartheid. We left serial killers to our country cousins in Dorset!" Sam was on the defensive, but as always there was that twinkle around the eyes that made me love him so much.

Jackie laughed, "Boys, boys, you came to hear my story - right? After all, I am now a historical figure, so my voice should be heard!"

I liked her a lot.

"Mind you" she said, "when he was eventually caught, and I realised who he was, I was so traumatised by the whole thing, that I used to turn the TV off every time it was mentioned on the news. Now I'm older, wiser and just happy to have survived, I rather wish that I'd listened to more of the details at the time. I do know that The Planner was so nicknamed because part of the thrill for him was the planning of the rape and murder. He travelled around, taking seasonal jobs in the UK and Europe. He would normally work in hotels or camp sites, because there were lots of people to choose from and sometimes the identity of his victim could change two or three times before he finally made his move."

"He would always make a male friend as well," I remembered, "so that he could frame them for the murder if everything went tits up. I think a couple of people went to prison for quite a long time before he was actually…" I stopped suddenly, I had suddenly realised who The Planner was.

"He did have a very close friend at the Holm View," Jackie remembered, "so that certainly fits, they were both barmen."

So, Hutch, the slimy, misogynistic toe rag, went on to become a notorious serial killer… it definitely fitted.

"You were his chosen one, I take it?" I said it gently, but forty years on, Jackie seemed to be able to cope with it.

She nodded, "I had arranged to meet Marsons, as originally Pete was going to be out for the day. He was going out with his boyfriend Max, I think. But for some reason that didn't happen, so he asked me to go shopping with him." She took a large swig from her glass of wine and continued with a grimace: "of course that would have ruined all my plans," she frowned. "So, I invented a girly lunch with one of the waitresses. Pete suggested that we could all lunch together in town. I don't quite remember how I talked him out of it, but I did it somehow, which meant I was free to go on my date with Marsons."

She paused, and we waited for her to continue with her story. When she did, she had changed tack slightly.

"I loved Pete! Oh yes, I knew he was gay, but it didn't matter to me. I was so naive that I probably believed that I could convert him," she laughed, remembering. "I was so jealous of Max, but I was sensible enough to know that to make a fuss about them would have probably ruined our friendship. So, although I would have preferred him as a husband, to have him as a very close friend was better than nothing."

"So, then you went off with Hu... Marsons?" I was so involved in trying to get her back to her story that I nearly dropped myself right in it, but Jackie didn't seem to notice.

"I did," she winced, "I was so determined to have a boyfriend, I abandoned the soul mate who had done nothing but encourage me ever since I had known him. I didn't even tell him about it, for fear he would talk me out of the plan. Nice friend eh?"

"We've all done it," I said, thinking of some of the mistakes Sam and I had made before we eventually got together.

"It was lovely to start with," she remembered, "walking along the beach to Uphill, chatting and laughing - he was quite good company - and I was in seventh heaven. I had finally found a lad who wanted to go out with me and that was basically all I could think of!"

"But it turned sour?" I think Sam felt he'd been quiet for long enough and he'd better let us know he was still awake.

"Yes, it did. We got to Uphill and I thought we'd go up on the hill, sit and make daisy chains and maybe smooch a little." Jackie shuddered in self-reproach, "Christ, I was a stupid little bitch!" She took another sip from the nearly empty wine glass. I thought she might need me to go and get her another but I didn't really want to stop her whilst she was in full flow.

"Just after we'd passed an old fishing tackle shop, he laughed and said that he knew somewhere quiet we could go. He disappeared down an almost impenetrable path thick with trees, shrubs and bracken. I followed him and within a minute we were in a clearing that was hidden from everyone - thick wood on one side and the old quarry on the other. He took me in his arms and we started kissing, but then he plunged his hands down inside my jeans and I started objecting."

Jackie looked at us, she was becoming visibly upset, but when I told her that we had got the general idea, there was no need to upset herself, she shook her head forcibly. "No, honestly I'm fine. It's taken me forty years to tell anyone this story, as they say in all those bloody self-help books, it will do me good to share."

"OK as long as you're sure?" I said doubtfully, and Sam jumped in to the rescue.

"Before you go on, I need a pee and I think another round of drinks is very necessary!"

Jackie nodded towards his disappearing form, as Sam headed off towards the bar. "He's a little bit gorgeous, your boyfriend, isn't he?"

I smiled and nodded, it's always nice to receive compliments on your own good taste.

"You two remind me of Pete and Max," she said, "the way you are with each other, it's like you were born to be together. They were like that too."

A horrible thought struck me, so I thought I'd better share it. "Look, I don't know if you know people who are likely to visit the Holm View, but if you do," I struggled for a way to explain it, "Sam's parents don't know about us. His dad wouldn't – understand."

Jackie nodded, "Enough said, they won't hear it from

me." She then whistled a soft sound of sudden realisation. "Goodness! You are very similar to Pete and Max, you share Pete's name, he's the son of the Manager of the Holm View and both Max and Sam have fathers who wouldn't like their son being gay. Whatever you do…"

"I know, I know, don't go out on the beach alone!" I held my hands up and grimaced.

Once Sam had returned with the drinks, Jackie had recovered her composure enough to continue. "At first when I felt his hands down my trousers, I just thought he was trying it on, I was a virgin of course and had very little experience of anything, even heavy petting. I pulled away in order to tell him that I wasn't quite ready, and I can still remember the look on his face to this day." She paused and looked squarely at us, "he was like an animal who'd had a taste of blood and was going in for the kill. It was a terrible look of raw…" She was struggling to describe it, "desire is not the right word - he didn't desire it - he demanded it. I was completely terrified by that look, by that face. I see it in my nightmares even now."

We both made sympathetic noises, but I don't think either of us had a clue what to say to her. She continued in a voice that was almost robotic as if she was trying to banish all the emotion. The memories were making their way directly to her mouth, without giving her brain a chance to process them.

"At one point I must have screamed because he hit me hard to shut me up. I felt his hands rip at my T-shirt and I think I sort of gave in and crumbled to his will. It was at that point that he was suddenly pulled away from me."

"Pete?" I asked, and Jackie nodded.

"I have no idea how he found me, I told no-one where I was going." She shrugged, it was still a mystery to her all those years later. "But suddenly I was free from Marsons' grasp. I remember looking up and he was lying against the gorse bushes having stumbled on the trousers around his ankles. I remember his willy had shrivelled and there was a pathetic looking condom hanging from it. He looked angry and terrified at one and the same time. Pete was standing over him with a small rock in his hand and I thought he was going to brain him." She shuddered, remembering her own reaction. "I really wanted him to do it."

She sounded almost guilty and Sam was quick to reassure her.

"That's understandable," he said.

Jackie nodded doubtfully, "I suppose so, but I'm not proud of it. Pete put the rock in his pocket and told Marsons that he would be quite happy to use it if he was forced to. He said calmly that we were leaving and Marsons was not to follow us. I can remember his face as he looked up at Pete, there was complete hatred in his eyes, he hadn't managed to achieve the kill and he wanted revenge…"

Jackie took a large sip of wine, but she looked relieved that a story that had been locked inside her memory banks for ten years shy of half a century had been finally freed and heard.

"Thank you for listening to that. As soon as you sent me that e-mail, I knew it was right to tell the story at last. Even my husbands don't know about it - it was somehow easier to tell two strangers. I apologise for putting you both through that, but it has definitely helped."

We both made noises to signify that there was nothing to apologise for and took huge gulps of our pints - I was feeling tense just listening to the story.

"What happened after that?" I ventured.

"Pete took me to the fishing shop and all the way there I was just begging him not to tell anyone. I felt stupid and dirty and that was all I could think to say. In the end he just told the old chap in the shop that I'd had a nasty fall and a taxi was called. Pete came with me all the way home, just holding my hand and whispering to me that it would all be all right. When he got me home, he repeated the story of a fall to my mum, who definitely did not believe it.

I think she was sure that Pete was responsible in some way, but I could never tell her. She's over eighty now, yet she still doesn't know and, please God, she never will."

"I guess that was the last time you saw him?"

Jackie looked stricken yet resolute. "It was, I can still remember the look of concern on his face as my mum closed the door on him. My last memory of Pete and it was so alien to the bright, funny, wonderful man that I should be able to remember."

I think we had just found out half the reason for Pete's bi-polar behaviour as he took Tony home, but what about the good stuff…?

"Tony said that he remembered that Pete was excited when he put Tony to bed that night," I said, "I don't suppose you would have noticed that."

"No, he certainly wasn't excited when he left me. It would have been something to do with Max though." Jackie took a sharp breath, "there was something though, earlier on in the day, when he asked me to go shopping with him, he was excited about something then," she shrugged. "No, I'm not sure I ever listened to what it was. I was just trying to think of a good excuse so that I could still go on my date with Marsons."

"When did you find out that Pete had died?" I asked.

Jackie looked bleak, "The next morning. I woke up feeling like shit, sort of fluey symptoms, shock I guess. My mum came up with a cup of tea and I asked her to ring in to let them know I was sick. She told me not to worry, they had worse things to bother about than me being off ill. She'd just heard on the radio that a lad who worked in the hotel had got himself stuck in the mud and drowned the night before. She was pretty sure it was the boy that had been responsible for 'my accident' the day before. Good riddance, she said."

"That was a bit harsh," I said irritated, "if you told her you had had a fall, why on earth did she think it was Pete's responsibility?"

Jackie pursed her lips. "I think she thought we'd been messing about climbing the rocks in the quarry, she had met Pete a few times and had quite liked him. However, she knew what a live wire he was, and I think she thought he had been egging me on to do something I wasn't capable of. You know what mothers are like, it could never be their own darling child's fault!"

Her words were heavy with emphasis. I guessed that years of looking after other people's children were responsible for that particular observation.

"Well of course in my groggy state I thought she meant Marsons, I mean he had been the one who had really been responsible. I felt so relieved that I would never have to see him again that I started sobbing. My mum thought I was crying on Pete's behalf and said that she knew I hadn't told her the whole truth the day before, he had been careless with my own safety in the afternoon and careless with his own life in the evening. Someone who continually plays with fire is eventually going to get burnt, that sort of thing."

I remembered her mother from my first dream - it was certainly the sort of trite mantra that I could imagine her saying.

"As we talked, I suddenly realised that we weren't talking about the same person, so I asked her who it was that had died. She looked exasperated, as if she had told me ten times already, but it was only then that she actually mentioned his name."

Sam exhaled deeply, and his voice came out as a throaty half whisper. "Holy hell! That must have been rough."

Jackie nodded and finally the tears came to her eyes. "I was inconsolable. She tried every platitude she had ever heard but interspersed it with her general conviction that he brought it on himself because of what he had done to me. Eventually I couldn't bear it anymore and told her that Pete hadn't hurt me, he had saved me!"

"How did she take that?"

"Well she wanted to know what I meant by that, but as I said, I couldn't tell her," a haunted look appeared around Jackie's eyes. "I do wonder though, if I had reported it the day before, as Pete wanted me to, or even told my mother on that morning, would they have caught him? Was I responsible for not preventing all those murders that he committed?"

I could understand the guilt and could see that however well she hid it, that question would always be in the back of her mind.

I murmured a platitude that she probably didn't believe and then moved the story on. "Tony said that there was a memorial for Pete, but he didn't see you there, I suppose you couldn't face it?"

"I was there," Jackie contradicted me, "but I went with my parents. I was completely terrified of seeing Marsons, but neither he or his friend were there. I kept away from the Holm View crowd as I couldn't have coped with questions, we hid at the back of the chapel and disappeared as soon as it was over."

"And like Tony, you never went back?"

She shook her head, but it was in agreement. "No, I never went back. I still haven't walked through the hotel doors, even after all this time. After a horrible week, I woke up one morning and realised that it was the day I was due to start my access course at college, the one that Pete had been so instrumental in organising. I suddenly decided, almost on the spur of the moment, that the one thing that would make him happiest as far as I was concerned, was if I was successful in the career for which he had given me so much encouragement."

"You quite like it, don't you?" I said with a cheeky grin.

"Guilty!" she laughed, "I do actually love it. Oh, I moan and groan about it because that's what us English do, but there isn't a week that goes past without at least one moment when I thank Pete for forcing me into it."

We moved onto more light-hearted subjects after that and due to efficient bar staff removing the empties, probably drank a lot more than we realised. It was a warm evening in the garden, Jackie was funny and intelligent, some of her tales of the nursery terrors had us aching with laughter. Apart from the echoes of a serial killer from the last century, it was the perfect summer night in the pub with friends.

It was lucky that the pub was in the station car park as it meant we didn't have far to go when we suddenly realised that the last train from Bristol was due. Sam extricated himself from the bench seating in a rather ungainly manner. "D'you know," he slurred in Jackie's general direction, "you should get in touch with Tony, I think he'd love to see you!"

Move over Davina McCall.

Jackie laughed and gathering up her bag and light summer jacket, was definitely on the wobbly side herself. "Do you know what Sam?" she said, "I might just do that!"

As we left her at the gate to the station, she gave us a little wink. "Just to say boys that I saw you earlier, trying not to laugh when I mentioned my ex-husband's name."

I was embarrassed and started to apologise, but she was taking it all in her stride. "None taken!" she laughed, "but for your information, when the little shit irritated me, I always called him Willie… he absolutely hated it!"

We all laughed, and then she was gone. Sam and I sat on the station waiting for the arrival of the last train to Weston. I started to think about all she had told us, about the brave man who was fearless in the protection of his friends and yet had died alone. I guess it was the drink, but I felt a sudden wave of anger on his behalf.

"Where were they Sam?" I semi-slurred. "Where were they when he died? He had been there for them both. In Tony's case, he had saved him from at least a bad beating and in Jackie's, he almost certainly prevented her from becoming Hutch's first victim." I snapped a remark at him, my face so close to his that I might have been going to kiss him, but for once that was the last thing on my mind. "So where were they, when he needed them?"

I could tell Sam was a little irritated and he was also slightly drunk. "Oh, for fuck's sake Rem! Jackie had been seconds away from being raped and Tony was so pissed up that he was throwing Z's in the planet Zogg!" He paused - his words heavy with meaning - "do you really think, after meeting them both, that if they had known he was in trouble they wouldn't have moved heaven and earth to be there for him…? Do you really think that?"

I didn't, but of course I wouldn't tell Sam that he had a point. The train arrived, and we got on and found a free seat for two. The train was crowded with commuters who had stopped on after work for a quick one, and youngsters who had abandoned the delights of Weston for a night out in the big city.

When Sam spoke again, he was more conciliatory. "If it's all upsetting you too much, maybe it's best if we don't go and see Max, after all. It looks like you will eventually find out the truth; your dreams are definitely heading you in that direction."

"God Sam! No, I really want to see him. Apart from anything else, I want to know what he looks like now, what he's done with his life after Pete. Did he ever get over him?"

"Good!" he laughed, sensing we were back on easier territory, "because I'm desperate to meet him and I haven't even dreamed about him!"

I had a feeling that Sam's relief would be short lived. I decided, in my drunken state and contrary to my earlier thoughts, that I needed to let him know about the crazy idea I had woken with on Monday morning.

"Also, I know this is going to sound a little crazy, but as I said yesterday, when I dreamt on Sunday night, I felt like I was part of Pete. I could feel what he was feeling, sense what he was thinking…"

"OK," Sam said it slowly, as if he was already slightly worried where this was heading.

"Well Sam," I paused, trying to shape the words in my head, which after six pints was a slight trial, "what if I can save him? What if with each dream I get more control over him and I can give him the strength to pull himself from the mud, or even stop him from going in at all? If I know exactly what happened just before he died, then maybe I could work out a plan to prevent it."

Sam looked at me like I had told him that I was pregnant with the President's babies. "Umm."

That was about all he could manage.

"You sound dubious." The master of the understatement was alive and well and travelling on a train to Weston.

"OK," Sam rubbed his face with both hands, trying to get his head around this latest madness. "Apart from anything else and there are about one hundred reasons why that statement is as mad as Madison Madman from Madhattan… What about the butterfly effect?"

I had already thought about that. "Pete was gay, he was never going to have children. It's possible that he could survive, and nothing would change in the world."

The train slowed for Worle Parkway and people got ready to leave the train. Once they had left, the carriage was only half full. Sam reduced his volume to an urgent whisper so that if there were any men in white coats nearby, they wouldn't feel it necessary to carry me away.

"What about Max, Jackie, Tony, Pete's mum and dad? Don't tell me that if you could change Pete's history, it wouldn't change theirs as well?"

He had a very good point and you know how irritated I got when that happened.

"Did you ever see the film, The Amazing Mr Blunden?" I decided to change tack, but possibly using a 1970s' ghost story for children that my gran had enjoyed, wasn't my best plan when it came to argue a case that went against all the laws of physics. When Sam merely sat there looking dumbstruck, I continued: "it was about two children who go back in time and save their grandparents from a fire that had originally killed them."

Sam looked stunned for a second and then laughed, loud and long. "Bloody hell Rem! OK I admit it, you totally had me! I really thought you were serious, you little fucker!"

I thought it best to laugh and pretend that I had been joking. Of course, I hadn't been. Looking back, knowing what I know, I wonder if I ever really believed it possible.

What I know is that I desperately wanted Pete to survive; I wanted the book to have a different ending; I wanted him to have had the happy life he deserved.

I was prepared to believe in anything at all that could have made it happen.

I also knew a certain fact as we stumbled down Station Road in a slightly alcoholic slalom. It was something I wasn't going to mention to Sam or Emily as it was possible had they known the truth, I would require the services of The Priory by the time Pete's story was completed.

I knew I would be witnessing the next instalment of the story that evening. I had realised, quite recently, that every time I slept in Sam/Max's room when I was drunk... I ended up going back in time.

22.

1977

I f Pete's childhood had been idyllic, the summer of '77 moved the idyll on to a completely new level. For one thing, he had discovered sex that was more than a guilty fumble or grope with his teenage friends.

For another thing, he had fallen completely and wonderfully, in love.

Max and he spent every moment that they could together. They would spend hours in Max's room listening to records or watching television on the fourteen inch black and white portable that sat on a small table at the end of the bed.

The picture quality wasn't that good, and every so often the thin circular aerial would slip from its position and the picture would either disappear into a snowstorm, or be gone altogether. On these occasions one of them had to leap up from their prone position on the bed and try to fix it. Pete was just amazed that anyone should have a television in their bedroom, so he was always more than happy to bounce onto his knees and attempt to tease the awkward aerial back into place.

Quite often this needed to be done with hands that were shaking as a result of the helpful tickles that Max was applying to his body. Sometimes retaliation meant that they ended up collapsing in an exhausted heap whilst static still raged from the small screen at the bottom of the bed.

The TV did manage to behave itself when Virginia

Wade played Chris Evert in the semi-final of the Wimbledon championship. Pete found himself split, Virginia was English, and it was Jubilee year, but Chris Evert was his favourite. His romantic teenage self had been enthralled when both Chrissie and Jimmy Connors, her fiancée at the time, had won their titles in 1974. This meant that they danced together during the champions' waltz and Pete, encouraged by his mum, lapped it all up. A fairy story played out in tennis whites.

In the end, after brainwashing from Max and Dan Maskell, the BBC voice of tennis, he decided he was glad when the English woman pulled off a bit of a surprise and beat the number one seed.

He had no such quandaries when Wade played the final against Betty Stove, two days later. After she had lost the first set, Pete banged his fist down in frustration on the bed with such force that the ripple effect caused the dodgy aerial to fall from its moorings. Both Max and he spent most of the second set trying to fit it back into place. In the end, the picture was restored, as was Wade's good form. They watched her receive the Wimbledon Ladies' Trophy in its one-hundredth year, from the Monarch in her twenty-fifth.

On pleasant summer days they went walking and cycling. Pete borrowed Mo's bike and the Deputy Manager was quite happy to let him. He had been relieved when Pete had started taking his brother under his wing. He was so busy running the Hotel, mainly as a help to his father, but increasingly as a buffer between the man and his staff.

Mr Edwards Senior was becoming more and more volatile and unreasonable, picking faults with the staff wherever he could. Mo spent a lot of time shadowing him, which meant there was a lot less time that he could spend with his younger brother. Max only had a few friends in Weston and they were away for the summer. Mo liked Pete and was happy to leave them to their own devices, which left him to run the hotel guilt free.

Pete for his own part wondered about Old Man Edwards. He had never liked the bloke, but it was almost as if something was troubling him. Pete even started to wonder if the Manager had discovered the truth about his relationship with Max. If he had, why was he waiting to make his feelings on the subject known?

Pete and Max still went out with Tony, Jackie and Helen for day trips when their schedules allowed. They spent days at the open-air swimming pool with its stunning art deco diving stage. Tony and Pete had wound each other up into a competitive frenzy over the summer until Pete eventually became the first to dive from the thirty-foot top tier into the water below. He resurfaced, feeling slightly red and water slapped, but jubilant.

Max and the girls contented themselves with the first tier, which at just over seven foot felt adventurous enough for them. Sometimes they chickened out completely and concentrated on the spring boards to the side of the main diving stage, which brought about friendly teasing from their more courageous friends.

Between the diving and swimming, they lazed in the sun by the side of the pool, listening to music on Max's transistor radio. The sounds of the summer of 1977 from "Strawberry Letter 42," to "Road Runner," "Ma Baker," "Oh Lori" and "All Around the World," accompanied them as they laughed, joked and ran to cool off underneath the fountain that dominated the shallow end of the pool.

When The Jam song was played on the radio, Max would turn it up to maximum volume. The genteel day trippers relaxing in deck chairs would mutter in disgust at the sudden disruption of their daydreams.

If not in the pool they were on the pier. Betting on the mechanical horses where the winner always seemed to be red or blue. Pushing coins into the penny drop machines and rolling wooden balls down an alley aiming for numbered hoops that sat at the end of the runway. They stumbled their way around the crazy house hooting with laughter. They teased each other mercilessly around the house of mirrors, where their features were deformed and their bodies stretched.

On the ghost train they scared each other more than the mannequins dressed as pirates and flip up skeletons could ever do. Everyone ganged up on Pete whilst driving the dodgems, once he had shown a kamikaze tenacity that was all his own. Alongside being crunched in retaliation by his friends, it also brought him yells of complaint from the staff who leapt from dodgem to dodgem with wiry grace and a bored arrogance.

After work at weekends they tended to go to Snoopys, mainly at Helen's suggestion. Pete, Max and Jackie would dance wildly to Donna Summer's "I Feel Love" and Candi Staton's "Nights On Broadway" and the boys would take it in turns to smooch with Jackie to the strains of "Float On." All the time Pete kept a wary eye on Tony, who would stand alone watching his girlfriend as she flirted with her drug dealing paramour.

Sometimes Starsky and Hutch would join them on these nights out and Pete was always aware of the blonde boy's growing interest in Jackie. He was pleased to see that Starsky was also noticing it, as the wiry barman seemed to join his friend just at the moment when Hutch was threatening to go too far.

Pete introduced Max to the delights of the theatre one night. The Playhouse in the Old High Street was showing a farce for the summer season. Trevor Bannister who played Mr Lucas in "Are You Being Served?" was playing the lead.

The comedy series was a bit of a favourite to both of them, although Pete felt he could probably survive the rest of his life without hearing someone asking him if he was free…?

Pete thought the farce would be a good bit of light-hearted fluff for a theatre virgin, and so it proved.

However, both of them agreed that the highlight had been a rather good looking young actor playing the stooge to Mr Bannister's wide boy, who had been stripped practically naked by a plot twist that no-one understood or cared about, and spent the majority of the second half, running around the stage with next to no clothes on.

"And I always thought the theatre was too highbrow for the likes of me!" Laughed Max as the orange curtains closed and the lights went back on in the auditorium.

"Things are moving on I can tell you!" Pete informed him, "time was when it was only the young ladies that showed any skin, apart from an old man in comedy under shorts. If this is the future, I like it!"

Afterwards they went to The Britannia, a pub a few doors down from the theatre, which was known locally as The Brit. Max had heard that it was the meeting place for "people like us," as he put it.

In the end, it was mostly full of a crowd of amateur theatricals and although some of them certainly fitted the bill, it felt slightly too cliquey for either Max or Pete to risk starting a conversation.

Around in a snug corner at the far end of the bar, Pete watched a young lad of about sixteen whose eyes couldn't tear themselves away from a dark haired muscular looking lad in his early twenties. The elder man was obviously part of the amateur dramatics club, but looked more like crew than cast and was completely oblivious to his young admirer. His attention was taken up by a good-looking girl who had wrapped herself around him.

Pete glanced at Max and then looked over at the young lad. You'll find someone like him one day, he wanted to say, and when you do it will be wonderful.

There were still nights when a crowd of the hotel staff would end up on the beach and Max would join them. Everyone seemed to accept that they were a couple, but nobody actually put it into words. Hutch would occasionally say something provocative when the Manager was around, but it was more to see the panic in Max's eyes and the glint of temper in Pete's, than a deliberate attempt to cause trouble.

However, Pete did wonder if it was those sorts of comments that were responsible for Old Man Edwards' increased irritability.

Sometimes it was after the trip to the beach and sometimes it was directly from work, but Pete always ended up in Max's room before the end of the night. Max's Dad and Mo never made an appearance before midnight, so they were safe to do what pleased them. What pleased them was to listen to music, make love, and lie together in the contentment of an experience shared.

One night they must have fallen asleep and didn't wake up until they heard the outer door of the apartment open.

"Is it Mo or Dad?" Max said, more to himself than expecting Pete to have the ability to see through walls and doors.

"I don't know!" said Pete, grappling for his clothes as silently as he could in the darkness.

"If it's Mo he'll pop in and kiss my forehead after he's cleaned his teeth and before he goes to bed." Max said urgently, then seeing Pete's look of bemusement through the night light, he shrugged, "he's always done it, since I was a boy."

They heard a door open, and close, somewhere along the corridor. "It is Mo. Go now whilst he's getting ready for bed."

"What about your dad?"

"He's either already in bed or Mo's left him at the bar in a drunken snooze - hurry!"

Pete pulled the rest of his clothes on and headed for the door, blew a kiss towards Max and opened the door slightly. There was no-one in the corridor, but just as he reached the door to the bathroom, Mo's door opened, so Pete took the most immediate action and hid in the room and locked the door. As Mo tried the handle of the door,

Pete shouted "Mmm mm mm," in the best impression of Max cleaning his own teeth that he could manage.

"Heck, you're late up Maxi," called Mo and Pete had to stifle a snigger, "OK, I'll leave you to it!"

Mo disappeared back to his room and when Pete heard the latch close, he risked opening the bathroom door slightly. Max had done the same thing and peered out of his bedroom. He pointed urgently at the front door and just as Pete was disappearing through it, shouted "bathroom's free!" to Mo and slammed his own door to cover any sound that Pete might have to make in order to escape.

Luckily there were no other hazards on his way home until he reached the top of the staircase that led to room seventeen. He was congratulating himself on the great escape, when a figure appeared from upstairs and they practically fell over each other in the hallway.

It was Tony, reappearing from Helen's room. When they had got over the shock of the encounter, they laughed long and hard.

"Well what have you been doing my skinny white gay boy?" Tony laughed, "or maybe I should say, who?"

As was their wont, they then talked into the ember hours of the morning. It made no difference to either of them that their passion took a different form, it was as irrelevant as the difference in their skin colour.

If one was worried about his friend risking the rage of a petty crook and the other was worried about the anger of their boss, then they were concerns that were acknowledged but never dwelt upon.

They talked their evenings through and relived the enjoyment in the telling.

There were no details that were too intimate to share.

***

A few days later, Pete had the whole day off; so he and

Max had time to themselves. They decided to ride the bikes along the beach towards Uphill and take the ferry across to Brean Down. The night before they had been to watch "The Spy Who Loved Me," and on their way home had been involved in an argument as to the identity of the best James Bond.

Helen, along with a waitress called Christine and Max had plumped for Sean Connery whilst Pete had gone for Roger Moore, as had Jackie. Pete had liked him since he and Tony Curtis had lit up the Friday night television of Pete's youth in "The Persuaders."

Tony, being his normal awkward self, had decided that George Lazenby was his man.

The argument was continuing the next morning as they cycled along the shallows of the incoming tide.

"But Roger is far more English and puts loads more comedy into it!" argued Pete.

"Nah! Who says he has to be English?" was Max's argument, "Sean is just so much sexier!"

They continued their argument, repeating many of the points three or four times before Pete, who was on the land side of the water, decided to point his bicycle in Max's direction. He forced him out into deeper and deeper water until the bicycle wheels could turn no more and Max was propelled into the sea. He stood up, the salt water dripping from his hair and every part of his body, as sodden as marshlands in the winter.

Pete was so busy laughing that he forgot to move out of the way and suddenly found himself pushed into the water himself. As they rolled around the shore looking like a Derek Jarman remake of "From Here to Eternity," they heard a sudden cry of warning and realised there was a great possibility of Max's bike floating away on the tide. After rescuing it, they staggered, spluttering with laughter back on to the beach.

"Look at me!" cried Pete, "I am absolutely soaked, you crazy boy!"

"Me!" Max was outraged, "I think you were the one re-enacting 'Duel' with bicycles!" They had watched the Steven Spielberg film together, through an aerial induced snow storm on late night television one evening, earlier in the summer.

"We'd better go back to the Hotel, dry ourselves and get changed." Pete laughed, but Max had a much better idea.

"No need! Follow me, Flipper!" With that he got back on his bike and led the way up the beach, struggling slightly as the sand got thicker and finer nearer the road. They rode up to the track by the dock where the boats were moored. Once they had passed the fishing tackle shop, he leapt from his bike and pushed his way through some dense shrubbery to a clearing below the quarry.

Pete followed him, looking more perplexed with every turn of his wheel.

"So why are we here?" he asked with comic irritation.

"No-one can approach us from behind as there is a quarry," Max was enjoying himself.

"Yep, I think I managed to work that one out."

"Very few people know this path and if anyone does, we can hear them approaching as soon as they hit the bushes."

"Agreed."

"And no-one can see us from the cliff top above, as the overhanging rock would mean that they would have to risk life and limb just to get a view of us."

Pete was beginning to realise where Max was going with this. "So you mean that you have brought me here to strip my soaked clothing from me and have your wicked way with me!" He said in mock horror, playing the ingénue from a melodrama.

"I will, if you will!" Max agreed and to prove his point peeled his still sodden T-shirt over his head and hung it from the quarry to dry.

Within minutes they had turned the rock face into

Wishee Washee's laundry and were standing nakedly facing each other.

"Loony!" Pete said affectionately and moved in to embrace his friend.

They kissed then, the sun dancing on the back of their necks threatening an uncomfortable evening, but they had no thought for it. Pete could taste a faint and heady mix of toothpaste and sea salt on his lips and could smell the scent of Lifebuoy and Brut mixed with a smell that Pete always thought of as Maxness. It was his favourite scent in the world. If they were to take his advice, perfumers would bottle it and sell it at Christmas.

There was a flat rock the size of a small bed and Pete lay down on it. It took two attempts, as the rock had been warmed by the sun like stones in a sauna. Once he had sorted their clothes into makeshift sheeting, he lay down again and Max straddled across his body. With the cries of gulls and clink of distant fishing boats married together with the warm air and the beautiful body that was engulfing him, Pete didn't believe he had ever been happier.

On Valentine's day he had been euphoric as he was jumping around to "Dancing Queen" and had shivers of joy rippling down his back as the hypnotic sound of "SOS" filled his ears. However, this was even more intense, it was like a combination of both sensations.

"I love you," he whispered into Max's ear as they lay together afterwards, making use of every inch of the rock.

"Back at ya!" Max grinned and kissed Pete lightly on the lips.

They held each other in silence for a few minutes. Pete staring directly at the blazing sun, creating psychedelic shards that ran from the epicentre of the burning disc to every boundary of his eye line. This, along with all that had happened before, created a drug like high that threatened sensory overload - but without the threat of the crashing downer afterwards.

Eventually Max shifted his position so that he was sitting upright, but straddled over the thin end of the rock. He lay Pete's legs across his own so that their penises were almost touching, a sort of recreation of what had gone before but, at this moment in time, Max wanted to talk.

"I've heard back from Auntie Sadie," he told Pete.

Following their conversation in Owen Owens, Pete had encouraged Max to try and find someone that knew his mum and could talk to him about her. Mo had once told him about an old friend of hers that he had always called Auntie, even though she wasn't related to the family.

Their father had continued to keep in touch and had taken the boys to see her regularly at her house in Cheddar until Max was a few weeks shy of his fourth birthday. There had been a huge row between the two adults and they had never visited Auntie Sadie after that.

Pete and Max had looked her up in the phone book, found that she still lived in Cheddar and Max had written to her.

"She's invited me over to see her!" Max grinned in delighted anticipation. "She's away for the whole of August, but she set a date for Friday 2nd September," he paused and looked shyly at Pete. "Would you come with me?"

Pete smiled, "Try keeping me away!" He said.

"You are the best thing that ever happened to me" Max said, leaning over to kiss Pete fully on the lips, Pete for his part held onto Max's head with his hands and sang gently and laughingly into his face.

"If Billy Bonds should ever write my life story..."

It was a bit of a joke between them, they had been listening to the Gladys Knight song and Pete had misheard the lyrics of the first line of the chorus. Now, whenever they sang it, they always replaced the actual words with the name of the West Ham United Captain.

Max was now in his element as one misheard lyric always led to another between them. Noel Edmonds was doing a slot about them on his radio one breakfast show, so there were always plenty to choose from. He treated Pete to a brief medley of a few he'd heard that morning when he was whiling time away whilst his lover worked. His senses were sharpened with the anticipation of the day ahead and his impatience was raging against the dilatory clock.

As he sung, his penis brushed gently across Pete's own and within seconds misheard lyrics were forgotten as other distractions arose...

By the time they had satisfied their bodies for the second time, their clothes were now dry. However, the salt had recreated the effect of an over enthusiastic laundry worker being let loose with a packet of starch.

The material crinkled against their sun blushed bodies and neither of them were overly sure that it was more comfortable than when the clothes were soaking wet. Yet neither of them were going to argue that the interlude hadn't been worth the itching sensations.

They retraced their steps back through the undergrowth surprising a small boxer dog and his human family as they emerged back onto the dusty track once again. Pete followed Max as he cycled his way down to where the ferry carried passengers across the river to Brean Down.

Whatever Pete had been expecting, the ferry was a slight downgrade from the one that had taken his parents and himself across to the Isle of Wight a few summers earlier. In fact, it bore no resemblance to it at all.

It was basically a wooden rowing boat that had to cross all of twenty feet of water, powered solely by the muscles of a craggy faced old boatman. Both the rowing boat and the man had seen better days, but there was no doubt of his ingenuity as he used every inch of the old boat to fit as much as he possibly could in a very limited space.

First both bikes were straddled over the back of the boat and then a family of walkers and the two lads were encouraged to climb on board. This was easier said than done, as the banks were slippery, and the boat was wobbly. The odds of someone performing a muddy face plant or one of the bikes disappearing to the bottom of the dirty river bed, would have been no worse than evens at any respectable betting shop.

The man himself, sprung on board with the agility and sure-footedness of someone half his age, circulated the tiny area taking ten pence from everybody and five pence for each bike. Within three strokes of his trusty oars he had propelled the boat to the other side of the river and had deposited his cargo on an equally muddy piece of land on the Brean side of the water. He then replaced them with six walkers, two wheelchairs and a pit bull terrier called Henry.

Pete and Max caught the bicycles that were thrown in their general direction. Once they had wheeled their way to a track, where it was possible to cycle with ease, they made their way down to the bottom of a large promontory that jutted into the Bristol Channel. This was Brean Down.

They chained their bikes to a wooden railing and started to climb the two-hundred odd steps to the summit. Once they had topped the irregular staircase, they glanced around them, taking in all points from their roofless church at Uphill on one side, to Exmoor, Wales and the Weston coastline on the others.

"Race you to the end!" Max laughed making sure that he had a head start on his rival. Pete was faster and soon soared into a lead, but Max had the advantage of knowing that the route was one and a half miles in length, so like the tortoise and the hare he had caught up with his exhausted friend by the time the nineteenth century fort was coming into view. Pete gave one more burst of energy and edged in front by sheer strength of will, before both of them collapsed together on the grassy slope that led towards the ruined fort and the sea beyond.

Once they had regained breath and composure Max

waved his hand, indicating the ruined fort in front of them. "That is called a Palmerston Fort," he said. "Lord Palmerston was Prime Minister in the 1860s and he had a load of these built to ward off the threat of a French invasion. The only shot in anger that was fired here though is when a young soldier blasted his rifle down a ventilator shaft exploding a gunpowder magazine below."

"Bloody hell!" said Pete, fascinated, "why did he do that?"

"The story goes that he was trying to commit suicide."

"Well that would be one way to do it," Pete agreed, then started to move. "Can we look round it?"

Max sighed, resigned to the fact that his comfortable relaxation on the grass would soon be at an end. A group of eight men identically dressed in khaki shorts and hiking boots, giving them the look of a scout troop for pensioners, were the only other people in sight. They disappeared back up the slope, nodding in politeness as they passed.

"There's not much we can look at," he said, "there is a rumour that it will be restored eventually, but at the moment lots of it is out of bounds. Anyway," he glanced as the last body disappeared from view, "wouldn't you rather lie here and kiss me instead?"

Pete pretended to give the idea a lot of thought, then teased, "Nah, I'd rather explore the fort!"

He then turned to face Max and completely contradicted himself with his actions, extinguishing the complaints that were on the lips of his friend as he did so.

By the time they had meandered in a slightly slower manner back to the steps, enjoying the late afternoon sun on their backs, then climbed down, collected their bikes and made their way back to the ferry, the ferryman had given up and gone home for his tea.

This meant they had to cycle the eight-mile detour around the winding country roads back to the A370. Nothing could dampen their spirits on that golden afternoon and they did so singing every chart hit that came to their heads. In so doing, they disturbed sheep, cattle and the members of a caravanning club who were enjoying a quick gin before supper time.

Once on the main road, they decided that their aching lungs could cope with some refreshment and stopping off at Hobbs Boat Inn, sat outside to drink a couple of pints of lager each. They filled their starving bellies with large plates of scampi and chips, following it with massive slices of Black Forest Gateaux.

They turned into the hotel grounds as the sky turned scarlet, the distant sound of the incoming tide accompanied the clicking of the turning wheels on their bicycles.

With aching limbs, they climbed the staircase to the apartment and once in Max's room they discarded the stiff and itchy clothing, which led to thoughts of making love for the third time that day.

"We will always be together, won't we?" Max whispered afterwards, his beautiful face crinkled in concern

"Never, ever doubt it," Pete answered him and then asked, "do you believe in an afterlife?"

Max shrugged, "Not really, my father once contacted a medium to try and get in touch with my mum, but I think they're probably all charlatans."

"Oh, there are definitely some of them, but I've always had a sneaking regard for it," he said. Then turning to face Max, he said with a sudden certainty, "I just can't believe that this is all there is, that after our life is done we just turn to dust."

"What, you believe in heaven?" Max was unsure but not derisive.

"Not the sort of heaven with white fluffy clouds, harps and angels - no," Pete said. "But I believe my spirit will live on after my death and that I will be able to contact the people I love," he seemed to think his thoughts through, "yes, I really believe in that."

Max seemed to be on the verge of asking a question, but Pete pre-empted it. "You sweetheart, would be the first person I'd try and talk to."

"Not for a long time yet though," Max said, and Pete nodded.

"Not for a very long time." he said.

The conversation took a lighter turn after that and soon, when even that had dried up and they were just holding each other, Max peeled himself out of Pete's arms and stood up.

"There's only one piece of music that can sum up this perfect day," he said, pulling an album out of its sleeve and placing it on the music centre. He put the needle ready to play the last song on the album and dropped it expertly on the gap between tracks. Within seconds the song started, and Lou Reed began to sing.

23.

It was quite bizarre, as soon as I woke up, I could sense a slight burn on my bum cheeks. It was from when Pete had sat down on the hot rock in the quarry, I was convinced of it.

I slithered out of bed and went over to the full-length mirror and attempted to look at my arse in the reflection. The fact that the curtains were drawn and there wasn't very much light in the room didn't make this the easiest of tasks, so I decided to give Sam a treat first thing in the morning. I shuffled over to his side of the bed and tapped him on the shoulder.

"Sam! Sam! Are my bum cheeks red?" I asked quizzically.

I thrust the aforementioned part of my body towards his face and waited for his response.

This came in the form of: "Oh for fuck's sake Rem, I'm asleep! Do you have to shove your smelly arse cheeks in my face?"

Now, quite frankly, there is not being very good in the morning and there is just being plain rude.

"Well you don't have to be vile," I said huffily and explained the reason behind my actions.

Sam groaned and held his head in his hands. "I thought you said you were joking about that?"

"No, you said I was joking, I just went along with it for a quiet life," I countered.

He shuffled himself towards a seated position and said

grumpily, "OK you've had another dream and you're even more convinced you can save Pete from his fate and run off into the sunset together…"

I guess it made me realise how daft it all sounded, but you know me, never give up on a lost cause,

"You just don't seem to realise how real it all seemed."

Sam grabbed my pillow with one hand and pulled it over his face. It might have smothered the sounds coming from his mouth, but I'm still sure I managed to make out: "Fu-ck-ing he-ell!"

When we had both recovered a little more of our equilibrium, kissed, made up and had breakfast, Emily reappeared from her chamber maiding tasks. She didn't need to suffer my arse cheeks in her face to realise I'd had another dream.

"Come on you two, your room now! I've got to hear all about it!"

The three of us sprawled on a bed made for two and I recounted my dream. As I told of their fight in the water, Sam whispered, "We did that too, without the bicycles, but otherwise exactly the same."

"It gets weirder," I said and continued with the story until I reached the part where Pete professed his love for Max.

Sam looked at me and said, "Please don't tell me that he said, 'back at ya'?"

I nodded, and Emily looked confused.

Sam blushed, obviously talking about that sort of stuff in front of your baby sister was way beyond his comfort zone. "It's sort of what we say to each other…" he confessed awkwardly.

"Yes, but that happens in dreams," Emily was completely unfazed by the revelation, "you project your thoughts into the mouths of other people…" she tailed off, "you're going to tell me that it wasn't like that?"

I nodded.

"Well for fuck's sake Rem, don't go on that beach

alone at night!"

It was said lightly, but I was beginning to tire of the joke. It was the travelling the wrong way up an escalator type of worry once again, and I was really beginning to get confused.

Were these dreams meant to lead me to saving Pete's life, as I had previously believed, or were they a warning? Was Pete reaching out across the years to tell me, his namesake, that something awful was going to happen to me before the summer faded into autumn?

The other thing I couldn't quite decide was this: were the dreams going to tell me the answer to all my questions, or did I need to find out the truth before I dreamt about it? Would Pete's downfall end up being my own?

One thing I had decided was that I'd better not risk getting drunk again before we went to see Max next week.

I needed cheering up and I had really liked the look of the place in my dream, so I asked Sam and Emily if we could take the ferry over to Brean Down. They looked at me quizzically.

"I don't ever remember that, do you Em?" asked Sam and his sister shook her head.

"Not in our life time Bro," she said. "Although I have heard something about a footpath being opened between Weston and Brean Down this summer." She scrunched up her mouth, "It's five miles each way though and quite frankly, I can't be arsed!" She then brightened, "I can drive you round there though!"

Be careful what you wish for.

In the end we did decide to go over to Brean Down for the day and it was just what I needed, OK the drive itself wasn't exactly what I needed, but Em's driving was improving... or I was becoming immune to fear.

The A370 was busier than it had been forty years ago, I wouldn't have fancied cycling down that road now, but the Hobbs Boat Inn was exactly where I had seen it and the caravan park was thriving. Em parked as near as she could to the Down. She even nearly managed to keep inside a single parking place. We headed up the hill and although I was tempted to challenge them both to a race once we had crested the steps, I decided that I was suffering enough of the past recreating my present.

In the present I really didn't need to recreate the past.

We walked the mile and a half to the end of the promontory, Sam and I stripped off our shirts on a day that was so like the one in my dream that I half expected to turn my head and see Max and Pete behind us. Seeing something as normal and loved as Sam's naked torso helped me though. The dream receded with every pace and I began to enjoy the brilliant company of my boyfriend and his wonderfully wacky sister.

Whoever had restored the fort to its former glory had made a great job of it. As we wandered around the gun emplacements, officers' quarters and main body of the fort, I told them some of the stories that Max had mentioned to Pete.

"It was from here that Marconi sent one of his very first broadcasts," Sam said. Not to be left out Emily told us that Brean Down had been one of the places where they performed trials to produce a bouncing bomb. I think she'd read it from the information plaques dotted around the area, but I gave her that one.

Sam and I explored some of the underground rooms that were dark and smelt damply of salt water, Emily had decided to stay over ground and no other tourists were down there with us. I could imagine two soldiers on night duty sneaking down there for an illegal moment of magic. I thought of Max and Pete, lying on the hillside above our heads, waiting for the last person to vanish over the rise, so they could kiss in the afternoon sunshine.

It seemed that Sam's thoughts were following my own, because after a wary look up the steps, he grabbed me in a clinch and smiled his special smile.

"Sorry for being such a Grinch this morning," he said.

"Just this morning?" I asked in affected surprise.

"I am struggling with all this too you know," he said.

"I know, it's all a bit X-Files isn't it?" I agreed, then referred to a comment that Sam had made earlier: "I don't want to 'ride off into the sunset' with Pete you know, it's just that the more I know of him, the more I like him. Combine that with the fact that I know he died a month or so after all the events that I'm witnessing. I suppose I want to think I could save him, even if the logical part of my brain tells me that it's all bollocks!"

Sam nodded gently in understanding, then his mouth twisted into a wicked grin, "You're trying to tell me that you have a logical side to your brain? Actually, are you trying to tell me you have a brain?"

I dug him in the ribs, "Shut up and kiss me." I ordered.

For once he did as he was told, and the cold, damp dark and airless place became paradise for a few moments. Eventually I dragged myself away from his lips. "I'm sorry for shoving my arse cheeks in your face first thing in the morning," I whispered in a conciliatory manner.

He smiled that twisted smile once again, "Well normally I wouldn't complain, but…" he trailed off as we heard Emily hollering above us.

"I'm bored and feeling left out…!"

We re-emerged and linked arms with her before dancing up the hill like Julie Andrews with a pair of the Von Trapp boys. Sadly, we lacked a pair of matching lederhosen made out of the bedroom curtains, but hey, you can't have everything.

The worries in my brain had receded like storms in a cloudless sky, but the clouds were still there, waiting to emerge on another morning.

We had a quiet night in when the three of us watched "Fantastic Beasts and Where to Find Them" in Sam's room. I limited my drinking to just one can of beer and if Sam and Emily noticed, they didn't say. To be honest, none of us drank much, the movie was good, and we were feeling wonderfully relaxed after a day in the fresh air. We sprawled across each other on the bed in comfortable companionship.

On Thursday, Ned disrupted our planned visit to town by asking Sam to work in the kitchen. It wasn't on a spying mission though, it seemed that Sam's argument had had the desired effect and his father was giving Mark a lot less hassle as a result. Sam was needed simply as a cover for the second chef, who had picked up a stomach bug.

I rattled around the apartment and with too much time on my hands, managed to get myself in a stew once again. As soon as Emily had finished her duties, she saved me from myself and we did wander into town. I kept away from talking about the mystery, in fact, she seemed to sense that I didn't want to talk about it. She rambled on about candyfloss nonsense for the whole of our trip into town… and I loved her for it.

Sam was working that evening, as well, and started early on Friday morning. In the end it was a bit of a relief from the boredom of my own company when I took over from Jack in the bar at four. Our changeover turned into a little bit of a gossiping session, which ended when Ned appeared and said sharply to Jack: "There is a function you are meant to be organising in the Burnham suite tonight, if you can tear yourself away!"

I tried to play the placatory card and said brightly: "Sorry Ned! My fault, I was just asking Jack to fill me in with all the details I needed to know for my shift." Well it was a slight exaggeration and Ned was having none of it.

"I think you should call me by my proper title when you are on duty Peter!" he reprimanded. I noticed he had dropped calling me Rem and replaced it with my own proper title.

He stormed out before I could apologise. Jack and I swapped looks. "That man could do with taking some lessons from his son on how you should talk to your staff," was his parting shot to me as he left the bar.

It was the similarity to the management situation from the last century that struck me: stroppy father, placatory son.

Whatever had been ailing Alf the week before had disappeared and he was there smack on the dot of six o'clock. After I had served his drink, I had a mini rush to deal with, so it was about twenty minutes later before I finally managed to get around to having a proper chat with him.

"Lad," he said as I approached.

"Hi Alf!" I said brightly, "you've lived in Weston quite a long time, haven't you?"

He gave me one of his "get to the point" looks, so I did just that.

"I wondered if you knew a Robert Morgan or Richard Townsend?" I asked, and Alf nodded.

His next comment was like a firework dropped onto a barbecue. He dropped it in a way that although I had no way of knowing it – I somehow felt an idiot for not having known it.

And it caused an explosion inside of me.

"Townsend was my wife's maiden name, Richard was her brother."

24.

Oh my God, bingo!

"But they were the lads who found the body of the bloke I asked you about the other day," I said, slightly confused; surely, he would have known about that?

"They did," he agreed.

"But… I thought you said you didn't know about the accident?"

Alf was straight back at me on that one: "No lad, you asked me if I knew the lad himself and I did not, you did not ask me if I knew of him…"

Lord, strike me down!

"OK," I gave myself some thinking time, it seemed that I needed to watch every question or phrase I uttered. It was like negotiating with two neighbouring nations at war. If every question wasn't exactly right, hostilities would be resumed and I would get nowhere.

"So, you didn't know Pete, but you knew Richard well?"

"I did, I was married to his sister." OK, too obvious and slightly patronising this time?

"What about Robert?"

"He was a stupid shit! Actually, they were both stupid shits… drugged up all the time, you know?"

I did.

"What about the night Pete died? Did you see them that night?"

"Why are you so interested?" It was a fair question and I gave him my stock answer, he seemed to accept it.

"I saw him the day after, he was in quite a state, worried but excited… not particularly upset though."

That saddened me a little, although Tony had said that there were a few people being unpleasant about Pete at his memorial, so it shouldn't have surprised me.

"But in Morgan's statement to the press, it made it sound like they were great friends, shouldn't they have been a little bit more upset?" I asked.

"That was a load of shit!" Alf said vehemently, "they were never friends, I don't remember either of them mentioning him before the day after his death. Apart from anything else, that whole statement was probably more than that idiot Morgan had ever muttered in his whole life… no lad, that was someone else's words, that was!"

"The press needing to beef out the story? They were faced with a couple of zoned out zombies as the only witnesses and monosyllabic grunts don't look good on the page?"

Alf grinned grimly, "Maybe. What I do know is that a few months afterwards they upped and opened a pub in Norfolk and no-one knew where on earth they managed to find that sort of money."

"You think they lied for someone and that person paid them to do it?"

Alf nodded in a non-committal way.

"So, you think it was murder?" I was trying not to get excited, the story about Pete going for a random swim and getting stuck in the mud had always sounded unlikely. It had become even less likely, since I had got to know him myself, and talked to the other people who had known him - but Alf echoed my thoughts.

"I don't know lad. Murder? If I remember rightly there wasn't a mark on him save for the natural lashing of the sea. How do you pick someone up and stick 'em in the mud without them putting up a fight?"

That was the point it always came back to whenever I thought about it. It was natural causes, a stupid mistake, a rash decision; but how did that equate with this latest information? Why did Morgan and Townsend lie and why would someone else want them to do so?

There was someone waiting at the bar, so nodding to Alf that I would be back, went and served a loud but lovely couple from Birmingham who I had met for the first time the weekend before. They were coming to the end of their week and wanted to tell me all about it. On any other day, I wouldn't have minded at all. I was just managing to pull myself away when another group came in, but it was all right, Alf wasn't going anywhere, and it gave me the chance to carefully form what I was going to say next, before returning to him.

"After I'd read the article about Peter, I tried to find out more about Richard and Robert on Google. The only reference I could find that might have fitted them were two people who were killed in a pub fire in Norfolk," I was pretty sure I knew the answer, but I was being particularly careful with Mr Tricky. "After what you've just said about them buying a pub, I guess that was them?"

Alf nodded, "Stupid stupid shits!"

"Well to be fair Alf, any pub can have a fire, it doesn't have to be down to negligence."

"No," Alf agreed, "this wasn't negligence, it was bloody arson!"

I was intrigued, but interrupted again by customers. I mean there I am, working in a bar and people actually want me to serve them? Ridiculous…

"Sorry Alf - you were saying?" I said, when I did manage to get back to him once again.

"It was a shit hole that place!" Alf seemed to have lost the thread somewhat, but I was hoping I could get him back on track eventually. "I mean, actually it was a nice pub when they took it over, but they didn't have a clue and after nine years, the only people that would go there were alcoholics and druggies. They were even known locally for doing a bit of dealing, if you know what I mean?"

"So, the place was struggling when they died?" I had a funny feeling I could guess where this was going.

"Closing more like," Alf said grimly. "The week before he died, Richie was down staying with us. Well you couldn't have had a more miserable house guest for the few days he was there. I mean, I know his business was failing, but you've got to try and look on the bright side, haven't you?"

The irony of the fact that this came from a man whose middle name was misery was not lost on me, but I merely nodded in agreement.

"Anyway, the last night he's with us, he says he's meeting some old school friends for a drink and did we want to go with him?" He took a sip from his drink before he continued. "Well to be honest, by that time even Pat had had enough of him and we stayed at home. The next morning, he seems so excited, completely different to how he'd been for the rest of his visit… I mean he was even talking in words that you could understand!"

I grinned and even Alf joined me on that one. His face quickly reverted to normal type as he came to the crux of his story. "He went back, and we thought we'd managed to cheer him up…"

Now that was a thought.

"… then a week afterwards we heard that he and t'other one had been killed in a fire. Pat took it hard, she was the eldest, he was the baby. She had always held out hope for him, even when the rest of us could see there was no hope to be had."

More bloody customers! Honestly what did they think this was?

I was back as quickly as I could, the clock was ticking round to seven o'clock. It always started to get busy then, with people coming in for a drink before they went into the restaurant for dinner. I was hoping I could get the final bit of information out of Alf before that happened.

Luckily, he went straight back to the point where we'd left it. "It was at the funeral and there was a lad there that Pat knew better than I did, he'd been a friend of Richie's since they were in kindergarten together. I think they'd drifted out of touch since Richie had become a pot head. The other lad was an electrician, had his own company, doing quite well. I'm sure he only went out with Richie when he was down for the sake of pity and old times."

"He was distraught, much more than you would have expected. He told Pat that he was so, so sorry - she was a bit confused to be honest. Then he told her. They'd been sitting drinking in a bar, think it might even have been in here actually. Richie was moaning on like he did about the state of his pub and the lad had said: "Do you need an electrician to sort you out a bit of faulty wiring?"

"Richie looked vacant apparently, well that was something he did quite well, so the other lad spelt it out for him. That's why he was in such a state at the funeral, he'd been joking, but the bloody useless shit had taken him seriously!"

"So, it was actually an electrical fault that caused the fire?"

"Actually lad it wasn't, probably didn't know an electrician that they could trust to do the job, or one that would even work for them by that time. No, they decided on an 'accidental' gas leak. Only trouble was when the fire investigators went in, they could still see traces of the rags that the idiots had used to block up all the ventilation in the kitchen, they could even tell that the hobs on the cooker had been turned on…"

"Not the cleverest bit of attempted insurance fraud then?" I ventured, and Alf nodded, "but why on earth didn't they get themselves away from the building?"

"Because they were stupid, stupid…"

"Shits?" I thought I was on safe ground there.

Alf nodded. "They found what was left of Ritchie's

body, just inside the kitchen, so they reckoned he misjudged the whole situation and turned the kitchen into a bloody bomb and then set it off. They don't really know if Robert was even in on the plan, he was found in his room upstairs, but the fire raged so quickly that he didn't have a chance to escape."

The seven o'clock rush was upon me, but there was just one more question that had been intriguing me in this whole sorry story. So, before I went to satisfy the thirst of the party of eight that had just started to amble through the door, I asked him, "Were they gay? Richard and Robert?"

Alf snorted, "Nah lad, I doubt it, they were so doped up that they probably couldn't find their weeners most of the time, let alone use them for sex."

"… stupid little shits…"

***

Due to our shift patterns, it was after I had handed the bar over to the night porter on Saturday night before I had the chance to talk to anyone about my chat with Alf. In the end it was Emily who heard the story first. Sam had worked three fourteen-hour shifts in a row, and had basically been merely a lump in the bed as far as I was concerned during that period.

"So, the two numpties, or at least one of them, came up with a plan to burn the place down and claim on the insurance, but got it all wrong and blew the both of them up, as well as the pub?" Emily had summed that part up pretty well, but it was the first part of Alf's story that really interested me.

"But how did they get the money to buy the pub in the first place?"

"So, you and Alf think they bribed someone with their silence?"

"Pretty much, but who would have that sort of money

and what was it that they wanted to keep secret that they were willing to pay for it?"

"Something about Pete's death then?"

I nodded, "Well there are bits about their statement in the press that don't add up, so why not that?"

"Who then? Who out of the people you've met would be rich enough?"

"Well the Edwards would have been, the father certainly and possibly Mo?"

"Because they found out that Max was gay and having an affair with Pete?"

I screwed up my face, "Pretty extreme even for the seventies I would have thought." Although thinking back to my latest dream, it might well have been plausible, certainly as far as the old man was concerned.

Emily nodded, and her face twisted into a grimace. "And how? Did one of them pick him up whilst the other one dug a hole? And how did they plonk him in it, without getting stuck themselves?"

And it always ended up back at that…

25.

S am eventually saw the light outside the hotel kitchen at three o'clock on the Sunday afternoon. By the time I had finished my shift an hour later he was snoring gently on the bed.

Fiona was in the apartment as I quietly left the room and went to the kitchen to pour myself a glass of water.

"Sleeping Beauty a little unresponsive?" she asked with a soft gleam of humour around her eyes.

"Yes," I agreed, "I thought I'd leave him to it, he's had a hell of a few days."

"That's the hotel trade for you," Fiona said, but not unsympathetically, then changing the subject, "looking forward to meeting up with Chloe?"

Sam hadn't wanted to tell his parents that we were going to Brighton to meet Max. For one thing it would have been quite a story to explain how we had found out about him in the first place. For the other, Sam was worried about telling his dad that we would be spending a night in the gay capital of England. I know, that friggin' closet again.

In the end we had decided to say that Chloe was going to be in London due to a work based meeting and we wanted to meet up with her for the night. Firstly though, we needed to Skype her and tell her this, and to do that I needed a boyfriend who wasn't in the middle of a sleepathon.

"When he does wake up, remind him that Uncle John

and Aunty Maureen are coming to dinner tonight," Fiona said. It was obvious I was being dismissed, so I took my water back to our room and propped myself against the head board. Then I listened to all the YouTube songs that Max had published, taking care not to disturb the comatose lump beside me.

They were good. "Tides" was becoming a bit of a favourite due to the subject matter and the connection I felt. However, I liked most of the stuff on there and I was really looking forward to hearing them in a live performance on Tuesday.

Nowhere could I find a video of him singing anything by Bennie Gold.

Sam eventually stirred at half past five, which meant it took an hour and a soothing shower before he was human. I can tell you that the afternoon Grinch was just as grumpy and immobile as the morning one.

We did have time to Skype Chloe and warn her of our deception and her part in it. We told her a potted version of our mystery, but there was more than enough information to get her legal juices flowing.

"I'll see if I can find any more information about The Planner for you, and Rem…?"

Yes, believe me, I knew.

She then told us her news. She had been mentoring the guy who was to be on the graduate scheme for her company at our university next year, and they seemingly had developed a very close relationship.

"We actually went on a proper date thingy last night!" she exclaimed. She was as excited as I had been early in the new year.

"And…?"

"And, it went very well." The gleam in her eye, visible even over Skype, gave the truth to exactly how well it had gone.

"I don't think that's what the company meant when they asked you to mentor him," Sam chided, but he was obviously chuffed for her.

Chloe flicked a finger in his general direction.

The clock was ticking around to dinner time, so reluctantly we said our goodbyes, clicked on the red icon and she was gone. Leaving me with so much stuff that I had wanted to tell her but was unable to.

I wanted to tell her that I had been unable to charm Sam's parents in the way she had.

I wanted to tell her that Sam seemed to be retreating deeper and deeper into the closet every day that he was in Weston.

I wanted to tell her that I really didn't like Sam's dad.

I wanted to tell her all those things. It was the first time since I had known Sam, that I wished he hadn't been in the room, just so that I could do so.

✱✱✱

The gathering in the Brean room that night was the same as two weeks before. We even sat, in a gloriously English institutionalised manner, in the same seats. But the atmosphere was different and that was entirely due to the man at the head of the table. He was in a definite long term bad mood about something. By the way he alternated looking between Sam and myself, I had a horrible idea that I knew what that something was.

Fiona did her best at being the gentrified English hostess, but she seemed to be as aware of her husband's mood as I was. I noticed her shooting encouraging glances in his direction from time to time, but she was having as much success as a sheep farmer in the Antarctic.

Maureen chattered happily about Rory and his partner Libby, the expectant mum, but she was getting as much support from her husband as Fiona was getting from hers.

I felt there was an argument just one misplaced word or phrase away. In the end, it came as a result of Maureen trying desperately to encourage her husband to join the conversation.

She was talking to me about Pete's death and I was desperately trying to work through the story, deciding what I could safely tell them and what it was best to leave out. I was tempted however, to tell them the whole story, dreams and all. After all I wasn't doing a very good job at charming Sam's dad, so what did it matter if he thought me a teaspoon short of a full set of cutlery?

"I know Fee thought that John worked here at that time," she nodded to her sister, "but you said it was earlier didn't you dear?"

John grunted in a non-committal way, but he didn't seem comfortable with the conversation. However, Maureen ploughed on heroically.

"He was a Saturday boy when he was about fourteen, the eldest Edwards boy was still at school and the younger one was mainly looked after by nannies…"

"For Christ's sake!" Ned butted in with quick anger. "Do we have to go on about a forty-year-old death, just because someone in this room happens to have the same name as the poor bloke that died? Can we not talk about something else?"

Jack had been clearing the starter plates and decided to speed it up a little and disappeared quicker than Alf's good humour when faced with a lollipop man. I thought he managed to do it with professionalism and grace, it seemed that his boss didn't agree with me.

"What about him for a start?" he said, gesturing to the closing door, "he's as useless as a colander in a rain storm!"

It was strange that within two weeks I had gone from willing Jack to make an idiot of himself, to defending him in front of his bosses. However, I had really started to like the young old queen and wasn't going sit back and listen to him receiving unwarranted criticism.

Probably not my best move in the circumstances.

"I don't agree Ned," glancing to check that I could call

him by his Christian name whilst off duty at least. His face gave me no clue, so I lumbered on regardless. "Jack's a brilliant barman from what I've seen, great with the customers, honest as you like as well. He was given twenty quid from that lovely Brummie couple yesterday. They told him to put it directly in his pocket, but he wouldn't do it. Once they had gone, it went straight into the pot."

Ned looked at me with something bordering on dislike and said, "And you have exactly how much experience in the trade?"

Fiona was staring at her husband, trying to will him into silence, Maureen and Emily were looking at their place settings whilst John was trying to look like he wasn't in the room. It was something he did with ease.

It was Sam that spoke next and the look on his face was the one that I had only seen once in all the time I had known him. It was exactly the same way he had looked on that Saturday morning, way back in December.

"If I say something Dad," he enquired, his tone quiet, careful and deadly. "Will I be hauled over the coals afterwards, for talking to you inappropriately in front of guests?"

The voice of the father mirrored that of the son, cold, quiet, calculated yet with the threat of anger being triggered by one more disputed word. "Say it anyway Samuel, I'd hate to think I was unable to take criticism from my own son." The words might have been mild, but the sarcasm within them was not.

"OK then," Sam paused, then launched… "What is the matter with you at the moment? First Mark and his entire kitchen management is not good enough, now Jack, and I must say I agree with Rem, he's brilliant. OK, he uses forty words when five will do, but the guests love him, he gets on well with the other staff and he works hard. As a boss, what's not to like? What is wrong with you?"

I was pretty convinced I knew the answer to that one, but I sure as hell wasn't going to use that moment to out

Sam in front of his whole family.

Emily though, had remembered something else I'd said the weekend before. She decided to share it with the group in support of her brother.

"Rem thinks it's because you've realised that Sam could run the hotel without you and you're feeling surplus to requirements, but Sam said…"

Perhaps it might have been better if Emily had reworded the sentence because she wasn't able to get to the point where Sam had refuted my argument and stuck up for his father. It also might have been better if she hadn't said any sentence at all that started with my name.

"Conrad Hilton himself thinks that does he?" he snarled with complete disdain. "Well in that case I'd better just sign the whole fucking place over to Sam here and be done with it - what do you reckon John?" He turned to his brother in law, "good business practice, or what?"

Poor John looked like a chicken in a foxhole, but took the question at face value. "Well legally speaking, there would be advantages in that…"

Maureen desperately tried to save the situation with gentle humour: "Good old John, always the solicitor!"

I think Jack must have been outside the door with that glass to the wall again, as the overdue main course was nowhere close to making an entrance.

Ned ignored his sister-in-law's attempts to bring peace to the gathering and said, his whole face twitching with anger: "Well in that case, whilst it still is my hotel, I think I can choose who to eat my dinner with." He stood up and turned back to face us. "And tonight, I would definitely like to eat alone!"

Fiona with her best Lady Mary face on, said clearly and with great command: "We are going to eat as a family Ned," he paused in the middle of his big storming out gesture and Fiona gently said, "please," and nodded at his chair. He sat down with slightly better grace and Fiona continued, "Sam, Emily, you will both apologise to your father."

They did so, but I was slightly appalled. Once again, I felt that their mother could have supported her children a little better. I thought that Ned had been the one that had completely over reacted and behaved like a spoilt child, whereas Sam especially had done nothing to apologise for. He'd even asked for permission to open his mouth in the first place.

Jack had definitely been waiting outside. Just enough time lapsed once the conversation had resumed with forced nonentities, for him to go to the kitchen and order up the full roast pork dinner with all the trimmings and return to the Brean room with it. To me that just proved how right Sam was in saying that Jack was good at his job. He even remembered the old catering adage: "Never try and serve food to people who are having an almighty bust up…"

It unsettled Sam though. He was quiet for the rest of the meal and as soon as he could afterwards, slipped upstairs to his room. I stayed with the family long enough for it not to look too obvious and followed him up.

He was sitting on his bed when I entered the room, still fully clothed and the look on his face made me want to hold him until I'd squashed the hurt from his body.

"Rem, what is the matter with him?" he pleaded.

This was not the time to tell him, so I simply held him until the necessary tears fell from his eyes and the sobs jittered his body against my own. The last time I had heard him crying like that, there had been a set of floorboards and a world of misunderstanding between us. At least this time there was barely a crack between our bodies and only two Hollister button down shirts separated him from me.

Later, as we turned off the light I knew that - spurred on by awkwardness - I had forgotten to be careful with the amount of wine that I'd consumed over dinner. Despite all my best intentions, I had once again drunk far too much to give myself a dreamless night.

26.

1977

On August 8th the whole of Weston celebrated the Queen's silver jubilee as the Monarch herself made an appearance in the town. Pete, Max, Jackie, Helen and Christine walked along the beach lawns where people had been waiting since dawn to get a good vantage point. As they looked for the nearest raised bit of lawn for them to get a good view over the heads in front of them, they heard Tony call, "Wait up!"

"My God! If it isn't Comrade Brezhnev himself! Why are you tainting your pure socialist soul with such flag waving propaganda?" Pete taunted.

"Well, it would be quite nice to see them in the flesh, before I make sure they are history," Tony laughed brazen faced.

"Hypocrite!" Pete said good naturedly, whilst the girls and Max set about beating Tony with plastic Union Flags on sticks. In the end, no-one really saw the Royal Party in the flesh. However, if the Queen had looked out of the window of her Bentley and through the crowds of the early birds, she would have seen six rather excited youths. They were jumping up and down at the back of the crowd waving macerated flags in her general direction.

The rest of the week followed the fairly well-set pattern where Max and Pete grabbed every moment they possibly could together. They went to the cinema to see the film version of "Are You Being Served?" and as they had when they'd watched James Bond, used the darkness like a rug to cover the fact that they held hands all the way through the film. The slight risk of it reminded Pete of an occasion, behind the bike sheds, when a borrowed cigarette morphed into a stolen kiss with a prefect, two years his senior.

They revisited their church on the hill and Max took his guitar along. Pete had convinced him that some of the Jam songs could sound just as good acoustically and he had added "Away From the Numbers" and "All Around the World" to his rapidly expanding playlist of three songs.

As Max sat, leaning against the wall, playing his entire repertoire twice, Pete was more than happy just to watch him. He loved the way his cornflower blue eyes seemed to mirror the lyrics that tumbled from his lips, the odd twitch across his cheek, or furrow that crossed his brow as he concentrated on picking out the correct chords. Pete joined in when "If Forever Ends With You" was played. Other than that, he was just happy being a one-man audience.

They managed two visits to their quarry during that week and even though one of the visits was in dank and drizzly weather, the warm summer rain falling on their naked skin failed to ruin the experience. Far from it in fact, the act of caressing the slick water across Max's skin, turned the whole episode into something that men in macs would pay good money to watch in the back of a side street cinema.

On the second occasion, whilst they were wheeling their bikes back on to the main path, they bumped into Starsky and Hutch as they walked towards the hill that would take them up to the old windmill.

"Hey watch out!" Hutch snapped as one of Pete's wheels threatened to leave a tattoo of dust and rubber on his leg. He then did a double take, "Well if it isn't Larry Grayson and his mate!" He flicked a limp wrist in their direction, "What a gay day!"

"Oh, for goodness sake Hutch!" Starsky seemed genuinely embarrassed, but Hutch was not going to drop the subject easily.

"Petey what have you been up to?" he enquired, peering into the gap that was being rapidly closed as Max let the last branch go. "Or should I say, what have you been up?" Well at least Hutch thinks he's hilarious, thought Pete, even if no-one else does.

He then questioned himself. Tony had said something similar a few weeks before and Pete had laughed... Hutch said it and he was irritated. Was he being harsh on the idiot, just because he didn't like him?

Starsky managed to pull his friend away and waving a slightly awkward goodbye, continued his walk with his mismatched mate beside him.

It was an encounter that Pete would remember later that summer.

The following Tuesday evening a large crowd of them made their way towards the dunes. They had a crate of beer that Mo had given them, and a few bottles of wine that they had all chipped in to buy at the local Liptons. Pete was pretty sure that Hutch had added a few more from the stock at the hotel, but he wasn't going to challenge him. He'd decided that the least contact he had with the bloke, the better he liked it.

Max had brought along his radio and they tuned it into the Radio Luxembourg chart show, as it was the only station playing pop music at that time of night. Tuning it in was quite a delicate task and once they had the aerial pointing in the right direction for a crackle free reception, they pounded the radio into the sand to hold it in place.

"Save me! Here we are in the middle of the punk revolution and what do we have in the top ten?" Tony moaned, "Showaddywaddy, Boney M and the Brotherhood of Man! So much for flippin' progress."

Mark Wesley, the DJ fronting the chart show, told everyone there was an important story that would be revealed in the news at the top of the hour.

"Bound to be the announcement that Ron Greenwood has got the England Manager's job," Smiler guessed, but Helen was not impressed.

"For goodness sake, how on earth could that be thought of as important!"

"It's the beautiful game Helen, of course it's important," said Tony. They were lying together on a rug in the deep sand just under one of the dunes, taking swigs from the same bottle of wine, wrapped around each other for warmth.

In the end, it wasn't anything about football, it was to break the news that Elvis Presley had died.

There was a murmur of surprise around the group and Pete felt a quiet twinge of excitement. It was the first time that a celebrity death had affected him. He vaguely remembered hovering around his mother's radiogram, listening to the funeral of Winston Churchill, without fully understanding what was occurring. He remembered the public outcry when Valerie Barlow was electrocuted by a hair dryer on Coronation Street, but this was different. This was someone that he'd grown up listening to and although he didn't consider himself a massive fan, that didn't seem to bother anyone else in the coming weeks. The number of people who'd been Elvis fans all their lives seemed to consist largely of people that had never mentioned the man in public before.

Tony Prince took over the airwaves for a tribute show, audibly moved. The show started with "Heartbreak Hotel" and broadcast deep into the night. Radio Luxembourg agreed to drop all the adverts from the show, which the DJ explained cost the broadcaster ten thousand pounds in lost revenue. It might have been a little mawkish but the group on a beach, an ocean away from Gracelands, were spellbound.

Pete looked around him. Max was sitting close, but they tended not to touch each other in public, they were still trying to work out the best way they could broach the subject to Max's father.

"I'm not going back to uni, I want to move in with you, get a job, maybe play the guitar at a few pubs in the evening to earn some more money." Max had been developing this fantasy over the last few weeks, and tonight he seemed more certain than ever that he wanted to make it happen.

Pete thought that he probably needed more than a three-song repertoire if that was going to bolster up his funds in any significant way.

"I Just Can't Help Believing," was being played on the radio for the second time already.

"I will talk to Mum and Dad about it," he agreed, "but I could also look to transfer my OND to Exeter and move in with you, if you'll have me?"

Max smiled in contentment. Pete knew that in all probability, neither of these things would happen, but he just loved talking about it with Max. The fact that they were discussing a future together made it feel more like a reality, even if in truth they would have to wait until time and training had run its course before they could make it so.

"What about your father?" Pete asked, "Do you really think it wise to tell him about us? He's just not going to understand, is he?"

Max grunted, but refused to be downhearted. "I'll wait until I've had a chance to talk it over with Mo and then I'll broach it with the man himself. I think it might be better if Mo is there as well, so that he can scrape parts of my body from the walls if it all turns to shit!"

Pete used the cover of their bodies to grab his boyfriend's hand in solidarity and stared at the party of people around him. Hutch was sitting with his arm around Jackie's shoulder, but Starsky was also there, so Pete reckoned that she was safe for now. Tony and Helen were involved in a spot of heavy petting and just as he was taking this in, he was suddenly aware that in the far distance, Dee and Dum were slouching down the beach. However, tonight they were not alone.

"Tony!" Pete whispered urgently, and his friend reluctantly pulled himself away from Helen who said slightly irritably, "Christ Pete! Can't it wait?"

Pete nodded his head in the general direction from where the danger was invading, and step by step was getting nearer.

Marlon Malcolm, larger than life and flanked by his two flunkies, was approaching.

By the time he arrived, the four friends were sitting around on the blanket chatting about any nonsense that came into their heads.

"Evening all!" Marlon might have been impersonating Dixon of Dock Green, but he had only ever seen the inside of a police station from the wrong viewpoint. There were a few mumbles of greeting but nothing that could have been described as welcoming. Unabashed, the drug dealer carried on regardless.

"What about my main man, the King?" he spoke with an American drawl, although the nearest he had come to visiting the country was a Kentucky Fried Chicken shop in the Locking Road. "I heard he choked on a hamburger… he just couldn't get it 'Way Down' far enough, uh huh uh huh uh huh."

No one laughed except for an embarrassed snigger from Dee and Dum. Marlon thrived on sycophancy, so he wasn't a happy man.

"OK Coon!" he glanced at Tony who stared at him, refusing to be outfaced.

"Pusher," he nodded, hanging on to politeness by the very tips of his finger nails.

"Now, there's no need to be offensive." Marlon pretended to be hurt.

"No Malcolm," said Pete, "he was accurate, you were offensive."

278

Marlon sneered, "Oh bum boy, you should be very careful of your pretty mouth, it could get you into serious trouble!"

Max might have chattered on at length to Pete in private, but he very rarely spoke in public. Tonight, as at that first picnic on the hill, when he spoke, it was worth hearing.

"I'm sorry Marlon, but it might be possible that it's you that could be in trouble." As usual Max's tone was soft, clear and polite.

"Oh Hallelujah! He speaks!" Marlon sniggered, "So bum boy's pretty friend, how do you work that one out?"

"Well you're trespassing really," Max said as gently as before. "My family own this area of the beach and it would be awful if we had to get security to escort you away - or maybe even the police."

Max was well aware that there were possessions on his body that Marlon Malcolm would not welcome being investigated too thoroughly.

He sniffed aggressively, "That won't be necessary." He grabbed Helen as if she was one of his possessions and kissed her deeply and hard. Pete saw her flinch slightly then relax into his violent embrace. Pete could also feel the tension in his friend, but was pleased to see Tony didn't react any more than that. The drug dealer stopped the kiss as abruptly as he had started it, ran his hand down the side of Helen's body as if to remind her of what would happen when they were alone, then retreated along the beach.

He clicked his fingers at his compatriots who trotted after him like two shabby mongrels behind a butcher's bike. He disappeared into another of the dunes that lined this area of the beach and although he thought he had hidden himself from view, Pete could see the wad of ten-pound notes that he peeled from his pocket and gave to the two lads.

Pete actually quite liked Dee and Dum, they were inoffensive, and their only crime was that they were both a bit thick and had got involved in a lifestyle they couldn't handle or afford. "What are they getting themselves into now?" Pete thought, but he had a horrible feeling that he knew the answer.

The drug dealer marched away, and Dee and Dum stayed where they were in the dune, transporting themselves further and further into a place from where a return journey would be tricky.

When Malcolm Marlon was far enough away, Tony laughed and clapped Max on the back. "Maxi my boy, I didn't know that your family owned this bit of the beach!"

Max grinned sheepishly: "To be honest, I haven't got a clue whether they do or not, but it got rid of him, didn't it?"

My God, I love you Max Edwards, thought Pete.

Eventually, everybody else left the beach and it was only Pete and Max who remained as the Radio Luxembourg Elvis tribute continued until just before four in the morning. The two lovers snuggled together. Pete felt Max's breath warm against his cheek. The body against his body was the most natural fit and as comfortable as family.

Tony Prince played "I Just Can't Help Believing," one last time as the night that Elvis Presley died slipped seamlessly towards the dawn.

27.

Sam was still affected by the family squabble when he woke up the next morning. This was obvious because I could hear the water bouncing off the shower room floor as I drifted slowly from the dunes on the beach below, to the bed in Sam's room. Metres away in distance but decades away in time.

It was seven o'clock in the morning and Sam was up.

I was very worried.

As he reappeared from the shower, he was patting his hair, drying it back from damp brown to natural blonde. He was completely easy about being nude in front of me and these days it didn't even occur to him to hide any part of his nakedness from me.

I think you could call that a bonus.

However, there was a definite sorrow around his eyes. "I need to get out of this place," he said, "I also need a really long walk, fancy the Strawberry Line?"

I had no idea what he was talking about. It could have been a completely obscure drug taking ritual that involved soft fruit for all I knew, but he wanted my company, so for me it was a no brainer.

We took the train line that was becoming as familiar to me as a dry mouth in the morning. In Sam's haste to leave the Hotel without seeing any members of his family we had caught the train in the middle of the morning rush. This meant that we had to stand along with a load of strap hanging commuters, some of whom had neglected to leave time for a shower before they left their houses. All in all, it was a relief when the train trundled its way into Yatton station and we could leave them to it.

The Strawberry Line, far from being anything dodgy, had in fact been a railway line that had transported the fresh strawberries from Cheddar over to the main line station at Yatton, from where it had been sent to the fruit markets in London. It had been closed in the cuts made by Dr Beaching in 1963 and since then had been turned into a ten mile walk through wetlands, orchards and ancient settlements.

Before anything else, Sam and I needed breakfast, he had been so desperate to leave his home that we had rushed out without so much as a sniff of a muesli box. We found a café that satisfied that in a fantastic all English, totally unhealthy but absolutely necessary type of way. I vaguely mentioned my dream, but Sam just looked at me bleakly and changed the subject. I got the message, this was a day when dreams were outlawed, talk of family was restricted and any mention of the hotel was subject to an all-out ban.

I certainly did not tell him about Pete and Max cuddling in a sand dune, exactly as we had done after our drunken pub crawl on my first Wednesday in Weston.

I didn't really want to think about it myself.

We ended up having a fantastic day. Sam had obviously decided that he needed fresh air and physical exercise to challenge his demons and it worked well for me too. We power walked our way to Axbridge and had lunch in a market square pub, before reaching Cheddar. We walked around the reservoir and then decided to walk back to Yatton, rather than cheating and getting a bus back to Weston.

We stopped off at the Railway in Sandford for a pint, but Sam wasn't in the mood for drinking too much and I was glad. I had a feeling that the last part of the story was probably but a dream or two away and I desperately needed to talk to Max before I got to that point.

As we arrived back in Yatton after twenty miles of hard walking, I must admit to being impressed by his stamina. Fifty hours of work, in four days, followed by a walk of that length is no mean feat. To be honest, I was so exhausted that I felt like I had taken a pedalo across the Atlantic.

I thought of Jackie as we ordered supper in the Railway Inn. I wondered if she had got in touch with Tony and whether anything would happen between them. We had exchanged friendly emails and I thought we would definitely keep in touch.

Even saying to myself "if I get through this," seemed ridiculously melodramatic, but I was becoming increasingly worried by the similarities between my relationship with Sam and our friends of forty years before. Even the way that Pete had stared at Max, as he played guitar at the roofless church, reminded me of my silent stalking of Sam on our first train journey down to Weston. There was that awful parallel between the two fathers in the stories as well. Both had a revelation to hear, how they reacted to it seemed to me to be the key to the whole mess.

We took a late train back to Weston and sneaked back into the hotel. Thankfully, Emily was alone in the apartment and we had a quick chat to her before we took our aching limbs to bed.

"Devil Dad is still in residence!" she exclaimed as Sam poured two glasses of water to take into our room. "He made Mrs H re-iron all the towels for the rooms on the first floor today and, honestly Sam, there was nothing wrong with them!"

As with me, Sam refused to be drawn into a conversation about it and merely kissed his sister affectionately and I followed him down the corridor to his room where we closed the door on the world.

He took me in his arms, "Thank you for today," he said, and I smiled.

"That's what I'm here for."

He seemed completely different to the man who had left the room that morning and although we barely had the energy for a kiss, we fell straight asleep, cuddling each other with such a feeling of togetherness that I believed that everything would be all right.

I hadn't really taken my first waking breath of the morning. I hadn't by then realised that my muscles were complaining about the long walk of the day before. I certainly hadn't got to the point of cajoling Rip Van Winkle into a spot of early morning loving, when that belief was shattered.

The events of that Tuesday morning were set into motion by the manner of my waking.

It started badly and went downhill from that point on...

28.

I was aware of two things. Fiona was knocking on the door and calling out Sam's name. The man himself was desperately trying to evict me from the bed by brute force.

In the face of my resistant "Oi!" he whispered in mild panic, "Get to your bed!"

I stopped myself from saying that I wasn't a dog who had just urinated over the soft furnishings, and moved with silent bad grace to my allotted space in the room.

I settled myself inside the cold duvet cover, unused for the last fortnight, save for the odd piece of ruffling up for the sake of misinformation.

Fiona entered the room carrying just the one mug of tea that she handed to Sam. Either I really was persona non-grata, or I was to be allowed to carry on snoozing once Sam had received his orders for the day.

"Hi Mum!" Sam said blearily, but I noticed in my huffy state that it was a brighter greeting than he had given me a few mornings earlier when I had woken him up suddenly. In my belligerence, I failed to consider the fact that his mum wasn't waving her naked arse towards his face…

"Oh Sam, sorry to do this to you, but Alison has caught this stomach bug and your dad wants you to cover reception today."

Sam groaned, as did I inwardly. "But Mum, Rem and I were going to Br… see Chloe today," he recovered the lie just in time and his mum crunched up her face in sympathy.

"I know love, but we only need cover until six, so we thought that you could take the train straight up to London. You'd still have time to meet Chloe for a late supper." Yes, enough time for that, but there wouldn't be enough time to take a four-and-a-half-hour train trip to Brighton in order to see Max performing in concert.

I was disappointed and angry, I was also completely pissed off with Sam who meekly shrugged his shoulders, took a sip from his mug of tea and said without rancour, "OK." I mean he could at least have had a hissy fit to show me that he was bothered by this turn of events, couldn't he?

His mother retreated to tell her husband that their plan had worked… OK maybe Alison was puking into a bucket somewhere, so that might be a little bit unfair, but reasoned acceptance wasn't high on my list just at that moment.

As soon as I felt she was far enough away, I went on the attack: "Brilliant!" I hissed, "so that's our plans completely ruined! Thank you, Ned and Fiona!"

Sam whispered quietly but with equal force, "Oh grow up Rem! These things happen… You can go on your own, you don't really need me there do you?"

"But it was to be our first night in Brighton, in a gay hotel, together." Oh yes, I actually did whine and I'm not particularly proud of it.

Sam threw his eyes up to the architrave and muttered unintelligible words to the ceiling. He went to take a shower and by the time he returned we were both entrenched in silent hostilities. It was the first time since I'd arrived that I'd seen him in a suit and hadn't wanted to rip it from his body and make mad passionate love to him. Yes, I really was in a mood.

I contented myself by lying on my bed, and to make a symbolic gesture, even if it was to an empty room, I stayed on the camp bed in the corner, rather than crawling back into the bed I had been sharing with Sam. I snatched out my phone and head phones and scrolled through my playlist to find something suitable. I didn't have to go far and within seconds I was silently yelling along to Anthrax, the only music that fitted my mood.

Eventually I dragged myself out of bed, showered and made my way to the kitchen. I still hadn't decided whether I was going to go to Brighton alone or not. I really wanted to meet up with Max, but I also didn't want to go on my own. I also wanted Sam to know that he had ruined my whole day with his pathetic capitulation.

Emily bounced in, she obviously had been busy cleaning her allotted rooms upstairs and had been nowhere near the reception area as she was very surprised to see me.

"Bloody hell Rem! Is he still not up?" She looked warily behind her in case there was a parent lurking before she whispered, "I thought you'd be on your way to Brighton by now!"

I explained the situation and she exclaimed: "That bloody man!" However, I could tell that she was meaning the father not the son. "I swear he gets crankier and crankier - he probably gave Alison a dodgy prawn just so he could assert his authority and stop you two going away!"

It is always nice when you are in a bad mood to hear views from someone that are slightly more barking than your own, so even I had to grin at that one.

"Thanks Em!" I smiled and gave her a hug, she squeezed me back and then quickly pulled away.

"But Cinders!" she said, "you shall go to Brighton! Just give me the chance to have a quick flash of my wand and change this delightful tunic into my professional woman in reception two piece and I will release Rapunzel from the penury of customer care!" OK she was completely morphing fairy stories here, but I didn't care. I could have snogged the face off of her.

Sam grinned at me in a placatory manner when he re-appeared in the apartment twenty minutes later. "Good old Em!" he said, "she told Dad that they were all going away for her Leavers Weekend at school, so the least they could do was to make sure I had a proper few days off beforehand. I'm not sure he particularly liked it," he saddened slightly at the thought, "but she didn't even give him a chance to argue with her logic! I've looked it up and the next train we can catch will get us there just after six."

I should have let it go, I should have cheered up and realised we were going to get the couple of days away together. However, I was still irritated by his mild-mannered acceptance of everything his parents threw in his direction. I was still, basically, in a strop and by the time we had packed our rucksacks and made our way to the station, Sam was in one too.

"Will you fucking cheer up?" he hissed as we boarded the train, bringing him a disapproving look from a woman who had cloned her style towards Theresa May, complete with the quirky shoes.

"When will you admit to yourself that your father knows about us?" I said angrily but quietly and without any blasphemous language that might upset Theresa any further.

Sam looked around instinctively and I blew out a breath of irritation. "Yes, that's right! Just check there is no-one around that you know, no-one who will hot foot it back to Ma and Pa and tell them that dear old Golden Boy is a confirmed poofter!"

Sam gave me the look, and said angrily yet firmly, allowing no room for response. "We are not going to discuss this here, understood?"

I did, but I couldn't resist one further dig, and Theresa, I'm very sorry for the language…

"Oh, fuck off then, make sure you close the closet door behind you!"

I retreated to Anthrax and Sam, who favoured Grime

when he was in a bad mood, put a selection on repeat and rammed in his earphones with a force that threatened at least a couple of brain cells.

Thus, passed the journey to Brighton. On a trip when I should have felt excitement and anticipation, I felt merely irritable with Sam and his family. Only Emily was spared from any acerbic thoughts that flooded my head.

We didn't even have a beer in our favourite buffet bar in Bristol.

We reached the Legends Hotel on Marine Parade and checked in. Ironically, with a nod of the head to my latest dream, the legend whose coloured canvas decorated our room, was Elvis Presley.

I didn't even get the chance to mention this to Sam. He shut the door and threw his rucksack on the bed and turning to me, said: "OK, let's get it over with. Let's have the fucking argument that you are so desperate to have!"

29.

I looked at him, feigning innocence and he spluttered, "Oh for goodness sake Rem! You've been itching for this fight all day. Let's sort it out now, whilst we're in private, and maybe - just maybe - we might actually be able to enjoy the rest of the time we are here!"

He had a point and I had been winding myself up all day, so I didn't need much encouragement.

"OK, if I must!" I took a deep breath. "Like I tried to say on the train. Why don't you just bloody admit to yourself that your father has guessed about us, maybe Em did let something slip, in which case you might as well tell him that you are gay. I mean you let him just walk all over you!"

"Oh I do, do I?" Sam said with a heavy sneer in his voice. "So that's why I've been in trouble for sticking up for Mark, then sticking up for Jack… and you, for that matter. But that's not good enough I guess, I'm still accused of being his pathetic little puppet!"

"But that's just it," I said, frustration leaking from every word. "You stick up for everybody else, but when it comes to yourself, it's yes Dad, no Dad, three bloody bags full Dad!"

"I'm sure it's difficult for you to understand Rem," and yes, the patronising manner did not help my mood at all. "But, that's the way it is in the Hotel trade, the customers won't come back next week, just because I wanted to go to Brighton today. If reception needs manning, then of course I'm going to help, if I'm around."

"It's not just about the work," I argued, "it's the whole way he talks to you as if you are an imbecile and to be frank, your mother is no bloody help. She doesn't support you, she even made you apologise to him, when he was so far in the wrong it was ridiculous!"

"Right!" Sam exploded, "So my father is a bully, my mother is pathetic, and my sister can't keep her mouth shut and has accidentally outed me to my parents." He paused and when he resumed there was ice in his voice. "It's very nice to know what a wonderful opinion you have of my family Rem!"

The sub-zero temperature of his tone quietened me then, but Sam had a lot more that he wanted to say.

"OK, so you've said your bit, it's my turn now. How the hell do you think it's been for me, knowing that you've fallen in love with someone else?"

Whoa! That was a thunderbolt from a clear blue sky if ever there was one.

"What do you mean?" I said quietly, temper trampled by confusion.

"Bloody Perfect Pete, that's what I mean," he said bitterly. "Ever since you've been aware of him in your dreams, you can't stop talking about him. It's like he's some sort of saint. I mean, you're even trying to work out ways to save his life! We're only here to see Max so you can find out if there's a chance that you can do just that. How on earth can I compete with a dead man who can do no wrong?"

I took a deep breath and tried to answer that one... I'd had A-level sociology questions that had been easier, I can tell you.

"Oh Sam, I guess I do love him in a way. I certainly feel a connection with him. I would like to believe that I could save him and let him have the life he so deserved, but even I can see that that is slightly on the cranky side of mad." I tried a lop-sided disparaging grin before getting to the nitty gritty of what I had to say. "But please don't think that I love you less because of him. You are so dear to me and so real, he is more like a character in a film that I have developed an affinity with. You know, the person you are desperately hoping will survive the bloodbath, even if you know that everything points to the fact that he won't."

He looked at me quizzically and seeing the truth in my face, visibly relaxed. He then opened up more than he had in the whole of our time together.

"Deep down inside me, I know you're right," he said. "I think that Dad has guessed about us. The whole thought scares me."

I made some sort of comforting noise and he continued.

"Do you know what really worries me?" It was purely rhetorical, and I had no need to answer. "It's the thought that if it's out in the open, he will send you away and we will have to spend the summer apart - the thought of that kills me."

I held his hand comfortingly, all anger done.

"Then, what if he never accepts it? I'm going to have to choose between him and you. I know you think little of him, but until the last fortnight, until he discovered this truth about me, we were so close. He was my absolute hero, in a solid, curmudgeonly but completely loving way. But I can tell you something Rem, if I had to make a choice, there would be no contest," he looked at me, beads of water pulling at his eyelids as he said softly and earnestly. "You are my life and I love every cranky breath of you."

I think it safe to say that I wasn't in a grump with him anymore.

He then paused, thinking about the wisdom of saying what he needed to say next. I gave him an encouraging nod and he continued.

"But do you know what terrifies me even more than having to choose between you and my family?" he said, I shook my head lightly.

"You are right, the whole of this dream scenario is totally mad. I don't believe you can save him, but I do believe you are dreaming this whole thing for a reason."

I looked at him, willing him not to saying it, yet at the same time, I believed it also.

"I think it could be a premonition Rem, the whole thing smacks of it. You sharing the same name, the similarities with our backgrounds, the same kind of connection between Max and Pete that we have. Rem, I'm just terrified that these dreams are warning you about your death…"

As you know, this idea had already occurred to me, but the knowledge that Sam had also thought of it, made it seem more real and totally explained his up and down moods of the last week. I had managed to convince myself as I now tried to convince Sam, that if it had been a premonition then surely, I'd be dreaming of my own death. I wouldn't be dreaming about the death of a man with my name, who had existed, and who had actually died forty years before.

We then proved the adage that there are few things better than making love after an argument. Later, as we walked through the summer streets to find food before going to the Kruz Bar, we were spurred on by other same sex couples doing likewise, to hold hands in the street.

Two hours in Brighton, we'd had a blazing row, made love and were now holding hands in public.

I felt properly gay.

***

I recognised Max as soon as we walked into Kruz. OK he was standing by an amp with a guitar in his hand, so I didn't have to be a member of Mensa to work it out, but the forty years since the seventies had been kind to him physically.

He still had light mousey brown hair, which apart from a vague threat of grey above the ear lobes, was unchanged in colour, although the cut was shorter, smarter and more like a bank manager than a rock star.

He was also still slim, the years had added muscle rather than fat and he was undoubtedly, a very attractive man.

He was busily setting up the equipment ready for his set and was talking to a man with rainbow dyed hair. It was teased into a pony tail, combined with a beard and moustache combo, in the style of Billy Connolly. I thought at the time he might have been a roadie, but found out later he was in fact Mr Kruz. Sam found a table second row back and I went off to the bar to buy some drinks. If I was right, the dreams didn't happen away from Sam's room so in theory I had a free pass to get as drunk as I liked. In practice though, I wanted to keep a clearish head for whatever tales that Max had to tell us.

He was good, there was no doubt about that. I think the word that best described his set was eclectic. He wove his original material around songs from every decade from the 1970s onwards. He did a decent stripped-down version of Clean Bandit's "Lullabye" and a cover of Dizzee Rascal's "Bonkers" that really shouldn't have worked from a white man nearing his sixties, but did so brilliantly.

He must have spotted us during the first half of his performance, the place was packed, but we were slightly younger than the general clientele, so that probably gave him a decent clue. As soon as he had soaked in the generous applause, he placed his guitar on its stand and walked over to meet us. We shook hands and told him how much we were enjoying it, he asked us about our journey, the hotel etc etc. So far, so normal.

He gave us a potted history of his career in the hotel trade. Then Max told us that he had retired early and played in bars and clubs for a little bit of beer money and also to give him something to do. My dad has always said that when people say things like that, it normally means that they've had a very impressive career, but didn't want to brag about it. I got every impression that it could well be true of Max.

It was probably that I had got so good at knowing what to mention and what to omit that I'd become a bit cocky when it came to the details of my story. It might have been because I hadn't been able to find his version of the song on YouTube which had left it at the forefront of my thoughts. Whatever the reason, he was just preparing to go back for the second half of his act when I asked him:

"Do you ever sing 'If Forever Ends With You' these days?"

Such a simple question but if I had told him the colour of the Queen's bedspread, his look would have said the same thing.

How the hell did you know about that?

30.

As soon as I said it, I realised what I had done. I could feel Sam's eyes boring into me and Max himself gave me another strange look before answering the call that Mr Kruz had mercifully given him.

"Oh shit!" I said to Sam as we sat back down, "what on earth do I say now?"

"Just tell him the truth," Sam said simply, "he looks like he can take it."

Even so, I fretted about it for the first couple of songs in the second half of his act. I soon relaxed into the music once again and decided that the worst that could happen would be that he would consider me a nutter and refuse to talk; but I also had a feeling that I knew enough information to convince him of the truth.

He played "Tides" third song up and from the first chord of the tricky introduction I was hooked. By the time it had finished I had goose bumps on every part of my anatomy. I looked across at Sam who also looked visibly moved. He reached over and grabbed my hand. Again - in public!

We stayed clutching hands, apart from the times we were applauding loudly, until the main act was over and he reached the encores.

"Thanks so much everybody," Max smiled and held up his hand to quieten the crowd. "OK, there are two new friends in here tonight that have requested a very old song, how they even know about it I have no idea, because it was a hit long before either of them first drew breath. However, I'm going to sing it tonight. It'll be the first time I've sung it in public for forty years; so please excuse the dodgy chords. This is a song that a man called Bennie Gold had a hit with in 1977, 'If Forever Ends With You' and I would like to dedicate it to the man who was the love of my life. To Pete."

It was beautiful. Suddenly I wasn't in a pub during the summer of 2017. I was in a bedroom in the 1970s and a naked lad was singing the song to his lover. His voice was still earthy and gentle, and the fingers meandered around the strings with the same delicate grace.

Completely losing our inhibitions Sam and I sang along with it unashamedly, bringing humorous looks from the group of fifty somethings on the next table. Eventually though, they joined in with the chorus as did half of the bar. Max finished his set and got a standing ovation from the appreciative crowd.

Sam went over and asked him what he wanted to drink and refilled our glasses whilst he was there. I then had an anxious half an hour whilst he went around chatting to all the regulars and selling a few CDs that he had on a table near to the door.

Eventually he was free to come over, he grabbed a vacant chair and pulled it around our table. He looked at me, those slightly faded cornflower blue eyes staring into my own.

"OK then," he said, "as I said, I haven't played that song for forty years and my version is certainly not on YouTube. So, tell me, how the bloody hell did you know about it?"

"Lucky guess?" I said hopefully, but erring I hoped, on the cheeky side of funny.

Max did laugh, but he also said, "Try again."

I told him the truth then. I told him about the dreams that had made his nineteenth summer as real to me as my own. When I eventually finished I waited for the contemptuous comments, but instead, it was him that surprised me this time.

"I had dreams like that too," he said.

I noticed the past tense and asked him when he had had them.

"For a few nights after Pete's death, it nearly sent me over the edge at the time," he admitted.

"Tell me," I had a crooked grin on my face, "were you drunk when you had these dreams?" Sam looked bemused.

"No, I was practically a prisoner in my bedroom at the time," he looked sad, then brightened. "Why? Do you only dream those dreams when you're drunk?"

I nodded, and Sam gave me a "you didn't tell me that" look.

I had a sudden thought, "The end of that perfect day when you took the ferry across to Brean Down, that was when he said to you that he'd find a way to contact you after his death, wasn't it?"

Max looked staggered, but enthralled. He breathed in deeply. "You really have dreamt about it, haven't you?"

I nodded and then said something that had just occurred to me. "Do you think that's why we only dream about him when we're sleeping in that room? Because that was the room where he made the promise? Or have you ever had dreams like that since?"

Max shook his head, "No, never," he thought about it for a few seconds, "you could be right." he admitted.

"Excuse me!" Sam was comically outraged, "I've slept in that room for nearly twenty years and never had a dream like that! What does that say about me?"

Max and I grinned in collusion, "Wouldn't like to say!" I laughed.

Mr Kruz was making obvious signs that the bar was closing so Max asked us to join him at his flat just around the corner for a drink. Now I suppose it went against all the advice we'd ever been given. However, I felt I knew him and besides; I was more desperate than ever, to hear his story.

Mr Kruz laughed as we helped Max with his gear and then trailed out after him: "I feel like chicken tonight!" he sang. Max gave him the finger with his free hand and they laughingly said goodnight to each other.

My original feeling that Max's career had been successful was enhanced somewhat when I saw his house. A three-story Regency town house on Marine Parade, a few buildings down from the hotel where we were staying. He had separated it into three large apartments and lived on the top story as he said it had the best views. He rented out the other two, which I imagined earned him more than his guitar playing hobby, however popular that might have been on the local music scene.

As soon as we entered his living room, the magnolia walls and high ceilings accentuated by the one wall in post box red, he disappeared to find cheese and wine. Within minutes we had a Moreland Road style midnight feast on the large glass topped coffee table, the base of which seemed to be a converted sledge.

He filled our glasses and I hacked myself off a large slab of Manchego. I decided not to mess about with preliminaries but to go to the heart of the story.

"When we talked to Jackie and Tony, they seemed to think that Pete was excited at various points during the day he died, and they thought it was something to do with you. I just wondered, did you meet up that night?"

"You've met Jackie and Tony?" Max was impressed, "how are they?"

"Fine, Tony has his own restaurant and Jackie ended up being a nursery school teacher," I took a swig of wine. "The career that Pete had encouraged her to follow."

Max smiled, "He was good at that, encouragement… It was all about other people with Pete, he had the best heart of any person I've ever met."

It was all about other people. I was suddenly struck by the fact that Pete wasn't so different to someone else I knew. Someone I'd argued with earlier, someone who wasn't a million miles away at that very moment.

"So, did you see him on the night he died?" I repeated, before we drifted off on an interesting but useless tangent.

Max shrugged and took a sip of wine, "No… but I heard him."

It was a slightly unsatisfactory answer, but I let it go, "Do you have any idea how he died."

"Oh, Christ yes," Max said sharply. "He committed suicide, and I've never quite managed to convince myself that I was completely blameless."

Suicide? I just didn't think it fitted with the man I thought I knew.

"Pete encouraged me too," Max said softly. "He encouraged me to meet up with my Aunty Sadie, a great friend of my mother." He saw the recognition on my face. "Christ this is weird, you know stuff about my life that hardly anyone else alive would know."

I apologised but he said quickly, "Don't be daft, it's just a bit strange that's all."

Sam tilted his head in my direction, explaining my nickname with a nod, "Rem said that you were due to go and see Aunty Sadie on the second of September, wasn't that the day that Pete died?"

I must say I had missed that, but Sam must have picked up on it when I recounted my dream as we were sitting on our bed with Emily the other morning.

Max nodded, "Yes, Pete was due to go with me, but suddenly the night before our visit, Mo decided that he wanted to go along. I decided that it would be a good chance to break the news of my homosexuality to my brother, hoping that he would be able to help me in telling my father later."

"How did Pete take that?" Sam asked.

Max shrugged, "Fine… he said that there was something he wanted to collect from town anyway. He was always encouraging me to break the news to Mo, he thought that he would be able to cope with it."

"And did he?" I asked.

"Not to start with, I told him on our drive to Cheddar and he just passed it off as a phase I was going through. He was sure I would get over it."

"But he was OK later?"

Max nodded. "We'd had a lovely day with Sadie, in fact she has been pretty much of a rock throughout my life since then. She must be about ninety now, but she still lives in her own house, in the middle of Bath. I see her quite a lot, even more so since I've retired."

Max must have noticed my slight impatience, it was nice hearing about Sadie, but I just wanted to move the story on. Max smiled at me and did just that.

"By the time we arrived back it must have been about seven o'clock. I was excited because I knew that Mo would go straight back down to work, and that Pete had the night off, which meant he'd be up as soon as he saw the coast was clear. However, when we got back to the apartment, my dad was there, and he was angry, very angry. A bloke they called Hutch had told him that I was having a homosexual relationship with Pete."

"Hutch!" I said, genuinely amazed. "Bloody hell! The guy has got balls of steel, I suppose you have to give him that!"

Max looked confused and I told him about Jackie, the attempted rape and the identity of Hutch's alter ego. "Bloody hell!" he said, "Desmond Marsons, The Planner? I've heard all about him, but never put two and two together, well, I never knew Hutch's real name, so I suppose there's no reason why I would have done…"

"Looks like he outed your affair with Pete as a smokescreen," I suggested.

Max nodded and expanded the theme, "You mean, he was worried that Pete would report him and thought that telling my father about Pete and me would create holy hell and he could disappear in the aftermath… Well he was certainly right about that." Max concluded bitterly.

"But why go to all those lengths?" Sam asked, "I mean why not cut and run whilst Pete was involved with helping Jackie? He was risking an awful lot going back to the hotel."

Max nodded but said, "It doesn't surprise me, he was a nasty piece of work, I wasn't overly keen on his mate Starsky either, but Pete quite liked him, I thought he was a little creepy."

I nodded, I had a strong idea who Starsky had grown old to become. I could sort of understand why the man denied it, but was there more to it than that?

However, at that moment I was more interested in what Max had to say.

"Hutch absolutely hated Pete, I wasn't there, but apparently Pete humiliated him one night."

"The card game?" I enquired, and Max looked astounded for a second and then laughed.

"God! This is weird!" he exclaimed again. "You saw - dreamt all about that?"

I nodded, "Hutch actually had quite a good body," I sniggered and held my thumb and first finger about a centimetre apart, "not much down below though!" I whispered confidentially.

Max laughed but Sam who already knew that story, wanted to get back to the crux of the matter. "So, Hutch sees a chance to get revenge and create a diversion in order to stop Pete reporting him?"

Max said bitterly, "Well he certainly managed that. By telling my dad about our affair he set in motion a chain of events that basically led directly to Pete's death." He paused for a second to let it all sink in, as much for himself as for us, I thought.

"Well, even though Mo hadn't taken it brilliantly when I'd told him earlier, he was fantastic in the face of my father's anger. He was even beginning to calm him down slightly when the phone rang, and he had to go downstairs.

As soon as he'd gone my father became vile once again and said some horrible things about Pete. I became so angry that I told my father that I was in love with Pete, he was my soul mate, I planned to quit university and move in with him. There was nothing he could do to stop me.

Sam whistled, "I guess that didn't go down very well?"

Max nodded grimly, "He hit me. No, he didn't hit me, he beat me practically unconscious. By the time he had finished with me, I could only crawl into my room, where I lay on the carpet and basically collapsed."

The emotion in Max's voice charged the whole room with an electricity that moved me to reach out for his hand. Sam had obviously felt the same connection as he did likewise on the other side, at exactly the same time. We must have looked like three people in search of a séance.

He glanced blearily but thankfully at both of us. "God! This is harder than I thought it would be."

I felt I should offer him a way out, but he shook his head violently, "No, no, it's fine; but this is a difficult bit so bear with me."

We nodded, then muttered platitudes. Taking a deep breath Max continued.

"At some point in the evening, Pete must have come looking for me, but he found my father instead. I have no idea what happened between them, the only thing I remember is hearing Pete trying to open my door, then shouting through it: 'Maxi, unlock the door and we can walk out of this place together. I love you Max and I know you love me!'"

I think both Sam and I were holding our breaths, the only sound I could hear as Max paused was the soft distant rumbling of traffic as it trundled down Marine Parade.

"I tried to speak, I tried to tell him that I was locked in my bedroom, I didn't have the key, but if I could only escape I would run with him to wherever he wanted to take me. I tried, but my father had literally knocked all breath from me and I could barely squeak. Within seconds, my chance to say anything had gone. I heard my father shout, he must have opened the door then and bundled Pete out of the apartment. I have never felt so lonely as I did in those moments afterwards. I eventually crawled onto my bed, over to the side that Pete always used to lay on and sniffing deeply, fell asleep smelling the scent of him."

"So, you think Pete then went down to the beach and committed suicide?" I said, doubtfully.

Max nodded. "You didn't hear the heartbreak in his voice." He looked at me, "maybe you will, when the time comes and believe me it won't be easy for you," he wasn't being cruel, simply factual. "But even worse than the heartbreak, was the hope. I think he truly believed that I would answer him, open the door and everything would be all right."

He stared at me:

"But I didn't… did I?"

31.

It was easy for me to say, but I said it anyway "You can't really blame yourself, you'd been knocked half senseless, surely it was your father who was to blame?" However, I knew deep in my heart, if it had been me - I would have blamed myself.

The laugh was bitter and meaningful. "Oh, I did blame him, I can tell you. I also spent the rest of his life making him pay for it."

The first bottle of wine was empty, and Max paused from his story whilst he opened another one and poured us all a glass.

"I woke up in the middle of the night in a terrible state, every inch of my body was aching from the bruises my father had given me, but that was nothing compared with the panic I was feeling. Someone, maybe Mo, had unlocked my door and I was able to get out and go down to the seafront. I just took one look at all the police activity and I knew."

He paused as if he was trying to remember the exact timings, but I had the impression that he had gone through this story, silently and to himself, many times over the intervening years.

"Mo broke it to me as gently as he could the next morning, but to be honest, they seemed more worried about the fact that the hotel safe had been broken into and a large amount of money had been stolen. They hadn't banked for weeks and most people paid in cash in those days, they had lost a lot of money and they weren't happy."

"But a man had died! One of their own staff had died!" I couldn't believe their priorities, but from what I'd heard of Old Man Edwards it didn't really surprise me, Mo had disappointed me though.

"I know, and I do think that Mo felt it, the old man... nah!" Max took another sip, "I went mad, crazy - in the end Mo had to force tranquillizers down me to settle me down. They locked the door again, then."

"Were you under the influence of tranquillisers when you had the first dream about Pete?" Alcohol did the trick for me, so maybe drugs had done the same for Max?

"No, I didn't dream until the night after. By this time, I was in a kind of catatonic trance, I wasn't eating or drinking. Mo would pop in from time to time and try soothing me, but he didn't bother with any more pills. Thankfully my father didn't come near."

"When you had the dreams, did you feel his physical presence or just see him? Could you talk to him?"

Max thought about it, "Are you saying that you've felt his physical presence?"

I nodded, and Max sighed, "Yes I did, I felt him, heard him, could talk to him. It should have been wonderful, but it was too soon. It sent me over the edge. I guess it was a type of depression, and the way I chose to fight that depression, was through revenge."

"Against your father?"

"Against my father. After the fourth night I came to terms with the fact that Pete was dead, and the dreams were all I was left with. I decided that I would do something about it."

"How did you do that?"

"They had stopped locking me in by now, I had become so inactive that I guess they thought it a waste of time. I went down to a pub called The Brit." I nodded at that, but Max was beginning to get used to my reactions, so he just ignored it and carried on.

"There was a young lad there, quite cute and very willing. I must have looked a state with my black eyes and bruises, but he didn't take much coaxing. I even told him what I wanted to do, and he laughed and came along for the ride."

"What did you do?" Sam was as intrigued as I was.

"We went back to the hotel and I sat on the ledge outside the dining room. I remember there were about three elderly couples at the window tables, eating their starters. I pulled off my shirt and dropped my jeans and pants to my ankles, then making sure that I was rubbing my arse against the windows, got the lad to suck me off there and then!"

Both Sam and I spluttered with laughter, as much as a release from the story that had gone before as a reaction to the present tale.

"I know rump steak was all the rage in the seventies," Sam the food buff sniggered, "but that was normally after the Florida cocktail, not with it!"

Max laughed before returning to his story, "Mo, my father and some of the staff got me inside somehow and sent the lad on his way. Within half an hour Mo was driving me to Cheddar to stay with Aunty Sadie and at least the dreams stopped then. But, even as lovely as she was, she couldn't contain me and within a week, I had decided what I was going to do. I moved away from Somerset and up to London, where my revenge continued in earnest."

"How?"

"Well the one thing my father couldn't cope with was the fact that I was gay, so I rented myself out to the first gay porn photographer that would have me."

"You did porn?" Sam drew in his breath in surprise.

Max nodded, "I did, any work I could get. I was luckier than most, the guy who looked after me, really cared for me. He was a bit seedy I suppose, but he kept me safe. He was definitely one of the good guys in my story."

"So, what did you do? You made sure your father received copies of your photos, I suppose?" I asked him, intrigued that the quiet, thoughtful lad in my dream would just run away to London and become the darling of Soho.

"Oh yes, it cost me a fortune in postage! I also made sure they knew where I was, so they could contact me and tell me to stop. Every phone call I received convinced me more and more that I was getting under their skin. Poor Mo was at his wits end, which was a bit of collateral damage as far as I was concerned. It wasn't ever him or Auntie Sadie that I was trying to hurt."

He tailed off as his brain re-ran old memories, then spurred on by another swig from his wine, started again. "Mo then came up with a good plan. He returned all the post from me unopened, to show that it wasn't affecting them. Although, I would imagine just receiving it would prove that I was still active, so it must have hurt them a little."

"I'm sensing that you didn't leave it at that?" I guessed.

Max snorted, "No, you're right. I took a load of my pictures and went down to Weston. I let myself into the flat whilst my father and Mo were busy at dinner and I wallpapered his bedroom with them." Sam made a sound that signified laughter and surprise at the same time, but Max wasn't finished, either now, or back in the 1970s.

"My father had bought a Sony Betamax video tape recorder, the year before, and I had bought down one of the spanking films that I specialised in."

"You really did the lot, didn't you?" I laughed.

Max nodded, "I'll have you know that my behind was a bit of a legend in its day!" He then returned to his tale. "I set it up and then phoned reception and asked the receptionist…"

"Was Helen still working there?" I interrupted, and Max nodded.

"Yep, I asked Helen to send my dad up, but not tell him that I was there. I started the movie and waited for him."

"You stood there whilst he watched it?" I was amazed by his bravery or foolhardiness, call it what you will. This was the man who had beaten him half senseless after all.

"He came in the room and I shouted "Surprise!" and pointed to the TV. I was just being spanked by a big black man. I was staring from the screen defiantly. To my father it must have looked like I was staring straight at him."

"Did he hit you?" I asked but Max shook his head.

"I made sure he couldn't come anywhere near me, so instead he pulled out the flex from the video and hurled it across the room towards where I stood. I just laughed and pointed to his bedroom. The sounds I heard from there were visceral, complete carnal anger and despair. I waited until I could hear him rampaging around the room, tearing at every poster he could reach. I then let myself out and went straight back to the station without even talking to Mo, something I would have never believed possible a year or so earlier."

"Do you think that all of this resulted in his death?" I thought it obvious myself, but Sam was after confirmation.

Max nodded. "Definitely. His heart wasn't the strongest in any case and during the next two years or so, I made sure that I put as much strain on it as possible."

"I guess it was Mo who told you about it?" I asked.

"Yep, he rang my contact number early in 1980 and when I rang him back, he told me that our father had died. He told me not to think about coming to the funeral and then…"

"What?" Sam and I asked together.

Max paused before answering, as if he was summoning up the courage to say the words. "He said, 'Congratulations! You killed my mother and now you have managed to do the same, to my father…'"

I think both of us inhaled a large breath of air. I now knew something that had been puzzling me, why two brothers who were so fond of each other, ended up not speaking.

"Did you ever speak again?" I asked, "Do you know where he is now?"

"He's dead." Max said sadly, "he died in the mid-eighties I think, car crash. I received a letter from a solicitor which contained Mo's watch. It was ironic really, I had bought him that watch one day when I was out shopping with Pete. It was the only thing he left me, but I certainly don't blame him for that. That's the only problem with revenge, you can't control who it affects, and it sometimes touches the people that you love most in the world."

"So, did you carry on with your porno career?"

Max laughed, "No, there was no point, was there? Mo's words gave me the wakeup call I needed. I got in touch with Aunty Sadie and she was much more forgiving than my brother. She knew what my father could be like, she had barely talked to him for years before they joined forces trying to control me. However, she never really liked him, I think. She was trying to save me from myself, she wasn't really interested in preventing me from hurting him."

"What happened then?"

"Sadie was quite a wealthy widow, so she was able to sell up her house in Cheddar and buy a property in the middle of Bath. I gave up the porn. I was lucky, I hadn't got involved in the drug side of the industry. I saw some of the lads who did, and it wasn't a pretty sight, they had to do more and more work just to get their next hit. For me it wasn't like that, I was doing it purely to avenge Pete and once I'd done that, I could move on... I was a bit of a callous shit, wasn't I?"

I would have said driven more than callous - but I'm sure his brother would have disagreed with me, were he still alive.

"I moved in with Sadie and she called in a few favours and found me a job with a big hotel chain in the city. I worked hard, did well and the rest as they say is history."

Once again, I noticed the reluctance to say how successful he had been, but I guessed, to own this building from a starting point of nothing, was proof in itself.

"You never saw Mo after you moved in with Sadie?" Sam asked.

Max shook his head, "No. I tried, Sadie tried, but he moved out of the Hotel and left the running of it to managers that an agency hired in, I think."

I remembered Maureen saying something about that on my first night in Weston.

"He just disappeared, I guess it was his revenge on me... now that I was desperate to talk to him, he wasn't having any of it. I made regular attempts to contact him, but any friends of his that I knew, either didn't know anything, or had been sworn to keep his whereabouts from me. The news of his death was the first I'd heard about him in years. It still makes me sad when I think about him."

"Did your background in porn ever come back to bite you on the bum..." Sam asked, and Max grinned at the terminology. "Like an actor making it big and then there's a big furore when the tabloids expose a shady past?"

Max laughed drily, "It's probably not quite the same in the world of hotel management," he said, "but there was this one occasion. I was dealing with a Japanese client in the nineties when I had moved into negotiating company expansion. He pulled out a copy of "Men in Uniform" from his briefcase and said, "Is it you?""

Sam and I gasped and laughed at the same time.

"I was slightly appalled to see it, more because I thought it might be a deal breaker than the fact that I was ashamed of it."

"And did he call the deal off?" I asked.

"No!" Max laughed. "He simply said "Nice arse!" Asked me to sign his copy and we went back to closing the deal!"

It was a good story to move us back to easier topics of

conversation and we talked about music from the last forty years. We then laughed when Sam and I recounted our tale of meeting and the Millennium Fountain and even managed a semi intellectual discussion about the effects on tourism brought about by Brexit.

There was only one more moment that evening when I saw the pain of his loss. Time might have healed him, but the agony of that Saturday morning, long before my life had even been thought of, would never leave him completely.

I had wondered ever since I first heard it, whether he had called his song "Tides" as a homage to the Bennie Gold tune that had been so important to them. He nodded.

"I did want a little snippet of that song in my tribute to Pete. I even used the same chords and wove the first line around it."

I hadn't noticed that, but Sam had always laughed that my own musical talent was similar to my namesake's. Max then became serious again, his voice was bone china brittle with loss as he said: "However, I mostly called it 'Tides' - because it was the sea that killed him."

We also talked some more about my dreams and everything I experienced whilst I was dreaming them. "You mentioned the day that Pete and I took the ferry to Brean," Max said. "Did you see what actually happened in the quarry?" I nodded and he continued "...so you've seen me naked and having sex?"

"Well to be fair, so has most of the gay population circa 1980 from what you have told us!"

Max laughed, humour fully restored. "Touché!" He then said with a mischievous twinkle, "I don't suppose you two want to join me and return the favour?" It was done cheekily and without any hint of sleaze, so it was impossible to take offence.

We smilingly declined, and he laughed, "Well you can't blame an old queen for trying!"

I laughed, "Don't give me that! I've got a funny feeling that you are successful many more times than not…"

He laughed deprecatingly at that and agreed that it might be so.

I thought it best not to tell him that not only had I seen him naked, but through Pete, I had already felt like I was making love to him.

Even if Sam had been up for it, which I thought unlikely, that alone would have made it all too weird for my battered brain to cope with.

In the end, it was five o'clock before we tore ourselves away and staggered the few metres down the road to our Hotel. As we let ourselves into our room, Sam gave a little laugh to himself, then shared his thought with me.

"Death by pornography - now that's one even Midsomer Murders hasn't thought of yet!"

***

The phone blasted into a beautifully dreamless sleep at about ten o'clock. It was Max.

"Goodness, the youth of today!" He laughed at my bleary tone. "No stamina!"

He then invited us around for lunch at one o'clock and after trying to semaphore the information to an unresponsive Sam, I just accepted for the both of us.

It was a wonderful afternoon. Max had produced a lunch of Bouillabaisse with garlic crostini seemingly out of thin air. We ate it with a light dry white wine, whilst sitting on the balcony overlooking the seafront with the greeny-blue sea heading off towards the horizon where it met the sky. Somewhere, tantalisingly out of view, lurked the French coast line.

Thinking about what he had said last night, I thought it a little strange that a man who had reason to hate the sea, should choose to look at it every day – but when I mentioned it, he said simply - "It's been good and bad for me, the sea. Mostly when I look out at it I can remember

313

the fun…"

Max and Sam did most of the chatting on that wonderful day. Sam was telling him about all the changes his family had made to the Hotel and I wondered that if push came to shove, would Sam be able to give all that up for me, and did I even have the right to ask him to do so?

After the soup came the cheese and we changed from white wine to red. I was being a little careful as I knew I would be sleeping in Weston that night and I didn't think I was quite ready for another dream. Although our visit to see Max had given us some answers, I still wasn't quite sure how it affected me. I was also sure that if I did, in some mad insanity manage to save Pete's life, it would change Max's irrevocably, so should I even attempt it? On the other hand, would I even be able to stop myself from doing so?

We stayed on the balcony until after five, when we had to tear ourselves away to catch the six o'clock train home. Once we were safely on board, I chatted my thoughts through with Sam. However, I kept away from the subject of changing history, as I knew he wasn't exactly comfortable with it.

"So, if I do have a fall out with my dad and he beats me half black and blue," said Sam, "don't commit suicide - just wait for my bruises to heal!" I think he needed to bring a little bit of levity to the subject and I was happy to let him.

I sat sideways in my seat, happy that once again I could partake in some not so secret stalking. Sam had downloaded some of Max's songs onto his phone. They had taken the place of Grime on his play list, which was basically a very good sign.

I thought about his light-hearted comment and now wondered if that had been the reason for my dreams, a warning from Pete that if it all became too difficult with Ned, not to despair. I wasn't entirely convinced. However, a starving vegetarian is unlikely to turn down a pork scratching, so I held on to it as a possibility.

Sam did manage to get a full twelve hours sleep that night. I think he needed it after the late night, the walk and hard work in the week before that. However, as soon as he appeared in the apartment kitchen, there was a message that he was needed on duty as the Deputy Manager had sprained an eye lash…

Em and I wandered down to the beach as I needed to get away from the building and she was desperate to hear news of our night away in Brighton. Once the story had been told, she said. "So, you think that was all there was to it? Pete committed suicide because he thought it was hopeless between him and Max? It doesn't sound very much like him, does it?"

I had thought the same thing even in the face of Max's certainty and I told her so.

She paused and then had another thought. "In which case why would Dee and Dum lie?"

I had thought about this too. "Well I suppose the Edwards' paid them. They wouldn't want it to become public knowledge that young Max was a homosexual and The Old Man had driven his lover to suicide."

"It was a bit of a waste of money in that case, when you consider what Max did afterwards," Emily said grimly then paused. "Just say, for the sake of it, that Pete didn't commit suicide, there are a few suspects that really didn't like him very much, aren't there?"

"Yes, but which of them besides Edwards would have been able to afford to pay Dee and Dum their hush money?" I asked reasonably.

Em gave me a knowing look. "Tony mentioned it," she said. "And you've just mentioned it in Max's story." I must have still had the confused look of a colour-blind snooker player, so she spelt it out.

"We've completely ignored the importance of the robbery…"

32.

When Emily returned from the last weekend she would ever spend at school, the three of us took a few bottles of wine down onto the beach and sat in the dunes chatting and drinking. The two and a half days that Ned had been away from the building had been a revelation. The strain around Sam's eyes had disappeared, I felt less tension and the staff seemed happier. Despite everything that his father had said about Sam's naivety and lack of experience, the place had run like clockwork.

Almost as soon as the Manager re-appeared the cracks started to show once more. Ned had barely parked the car before he questioned two of Sam's decisions. That was one of the reasons we had headed for the beach as soon as possible. Also, if we had hung around the hotel for a few minutes more, his father would have been sure to decide that Sam desperately needed to hand paint the hotel logo onto the beer mats...

Sam and I had stolen a few moments whilst the family were away and had decided that as soon as Pete's story had reached its conclusion, we would finally tell Ned and Fiona about our relationship.

So that was the other reason we took the wine and went down to the dunes to drink it. I had never in my life before gone out specifically to get drunk, but on that Sunday night, I did just that.

I was just about as ready as I could have been, to find out the truth.

33.

1977

The day that Pete died started in such an ordinary way, not so dissimilar from most of the other days that summer. The weather forecast said that the day would start bright and sunny, but would turn cloudy, with a storm arriving by nightfall.

The only problem that Pete faced early in the morning was the fact that the rotary toaster was on the blink and kept burning dark edges around the crusts of the bread. The waiting staff had to irritate the chefs by running into the kitchen and toast batches of bread underneath the main grill, which the chefs in their turn, were trying to use to cook bacon.

Tempers were running a little high, but as so often happened, all was forgotten by the time everyone sat together eating breakfast after service was over. At this point in time the sun had burnt away the early morning cloud and was shining with optimism, brightly in the sky.

Spurred on by the sunny weather, the window cleaning firm the Edwards' used had arrived. They had just started setting up their ladders at the other end of the dining room, clattering wood against the walls as the Hotel staff ate their breakfast.

Pete's body was aching slightly, but it was merely muscle memory of the night before. Max had broken the news to him that Mo wanted to go and see Auntie Sadie with him and thought that the old adage "two's company, three's a crowd," might well apply. Pete was slightly disappointed, but only because he resented any hour that he couldn't spend with Max. However, he guessed that he would get to meet Sadie eventually and thought that it was a good chance for his boyfriend to talk other matters over with his brother. This would pave the way for a showdown with Old Man Edwards, eventually.

To make it up to him, Max had wasted precious few minutes on talking the night before. Their love making had been the most intense that both of them had experienced and had continued until well after the midnight curfew they normally allowed themselves. Running the real risk of meeting Mo, or The Old Man, in the corridor. Pete eventually pulled himself away, step by reluctant step. However, on this occasion he escaped without incident.

Tony had returned from Helen's room a little while later and in their normal way, they talked through their evenings until one of them dropped off to sleep.

However, there was one plan that Pete hadn't even talked over with Tony yet, he wasn't exactly sure why, but up to that point he had shared it with nobody. An idea had formed in his brain after the conversation he and Max had shared on their first trip into town together.

A few days afterwards, Pete had taken the elastic band that he had laughingly wrapped around his friend's finger. Much to the amusement of the staff in Rossitters, he had triple wound it into shape and used that as a form of measurement to order a proper piece of jewellery that wouldn't be made of elasticated rubber. Since then, he had been paying for the ring in instalments, secretly every week. Today, the last payment was due and when Max returned from Cheddar tonight, Pete would give him the gift his friend dreamed of, but had never believed he would receive.

He asked Jackie if she wanted to go into town with him, but she seemed unusually distracted and even when he told her the reason for his visit, she didn't seem overly impressed. He was a little bit disappointed, after weeks of keeping it a secret, the first person he told treated it with mild boredom. It was similar to the way people may react when you discussed your medical problems with them.

She merely said that she had agreed to meet Christine for lunch. After he had suggested that they all went into town, did shopping and had lunch together, she said, in an offhand manner, that Christine wanted to chat to her about girly stuff and that he'd probably be in the way.

Jackie may have guessed that Pete was a little disappointed and mouthed "Smiler!" to him, intimating that it was Christine's obsession with the second chef that was behind the planned lunch time chat.

Knowing when he was being dismissed, even if he was slightly suspicious of the reasoning, Pete let the matter drop. He did think about asking Tony, but he still had an hour's prepping to do for tonight's service. Now that Pete had decided to collect the gift today, he just wanted to go in and purchase it. He was desperate to see if it was as good as he dreamed it would be.

It was. When the man in Rossiters opened the case, and showed him the simple nine carat signet ring in yellow gold, it outstripped all of his hopes. He had originally wanted a simple engraving of their two initials. However, the salesman had suggested that it might look like it stood for a Member of the House of Commons or a time in the afternoon - depending on which order you placed the initials.

In the end they had decided on M & P with the tail of the final letter swirling around in a circle that surrounded the lettering, but didn't quite meet up with itself. On the side that would be hidden from view, trapped against Max's skin, he had thought about "With Love," played with "Forever," but in the end settled on their very own, "Back at ya."

His enthusiasm was contagious, and the salesman was grinning as Pete clasped his hand, thanked him for the twentieth time and waving a farewell, left the shop. The exhilaration from the purchase and the anticipation of Max's joy when he opened the box later, made Pete run down the High Street. The blazing late summer sun magnified his feelings of complete and undeniable happiness.

He then did his rounds of the High Street record shops and eventually bought "Nobody Does It Better," by Carly Simon, for himself and the Boomtown Rats, "Looking After Number One," for Max. On a day that was threatening to bankrupt him, he went the whole hog and treated himself to a soup and sandwich lunch in Owen Owen. He felt a simple excitement of just being back in the place where Max had first opened his heart to him. There had been no way back for Pete after that day… and he felt like the happiest man in the world because of it.

Pete gently hummed the James Bond theme song to himself as he walked home. The lyrics made him think of Max and he grinned as he thought of how their fingers had found each other's in the cinema as they watched the film, just inches away from their friends, hiding in plain sight, camouflaged by the darkness.

He watched the water slowly retreating as he made his way along the promenade, as benign and non-threatening as an elderly aunt. It gave no indication of future events, when the tide would turn and once again cover the damp sand.

At first when he got back to the hotel, everything seemed normal. Tony wasn't in their room and his chef's clothing had been thrown on the floor in an untidy heap. The West Indian was a little bit of a tidiness freak and it had been another cause of good natured bantering between them, so it was unusual, but nothing more than that.

He plugged in the old Dansette record player that Tony and he had eventually clubbed together and bought from a junk shop earlier in the summer. Of course, it had led to lengthy arguments between them. However, on this afternoon, Pete took the opportunity of solitude to play the Carly Simon record as loudly as he liked and without any teasing from his friend, the self-appointed Chief Inspector of the Taste Police.

He was just turning it over to sample the B-Side, when there was a knock on the door. It was Christine and she had gossip to share.

"Hi Pete, I could hear you were back! I don't suppose anyone has told you what has happened?" Pete liked Christine, but if you gave her a secret recipe, half of the bakeries in town would know about it before you'd had a chance to weigh out the flour. She was never more delighted than when she had a juicy bit of news to spread around, especially if it was bad and it had happened to someone else.

"Tony only went and caught Helen in the laundry cupboard..." She paused before the crux of the matter, just to give it a heightened sense of tension, "she was at it with Del from the window cleaning company!"

She grinned and waited for all the obvious questions to which she had all the answers, but Pete failed to ask any of them. He just felt a horrible sense of the agony his friend would be feeling. Within seconds, his own sunny mood was fading. He became slightly irritated with the girl standing in front of him, who was so delighted with the thoughts of someone else's misfortune, that he had a sudden desire to burst her bubble.

"How's things with Smiler? Have you melted his heart of misery yet?" He knew damned well that the answer was in the negative, but he was maliciously pleased to see the gloating grin fade from her features. "That one's for you, Tony," he thought to himself.

"Not yet," said Christine, slightly annoyed that Pete had changed the subject from the gossip she had given him. There were loads of details that she had heard, guessed and quite frankly, made up - that she still wanted to tell him. "But I'm working on it!"

"Not in my life time," thought Pete grimly to himself. However, he decided to humour her, hoping to get rid of the girl as soon as possible. He wanted to find Tony and let his friend use him as a shoulder to cry on.

"How was your lunch with Jack?" he asked. "Did she go home afterwards, or did she come back here with you?" He was thinking that if it was the latter, he would grab her, and they could go looking for Tony together. In the back of his mind, he rather hoped that he would dump Helen, especially after this latest development, and take up with Jackie instead.

Christine's reaction was upsetting and slightly worrying. She looked mystified. "I didn't meet Jackie for lunch," she said, "I was going to go shopping on my own, but then all hell broke loose, so I stayed around." She was trying to get the subject back on track, Pete had to give her that, but he was now quite concerned, so he didn't allow her to side-track him.

"So, you were never going to meet her?" He asked, and she shook her head. Dismissing her in a way that was as close to rude as Pete was ever likely to manage, he grabbed his keys and unplugged the Dansette, before leaving an ever-hopeful Christine in the doorway with her mouth open.

He went straight round to reception and Helen was on duty. She looked a little bleary eyed, but it wasn't her that Pete intended to waste any sympathy on. He had two friends that he was worried about and he wasn't entirely sure which one needed him most.

"Where is he Helen?" He said, slightly sharply and the receptionist snapped her head up from the booking sheet.

"I don't know Pete," she seemed genuinely worried, "he stormed out and I haven't seen him since: talk to him for me, will you?"

"What have you done Hels?" They both realised that it wasn't a question he needed answering, so Helen simply repeated her entreaty.

"Find him Pete, talk to him?"

He left the building with no particular plan in mind, except maybe to walk into town and trawl through the pubs that allowed unlicensed drinking throughout the afternoon. Pete was about to retrace his footsteps, of only half an hour earlier, when he saw Hutch just in front of him, heading for the beach. He had been on bar duty until two-thirty, but now he was a man with a mission. Hutch was completely oblivious to the fact that Pete was only about twenty feet away. He strode towards the gate with the determination of a man with a deadline to keep, or maybe a rendezvous with someone?

It suddenly all made perfect sense. Jackie's air of distraction this morning, her quickly invented excuses and her desire to shut him out of her plans. Pete suddenly knew exactly which of his friends needed him more and he abandoned his plans of walking into town. Was he being ridiculously overprotective? Was that why she hadn't told him? It could have been a completely innocent date between the two of them, but Pete knew what Hutch was like with women, he'd seen him in action and he didn't want that for her. He wanted the best for her, and in his view the blonde-haired sleaze ball was a few miles short of that.

Taking care to keep a little distance between them, he followed the barman onto the beach. He thought about catching up with Hutch and asking him directly, but he knew that he was the last person the man would give an honest answer to; and he didn't want Jackie left on her own, waiting for a date who never showed.

Hutch was moving quickly. Pete drifted into the dunes and onto the golf course, in case the man he was tailing should turn around. This made his route more circuitous and he practically had to run to ensure that there was never more than forty feet between them.

Once they had reached the boatyard, Hutch went

through the gate, but didn't go up the hill that the picnic party had climbed earlier in the summer. Instead he went along the track, over a stile and into a field that led down to the estuary. The field was open, and it was therefore much more likely that Hutch would see him if he should turn around, but the man was so intent on his destination that it seemed unlikely he would do so. However, when Hutch had reached the end of the journey, which seemed to be in a dune by the estuary itself, secluded and slightly hidden from view, he did start to look around him. To avoid being seen, Pete kept to the bushes that ran down the side of the field and waited, just as the barman was waiting a few feet away.

Jackie was not there.

Pete was sure that she should have arrived by now.

So, by the looks of things, was Hutch.

With a sudden and awful sense of realisation, a few things tumbled from Pete's memory like a load of coins cascading from the penny drop machines on the pier.

How he'd been glad that Jackie wasn't alone with Hutch on the beach on the night that Elvis had died.

The sense of comfort he felt by the fact that someone besides himself always kept a wary eye on Hutch when they went dancing at Snoopys.

So, Jackie had got herself a boyfriend and that was a good thing, wasn't it?

However, Pete had a strange sense that all was not right, and he moved away from Hutch as silently as he could. If it was all so innocent, then why had Hutch been sent on a fool's errand? That was one of the questions bothering him. The other one was… where were they?

A sudden memory. Max holding onto a branch as Pete careered Mo's bike into Hutch's leg.

And the man who was with him.

Then, a sudden realisation crashed its way into Pete's brain.

He tore along the field as fast as his legs and the

uneven territory would let him move. Hutch was already hidden from view in the dune, so it was unlikely that he would turn and see him, but he didn't care anyway. Hutch was not a concern to him.

Not anymore.

He vaulted the stile, like an ungainly hurdler who would never qualify for an Olympic team, and ran down the road until he reached the shop that sold fishing equipment. He turned through the bushes on the hidden track, not caring when branches caught him in the face or stabbed him in the stomach.

He was sure that he could hear a cry.

He was sure he could hear a scream.

In next to no time he emerged into the brightly sunlit clearing in the quarry.

The first thought that entered Pete's head in a slightly bizarre fashion was that Starsky was wearing one of Hutch's shirts over his T-shirt.

He wasn't the soft spoken, gently humoured man that could easily get lost in a crowd, not at this moment in time.

Starsky was tearing at the clothes of a girl whose screams had camouflaged Pete's entrance. His trousers were around his ankles and he was attempting to force himself into her. The last of her resolve had crumbled and she almost seemed to be waiting for it to happen.

Before the rapist knew what was happening, Pete crossed the quarry and pulled him back from the girl. As Starsky was forced backwards, his trousers became like a lasso and they tripped him. With an agonised scream he tumbled to the ground, his naked excitement shrinking with the realisation of defeat.

Pete glanced hurriedly around and found a rock, small enough to handle, yet big enough to scar. He quickly bent down to pick it up and held it above Starsky's head.

"Do not think about following us," he said, his voice trembling with temper, "I will use this, I will bloody well use this… if you do!"

Quickly grabbing Jackie and helping her to her feet, all the time glancing over his shoulder to make sure that the barman wasn't planning on making a move. Pete rearranged her clothing as gently as he could, whilst muttering soothing noises and phrases: "You're all right Jack. You're going to be fine sweetie." Just as he had managed to get her moving and they were beginning leave the clearing, Starsky started getting to his feet.

"Don't you fucking dare!" Pete turned and pulled the rock from his pocket, holding it above his head. Starsky shrank back and Pete used the opportunity to help Jackie into the bushes, using one arm to hold the branches back and the other to guide her through as she stumbled on the foliage beneath her feet. He took one last look back, but as far as he could see, the barman was not following them. He felt a sudden sense of disillusionment and sadness. The place that held so many tender moments for him, had changed before his horrified eyes. It felt like the whole clearing had been raped itself by the brutality of the act he had just witnessed.

Jackie wouldn't go into the shop until he had promised not to report the attack. He gave way to her, just to coerce her into the safety of the shaded interior. The man behind the counter looked at them, obviously suspicious of his quickly made up story of an ill-advised climb, but rang for a taxi nonetheless.

All the way back in to town, Jackie clung on to Pete like he was the lone piece of flotsam floating in a stormy sea. All she could say to him was, "Don't tell her, please don't tell her!" He muttered encouragements and held her tightly, willing the memory of the attack to leave her, yet knowing that it was an impossible ask.

Jackie's mum looked at him, stone faced in front of the stone effect wallpaper. The air in the hallway was dank with disbelief, and alive with an unspoken accusation. She didn't believe a word of the fiction that was falling from his mouth. Her whole body language seemed to be saying that you didn't end up looking the way her daughter did because of a simple slip on the rocks.

Mrs Trevellyan ushered him quickly out of the house and the last time he saw Jackie she was sitting slumped on the stairs looking bleakly in his direction.

He walked towards the High Street aware of the change in his mood since he had last been in that road. It had only been a few hours, yet it felt like a lifetime in terms of the event that he had just witnessed.

As he passed Rossiters he was reminded of Max and the surprise he had waiting for him on his return from Cheddar. His spirits lifted immediately, and he resolved to talk to Jackie tomorrow, even if he was going to face a struggle trying to sweet talk her guard dog before he could reach her. He would persuade her to go with him to the police station and report it. It would give the bastard a few hours to escape, but Pete managed to convince himself that he wouldn't be able to get too far and besides, he wouldn't do anything without Jackie agreeing to it. He had promised her that, and he would not break his word.

Pete's thoughts drifted from one friend in trouble towards the other one. He returned to the idea that Tony would have gone to get plastered somewhere. There were a few pubs he knew that had a reputation for opening all afternoon and he struck gold in the second one he entered.

As he walked through the door, the three old men that constituted the crowd, covered their drinks with their hands. It wasn't the best disguise in the world and Pete was pretty sure that if he had been the police, he wouldn't have needed the wit of Columbo to work out their guilt. They looked at him, satisfied themselves that he wasn't the constabulary wanting to charge them for out of hours drinking and resumed their supping with barely a blink of the eye.

The landlord removed the Racing Times from in front of his face for long enough to tell Pete that Tony had been there all day until about twenty minutes ago. He had been getting increasingly agitated the more he drank and when he had reached the point when the landlord had decided that he needed to leave, he had phoned someone and then left the pub straight away on his own accord. The only person Pete could imagine Tony phoning in that sort of state was Helen, so he asked to use the pay phone and followed suit.

"Oh, Christ Pete! Thank God you've rung. Tony's just phoned me, completely off his rocker with booze. He says he's going to Marlon's surgery in The Feathers and he's going to tell him all about us. You've got to stop him, Marlon will kill me if he finds out what I've been up to with Tony."

All Helen seemed to care about was herself, it was Tony who was just about to enter Hell and all she was worried about was that her dishonesty was about to be exposed. Her whole attitude seemed to be that Tony was over reacting and it irritated Pete, "You've been risking it all summer, Hels, what the bloody hell gets into you? You had a fantastic man who loved you to bits and you've treated him like shit!"

Helen's worry turned to a quick anger, "Oh for God's sake Pete, I don't need a bloody lecture, I need you to find the stupid idiot and get him back here to sober up before he does any damage!"

"OK, I'll do that Helen, but just in case you're interested, I'm doing it for Tony, not you, because you…" Whatever else he had wanted to say to her was lost in the dialling tone as she had slammed the phone down on him.

As Pete entered The Feathers, he could see Malcolm Marlon at the bar blatantly doing business with a young man with grey skin and no teeth. Just lurking by the bar waiting to talk to him was Tony. Malcolm Marlon was well aware of Tony's presence, but Pete could see that he was playing with him and making him wait. He felt a stab of anger on his drunken friend's behalf. He devised a plan that besides helping Pete in extricating Tony from the pub, held the added bonus of causing Malcolm Marlon a little bit of trouble.

There was a large man drinking a pint by the door. He had a tattoo with the legend, "Hard as Nails" in the middle of a multi coloured design that made a collar around his neck. Pete thought about having a needle imprinting a pattern into that part of your body and decided that the phrase probably wasn't overplaying the truth. He was looking at a substance he had just bought, a dubious frown creasing his large features.

"All right mate!" Pete greeted him, and the man mountain grunted. "Clever of you to check anything that he," he nodded his head in Malcolm Marlon's direction, "sells you." He lowered his voice conspiratorially, "I've heard he's got a reputation for substitutions, if you know what I mean."

He left the mountain checking his purchase more carefully and went over to Tony, just as his friend had been given the nod that the pusher was happy to listen to whatever he had to say at last.

"So, Anthony, what is it you want to say to me?" Malcolm Marlon asked him with the tone of voice that he loved to use when talking to people that he felt were inferior to him.

"I just wanted you to know that…" However, Pete decided not to let Tony finish the sentence.

"…that he thinks you're a jolly fun chap to be around!" Pete realised he had turned into Jerry from "The Good Life," but he was just desperate to say anything that would stop Tony confessing. Malcolm Marlon's cohorts were all around and although they say that confession is good for the soul, in this case it wouldn't have been any good for Tony's ribs, limbs or face.

He put his arm around his friend's shoulder and tried to encourage him away from the bar. Malcolm Marlon had other ideas.

"Now Anthony, don't let the sissy talk for you," he

stared aggressively in Pete's direction. "What is it you want to say to me?"

"I think we should go Tone," Pete said urgently.

"And I think you should talk to me," there was a hard decisive edge to the pusher's tone.

"Well I would like to talk to you!" Night had suddenly engulfed the bar as The Mountain from the table by the door had stood up and by approaching, was blocking every inch of daylight. "What is this fucking crap you've sold me?"

He nodded at Pete as if to say, "Get out while you can, the shit is just about to hit the fan," Pete did not need telling twice. He hauled Tony with as much strength as he could muster, towards the door and through it. Pete looked back in time to see Malcolm Marlon with a look of panic in his eyes being faced down by the man he had just conned.

When they reached the comparative safety of the end of the road. Pete screamed "Yee Hah!" at the top of his voice. "Tony my drunken West Indian soul mate, I do believe that Malcolm Marlon Brando is just about to get exactly what he deserves!" Even from thirty feet away they could hear the shouts and general confusion of a bar room brawl.

It was not an easy journey along the sea front. Tony could barely walk, and Pete kept falling over his trailing legs. However, he didn't care, he had saved his friend and Max would be home soon. He babbled happily to Tony about what he had bought Max and how he couldn't wait to see his face when he opened it later.

He tried not to think of Jackie. The day at last was taking a turn for the better.

Somehow, they managed to reach room seventeen and Pete rolled Tony from his shoulder and onto the bed.

Released to the comfort of the fabric below, Tony looked up at Pete. "I love you my skinny white gay friend," he slurred.

"Love you too, Tony." Pete said and lightly kissed him on the cheek before leaving the room. Then he went down to the kitchen and made up a story about Tony vomiting his heart out upstairs. He was pretty sure that it wouldn't turn out to be a lie by the end of the night, it was only that he had substituted the alcohol with a dodgy curry.

Giuseppe looked at him from underneath eyebrows that were worthy of Denis Healey. His look told him that he knew exactly the state that Tony had been in when he had returned from the laundry cupboard that morning. It also told him that he didn't believe a word of it, but because he sympathised, he was happy to pretend he did.

Pete was meant to be off duty that night, but all thoughts of his impending meeting with Max were put on hold somewhat when the Head Chef asked him to help in the kitchen as a replacement for his ailing roommate. There was an unspoken bargain in the request and Pete knew that it would be churlish to refuse.

He fetched a uniform from the laundry room, thought about what had occurred there earlier and took a chef's jacket and a pair of trousers from the bottom of the pile.

He couldn't resist a little more mischief as he was in charge of dishing up the vegetables alongside Smiler. "So, how's it going with Christine?" he asked, "reached second base yet?"

"Don't be fucking ridiculous Pete," snarled the curmudgeon, "I'd rather snog you!"

"Thanks sweetheart, I'll take that as a compliment!" He laughed, and Smiler grunted, but there was definite humour, albeit well hidden, behind the eyes.

As soon as he had been released from his duties, Pete ran back to Strangeways for a quick shower and change. He then checked that his sleeping friend was not lying on his back, and likely to choke on his own vomit. He picked up his gift and the record by the Boomtown Rats, and headed back across the yard to the main building. With every step of the staircase his excitement increased. He hadn't seen Max for nearly twenty-four hours and young and in love as he was, it felt like a lifetime to Pete.

He gave his trademark knock on the door, but when it swung open, it was not Max's face that he saw.

It was the face of Max's father.

"Well well Mr Abrahams! Come in, I've been wanting to have a word with you." The words were cordial enough, but the tone was hard, angry and full of bile.

"Go into the lounge and wait for me." Pete was tempted to run back down the stairs, but he was worried about where Max was. If this was to end up the way he thought it might, he wanted to take Max with him when he left.

Heart pumping, he walked past the Manager and into the lounge. He knew this was a ploy the man liked to use. The longer he kept you waiting, the more trouble it meant you were in.

He walked towards the window and glanced out of it. He didn't have any particular desire to see what was going on outside, but it was something to do to keep him from thinking about the horrors awaiting him on Edwards' return.

The weather forecast had been correct, and the lovely late summer's day had turned to rain with the fall of night. A car drove into the car park and lightened on a man walking towards the gate to the beach. He was the only person in evidence and on such a stormy night. Pete was surprised to see even one person thinking that a walk on the sands was a good idea.

Pete called Max's name in the hope that he would appear before the father returned and then they could leave together. Not a sound answered his call and he thought he'd investigate along the corridor to find out if his lover was in his bedroom.

As he opened the door, he saw Edwards waiting outside. He had obviously wanted to make him wait much longer, but was allowing him no chance of an escape. His face was scrunched into a mask of pure poison, he had stopped even trying to hide behind a façade of respectability.

Pete now knew for sure that he was in big trouble.

He was pushed back into the lounge by the elder man who had decided that he couldn't wait any longer to make his opinions known.

"You fucking stupid Nancy boy! How dare you come into my hotel and bring your repulsive sexual practices into my home! How dare you sodomise my child. It is morally reprehensible and it's not even fucking legal!"

Pete bit back, "It is legal, you moron!" There was no thought in his brain for trying to keep his job, he just needed to get out of this room, find Max and take him back to his own mother and father as soon as possible. "Where have you been since 1967?"

"Are you twenty-one?" Edwards ranted, "Is he?"

Pete gasped, they were both under the legal age. Did that make a difference? It suddenly seemed ironic that he had thought about going with Jackie to the police, as a witness. Now it was possible that he could be going as the accused.

"It doesn't matter, I love him, and he loves me!" Bizarrely he realised he was still holding the Boomtown Rats record in his hand, he waved it as he talked. Edwards knocked it from his hand and Pete watched as it flew across the room and slid under the sofa.

"He doesn't love you, you pathetic little sodomite!" There was an angry laugh in a voice of pure disdain. "Do you really think that? He told me that he can barely bear to look at you."

"No!" Pete couldn't believe it, wouldn't believe it, he knew the man was lying… Max was the most lovely, truthful man he had ever met, he knew that he wouldn't lie to him, he knew that he loved him.

Edwards pulled Pete towards him by his shirt and spat in his face. "You are going to leave this place tonight, and… if you leave here without preamble or argument, then I may not call the police, but if you ever try to see my son again, then I would be more than happy to inform them and see you charged!" he released his grip slightly, "Do I make myself clear?"

"You do," Pete's voice was as clear and sharp as broken crystal. "However, if you do that, then you must be prepared to see your son in jail also. Because I know that if what we have done is illegal, he loves me too much to let me suffer alone. Just think of the scandal, how good would that be for your precious hotel?"

He paused then shoved the older man away, "I am going to call him now and you will never see either of us again."

Pete left the room and marched down the corridor. He tried the door, but it was locked and there was no key on the outside. "Maxi, it's me!" He called, "unlock the door and we can walk out of this place together. I love you Max and I know you love me!"

He listened and convinced himself he could hear rustling inside, but other than that there was the loneliest sound in the world… silence. Edwards had followed him down the corridor and was standing in front of him triumphantly. He pulled him away from Max's door and whispered viciously into his ear. "You see, I told you that he is not a pervert!" He had reached the main door to the apartment and opened it with his free hand. "Leave now, because if I ever see you again…" he left the final threat unsaid as he opened the door and manhandled Pete out of it.

Pete stood on the wrong side of the door and wondered what he should do. Why hadn't Max answered him? Had The Old Man threatened to report him to the authorities and had he succumbed to the ultimatum? He couldn't believe it, from the very first day when Max had stood up to Hutch he had known he was stronger than that. Was he even there? Had they already sent him away and had Pete been calling to an empty room?

Yet he was sure he had heard some sound of life inside.

He stood for a while in the corridor wondering what to do, when he remembered the man who had been walking down to the beach on a rainy night. He suddenly realised who it was and knew that he would help him. He ran down the stairs and into the open air. Pete was pleased to feel the cool of the night on his face, after the heat and oppression of the apartment upstairs. The rain was easing, and the angry clouds were being blown across the sky by a stiff breeze.

As he entered the beach, he saw a solitary man standing on the edge of the shore. The night was chillier than the summer nights when they had partied on the sands or laid in the dunes chatting and drinking. Pete didn't have a coat and after first blessing the cool air, he now shivered. He was unsure, however, if it was because of the cold or the fact that the man now standing just a few yards in front of him would help him to be reunited with Max. He ran up to him and shouted, "Mo!"

But the look on the face of the man who turned around was not the face of the Deputy Manager, a man who was known for being tough but fair.

It was the face of a man who was trying very hard not to descend into madness.

It was a face of pure loathing.

34.

1977

"You raped him!" Mo spat it out, phlegm descending onto the sand.

Pete couldn't believe it, was he trapped in some nightmare? Would he suddenly wake up in his parents' house with Max sleeping beside him?

"No!" he cried, "I love him, Mo, I love him!"

Mo was on the verge of tears. "Don't!" he whispered, "don't even say it. I have just seen your friends. They told me everything."

Pete was confused, Tony was in an alcoholic slumber and Jackie was…

"How…? Who…?"

"Barry Grounds was one of them"

Pete stared at him, "I have no idea…"

"I believe you call him Hutch," realisation dawned on Pete and a sick feeling spawned in the pit of his stomach, which worsened as Mo continued. "Him and that drug dealer friend of yours."

"Marlon?" Pete couldn't quite believe what he was hearing. "We're not friends. What on earth have they been telling you."

"Grounds said that you'd been hitting on Max for weeks, even though he kept telling you he was only interested in friendship…" Pete opened his mouth to speak but Mo held up his hand. "Don't!" he said, "Just don't! I can't bear the fact that I allowed you to see him, encouraged you to befriend him… I thought you were all right, I'd heard the rumours about you, but I thought you were OK."

Pete was trying to think of something to say but Max's brother continued. "I should have known that all you lot are the same!"

"Mo!" Pete put an arm out, but the Deputy Manager pulled away from him as if he was infected with nuclear waste.

"Your other friend, the pusher, said that you asked him for a drug the other weekend, something that would make someone "compliant with your wishes" - I think that was the way he put it." The pain in his face was unbearable, Pete wanted to put an arm around him, but the anger that was also there, stopped him.

"It's rubbish Mo! Hutch just hates me, and Marlon is getting revenge because I fucked up a deal for him…" Even as he said it, Pete realised that it sounded like he had been in business with the man. "I mean not like that…"

"His face was in a terrible state," Mo shuddered, his heart was breaking, but not for a drug dealer with bruises. "He said that he'd threatened to expose you and you hired heavies to beat him up."

Pete wanted to laugh, but in a humourless way at the bizarreness of it all. "For God's sake Mo! How on earth have I got the money to pay to get someone beaten up? They're lying! Surely you can see they're lying!" He heard the pleading tone in his voice and hated himself for it, but he needed to make Mo understand. However, the Deputy Manager replied with a statement that had convinced him that Pete's enemies were speaking the truth.

"They knew about the mole on Max's buttock." Mo stated it simply, the way he would ask a customer if there was anything they wanted from the wine list.

"What?"

"You told them about every inch of Max's body afterwards and how you had…" Mo trailed off, he couldn't say the words.

A sudden and horrible realisation crept up on Pete. Those late-night chats with Tony, who must have shared pillow talk with Helen… who in turn was very good friends with Hutch.

Oh God Tony, what have you done? thought Pete. However, it wasn't his friend he blamed, it wasn't even Helen. It was Hutch. He had waited all summer to get his revenge for his card game humiliation and he had done so… in spades.

"You even told them that I have always kissed Max on the forehead before bedtime… and that I still do." Mo was like a glass full of rage teetering on the edge of the table, on the very point of falling to the floor and exploding.

"They thought it very sweet…" The voice shook at the memory of the mocking and the glass wobbled in preparation for the final journey.

"Please, Mo! I love him, surely you can see that!"

The glass hit the floor.

"You never loved him…! You loved the power you had over him… you… sick… pervert!"

"What did Max say Mo? He was going to tell you about his feelings on the drive over to Cheddar." Pete just hoped that the fact that he knew about Max's plans may just convince Mo that he was telling the truth. But Mo believed he had heard the truth from a misogynist liar and a drug dealer, he didn't even believe his own brother.

"Oh…" His voice was bitter and full of scorn. "Of course, he said that he loved you. Apparently, victims quite often fall in love with the people who have abused them."

Pete could guess where he had got that bit of tuppeny wisdom from. He wanted to tell Mo that he wasn't the rapist around here, that he should look a little bit closer to Hutch for that person.

However, it wasn't his secret to tell, and he knew he couldn't break Jackie's trust.

He was suddenly aware of the object in his pocket. It

lay trapped between denim and cotton and he could feel the pull of it against his leg as he moved.

"Look," said Pete, reaching into his pocket and pulling out the present he had hoped would make its first appearance at a much happier time. He forced the agony from his voice and tried to be calm and reasonable.

"I've saved up all summer for this. We went into town one day and saw a young lad buy his girlfriend an engagement ring. Max said that he wished that he could have been that girl, could have received a present from someone to show him he was the most important person in their world. He also thought that it would never happen. I wanted to show him that he was wrong. I wanted to prove that I would always love him."

With shaking hands, he unwrapped the box and passed the ring over to Mo who took it like it was a piece of pure evil.

He looked at it closely and then looked at Pete, but the anger hadn't died, it had intensified.

"It is all about power with you, isn't it?" he asked, "the drugs to make him bend to your will, the bragging about it to your friends afterwards and the ring which you only bought to prove that he was wrong! It is all about power," he repeated, then giving Pete a strange look he said: "Well at least I can make sure that you never get to give him this horrible piece of tat."

He lifted the ring in the air and threw it to the edge of the water where it landed, invisible under the clouded night sky.

"No!" screamed Pete and without thinking ran towards the water. As he neared the edge, his feet began to stick in the soft mud, two paces later and he had decided that it was too dangerous and the gift that he had slogged for and saved for, had gone forever.

It was then that the untimely moon decided to appear from behind a cloud for the first time that night. Pete saw the jewel shining a mere six feet beyond him. He took one step and sunk a little more, then another with the same result. He needed only one more step and he could reach it. Without a thought, he pulled his front leg from the mud, moved forward and pulled his other leg to join it and planted it in the soft earth. For a moment it held him, but as he leant to pick up the ring, the land gave way and sucked him downwards. Suddenly, the only parts of his body that were free from the mud were above his armpits.

"Mo!" he shouted, turning his head towards him. "Mo, I'm in real trouble here!"

The man on the beach stood stock still for a while and then slowly turned - and walked away.

He shouted again, but the man carried on walking, step by murderous step away from the drowning man… as the tide came in.

Pete tried to use the water to soften the sand and free himself, but he was in too deep and escape was no longer possible. He tried shouting to anyone, but the revellers who crowded the bars less than a quarter of a mile away, were all indoors on such a damp and dreary night and were useless to him.

Once he realised that the water would come quickly and engulf him, he soothed himself. He would not die screaming like a coward or begging forgiveness like a hypocrite. He would accept it and think of all the wonderful things that had blessed his nineteen years. He would run through his life story the way he would play a Greatest Hits album.

He thought of his parents and his resolve almost weakened. So he thought instead of the joy that they had brought each other. He thought of his childhood, his last Christmas… and Abba.

He then thought of Max. Max loved him, even Mo had admitted that. As the incoming tide started to invade his nostrils, he thought of his promise to Max on the night that ended their perfect day. He knew that it was not the end, could never be the end. With his dying breath Pete swore that he would one day see Max again and he would wait for that day, however long it took.

He was suddenly aware, almost for the first time of a strange presence inside him.

He exhaled one last time and whispered one word.

35.

I am inside Pete as he runs towards the water.

I am trying to stop him, but his will is so much stronger than mine.

As we become cemented in the soft mud I am working with him trying to free him, trying to free us.

I know that Mo has deserted us, I know that it is only myself and Pete that are left to fight this unyielding enemy.

I also know that it is stronger than us.

I can't save you Pete, I cry, I can't save you!

As the water flaps around his nostrils, I think I hear him breathe one word to me…

"Go!"

36.

S am was holding me, trying to soothe the tremors in my body, but he couldn't do anything about the terrors in my heart.

I could taste a mixture of salt water and bile in my mouth, and my sinuses were aching as if they have been starved of air. I felt sick and my head was pounding. I had no idea if I had been close to drowning, or I had the worst hangover ever.

But Sam was close, pulling me towards safety, helping me, saving me. I could feel the comfort of his body as I shivered with cold in a warm bed. He whispered to me. He was telling me that everything will be OK.

But how?

"I couldn't save him Sam, I couldn't - save - him."

He crushed me towards him and whispered gently in my ear. "Oh sweetheart! You were never going to save him, were you? I'm just glad that you survived. You have been writhing about choking for air for the last quarter of an hour. I thought you were drowning in your own vomit. I was trying to wake you, but nothing seemed to work."

He settled me on the bed and pulled his body up on his arms so that he was staring into my face. His eyes were full of concern… and terror.

"I thought I was going to lose you."

I tried to pull myself up so that I could kiss him, but I was unable to do so, in the end he bent down to kiss my lips instead.

There was a knock on the door. Oh, for fuck's sake, the early morning tea tray had arrived…

I was not sent to my corner of the room and at first, I thought that this was an improvement. However, Sam jumped up and ran to the door before his mother could enter the room and catch me naked in his bed.

I could hear the conversation vaguely through my post-drowning bleariness.

"Oh darling! You didn't have to get up, I would have brought it in. Is everything all right? I thought I heard crying and screaming." I could almost feel Fiona trying to peer around the door; but Sam only had the door open a few centimetres under the pretext of hiding his nakedness from her.

"Rem had a really bad nightmare." He felt around the door and his hand returned carrying a mug. It was obviously hot as his other hand grabbed it by the handle quickly and he shook the burning sensation away. "I guess Dad wants me to work today."

"Oh yes love! We're really sorry, but Bev has just rung. Bakers are having the first of their Christmas tastings today and someone has dropped out last minute. They wondered if your dad and I would be able to get away, your dad is quite keen to go."

Christmas! In July? I was dubious, but Sam seemed to think it quite normal. He firmly closed the door on Fiona, put the mug down on the bedside table and crawled back on top of the bed, before enveloping me in his arms once again.

"I'm sorry Rem, are you going to be all right?"

I nodded, "Just a bit knackered really, you go to work, I might try to get a bit more sleep."

"We'll talk about…" He paused, searching for the right words, "your dream later, OK?"

He looked at me, checking to see that I wasn't going to go off on one about his parents and their increasing demands on his time. I was probably being harsh, he actually looked at me with deep concern and I loved him for it.

I didn't really sleep. I took tablets but for once they didn't do the trick. My headache stayed happily banging at my temples, whilst my brain tried to come to terms with all that I had witnessed.

Sometime after eleven when Emily had finished her rooms, she popped in to see me. I was feeling better physically, if not mentally. "Sam asked me to check that you're all right, he is really worried about you. What happened?"

I told her the final chapter of the story and she looked concerned, amazed and angry at various times during the recounting of it. When I reached the end and the moment when it seemed that Pete was pushing me away from the sea and Sam was pulling me from it, she held my hand tightly.

"So, it was Mo? Mo killed Pete?"

I nodded, there were arguments that he simply left him to die, but I shared Em's opinion.

"Will you tell Max?"

It was a question I had asked myself all morning. "I don't know. On one side, he has been blaming himself for the way he treated his brother for about forty years. It even occurred to me that he thinks he might have been a little bit responsible for Mo's death as well as his father's, so it might help to give him…" I struggled not to use the awful cliché, but then decided that my addled brain couldn't think of anything better, "closure… Then on the other hand, I'm telling him that the man he idolised actually killed the love of his life." It was too difficult a question for my state of mind, I finally settled on, "I'll see how I feel, if and when the time comes."

Em nodded and then said, "I thought you said Jackie told you that Hutch was The Planner?"

That was something else that I had thought a lot about that morning. "D'you know, I'm not actually sure she did.

She always referred to him as Marsons or The Planner, I think. I just assumed it was him." I grinned ironically, the nearest thing to a smile that I had managed all morning.

"I never for a moment thought she was actually talking about Starsky. In fact, I thought he had grown old to become your Uncle John!"

Em drew in her breathe, "Really?... Why?"

"He looks a bit like I could imagine Starsky would have looked when he had grown older, even now your Uncle John hasn't managed to grow a beard and moustache properly. Starsky was studying law, they both had the same talent for anonymity." A little spark of naughtiness reared its head briefly. "They were both a little dull…"

I trailed off vaguely then thought of another reason. "Also, your uncle was always a bit edgy whenever 1977 was mentioned. I thought that it was because he didn't want it known that he was once a friend of The Planner."

Em laughed, "Oh no, that's just Uncle John, he's edgy about everything!"

She looked at me, concern and relief waging a tiny battle around her eyes. "You're looking a little better… Am I a force for good?"

I laughed genuinely, "You most certainly are! It was good to talk about it, it's been driving me crazy all morning, bashing it around my head."

From quite a young age I have kept a diary. If I've had a particularly bad day, I always feel better once I've written all the dreary details down… this felt a bit like that.

She smiled and feeling comfortable that she could continue dissecting what I had told her, continued.

"It makes more sense though, doesn't it?" she asked and then answered her own question. "Up to now we've thought that Hutch attempted the rape and then went back to the Hotel to discredit Pete, which seemed like an incredible risk. Now we know that it was Starsky," she paused to get her thoughts in order, "I think I can guess what happened."

"Go on."

"I read up on The Planner and I think you told me yourself, he always had a stooge who he could use as a scapegoat, if things got a little tricky."

I nodded, "Carry on."

"Hutch was his stooge. He had organised him to go and wait somewhere that he was unlikely to be seen, but near enough that he could have been noticed in the general area of the attack, when the police started investigating."

"Yes!" I said, I was almost getting excited, it was a definite improvement on the state I'd been in all morning. "Pete also noticed that Starsky was wearing Hutch's shirt."

Em nodded, "Well it was before DNA was discovered, but do you think that a bit of that shirt would have been found snagged on a bush afterwards?"

I nodded, "So he was definitely planning to murder Jackie, not just rape her?"

Em agreed. "I think she would have been his first victim," she said.

A shiver ran down the back of my spine when I thought of the lovely lady so full of life that I had met in the pub out at Yatton. If it hadn't been for Pete and the way he always put others before himself, the way he worried about his friends, I would never have met her.

"So," Em was warming to her theme. "Starsky has Hutch in place, probably by telling him where he's going with Jackie and promising him a bit of the action if he wants to meet them after work."

I frowned, "You think Hutch was in on it too? From what I remember The Planner operated alone."

Em shook her head, "Oh no, nothing like that. It was just to get Hutch by the estuary, where Starsky needed his fall guy to be. Starsky probably joked that he would get Jackie away from Pete, her guard dog, and they could fool about with her in private. Hutch was sleazy and liked to demean women, but she would have been a notch on his bedpost rather than a rape victim, I think."

"So, he has Hutch in place, he has Jackie where he wants her and then Pete appears."

"Exactly!" Em seemed to have sorted her thought processes and was steaming ahead. "That completely messes it all up for The Planner. He guesses that Pete will encourage Jackie to report it. I can only think that he just hopes she will be in such a state that Pete will have to wait until the next day before she is well enough to do so."

"A bit of a risk though," I frowned, but Em was not to be discouraged.

"It is, so he finds Hutch, spins him a story that Perfect Pete has turned up and sabotaged their plans once again. Wouldn't it be nice if he got a bit of his own medicine? If someone was to tell Old Man Edwards about him and his boyfriend, that would do the trick!"

"But what does he do then?"

"He hides out, I guess. He sends Hutch to do his dirty work then conceals himself somewhere he can see what's happening, so that if the worse comes to the worse and the police start arriving, he can head to the hills."

"But why bother? Why not go just as soon as Pete has taken Jackie into the shop?"

Em grinned at me like a magician on the point of telling me exactly what card I was holding. "I told you, it was the robbery that was important." She screwed her face up into a small frown, as if the card was the wrong one after all. "OK, I might not have got the reasoning quite right…"

I gave her a look of bewilderment, I mean, I nearly drowned in my bed earlier. I couldn't be expected to keep up, could I?

"Starsky probably tells him something close to the truth, except he would have said that Jackie really wanted it, then started crying rape when Pete turned up. 'I was just getting her warmed up for you, Hutch.' or something awful like that," Em curled up her nose in distaste. "Hutch was such an idiot he would have fallen for it. Starsky then says that he needs to leave before the shit hits the fan, but why should they go without the money they are owed? They then come up with a plan for him to hide out whilst Hutch goes to the Hotel and causes a diversion. This has the added bonus of Hutch getting his revenge on Pete at the same time. Then, when everyone is cosy in bed, they can break in, take the money and fly away to wherever they want to go!"

She sat back, very happy with her pronouncement - just like her brother... They both wanted to be Jessica Fletcher.

I didn't want to burst her bubble and in all probability, she had got it about right, but...

"Max said that there was a lot of police and ambulance activity when he went for his walk on the beach in the middle of the night. Surely if Starsky and Hutch had seen them arriving, they wouldn't have hung around?

Em scowled slightly, then brightened. "They had either broken in already and fled, or they were in the middle of breaking in, heard the sirens, panicked, then realised that the sirens were nothing to do with what they were doing..."

"Or?"

"Or, they've got balls of steel and they hung around until it was all over and did the job, then. Whichever it was, the Hotel was broken into and the only reasoning that really makes sense is that they were responsible."

It did add up, I guessed, but it brought another question to my mind. "I wonder if they ever found out that the lies Hutch told, along with that other drug pushing bastard, led directly to Pete's death?" I shrugged. "They probably wouldn't have cared even if they had known."

I have always thought that hate was a futile emotion. But, just at that moment, I felt it in a way I never had before.

Em stayed with me for an hour or so, chatting about her weekend away. Speech day had been long, dreary and she had been "Sweating like a P-I-G for two hours in an airless marquee."

The aftermath of the ball had been much more successful as she had ended up down at the cricket pavilion with a lad that she had fancied for a long time… There were similarities between us, I thought, first lust and the use of sporting facilities…

I must have dozed off at one point and when I awoke, she was gone. I padded out to find her and she was watching TV in the lounge. She asked me if I was hungry and I realised that I was – the physical effects of my dream had receded, now all I needed to do was sort out my mental welfare and I'd be fine. I had a horrible feeling that it would be trickier to fix.

Em cooked me a mid-afternoon snack. Actually, cooking is rather a grand term for what she did, she microwaved a macaroni cheese. Em did not share her father and brother's passion for food, unless it was eating the stuff.

We watched late afternoon quiz shows and then she announced that she was going to ring one of the waitresses and tell her that she couldn't go to the cinema with her after all that evening.

"Why on earth not?" I asked.

"I'm not leaving you," was the reply.

"I'm fine Em," I assured her, "I could do with a few moments without you prattling on, to be honest!"

I didn't mean it at all, I loved her company, but my rudeness did the trick: it convinced her that I was returning to my normal self.

As soon as she had gone, I regretted being so magnanimous. I started thinking and over thinking the whole situation and ended up landing straight in the middle of a worry that I hadn't even considered before.

OK, Pete had died that day at the hands of his lover's brother. Sam did not have a brother, so maybe that wasn't the point of the dream after all. I hadn't been able to save

Pete, so obviously that wasn't the point of the dream either. However, Pete's lover had also been in the wars that day, beaten half to death by his father when he found out he was in a gay relationship.

Sam and his father did very much exist, and we were planning to tell his parents of our relationship very shortly.

Was it Sam that I should have been worried about?

Ned wasn't like that though, surely? Bad tempered, pompous and a bit of an arsehole maybe, but a maniac who could commit filicide?

By the time that Sam had got a minute to pop up and check out how I was, I had got myself into a complete state. As soon as I saw him, I ran over to him and enclosed him in a massive hug. He held onto me and he could probably feel me shaking. He held me closely for five or ten minutes, calming me and soothing me. Once I had stopped shaking, he continued to hold me. By this time, we were just enjoying the closeness of each other.

And then we kissed.

That was when Armageddon arrived in Weston.

"What the fucking hell! Samuel!"

We broke away from each other like we had been stabbed with a cattle prod. I could see Fiona standing in the doorway, there was panic in her eyes and she was watching the man who was standing in front of her. Shouting.

"You fucking pair of Nancy boys, what the hell are you doing?"

My illogical thought was: "Oh my God! He didn't know that we were having an affair. He must have done. I was so sure he did…"

Then I remembered hearing the expression he had just shouted in our general direction.

I had heard it in my last dream.

I then thought about how bad tempered he had been in the last few weeks, if he hadn't known about Sam and me, then what on earth had caused it?

I thought: apart from the first time we met, he has barely been able to say a word to me. Sometimes it felt like a struggle for him to even look in my direction.

However, it now appeared that it wasn't because he had guessed I was gay.

I remembered the look on his face when Sam mentioned Tony's name in the middle of the gammon and cauliflower cheese dinner. I thought at the time he was just angry with his son for refusing to spy on the Head Chef.

I thought about who was near to Jack when he dropped the cutlery on my first night in Weston.

I was pretty sure that it had happened after I had given the family one particular piece of information.

My real name.

37.

"Hello Mo."

I vaguely looked around me. Sam hadn't heard the details of my latest excursion into 1977 so he looked frightened and baffled. Fiona couldn't seem to understand why I was calling her husband by the wrong name.

But Ned… or Mo, he knew.

He looked at me and said very slowly. "I want you to go and get your things and leave my hotel immediately. You are no longer welcome…"

I was reminded of an evening in this room about forty years ago, when another man with my name was told the self-same thing. I wasn't being threatened with arrest, but I was under no illusion that if he could have used that ultimatum, he would have done so.

He turned to his son and said, his voice ready to cut like an unsheathed knife. "You have let me down, Samuel, in fact you have let the whole family down. At this moment in time, I am ashamed that you are my son."

I turned and looked at the face of the man I loved. A man who was so much more respected by the people who worked for them than his father was. The man who would drop everything at a moment's notice and would do any task that was necessary to make the business run smoothly. The man who loved his mother, idolised his father and would have chased after heaven just to give it to his sister.

I saw the face of a man who was falling apart thinking

he had somehow shamed them.

I became angry.

"You murdered a man!" I screamed, "You murdered a lovely man and you stand there and tell Sam he is a disgrace!" I was choking over my words and the last of them were barely audible through anger, phlegm and spit. "How can you live with yourself?"

He walked towards me and I reversed in the direction of the french windows, not because I was frightened that he would hit me. I was more worried that he would be able to shut my smart mouth, before I got a chance to say what I wanted to say.

"You are an idiot Mo!" I yelled in his face, "you believed a man who helped a rapist become a serial killer, you believed a drug pushing scum bag and you supported a man who was a complete bully!" I paused, I wasn't even sure if my words were coherent, I just knew that I had to say them. "You believed them, even though the brother who idolised you told a different story. You believed them over a man who had worked hard for you and actually liked you. How stupid are you?"

I saw Mo walking towards me, his face an advertising hoarding full of hate. I was aware of Fiona and Sam, but they seemed to be playing a bizarre game of statues. They weren't moving at all.

Mo raised his arm, but I could tell there was a brief conflict, I could see it in his eyes. I had never once in my life, wanted to give or receive physical violence, but I needed him to hit me so badly that I gave him one last taunt.

"That's right Mo! Beat the living crap out of me!" The last phrase cracked and choked and came out as a whisper. "Prove to me that you are your father's son…"

He didn't punch me. He went to grab me, I think more to shut me up than to actually cause me physical harm. I pushed against him and continued with my vile rants directly into his face.

"Oh of course, you can only watch a man die, you don't even have the balls…"

I pushed hard against him and he pushed back much harder than I believe he meant to.

He was a big powerful man and I was not. I was launched towards the open window. My trailing foot hit the slight ledge between the carpet and the outside air and I continued my journey towards the security rail with an upward trajectory.

As I hit the rail, I expected to bounce back, but it had been there a long time and there was rusting where the upright met the floor. It wasn't enough to tear the railing away from the stonework, but it was enough to bend so that I could continue my journey over it.

As I realised that I had not reached my destination just yet, I grappled desperately to find something to cling on to. My shirt caught on the edge of one of the curves and my flailing arm managed to get purchase. However, my upper body strength was not as good as a young man's should have been. I knew that I wouldn't be able to hold on for too long.

The wrought iron pressed at my hands, prising my fingers apart and I began to lose my grip.

Slowly, I slipped away from the balcony.

I saw the canopy before I felt it. I slid into it more than dropped onto it and for a brief second, I wondered if it would hold me. It did - but I knew that it wouldn't be too long before my weight pulled it away from the wall. I could see myself cascading down the side of the hotel like Elmer Fudd in a tree, hitting every branch until he reached the bottom, where he would get up to lose another day. I knew that unlike the cartoon, I wouldn't be getting up and going anywhere.

I looked up and I could see Sam leaning over the misshapen ironwork. He was leaning further than a health and safety evaluation would have considered sensible. It didn't really matter, he looked miles away and I felt that I had more chance of climbing up the Eiffel Tower wearing a pair of ice skates than I did of actually reaching him.

I looked up at his face, but I could not see it clearly. I wanted to shout out, "I love you Sam… I'm so sorry for being such a dick!"

I tried to get a bit of purchase on the canopy, but it shuddered away from the wall slightly. It was only a little movement, but it caused me to slide to the edge of the material. I felt my legs scrape against the bottom bar, as they crossed the edge and flailed wildly in the empty space.

I looked down then and I could see the human ants as they glided across the grass. They were so intent on enjoying their evening beers that they were completely oblivious to the drama that was occurring above them.

I thought illogically, "Shouldn't someone be running to fetch a mattress?" Then on the verge of insanity, "Why is no-one blowing up a bouncy castle?"

My legs seemed to be weightless, but the weight of them was pulling the rest of my body closer to the edge.

Looking down had been a very bad mistake. My arms felt bereft of all power. They were shaking, and the tremors went all the way from my shoulder down to my wrists. My hands were clutching desperately into the plastic fabric and my knuckles were beginning to go numb. My stomach felt hollow and empty - like an elephant had kicked all the air from inside me and my head was feeling like I had inhaled an entire humidor of Cuban cigars. For one brief moment I had an intense desire to unclench my fingers and fly as a bird would fly.

People have told me since, that adrenalin is an incredible thing. It can fill you with the power to do things that you were sure you weren't capable of. I have never told them what I believe to be true. I do not want to see that look in their eyes, or sense the condescension as they nod and quickly change the subject.

I know in my own mind that as I clung there, an interested but useless observer to the dying of my life… I heard a familiar voice.

I had heard it in my dreams many times over the last few weeks.

He was telling me to trust him, to use him and he would help me to crawl to safety.

I felt a strange power occupy my body. My arms stopped shaking, my legs stopped flailing and my whole being seemed to assume a purpose. To crawl, millimetre by millimetre, and climb the canopy before the whole thing parted company with the wall and crashed someone's party below.

Adrenalin is an incredible thing?

All the time I was climbing I could hear his voice in my ear, telling me that everything would be fine. It was just like climbing the stairs to bed, no big deal really.

As I reached the top of the canopy, I was running out of things to hold on to. By the sound of the creaks and groans of the framework below me, I was also running out of time. I looked up trying to find anything to cling on to and saw Sam stretching out too far... far too far. He was resting his weight on a piece of wrought iron that was no more solid than an iceberg floating in a warm bath.

He was being far braver than was sensible, simply because he wanted to save my life.

The thought gave me an added impetus. I risked pulling my legs up on to the crossbar of the canopy framework. I tentatively pulled myself up to a semi-standing position. All the time I told myself that looking down was not an option. Instead I looked up and saw the arms with the golden flecks of hair stretching to reach me. I stretched also and clasped his hand, I felt my weight pull at Sam's resolve. I dropped about ten centimetres and wondered how much leeway Sam actually had before he plunged to his death, taking me with him. I also wondered how much strength was still left in the battered railing, and in Sam himself.

My feet found a semi-purchase on the wall. I heard the

voice again and felt that strange power within me. I could also feel the strength of my boyfriend above me, pulling me. With his help, I began to walk up the wall.

In the same way my dream had ended, Pete was pushing me to safety and Sam was pulling me from danger.

Slowly, slowly, centimetre by centimetre, I climbed. The railing shuddered but held. But Sam was still leaning out too far. I had reached the edge of the wrought iron which was now practically horizontal. I grabbed at it with my free hand and half pulled myself and was half pulled by Sam towards safety.

With one last burst of the power from inside me, I threw myself over the edge of the piece of iron that had formed the safety barrier. Letting go of Sam's hand, I fell towards the security of the thin strip of concrete beyond.

My trailing leg trod on railing rather than concrete and I felt the wrought iron finally give in to gravity and it disappeared from underneath me. I sprawled in an ungainly fashion with my knees jarred against the concrete outside and my head butting against the carpet inside.

I then heard a terrible scream and there was only one thought in my head.

Sam had been leaning too far out.

38.

I lay on the floor trying to get my breath back and at the same time I tried not to think too much about that scream.

Fiona had been sitting against a wall just to my left, holding her husband. The whole of Mo's face looked white from the snowy hair, down the alabaster skin, to the beard below. He looked like a Santa Claus who had heard that Christmas had become bankrupt, and he'd been given his P45.

On hearing the scream and then seeing me land on the lounge floor, Fiona had got up quickly and moved past me as if I wasn't there. Just about managing not to stand on me, she went out onto the balcony to find out exactly what the cry had signified.

I couldn't move, could barely breathe and couldn't get rid of the sick sense that I had killed her son.

I looked across at Mo, who looked into space, he seemed completely oblivious to the fact that I had crashed landed on his carpet. His face was completely empty, like a lunch box after the picnic had been removed.

I waited for the cry of anguish that would have told me the horrible truth, but it didn't come. In fact, nothing happened for a minute or so and I was beginning to wonder if Fiona had silently thrown herself off the building following her son to his death. Then, I saw the glimpse of a shadow cross the path of the french window and Fiona reappeared.

Sam was with her! He had somehow managed to throw himself onto to an iceberg as the Titanic went down. He looked amazingly healthy for a man who had been dead in my mind, just a few seconds earlier.

It seemed to be more a case of Sam helping Fiona back into the room, than vice versa. I pushed away the last vestiges of my grogginess to stand up and greet him.

On seeing me, Fiona immediately left her son and went back to holding her husband.

"Are you OK?" Sam asked me, and I nodded.

"Are you?"

He seemed surprised by the question. He looked at me as if he was my GP and was assessing whether I was a good candidate for care in the community; rather than my boyfriend sharing the intimate knowledge that we had both been centimetres from death.

Dr Morris looked at me again and decided that I might not have been telling the whole truth.

"There are some sedatives in the bathroom, I think you should take some to help you get some rest."

I was sure that he was going to write a prescription at any moment. My only surprise was that he didn't have a black bag with the tablets ready and waiting.

I allowed myself to be led by him from the room. I glanced back, and both of his parents were still sitting on the floor. Mo still seemed to have no knowledge of my existence and Fiona gave me a strange dismissive stare.

After I had taken the tablets, he led me with the same professional courtesy along to our bedroom.

I thought that once we were inside the room he might have held me like I had been aching to hold him. However, he merely waited for me to get undressed, then guided me in the same caring but anonymous manner towards the camp bed in the corner.

I slept a dreamless, drug induced sleep and woke up when it was once again light outside. My phone told me that it was eight-thirty in the morning.

As I lay there trying to shake the terrible sense of depression that was threatening to take me over, I had only one thought in my mind. The almost robotic, completely emotionless way that Sam had dealt with me the evening before. I decided that he must have been shocked from the ordeal we had both just been through. He had been strong, heroic and fought to save my life after all. Surely that was a good sign?

I suddenly realised why he had been so confused. He would have had no idea about the way Pete's story had ended. I hadn't had a chance to tell him about my final dream the day before. I had been shouting abuse towards his father that would have made absolutely no sense to Sam or Fiona. No wonder they had looked at me like I was slightly deranged.

I looked over towards Sam's bed. He was not in it, at that moment, and the tell-tale neatness of the duvet led me to believe that he hadn't slept in it at all the night before.

There was an envelope, addressed to me, on the table by the side of the camp bed. I leant over and tore across the top of the paper and released the letter from inside.

39.

D^{ear Peter,}

ear Peter,
    I am going away.
        By the time you read this, I will be gone. There are a few reasons for this: My family will soon know exactly what I did in 1977 and being an old-fashioned type of man, I need them to respect me as the infallible head of the family - not as an idiot who believed two losers over his own brother.

One of the things that you were right about is the fact that I am slightly jealous of Sam. He is going to become a much better manager than I have ever been. He has a natural affinity with people, a great eye for business and is not frightened to tackle injustice head on - I have been on the losing end of a couple of arguments these last few weeks and I have been so proud of him. I am sure he would never have been taken in as I was, all those years ago.

However, all this being said, it does pose a problem, because I am a control freak. Giving Sam more and more authority might well be the right thing to do, but it would be impossible for me to do it.

He is, in truth, probably a couple of years away from being completely ready, but with the help of his mother and the rest of the management team, he is going to have to step up a little earlier than anyone thought he would.

You see, Peter, the third and final reason I am going away is…
You.

I would be vilified for this by the PC Brigade, but I just can't cope with the fact that my wonderful son is a homosexual. I could have coped with him having many unattractive qualities, if only he had been straight. The worst of it all is that I didn't have a clue that he was that way inclined, I missed it with Max, how could I miss it again with Sam? I know I shouldn't, but I blame you for this. I keep thinking that if you hadn't turned up and turned his head, he might have made a go of it with Chloe by now. To think that I originally wasn't sure about her because she was the daughter of immigrants…

I blame the fact that he was gay for turning Max against his family. It changed him from an innocent boy to a man I would have crossed the street to avoid. Because of his obsession, I have seen pictures of some depraved acts which conceal themselves under a banner of homosexual love. It is not something I want for my own son.

I am not sure how much you know about the fall out after Pete's death, I will explain a little of that later. I am sure that you would say that it is the way his family dealt with his homosexuality rather than the homosexuality itself that caused him to behave this way, but I would beg to differ.

It is much better that I leave, then if you must become the love of Sam's life, at least I won't have to witness it.

I am aware that I came close to killing you tonight. I could say that I was merely trying to get you away from me, that I had no idea we were so near the window and that I had pushed with greater force than I had meant to. All these things are true, but I guess that they are all weak excuses.

I know that I have not treated you well since you arrived at my home. I know that I have barely talked to you, looked at you and scarcely acknowledged your existence. After all I've just written I'm sure you are assuming that the reason behind this was because you are a homosexual. Believe me, I had no idea before last night that this was the case, I would have not let you share a room with my son if I had known.

No, it was not your sexual preferences that made me treat you in that way. It was from the moment that you told me your real name. Poor Jack, he was the only person who noticed my shock, my arm knocked his as I jumped in surprise and it caused him to drop cutlery onto the floor.

At first, I was able to shrug it away. I told myself that it wasn't the most unusual name in the world and that it was only a very strange coincidence.

However, it helped me decide that I didn't like you very much.

Then one morning I just popped up to the flat as I had left my mobile phone in the bedroom. You were telling Sam and Emily about a dream you had had. You were mentioning names of people that I had barely thought about in forty years. I started reliving that time in general and one evening in particular.

This led to me behaving in a manner that I am not proud of. I have always tried to be tough but fair, the sort of manager that would not tolerate any nonsense, but one who was always there if my staff needed any help or encouragement. I became a bully. You were absolutely right in what you said tonight. I became my father.

Another thing that you got completely right was your assessment of my behaviour on the night that Pete died. I was an absolute bloody gullible idiot. Again, I have no idea of how much you know as a result of your dreams, but I'm hoping that by telling my story to someone I don't really know or particularly care for, it will act as a cathartic release. I will then try never to think of it again.

I didn't like Barry Grounds at all. He was always a sarcastic sleaze ball who loved slagging off the family whenever he could, in a way that annoyed me, but was never direct enough to enable me to tackle him about it. I should have just got rid of him, but he was quite a good barman and we needed all the staff we could get as my father had a habit of upsetting them.

So, when he and Malcolm, who was a man I only knew by reputation, came to tell me that Pete had drugged and raped my brother then bragged about it afterwards, I should have known that it was complete shit.

OK, they were very persuasive, they gave me descriptions of parts of my brother's body that they had no way of knowing about. They gave me the name of a drug Malcolm had supplied and said that Pete had laughed about using my brother, had said he had tricked him into believing he was in love and was planning to dump him as soon as he had had enough. It was very plausible, but I was normally quite good at sniffing out fictions and would have sent them on their way in no uncertain terms, but for one thing.

I desperately wanted it to be true.

I didn't want my brother to be gay.

On our way to see an old friend of my mother's that morning, he had opened his heart to me, told me of his relationship with Pete, actually told me that he loved him… and I brushed it off as a phase he was going through. I explained that as he had been at an all-boys school, then just finished his first year at university where he had mostly male friends, he was just not used to female company. He would eventually find the right girl for him and everything would be fine.

In my heart of hearts, I didn't believe a word of it.

I quite liked Pete, that was the pity of it. I had heard rumours about him, but I tried not to think about them. But I certainly didn't want him to be my brother's lover.

When my father found out about it and reacted in his typical manner I tried to placate him and because I had had years of practice, I was just managing to do so, but I wasn't happy about it. I would protect Max to the ends of the earth, but I wanted him to be normal.

When the phone rang, and I was asked to come downstairs because there were two men who wanted to see me, I was dubious about leaving my father and brother alone, with good reason as it turned out. The receptionist simply said that the men had information about my brother. I knew I needed to hear it. I left them together without a second thought. As soon as they told their sordid tale I knew that I needed to believe it.

If I had realised that my decision would cost me my father, my brother and the life of the man who loved him, along with a great deal of money - I hope that I would have changed my actions. Even now, with all that has happened, I'm not convinced that I could have done so.

From what you said last night it seems that you know about what happened on the beach, and any details that you don't know, you won't find out from me. Suffice to say, I left Pete to die. As soon as I had done so, I walked back up the sands. It was an awful evening weather wise, so I was happy that no-one would have seen what I had done. But, Townsend and Morgan had been searching for a private place to partake in their drug taking habit and I practically bumped into them as I reached the dunes before going back into the hotel grounds. They had arrived late on, so hadn't seen that much. If they had been clean and slightly more intelligent they might have had the wits to run into the sea and they might even have been able to save Pete's life. But they were neither of these things. However, they had seen enough to realise that I had left a man to die when I could have easily saved him.

I could see my future in tatters. I would have faced a charge of manslaughter at the very least. I came up with a plan. I offered the two druggies a great deal of money and gave them a blow by blow account of the story that they had to tell if they wanted to receive it. Even after that, there were a few dodgy moments, they didn't always follow the script. However, there were no signs of foul play and in a way, using Morgan and Townsend was helpful, the police and press were happy to categorise Pete by the company he kept. Basically, he was considered to be a drugged-up idiot who under the influence, went for a late-night swim and paid the price for it.

Especially now I am a parent, I shudder to think what his own parents must have gone through. The authorities would have tempered the story when they informed them about his death, I'm sure. Max told me later, in one of the rare moments when he wasn't trying to destroy the family, how close Pete had been to his mum and dad. Thankfully they found it too painful to come anywhere near the hotel. If they had heard the rumours that circulated afterwards, they would have known it was all rubbish and would have probably searched harder for answers.

I went back to the apartment, leaving Townsend to phone the police. I was in a bit of a state. I had let a man die, and been forced to leave two idiots to deal with the authorities. They had the power of my freedom in their hands. The worry of that situation was superseded by another when I got back to the flat. My father was drunk on the settee and when I went to check on Max, his door was locked. I searched my father's pockets and found that he had the key to the room. So, I unlocked it and went over to check that Max was all right. Even in the faint light I could see that his face was covered in cuts and bruises. He looked as if he had suffered such a severe beating that I put my hand in front of his mouth to check he was still breathing. I left the door unlocked, got my father into bed, poured myself a huge whiskey and went to bed myself.

When I woke in the morning and discovered that Grounds, Marsons and a load of money had disappeared, I realised that I had been taken for the biggest idiot ever. Grounds had simply been creating a diversion so that he and Marsons could make off with the cash. This feeling was confirmed to me when I broke the news to Max of Pete's death. He went completely to pieces, so much so that we had to tranquillise him and even I agreed on locking him in his room – for his own protection. He had not been raped by Pete, I now knew this for sure, he had loved him and although I might not have liked the idea, I could no longer resist the truth of it.

Over the next week or so, the situation got worse and worse, if that was at all possible. Max was convinced that Pete had committed suicide, blamed my father and with a sense of righteous outrage decided to make him pay for it in ways that even in my hope for closure, I will not explain. I will only say that my gorgeous brother reduced himself to little more than a homosexual whore. With every sordid act he embarked upon, I felt the guilt of my actions more and more keenly. As I saw my father's health deteriorate over the next few years, I felt a hideous responsibility.

My father was not an easy man, but he was not an ogre. I believe that he was never quite the same after my mother died. He bullied people as part of his rage against the injustice of her dying and Max tortured my father as part of his rage against the injustice of Pete's death.

I knew my father better than anyone and I loved him despite all his failings. When Max would not stop his awful revenge, even though I pleaded with him that it was killing our father, I suddenly stopped seeing the beloved brother and saw a selfish lout instead. He was becoming a bully himself.

It didn't matter how many warnings we gave him that my father's health couldn't cope with his outrageous behaviour. He continued his crusade until my father's heart could take no more, and I found that I could not forgive him. Maybe I was projecting my own guilt on to him, but suddenly he wanted to talk to me and I didn't even want to breathe the same air as him.

I wanted to get as far away from him as possible, so I left the hotel in the hands of an agency and I went around the world. Finding work with my experience was not difficult and I began to forget about the hotel and Weston-super-Mare. However, I had kept a mailing address and every so often, my letters were forwarded on to me. Max kept trying to re-establish relations, but he never once admitted to regretting how had he treated our father. I became more and more angry with him and it was always a terrible reminder of what I had done to send us down this road towards hell in the first place. I eventually decided that with the help of a friend of mine, I would kill myself off, so that he wouldn't need to try and contact me anymore. I sent a letter and a watch that he had bought me for a birthday in happier times, and it worked, I never heard from him again.

In conjunction with killing myself off, I decided to change my name in celebration of what I hoped would be a new life. Because of my surname, I had been called Ned or Neddie as a nickname at school, so I decided just to flip my name over and Maurice Edwards became Ned Morris. Such is the joy of having two Christian names.

Early in 1987, I was working in a hotel in Paris, which was as near as I had been to Britain for years. I was given a long weekend off as I had worked the whole of Christmas and New Year without a break. On a whim I came over to England and almost without thinking, took a train to Weston and walked over to see how the old place was fairing under new ownership. I had decided to sell it a few years before as the managers were running the place into the ground, and I had no idea at that point that I'd ever want to run it again.

I walked into the bar and fell in love. Not with the hotel, although they had made a lot of improvements. It was the young lady behind the bar to whom I lost my heart. I started chatting to her and I realised that she was as intelligent and funny as she was beautiful. We talked until the bar became too busy and then I satisfied myself by watching her as unobtrusively as I could.

I became aware of a party on a table near to the bar stool I was sitting on, a man with his back to me was bemoaning the fact that his pub in Norfolk was failing. His friend laughingly suggested that maybe an electrical fault would be the answer to all his problems. I thought no more about it until I went to the loo and the publican with money problems walked in. I had seen no-one I remembered from the old days until that point, but he recognised me straight away. His face suddenly spread into its first smile of the evening, but it wasn't a pleasant smile of remembrance, it was a threat: "Hello Mo!" he said. I couldn't believe my bad luck, of all the people I should run into, I had to run into him.

I could almost see the cogs working in the bit of brain that he had left. He suddenly started saying that he and Morgan could really do with some more money, their business was failing, and it would be a pity if they suddenly remembered what had happened all those years before.

First of all, I wasn't too worried. If they had reported me, they would have no proof that I had done anything wrong.

But he had said that as well as going to the authorities, he would go to the papers, it could be an interesting story, he thought.

Max could well find out that I was still alive, he would wonder why I had killed myself off and I had a feeling that he would guess that their story was true. Although I still blamed him for what happened to our father, I was happier that he thought me dead, than responsible for his lover's death.

Also, I was desperate to be able to live in Weston once more. I wanted more than anything to have a chance to talk to the barmaid again.

On a whim, I agreed to his demands. I asked him to give me the address of the pub so that I could come over and talk with him, and Morgan, to sort something out.

He gave me two weeks.

I went a day later.

I watched the pub for a week to see their daily routine. I had remembered the conversation I heard and the joke his friend had made. If there was to be a fatal fire, it would emerge that a fraudulent claim had been discussed. There would be no shortage of people ready to believe that they were desperate enough to try it and stupid enough to bodge it up. Because of his friend's comment, an electrical fault would have been perfect, but a "gas leak" was so much easier to organise.

Townsend had a habit of being first up in the morning. He went straight down to the kitchen and lit a cigarette as he went through the door. On one morning out of the seven I watched, he had the cigarette lit when he walked through the kitchen door, but every other day he sparked the lighter as he opened the door. It was fairly good odds I thought, so I broke in on the eighth night and found bar towels that I stuffed into every place the air could escape. I turned the gas on and left. A few hours later I saw a fireball envelope the sky and I watched death from a distance, for the second time in my life.

The whole experience affected me more than I expected. I decided to leave England again. I had no real worry that any blame could be traced to me, but I was aware that I was still recognisable as Mo Edwards and I was no longer that man.

Even then I was torn, I was desperate to see the barmaid again but in the end, I decided to wait a couple of years and hope that no suitor beat me to it in the mean while. However, just when I thought I'd waited long enough and I no longer resembled the man of my youth, I met a girl in Cairns and we started a relationship. It lasted for three years, but I would always compare her to the barmaid in the Royal Holm View and she would always come up wanting. When finally, I decided that the relationship was going nowhere, I left her one morning and flew back to England. I had no idea that I would be able to find the barmaid, or if she would be single when I did, I only knew that I had to try.

When I walked into the bar and she was standing there, I couldn't believe my luck. When I found out that she was a co-owner of the hotel, I decided that it had to be fate. The rest as they say is history.

I have had a wonderful twenty-four years since then. Fiona and I have brought up two wonderful children and only a freak of nature is forcing me to leave them.

I haven't told Fiona of my decision. That would be much too difficult to do. Better that I just go, and she wakes up to start a new life without me.

If I was to stay and say goodbye to her properly, I would tell her that she was the piece in the puzzle that changed my world from a bit of a mess to a beautiful picture.

I would tell her that twenty-four years of her, was probably more than I deserved and so much more than I expected.

I would tell her that I returned for the barmaid, not the bar, and stayed for the hotelier, not the hotel.

I would tell her that I love her.

I may not have taken to you Peter and I certainly don't approve of your lifestyle, but I do believe that you are an honourable man. Look after Fiona for me and my sweet angel, Emily.

I will not ask you to look after Sam, I am sure that is uppermost in your thoughts for the future anyway, but forgive me if I try not to think about it.

Sincerely
Ned

40.

I have never understood people who categorise others because of their sexuality, ethnicity or anything else for that matter. To run away from a family whom you love and who love you, just because your son is gay, seemed to me to be the most pathetic of excuses.

To be honest, I thought he needed to man up.

However, I couldn't say that I was sorry he had gone. Maybe the fact that he had, whatever his excuses, nearly pushed me to my death the night before, somewhat coloured my judgement. I thought the whole family would be better off without him. However, I wasn't sure that the rest of them would see it in that way.

I lay in bed for a while, my thoughts jumping and dancing like a Palomino horse performing dressage. It was the cold and clinical way that he had dispatched Richard and Robert, and the lack of guilt he felt about it that affected me. He had done it simply to avoid paying them any more money, and to prevent his brother finding out that he was still alive.

I considered telling Alf that his brother-in-law wasn't the complete idiot he took him for. He was murdered, rather than died as a result of his own stupidity. However, I was aware of the hornet's nest it would disturb… and for what? Was it better that the family remembered him as a plonker or a blackmailer?

I decided that whatever happened, I wouldn't tell Sam, Emily or Fiona about that particular passage in my letter.

The door opened, and Sam poked his head around the door. I was so pleased to see him and smiled a broad smile of welcome. However, the Doctor was still on duty and a professional icy calm answered my enthusiastic greeting.

"If you are feeling well enough, the police are here, and they wish to interview you," was all he said before he closed the door and left me to it.

I dressed quickly and went down the corridor to the lounge. I experienced a brief flutter of nerves as I walked through the door of the room that I had tumbled from the night before.

Fiona and Sam were both sitting on the settee and I sat on a chair as far away from the window as I possibly could. A kindly policewoman was there and explained her presence. Apparently, the fact that I had been clinging to a canopy on the side of the building hadn't been lost on the watching public the night before. Was I able to give her my account of what had happened?

I merely said that I had been pratting around inside and had fallen against the railing which had given way and catapulted me out into the evening sky. Luckily, I had been caught on the canopy and had managed to pull myself up far enough so that Sam had been able to help me to safety.

Fortuitously, when the railing had disappeared from under Sam and myself, it had been held by the thinnest piece of metal and had hung from the balcony rather than plummeting on to the general public below. Maybe they had all scattered anyway, to avoid being squashed by a falling teenager, but it would have made a terrible mess of the lawns. The maintenance men had been called from their slumbers to make it safe the night before. The canopy that had saved my life was still standing and would be checked out later that day.

The policewoman gave me the briefest of lectures about the dangers of playing near an open window and I felt like a disobedient nine-year-old. She then informed Sam and Fiona that they would probably receive a visit from a Health and Safety professional who would be interested to check the security of the rest of their railings in other rooms.

Once Fiona had shown her out, she re-joined Sam on the settee. He had been barely able to look in my direction during her absence and I was beginning to become worried.

I felt like I was facing a disciplinary panel and as it turned out, I was.

"Thank you for backing us up in front of the police," Fiona said, and I nodded that it wasn't a problem.

She held my eyes with an icy glare. "However, I think it's best if you leave… as soon as possible would be good."

I stared at her and then at Sam who was still trying to avoid my gaze. I felt like calling out to the constable that I wanted to change my story. If I could have forced myself to go anywhere near that bloody window, I might well have done so.

"The abuse you gave my husband last night was totally unacceptable, considering the fact that we have taken you into our home for the last few weeks."

I was angry and upset, but I was not out of control like I had been the night before.

"Excuse me Fiona, but he tried to push me to my death!" I thought it a fairly important point to mention, but Fiona did not agree,

"Don't be ridiculous you stupid little boy!" She was in full outraged Lady Mary mode and if I hadn't been on the receiving end, my gay sensibilities would have loved it. "You taunted him in a way that was unbearable to watch. You then pushed against him and he simply pushed back. It was hardly his fault that the railing gave way, no one could have predicted that."

I felt like suggesting that we would wait and see what the health and safety report said about that, but decided against it.

Lady Mary had not quite finished. "My husband was so

distraught about what happened, that he has left us. We don't know where he has gone or if he will ever return. That was the direct result of your horrible diatribe. I hope you are happy with yourself… but I would very much like you to leave now."

I looked in the direction of my lover, my safety net in so many ways, literally so the night before, but Sam had left the building and been replaced by the inscrutable Doctor Morris.

He spoke for the first time since I had entered the lounge. "Mum, do you mind if I speak to Rem in private?" Fiona nodded and got up as if to leave but Sam stopped her. "No please, it's fine, we'll go to my room."

As we walked along the corridor I had decided that it would all be fine. Sam would just say that he was supporting his mother. We would wait a few weeks, until it had all calmed down. She would realise that she was overreacting and projecting the anger that she felt for her husband, in my direction.

As they say in Family Fortunes. "Aagh Uugh!"

Once we had closed the door to his room, I attempted to pull him in for a kiss, but he held up his arms in a defensive gesture and said calmly. "I'm sorry Rem, this is not going to be easy."

"You can't agree with her," I pleaded, "after what he did…"

Sam interrupted my flow. "Two of the people I loved most in the world broke my heart last night," he said simply.

"How did I…?" I tried to interrupt but Sam wasn't in the right frame of mind for listening.

"My father told me I was a disgrace to the family, just because I was gay."

I nodded and said, "I know, and I said…"

"Yes! What did you say, Rem?" Sam snapped, the calm façade cracking for a moment. "I thought you were going to tell him that you loved me, you might even have mentioned a few of the qualities that you loved about me. It would have been nice if you could have supported me just a little bit."

I was lost for a moment. I had thought all of those things. Surely, I had said them?

"But I did!" The unattractive pleading tone was back in my voice.

Sam stared at me in barely concealed frustration.

"You did not! You are so obsessed with Pete that you even called him Mo and then started prattling on about how he killed a lovely man and how stupid he was. Are you starting to confuse reality with your fucking dreams?"

I suddenly realised that I still hadn't told him about my final dream and how I knew who his father actually was.

"I've not told you how Pete died," I said.

Sam's anger was quick and unexpected.

"I don't give a fuck about it! Can't you get that into your head?" The words snapped at me like a flexed cane. "I told you in Brighton how I felt knowing that you were in love with a dead man. I also told you that I can't compete with how perfect you think that man was."

I remembered it well. I had also remembered what I said to Mo, and I knew exactly how I had confirmed all of Sam's suspicions.

"It was all about Pete." Sam's anger had been replaced by sadness. "My dad had just said one of the most hurtful things he could have said to me. At a time when I most wanted your support, the way you answered him was to pretend he was responsible for a death forty years ago. How do you really think that made me feel?"

I tried one last time.

"The reason I got so angry was the fact that he was treating you in that way. But I had also just realised who he was, so all of those things about Pete, just flowed out because of it."

Sam nodded sadly, "And that is exactly what I was talking about. You have become so obsessed with that story, it's taken you over, Rem. I thought it was fun to start with, but it's not fun now. I just feel that there is little room for me in your life." He held my gaze for a moment, those wonderful eyes giving me a final flash of what I was just about to lose. "I do really think you should go now."

"But…" I was trying to think of something to say that would change his mind. "You saved my life last night!" I thought it best not to add the bit about Pete's involvement.

Sam looked genuinely confused. "You might have hurt me deeply, but I wasn't going to leave you to die, was I?"

Not so much of his father's son.

***

He left the room and I realised that there was little point in hanging around. Not to labour the point, but I felt like I had done enough of that the night before… Sam wasn't in the mood to change his mind today. Maybe, in this particular case, absence would make the heart grow fonder.

I packed and left. I would have liked to have said goodbye to Emily at least, but she was still spraying extra thick bleach into a toilet somewhere, so I thought I'd text her later and maybe we would be able to talk.

As I struggled down the back stairs with all my luggage, a figure who was flying down the staircase two steps at a time had to perform an emergency stop to prevent from crashing in to me.

"Goodness Pete!" Jack said and then noticing my overloaded state for the first time: "Oh you're not leaving us, are you? I thought you were staying for the whole of the summer."

I smiled painfully, "Change of plan I'm afraid Jack." I balanced a bag on the stairs so that I could shake his hand, "I'm glad I bumped into you though, so that I could say goodbye."

"More the other way around actually," Jack grinned,

"Oh I'm really sorry, I've enjoyed working with you." He stopped as if he had a sudden thought, "I keep meaning to tell you, but you know how it is, memory of a goldfish!" He laughed deprecatingly. "I was telling Martin, the man I live with, about you. He said that there was a really nice bloke with that name who worked here ages ago, when he was the second chef. Isn't that a coincidence?"

I just about managed not to call him Smiler. Instead I said neutrally, "Martin is your uncle?"

"Well!" Jack grinned conspiratorially, "Not so much of an uncle if you know what I mean!" With that and a shout of "Good luck!" he disappeared down the stairs towards his lunchtime clientele.

***

It was a beautiful day as I walked along the seafront, but I was a complete mess. It seemed that I had ballsed it up totally with Sam and I wasn't overly confident that I'd be able to talk him round.

I had not quite reached the old lido where Pete, Max and their friends had spent many a happy hour in the summer of 1977, when suddenly a baby blue Fiat 500 screeched to a halt in an empty car parking space to the side of me. There were a family in the next parking bay who were busy emptying their Volkswagen estate ready for a day on the beach. Father had just pulled out Grandma's walker when Emily parked, and it was only good luck and well-maintained brakes that prevented the poor old lady being knocked into the middle of the Waitrose picnic that was still sitting in the boot. With what was becoming her trademark wave of apology, Emily left her car and ran over to me.

"Rem! Sam's just told me that you're leaving and that the old man has done a bunk too, what in hell's name is going on?"

We sat on the beach wall and I told her the story as the

Volkswagen family passed us. Grandma tutted vociferously in our general direction, but other than that, she was none the worse for her ordeal.

By the time I had finished my story, Em was staring open mouthed, looking as if she was lying in a dentist's chair, obeying instructions.

"Bummer! I go out to see one shitty film and all hell breaks loose! I wondered where Dad was and why Mum and Sam were shut in the kitchen having a confab when I came home last night! I thought it might have been the night of the big confession, but I never expected anything like that!" She looked at me and smiled, "don't worry Rem! I'll talk to him… we'll talk him round!"

She then changed tack: "I can't believe that Dad has lied to us for all these years, and that he had another life before us." She thought for a moment. "He never talked about his childhood. I had the vague impression he was brought up in care. Any stories were always from the years he went travelling."

"Well to be fair," I said, "that was when Ned Morris was born."

"What a wanker!"

I should have said that she was being unfair etc etc, but as I've said before, it's always nice when someone is being more unreasonable than you're actually being yourself, so I didn't argue with her.

Then she suggested that we turned tail and went back to the hotel and tried to talk to Sam together. However, I said that I thought it would be better to leave him alone. I said that I would try and ring him tomorrow, in the hope he would have calmed down, and might well be missing me.

Em nodded a little doubtfully, she was always one for the direct approach. When she realised that my mind couldn't be changed, she offered me a lift to the station. Although I had had one near death experience in the last twenty-four hours, I was grateful for the company and willing to risk another, so I accepted.

We stood on the station with that awful expectation of farewell that makes it impossible to start a new conversation for the fear that it will be cut short by the train's arrival. In the end we resorted to hugging each other and she whispered that it would all be all right, she would talk him round, she'd tell him exactly who their father was and why I'd reacted in that way. He'd never been able to resist her arguments in the past, why would he start now?

I waited until two men who were a similar age to Max, helped an old woman onto the train. The slightly elder of the two men called her "Mum" and I wondered about their story. Could that have been Max, Pete and his mother, if fate and Mo hadn't intervened that night?

I waved and blew kisses to Em as the train pulled away. As soon as I was without her, I missed the madness of her irrepressible good humour. It also gave me a chance to think and go through what I needed to say to Sam, if he ever gave me the chance to say it.

The thought that he might not give me that chance, combined with the familiar sights that I had always experienced with Sam beside me before, made me unable to stop myself. Suddenly, I was crying like a small baby deprived of his mother's breast.

"Are you OK?" The older of the two men leant across the train corridor and looked at me, concern hovering around his eyes. "Missing your girlfriend, I suppose?"

He wasn't being nosey, just nice. I was pretty sure of his circumstances, and besides, I had just finished three weeks of being closeted. I wanted someone to know about me.

"No, that was my boyfriend's sister," I said and then by way of explanation, I added, "he's just dumped me."

He nodded sympathetically, taking in the information. "Men, eh! I have a terrible time with this one over here!" He nodded at his boyfriend in the window seat.

"Oh no!" his boyfriend said with mock concern, "I'm

in trouble again!"

I wiped at my eyes with my sleeve and my new friend held out his hand to his partner. Without a word passing between them a tissue was produced and handed over to me.

I thanked him, and their obvious closeness started me off again, it was something I'd felt I had with Sam and it just brought it home to me what I might have lost.

"What a nice young man," the old woman said in the loud clear tones of someone who is slightly deaf. "Has he got hay fever or is he a bit soft?"

The man gave a moue of apology and I smiled back a watery smile to assure him that I wasn't the least bit offended. On the contrary, the whole incident had made me feel a little better, and I managed the rest of the journey to Bristol without a further risk of soaking the upholstery.

I waited whilst they escorted Mother from the train and I thanked them all for their kindness.

"If he's got half a brain, he'll come back!" The mother was obviously not quite as deaf and certainly not as unaware as I had first thought. Her son and his partner smiled and showed they were crossing their fingers as they took an arm each and escorted the old lady towards the subway. Dorothy with her Tin man and Scarecrow for the blue rinse generation.

I had quite a wait for the Salisbury train and could have downed a pint with ease, but I resisted the charms of the Buffet bar as I feared it would start me off again. I would have been painfully aware of the completely different circumstance and mood I had been in the last time I was there.

By the time I had reached Salisbury, I was in that sort of state anyway. I have never been the type of teenager who has relied on the taxi of Mum and Dad. However, as I sat in the Pumpkin café, morosely sipping a coffee, I realised that I just couldn't face the thought of a twenty-mile bus ride. I rang my dad and on hearing his voice, broke down completely. Within half an hour he had given his excuses to his boss, collected my mum from her work and arrived at the station.

This was very unusual.

As I have mentioned before, I have always had a slightly remote relationship with my parents. All that changed that day.

I asked my mother about it afterwards and she was surprised and said simply: "Well my love, you were such an easy child, we never had to worry about you like our friends had to do with their children. Your dad and I were slightly concerned at Christmas, but even then, we had an idea of the reason behind it. Once you had come out to us, it was business as usual. That day when you called your dad, we knew that you really needed us, probably for the first time in your life."

They were wonderful that day, supportive, practical and loving.

Once I had got back to our house in Shaftesbury I told them the whole story of the three weeks I had been away. When I finally reached the bitter end of my tale, my dad let out a small breath. "Peter…"

"Yes Dad," I said, but he looked at me with a strange expression. He might be well known amongst his friends for having a vague manner that hid a quite brilliant brain, but this was a bit extreme, even for him.

He'd only mentioned my name five seconds before.

He suddenly realised my confusion.

"Sorry Pete," he smiled, "I didn't mean you…"

He then dropped a small bombshell.

"I was talking about your Uncle Peter…"

41.

I felt like I had somehow fallen into Soapland and had awoken to find an unknown uncle in the shower.

"Uncle Peter?" I repeated slightly stupidly.

"Yes," my dad seemed surprised. "Surely you've heard me talk about him? The brother I never knew? He died before I was born, drowned in Minehead, or somewhere like that, in the West Country."

It suddenly all seemed to slip into place, that one turn of the Rubik's cube that aligns all the colours. "Weston-super-Mare possibly?" I said gently.

He grinned at his own vagueness, "Oh God! I suppose it must have been," he said.

"Tell me about him," I asked.

"To be honest Pete, I don't really know that much. It was a bit of a taboo subject in our household. Even years later the thought of him would upset your grandma so much, that we kept away from the subject. I never knew him, so he wasn't really a part of my story." He thought, before adding, "If he hadn't died, neither you nor I would be here though, I do know that."

Right, so that made the thought that I could save Pete and not change the lives of anyone else, look just a little bit silly...

"I'm sure you've heard these sad tales of couples who have lost a child and it has torn their relationship apart?" I nodded, and he continued. "Well, according to your granddad it was completely the opposite for my mum and dad, they became almost inseparable, clinging on to each other in grief." He cleared his throat, "They stopped taking precautions, I'm not sure if it was a conscious desire for a replacement, but they got one… me."

This was an awkward question and one that might have threatened my newly found bond with my father, but I asked it anyway. "Did you ever feel like a substitute, Dad?"

He looked at me, he wasn't upset, just amazed that I would need to ask the question. "No," he said firmly, "No, never. Apparently, I was a completely different character to Pete, which probably helped, but my mum and dad gave me a wonderful childhood. There was never any question that I was second best. You remember her, don't you? You were seven or eight when she died, I think."

I nodded, and I started to associate the woman I had loved with the one I had heard about in my dreams. I could suddenly see her very clearly. "I remember she smelt of Yardley's Lily of the Valley and that they were her favourite flower. I remember that she always kept chocolate for me in her pocket and the dog used to nudge her with his nose trying to get at it. She was kind and funny… and she treated me like a grown up even when I was young…" I took a sharp breath. That was exactly the way Pete had described her to Max.

"She loved you so much!" My mum had been quiet for a while and when she spoke I could see she was slightly teary. "When I seduced your father," she smiled, and he grabbed her hand and smiled back at her. "Practically everyone disowned me. Even people who were meant to be my friends treated me like some sort of pariah." She gazed at my dad, I had never realised before how much they still loved each other. I suppose as a child you try not to think of such things.

"Your grandparents would have had more reason to hate me than anybody, but they were the most supportive, lovely people you could ever wish to have met. When the chance of a research job came up, they encouraged me to take it and said that they would love to look after you. I have never seen them happier than they were during the last six or seven years of their lives." She smiled at me, "they would be so proud of you now, Pete, they really would."

My dad exclaimed, making both of us jump. He wasn't a man who was normally given to excitement, so it was slightly out of character.

"You did know about Pete!" He said, poking at the air with his finger. "I remember it because we both found out about him in exactly the same manner." He paused making sure he'd got his facts straight before continuing. "When I was a kid, I had been sneaking in my parent's room and saw a photograph album that she had tucked inside her bedside table. One day, when I came home from work, my dad grabbed me and said you had done the self-same thing and were asking questions. He was worried about upsetting Mum, so I told you that the man was my brother, but not to talk about him to your gran. He had gone away and couldn't talk to her anymore." I was obviously looking blank, so he added, "I told you that it made her sad."

No, I didn't remember it at all.

"You said that if she wanted him to talk to her, she should just ask him. And then you said something that was quite strange." He caught his breath on the implication of what he was just thinking. "And given what you have just told us, even stranger."

"What was that, Dad?"

"You said that you were sure that he would talk to you one day."

Spooky.

Something then occurred to me. "So, I suppose I was called Peter because…?"

Mum nodded, "Yes, it was the only time she ever mentioned him to me and I asked questions about him that obviously upset her, so I never asked again. However, we called you Peter in memory of the uncle you never knew."

I thought, but didn't say, "I got to know him in the end."

We talked long into the night about family matters we had never mentioned before. My father found the photograph album and I saw pictures of Pete growing up and at his eighteenth birthday, the year before he died.

"Gosh," My mum said, "you do look like him." It reminded me that both Tony and Jackie had said similar things; to be honest, I still couldn't see it.

I'd had a few strange days recently, and that was certainly another of them.

It was the day I lost my boyfriend, found my parents and discovered that the ghostly figure in my dreams was my uncle.

Just another day in Soapland.

42.

I tried to text Sam the next day, but received no reply. I phoned him, and my call went straight to voicemail. I left messages, but he didn't get back to me. I chatted to Em, but he was refusing to talk to her about it. "He is stupidly busy at the hotel," she explained, but we both knew that if he had wanted to, he could have spared thirty seconds to send a text.

Over the next few days I received texts from her that started with "Still trying! Keep up hope!" through "Duh! My brother is a stubborn arse!" to "Sam can be such an idiot when he wants to be! I am not talking to him!"

I skyped Chloe and she had told me all about her love life with Adam, which was going so much better than mine. I said that I couldn't wait to meet him. I then told her the whole sorry tale of events that had occurred since we had talked the night before we went to Brighton.

"Don't worry Rem, leave it with me, you know what I'm like - the voice of reason in a beautiful Anglo Chinese female form - I'll soon talk him round!"

I waited with bated breath until the next day. If it had taken that long for Chloe to contact him, he must have been really busy. I knew in my heart of hearts that if she couldn't get through to him, then no one could.

So, it turned out to be option two then...

"I don't know what's the matter with him, I do think he's missing his father and feels let down by him in so many ways... I didn't tell him how much I knew by the way." I had asked her to be a little careful. I didn't want Sam to think I was washing his family's dirty linen in public, even if the public in question was Chloe. "When I talked about you, he went all Princess Di on me… you know: there were three people in our relationship…"

Before she disconnected she did tell me something that interested me. She had been doing a little digging into the crimes of The Planner. Looking at the timescale, it seemed that he had gone straight from Weston over to France. His first crime was committed over there about twelve months afterwards. It wasn't discovered until he was caught much later, and he admitted to a total of seven rapes and murders. By the time all this had occurred, a man had spent seven years in a French jail for a crime he didn't commit.

The man's name was Barry Grounds.

As the lies he told led directly to Pete's death, the irony of the situation was not lost on me. He had got away unpunished for the crime for which I believed he was culpable.

He then ended up serving seven years over a crime for which he was innocent.

I hoped rather maliciously, that he hadn't received a centime in compensation from the French Government.

***

Apart from that it's probably wise to draw a bit of a veil over the next few weeks. When Mum and Dad weren't around giving me moral support, Dean came over or forced me to go out to the pub with our crowd of friends. Mandy and Gemma were devastated that I'd broken up with Sam, but they seemed more worried that they would never see him again, than the effect it was having on my mental health.

On other occasions, when Dean came over, I would talk, he would listen and then we'd just lie there hugging each other. It must have been as entertaining as a weekend in a leper colony for him, but he bore it with a stoicism that only a true friend would.

As I entered my fourth week of misery, Chloe broke it to me that Sam had said he was too busy at the hotel, to return to uni. He was going to either drop out or, if possible, miss a year. After this news, I began to think that I should snap myself out of it and ask for a few hours in the pub. This would give me something else to think about and earn myself a little money in order to slow down my ever-growing debts. Just as I had decided that Sam would never get in touch with me again… he did.

My phoned beeped to tell me I had received a text and I picked it up with less enthusiasm than I usually did. Constant disappointment had ground me down somewhat. When I saw that it was Sam, I experienced what my uncle would have called "that bubble-gum popping moment." However, they were soon burst by the only piece of text that I could see under his name. It read, "It would probably be too much to expect…"

I guessed that he had found out that I had told Chloe all about his family secrets and he wanted to tell me that he didn't appreciate it. I clicked on the icon with a good deal of anxiety firmly in place.

I didn't quite believe the text the first time I read it. I ended up reading it through three times to ensure that it wasn't some sort of cruel mirage. "It would probably be too much to expect that you would still want to talk to me but if you do, please ring me."

Over the weeks I had decided, depending on my mood that if he did get in touch, I would.

a) Ignore him completely. Forever.

b) Answer his call and tell him what I thought of him. Then ignore him completely. Forever.

c) Ignore his call, then when he had lost all hope, ring him back and talk to him with a great deal of reluctance.

I called him back straight away…

43.

Sam arrived the next morning. As soon as I heard the doorbell, I hurled myself down the stairs like Greg Rutherford in front of a sand pit. When I opened the door he looked nervous, I was reminded of the day in Moreland Road at the beginning of the year. Well, that day had gone pretty well in the end, so I was quite hopeful. I decided that I had waited too long for this moment to leave anything to chance, so I pulled him towards me, kissing him fully on the lips.

He certainly didn't struggle and when we did finally pull apart, he actually managed not to glance behind him to check that no-one had seen us.

It was definite progress.

My parents had gone to work but they had been as excited as I was the night before.

They had even cracked open the Prosecco.

"I've missed you!" I said. He started to look a lot less nervous, but began nodding behind him furiously. I briefly wondered if he'd received a course of slow acting electric shock therapy, before realising that he was trying to focus my attention on a silver-grey Volkswagen that was parked in front of my house.

"You haven't!" I said.

His smile said it all. "I booked an intense week's driving course the minute I discovered that little Sis had beaten me to it! It was just typical I chose to take it the week that all hell was breaking loose at the hotel, but Mum insisted I went ahead with it."

I grinned, he was as pleased as a turkey in January and I was chuffed for him.

On the phone the evening before, we had batted apologies back and forth like a battered ball in a table tennis tournament. So all of those had been said and accepted. I just wanted to drag him upstairs to my room, but I knew there were still things we needed to say to each other. After I had made some coffee, we took it into the lounge where we could talk.

"You remember that night on the balcony?" Sam asked, and I nodded, I was not likely to ever forget it.

Sam was sitting on the sofa and I was lying across him with my head on the arm of it, looking up at him. It wasn't the traditional seating arrangement for a round of peace talks, I'll give you that, but maybe they should try it in the Middle East.

I nodded grimly, "I thought I had killed you, I really did."

His hand found its way up my tee shirt and gently caressed my skin as an expression of understanding. However, I knew that he needed to stop that soon, or this peace summit would be curtailed in a way so far unheard of in the history of the United Nations.

"As you hit the rail with your foot, I felt it give way. I had just enough time to launch myself backwards... It was quite close though."

He has a gift for understating the facts.

"Once I had got you to bed and my mum had helped my father into their room, we had to contact the maintenance men to make the railing safe. Once that was sorted, we went to the kitchen to talk. She understood that I was gay, but she didn't think that you were right for me."

I grinned ironically, "I sort of got that impression the next day."

"I talked to her for ages. To be honest, I talked mostly about you and how much I loved you."

I smiled encouragingly.

"But I also said that I thought it was hopeless. I explained the dreams you had been having, and how I was convinced you were obsessed by Pete."

I knew I had to say it. I knew I had to tell him one of the things that had been bothering me for the last month.

"I just don't understand it." I said, "Pete was dead. I just don't understand why you were so jealous."

He stared at me, but there was no anger or irritation in the glance, he just needed me to understand.

"You have never seen the look on your face whenever you mentioned him, but I have. It wasn't like he was dead to you," he paused and then added, "don't forget, at one stage you were definitely hoping that you could change history."

"He was my uncle," I said simply.

Sam stopped to take in the new information, then nodded as if to himself. "That suddenly makes a lot of sense," he said. "The first day we met, you told me that your dad was very young when he fathered you, but conversely, his parents were well into their forties when your father was born. They'd had a family before?"

"Pete," I nodded, strangely pleased that he'd remembered the tale I told him in the infancy of our friendship. "My dad said that I knew about him, but I certainly didn't remember." I glanced at Sam, "I do understand why you were confused, jealous and everything else for that matter, I was struggling with it myself. It's only now that I realise… Pete and I were the same age - it was less of an uncle/nephew relationship and much more like a brotherly thing." I stopped to take a breath and thought of something else. "Dad reckons that if Pete hadn't died, neither he nor I would exist."

Sam grinned cheekily, "So the idea that you could change the past and not invoke the butterfly effect…?"

"… I don't think I thought that one through" I admitted self-deprecatingly. I paused to give myself a chance to decide whether Sam was ready to hear what I wanted to tell him. In the end, I blurted it out before I had really reached a decision.

"When I was hanging on to the canopy for dear life," I began, warily looking at Sam's face for signs of a resumption of hostilities. "I'm sure I heard Pete's voice. I definitely felt some sort of force pushing me upwards. All that time I was sure that I was meant to save his life, I now believe that he was meant to save mine."

Sam didn't waver. He didn't talk about adrenalin. He didn't mention the brain behaving strangely when faced with stress, and he said nothing about me needing a course of anti-delusional drugs.

He simply nodded and held my hand.

We remained silent for a few minutes, but it was a comfortable silence, not an angry one. Eventually I asked him, "Did you hear your father leave?"

Sam shook his head, "Not a thing! OK, so Mum and I were quite involved in our heart to heart, but we heard nothing."

"So, when did you realise?"

"Mum went to bed, I was just tidying the dirty coffee cups and trying to work out whether you and I had a future together." I winced slightly, and he gripped my hand tighter. "Suddenly I realised she was standing in the doorway. I was about to make a quip about it being two in the morning and hadn't we had enough Mother/Son bonding for one night? Then I really saw her…"

It was my turn to squeeze.

"Oh Rem, her face was like a pencil sketch, all the colour had drained out of it. She was using all her self-control just to be able to stand there. She told me that my dad had left. I of course, said all the things you say: it had been a weird old night, he probably needed some air, he'd be back, she wasn't to worry…"

"…but?"

"She was holding the office box where they kept our

passports, she pushed it towards me, but she didn't need to. I could see straight away that there were only three passports inside."

He twisted his signet ring around on his finger, something he always did in moments of stress.

"I ran over to her and hugged her." he breathed out a disapproving sigh. "It was the first time in my life that I'd had to be the strong one in our relationship and that was all I could do."

"It was probably exactly what she needed you to do," I said encouragingly, and he smiled a half-smile of gratitude.

"We hugged for ages and then we started to talk again." He glanced at me and grinned gently, "Mum blamed you, of course… but I knew that it was my fault."

More hand squeezing was necessary, I decided.

"I was so angry with him for doing that to my mum just because of his homophobia." His eyes shone in anger at the memory. "I was still his son, why did it matter a fuck who I… fucked?"

He glanced at me. "The more Mum and I talked, the more my anger with him merged with my…" he searched around for a word and borrowed one of mine from earlier, "jealousy of you and Pete."

He looked at me to check that I was OK, but there was no point trying to clear the air if you weren't prepared to hear about whatever had made it polluted in the first place. I nodded encouragement and he continued.

"Sometime later, just as it was getting light, Mum said that she didn't think she could bear to have you around and by this time, I was beginning to believe that she had a point. We would be able to grieve better as a family, without you."

He laughed grimly, the introduction to another memory. "Emily was so cross with us both when she returned from taking you to the station. She accused us of everything, starting with ruining your life and ending with blaming us for her poor A-level exam results. I tried to tell her that she had taken the exams before any of this had happened and the results weren't due for another month, but you know what she's like - never let the truth get in the way of a good rant!"

I grinned, "I absolutely adore your sister!"

He nodded and crinkled his nose in agreement, "So do I."

"When she calmed down, she eventually told us about who had killed Pete and the real identity of our father." He glanced at me: "She was trying to explain your anger on that awful night."

"It didn't help though." It was a statement and Sam shook his head in agreement.

"No. My whole world crashed around me. Everything I had believed my whole life had been exposed as a lie and as for my mum…" he rubbed his hands over his face as he remembered. "Oh my god Rem, she went to pieces, I have never seen her like it before and never want to experience it again…"

"She realised that she had never really known him?"

"It was more than that. She demanded that Emily and I told her the whole story from your very first dream to our visit to see Max. By the end of our tale she had convinced herself that he had never loved her, she was just a means to an end. He had lost the Hotel once and had been determined to get back what he believed was rightfully his."

Poor Fiona. I could certainly imagine that by inadvertently exposing her husband's double life, she wouldn't feel like buying me a jeroboam of bubbly for my birthday, any time soon.

I also remembered that I owned something that might just help her.

"Your dad wrote me a letter." I said and when Sam looked up sharply, I quickly explained, "I think he found it easier to write to someone he didn't really care about."

I would work out the paragraphs in the letter that

would help them and the phrases that were better left unread. The truth of it was harsh. It may well be that there was enough in it to convince Fiona that she was more than just a convenient means to an end. However, there would be nothing to persuade Sam against the fact that his father stopped loving him, the moment he discovered his son was gay.

Maybe it was a truth he needed to accept in order to move on.

"All my life I had admired him and loved him," he continued after a brief pause, "I suddenly found myself hating him. I also found it difficult to separate my feelings for him, with my feelings for you. I suppose I blamed you for the fact that the whole sorry mess had been exposed. Chloe told me I was deflecting my anger against my father on to you. She was right…"

"Now that," I said with a wicked grin, "Is something I must tell her…"

"Don't you bloody dare!" he laughed.

We were going to be all right. I knew it at that moment. If we could banter, even in a tentative, baby steps type of way, whilst discussing the worst period of our lives… we were definitely going to be all right.

"I think the hotel saved Mum, it definitely saved me and probably Em too, during that time," he said. "We had something to concentrate on, something we could do that would stop us focussing on the huge crater Dad had left in our lives by leaving. Even the fact that we'd had a man hanging from one of our canopies didn't put the paying public off…" He looked at me and we gave each other a little grin. "We all worked ridiculous hours, but at least when we did get to bed, we were too knackered to think."

I thought it was time, I scooted my legs from Sam's lap and shuffled my body towards his so that I could enclose him in a hug. When he continued to speak, his breath ruffled the top of my hair.

"Everybody was telling me how daft I was being. Em

told me every day, Chloe skyped me whenever she could get hold of me and did the same. Chris and Dan did likewise. Even Jack gave me a lecture on how silly I would be if I let you go."

"Jack?"

Sam nodded, "A little bit of a fan of yours, is Jack." Considering how I felt about him when we first met, I was strangely pleased to hear that. "We shared a bit of wacky baccy one night," I glanced up at him and raised my eyebrow, he laughed. "No honestly, we only shared a joint, he's perfectly happy with his 'Uncle' Martin, who I think might be…"

"Pete's friend Smiler, the second chef from the seventies!" I laughed, then sobered as a question struck me. "So, who on earth convinced you that you were being a stubborn old goat?"

Sam ignored my jibe and smiled slightly. "Pete," he said softly.

"You had a dream?"

"I had a dream." he confirmed. I wasn't quite sure whether he was quoting Abba or misquoting Martin Luther King…

"That night I smoked the dope with Jack, I dreamt about Pete."

I was excited, at last he had experienced what I had experienced. "It was just like watching a movie, wasn't it?"

Sam shook his head. "No for me it was much more like a conversation. I even dreamt that I asked him why it had taken twenty years for him to talk to me."

"What did he say?"

Sam snorted, "He said that I was unresponsive!" I laughed smugly, but apparently Pete had been quite scathing about me too. "Don't get all pleased with yourself," Sam teased, "he said that he was only able to contact you when you were pissed!"

I grinned, but then sobered when Sam continued. "However, I have started to wonder if there was something else as well, something that helped to cause the very first connection."

"What?" I asked, slightly perplexed.

"Do you remember the very last words you said before we went to sleep that night?"

There was something niggling at my brain – we had just made love, in which case… With a lurch, I remembered my exact words.

"Back at ya…"

We were silent for a second whilst that sank in. "So, what did he say to you that convinced you to talk to me again?"

Sam sobered, "He said that he had lost the love of his life because of events that could have so easily been avoided. There was only one question I needed to answer. Did I love you?"

I smiled at him "… and?"

He grinned, "I'm here aren't I!" He paused still unsure of what to make of the fact that he could remember every word of a conversation he had experienced whilst sleeping. "I told Pete that I couldn't imagine waking up in the morning and not needing you to be there by my side. I told him that even when I was angry with you and really wanted not to love you… there's just something about you that made it impossible."

I think we've established before that he's got a pretty good line in flattery…

Sam laughed, remembering what had happened next. "He then said that if I was risking what we had because of stubbornness or pride, then I was a bit of an idiot!"

I wasn't going to argue with Pete on that one. However, on that occasion I decided not to mention it.

He held my hand and I remembered how I felt that day in Moreland Road when Sam first said that it was me that he loved.

"He also said that he knew that you loved me more than you could ever love anyone else," he smiled a nod of acknowledgement, "Living or dead." I looked up at Sam and stretched to kiss him on the lips.

It was as good a way as any to prove I was in full agreement.

Good old Pete, even from the grave he was still able to improve the lives of people he cared for.

"Mind you," he paused, a wicked grin playing around his eyes, "I did tell him that you are far too freakin' cheerful in the morning!"

"It's not me that upsets you," I countered, "It's the screeching that comes from Stage School Stacey! That girl has got to go!"

He nodded agreement and then said gently, "I do understand why you felt the way you did about him, uncle, brother or no relation at all. If I had kept dreaming about him like you did, I think I would have done the same. He was an easy man to love."

"Hell!" I said with mock horror. "You're not thinking of sampling the dreaded weed regularly, are you?"

He laughed and squeezed my hand. "No thank you, I think I'll stick with you, if that's OK?"

I kissed him full on the lips once again. This time it was to tell him it was more than OK, in fact, in my mind it was a no-brainer.

It was my turn to offer a bit of understanding. "I realise how difficult it must have been for you as well," I said gently. "Coping with me and my irrational feelings for a dead man, even if he did turn out to be my uncle. It was all a tad bit weird!"

"Talking about uncles and weird happenings…" Sam grinned, "we nearly slept with mine!"

I remembered Max's cheeky request when we were in Brighton and laughed. However, I stopped suddenly when I had another thought. "Your Uncle Max loved my Uncle Pete and now, here we are, together ourselves… it really does have to be fate, doesn't it?"

You really don't need the help of any TV detective to

work out what happened next.

As we lay in my bed afterwards, Sam asked me if I would go back to Weston with him. He said airily that he wasn't much bothered, but he could do with another half-decent barman…

"What about your mum?" I asked.

"She's a bit busy to run the bar full time…" he said straight faced, then grinned and winced as I tweaked his nipples to pay him back for his deliberate misunderstanding.

"We spoke about it last night," Sam admitted once he had recovered, "she said that she liked you a lot before the madness kicked off." He looked at me and I could feel the full force of those wonderful eyes. "She knows it may be awkward. You will always be linked in her mind with my dad walking out on us. But, she also knows how fantastic you make me feel, how happy I am when you're around - and conversely - how bloody miserable I am when you're not there."

Yep… he has a pretty good line in flattery.

I rang my mum who was so pleased for me that she didn't mind that I was walking out on them yet again. Both my mum and dad really liked Sam and when I threw the phone over to him, after he had indulged in a spot of frantic semaphoring, he invited them down to stay at the hotel.

I quickly packed and put up with some teasing from Sam about the amount of luggage I needed. I was on a roll. This time I wasn't going to have to struggle on and off trains and I was determined to make the most of it. However, I did stop short of sliding the chest of drawers down the staircase.

As we drove out and met the main road at the Tesco roundabout, Sam turned left towards the Royal Chase instead of right towards Gillingham.

"No, you numpty!" I cried, "You should have gone right there… Thank God they didn't test you on directions!"

Sam just smiled enigmatically, "Oh, did I not tell you? There was one other thing that Pete said to me, when I dreamt about him."

"What on earth was that?" I said.

"He asked me to go and get Max…"

Epilogue (i)

It was a little bit awkward with Fiona at first. Like two people faced with the best Dartington Crystal at a drinks reception, we were almost too careful with our movements lest we were responsible for a chip or a crack. Eventually, I plucked up the courage and approached her with carefully selected pages from the letter her husband had left for me. It seemed to help her a little and in doing so helped us to forge something of a friendship. We weren't exactly smashing the Dartington together like they were two steins in a bierkeller, but neither were we worried about lifting them to our lips in case they should crumble to dust before our eyes.

Fiona even admitted to me, in a long cathartic conversation, how she had convinced herself that their whole marriage had been built on a lie. The last page of his letter refuted that argument and gave her a glimpse of how he really cared about her. She might have still felt abandoned, but at least she no longer felt used.

There was another thing that helped Fiona move on with her life.

Max.

A little bit like myself at Moreland Road, he moved in for a night and stayed forever. Perhaps he had become bored with life on his own and the sudden discovery of a ready-made family was the boost he needed. He moved into Sam's room and it became his own once again.

Max and Fiona developed a bond very quickly. Maybe

there was something that reminded Fiona of her husband, but he was also different enough for it not to be too painful. They developed one of those friendships between a gay man and a straight woman that are quite unique and wonderful. My parents also became good friends and frequent visitors to Weston. Family dinners in the Brean room became something special.

Sam, who had inherited his father's ideology of not relying on the staff to run around the family, had moved it on somewhat. He would produce all the food; Emily and I would clatter it towards the table whilst Sam looked on like a fussy Maître D who had been lumbered with the Chuckle Brothers on the night of a gala dinner. Once it had somehow found its way onto the table, everyone then just pitched in and helped themselves. Later, we would clear the room and all bundle into the cavernous hollow of the Hotel kitchen, after it had closed for the night. Once there, we would do the washing up whilst laughing and balancing glasses of brandy on the shiny stainless-steel tables. Even John seemed to have discovered a sense of humour, I started to see the man that Maureen had fallen for, rather than the man I had believed him to be.

Emily was pleased to have me back. I would have liked to have said that her driving had improved, but this is an epilogue not a political manifesto, so I'll probably have to stick to the truth. However, whatever the accuracy of her talent for clutch control, she was my confidante, my friend and my co-conspirator when it came to teasing Sam mercilessly...

Sam. What can I say about that man that won't have you running to find a nausea suppressant? Whatever I say, it's going to sound like the lyrics to a second rate West End musical but quite frankly, I don't care. I love that man with every heartbeat that bangs behind my chest. We laugh, love, chat and banter... Then laugh and love again.

I still remember the moment when I heard that cry of surprise and thought he had fallen from the railing; I still recall the train ride when I thought I had lost him forever, and needed to rely on tissues from friendly strangers. I remember, and I am determined not to put ourselves in such jeopardy ever again.

In the end, Sam did return to university in September. Max had decided that he wanted to stay in Weston and was happy to help Fiona run the Hotel whilst Sam was away. Fiona was keen for him to finish his degree, she wanted Sam to have the complete university experience, before he returned to harness himself to the hotel for the next forty years. We didn't mention her reasoning to Chloe.

We might have got away with it, even if we had. When she returned to Moreland Road, Adam came with her and I have never seen her happier. He is a lovely Yorkshireman - tall, dark and bloody gorgeous - if you know what I mean. He is also kind, funny and he completely gets Chloe. He obviously adores her, but he also doesn't put up with too much nonsense. The house was a very happy place that year.

The boys returned from Brentwood. They turned the attic rooms into their own private apartment. They used my old room as a study and slept together every night in Chris' room. We still heard tales of threesomes at the summer camp, but as Chloe has said, there is no hard evidence that would stand up in a court of law...

Talking of which, Dean eventually had his wish granted. One day, early in the new year, Fiona closed the hotel to the public. Sam organised a huge party for all the staff, our friends from Shaftesbury and university, along with the various new friends we'd made over the course of the year. We consumed enough alcohol to keep the inhabitants of a small Scottish island happy for many a month.

Aunty Sadie made one of her trips down from Bath, and the sight of a ninety-year-old woman dancing to "Uptown Funk," on the wild side of midnight, will live long in everyone's memory.

In the early hours of the morning when all conscious thought had been banished like a royal wife in Tudor times, Dean suggested a threesome. What can I say?

I thought he was offering us a new brand of chocolate bar from Cadbury.

So far, we have not seen or heard of Sam's dad. I don't hold him responsible for what happened to me, and maybe even Pete's death could be attributed to a moment of madness if you were feeling charitable. However, what happened in Norfolk, that was murder. It is the one secret that I won't share with anyone. Other than that, Sam and I can talk about him without fear of a row, and that is about as good as it needs to get.

A few weeks after the Christmas party, when Sam and I were back at uni, Fiona went to a hoteliers' conference. She told us that she had been especially impressed with a talk given by a couple who had run a hotel in Torquay for the last twenty years. They staffed it, completely, with men and women who were victims of domestic abuse. The hotel provided them with a safe haven, employment and a support group that enabled them to move forward with their lives.

Fiona said the woman had reminded her, slightly, of Joanna Lumley.

On the night of September 2nd, forty years to the day that Pete had died, Sam and Max had decided to hold a proper memorial for him. They reasoned that it hadn't been done correctly at the time and they wanted to put that to rights. Mum and Dad visited especially for it, and my dad said it was strange remembering a brother he had never actually known, but was glad that he had done it.

Tony and Jackie turned up together, and were obviously as pleased to see Max again after a forty-year hiatus, as he was to see them. They arrived hand in hand, and Sam in full Cilla Black mode, couldn't stop crowing about his match making skills. He has done the same thing on all of their frequent visits since.

That was also the first time we met Jack's "Uncle" Martin. The man Pete described as a twenty-eight-year-old who was going on eighty-two was now a sixty-eight-year-old with a lover half his age. Talk about a life lived backwards!

I invited Alf and Pat. Even though I had never told him what I had discovered about his brother-in-law's involvement with Pete's death, he was a canny old bugger and he knew there was something I was keeping from him. He and Smiler got on like hot dog and onions in a torpedo roll… The air was frequently punctuated with moans and groans and the agreement that everything was in fact - shit.

I thought it would be a bit too much to expect Fiona to attend, but encouraged by my mum, Emily and Maureen, she stood at the edge of the water and watched Max throw a wreath into the shallows.

Sam and I had clubbed together and bought Max a small gift to mark the occasion. It was a simple ring of nine carat yellow gold engraved with the two letters M & P. The tail of the final letter swirled around in a circle that surrounded the lettering, but didn't quite meet up with itself.

After he had thrown the wreath into the water he subconsciously rotated the ring around his finger. There were three words engraved on the inside of it, invisible to all, trapped against his skin. We had thought about "With Love," played with "Forever," but had always really known there was only one inscription that could have been used.

We raised a glass of champagne to the man who some had known only briefly, some had never met at all and some of us only knew through the power of a strange dream. As I stood and watched the simple display of foliage and flowers bobbing on the tide I thought about him. A man who in life was full of a desire to make things better for everyone he loved, and in death was managing to do exactly that.

We all stayed on the beach until late into the night, a similar party to those that Pete and his friends had had during the summer of 1977. Max had brought down his guitar, and his version of the song that will always bring thoughts of my uncle to my mind hovered over the beach. He played a few more songs, but didn't play "Tides." When I asked him about it later, he said that it didn't feel relevant any more. After everyone else had disappeared back to the hotel, Sam and I wandered over to a dune and sat cuddling as Max and Pete had done on the night that Elvis Presley had died. My body against his body was the most natural fit and as comfortable as family. We lay together as the night slipped seamlessly towards the dawn.

Epilogue (ii)

How I curse the tide that took you from me
I curse the cruel and taunting sea
The only thing left to ease the pain
would be to hold you in my room again.

It had never been questioned that Max would move into Sam's room. When we were in Weston, Sam and I lived in a large room up in the staff quarters. I never dreamt about Pete again and although I missed him at first, it was probably a good thing overall. Pete had done what he needed to do and like any good mentor, was giving us the chance to build a future, unaided.

I often wondered whether Max experienced what Sam and I had experienced in his room. With Sam it had been after he had smoked pot, and with me it happened when I was dozy with alcohol. I must say I hadn't noticed a tendency for vodka bottles to disappear and Max's room never smelt like an opium den, so I guessed that either nothing was happening, or if it was, Pete's promise from the past was enough to make it so.

One day, I had wandered down to the apartment kitchen and Max was in there alone, drinking a mug of coffee. I decided to broach the subject.

"Max?" I enquired, and he looked up from the paper he was studying.

"Oh! Hi Rem."

"Can I ask you something?"

"Of course," he smiled and folded the paper in two, letting me know I had his full attention.

"Do you ever have those special sort of dreams, like I had?"

He paused for a moment, teasing me a little.

"Oh yes" he said and smiled.

I hesitated, then asked him a question that had been on my mind for a while.

"I hope you don't mind me asking... But, is it enough?"

The smile he gave me was better than any polygraph test. It was a smile of complete and absolute happiness.

"Oh yes..." He said again.

Acknowledgements

Weston-super-Mare is my home town and has a very special place in my heart. Many of the incidents, and day trips mentioned in the book, are a result of my memories growing up there. I'd like to thank my mum, dad and sister Nicky, for giving me the best childhood a boy could have had.

Most of the places I mention exist, or existed. However, the Royal Holm View Hotel is a figment of my imagination. If you know Weston, you will probably have worked out that I have built it on the site of the Royal Hospital, or the Sanatorium as some people will remember it. The building has since been converted into residential apartments called the Royal Sands.

I apologise to anyone who owns one of these flats, that by turning the building into a hotel, I have made you homeless. Fortunately, it's only in my imagination!

I would like to thank several people who read the book in its infancy: Alexis Batt, Nicky King, Angus Bramwell, Pam Godwin, Louise Smith, Chloe Quance, Richard Brookes, Yvonne Newnham, Anna Difazio, Caroline Doman, Bobbie Mato, Anne Andrews, Polly Warner and Emily Pithon. The encouragement I received from you all gave me a determination to see my book in print. Thank you so much.

I would also like to thank Emily for the cover design. If you would like to see a talented artist in all her glory, visit the Emily Pithon cartoonist website.

Finally, but certainly not least, I would like to thank my partner Ian Lawson, for all his love and patience. Not least when it came to anything technical. I have lost count of the number of times I have snapped:

"This stupid computer! It's not doing what I've told it to do!"

With one click he has always managed to retrieve the situation and never once mentioned those awful words:

"User error!"

Printed in Great Britain
by Amazon